Divine Wreckage
A Novel

Divine Wreckage

A Novel

Reynald Arthur Perry

Divine Wreckage

ISBN-13: 978-1-970003-02-4

Red Dashboard LLC Publishing
Princeton NJ 08540
www.reddashboard.com

Perry, Reynald Arthur, author.
Divine wreckage / Reynald Arthur Perry.
pages cm
ISBN 978-1-970003-02-4

1. Gods--Fiction. 2. Human beings--Fiction. 3. Death--Fiction. 4. Mothers and daughters--Fiction. 5. Fathers and sons--Fiction. 6. Brothers and sisters--Fiction. 7. Science fiction. 8. Action and adventure fiction. I. Title.

PS3616.E7943D58 2016 813'.6
QBI16-900068

For Caitlin—

You are a thing of forever, now.
Rest easy,
my silk and sugar.

Prologue
Cape May, 1937

Philip Ashwood finds a spot amid the dune grass and sand fleas and sits down, just behind a blown-over fence sandblasted bare save for a few specks of old whitewash. He's stuffed his pockets full of penny candy and he has a copy of *Astounding Science Fiction* rolled up in his fist. He pushes a half-drunk bottle of orange Nehi into the sand and looks out over the beach that spreads out below him to the deep blue sea and the pale blue sky beyond.

It's too early in the season to go swimming in that water, he knows. Only a couple of days before, he had taken his shoes off and, with trousers rolled, stepped into the surf. The sea was so cold that he felt as if his feet were boiling, a pain that penetrated down into the marrow of his bones. He'd been astonished by that, how something could be so cold that it burned. He wondered if it was like that in Hell (though why he thought of Hell he wasn't sure—his family had little time for church and religion) or in outer space. He'd made a clumsy run for the dry beach and forced a laugh through his chattering teeth to keep the tears away—at nine years old, he was getting too old to cry.

Philip reaches into his pocket and fishes out a piece of bubblegum. The familiar, sugary scent reaches him even through the waxed paper of the wrapper. This gum is something new, though, something he had never seen before he spied the opened box full of them at the candy and cigar store. He slowly unwraps it, careful not to rip the folded comic tucked around the thick, powdery pink rectangle. He sticks the gum in his mouth, reads the three-panel joke—something about a kid eating his dog's homework—checks out the ad for a secret spy decoder ring and then looks to the bottom margin, where there's a fortune, just like in those cookies they give out at the Chinese restaurant. It's a pretty lousy fortune, he thinks. "Once every lifetime, we're swallowed by the whale." He would have preferred something funny, something like, "Help! I'm trapped in a bubblegum factory!" This one is just a little bit scary, though he can't figure out why, and that only scares him more.

Swallowed by the whale—Philip has never seen a whale, just dolphins. In the past, he watched as they swam parallel to the shore, their blue-grey backs shiny and smooth in the sunlight. At the time, he was thrilled but now the memory seems tinged with underhanded menace. He looks up from the comic and casts his worried eyes toward the sea.

Instead of dolphins out in the ocean, he spots a little girl down on the shore. She wears a yellow swimsuit and walks from tide pool to tide pool, picking up starfish and putting them back, her tiny feet leaving bird tracks in the waterlogged sand. Philip forgets the comic and turns his head to watch as the little girl walks into one of the bigger pools. The water goes up past her ankles—with the sun directly overhead, Philip imagines it must be plenty warm by now. He watches her crouch down until her bottom is almost in the water. She runs her hands just under the surface of the pool, skimming for something he cannot see. Then she's standing again and throwing whatever it was she had skimmed up into the air. Philip can just barely see little pale yellow flashes of light and hear soft, flat pops, like firecrackers. She stands there for a moment, stock-still and serious, then claps her hands. Philip hears her laughter, clear above the sound of the surf, carried to him on the breeze as if she were there in the dune grass with him, laughing in his ear.

"Janey!" he hears someone, a woman, call from further down the beach. "Jane, where are you?"

A sudden breeze takes the bubblegum comic from his lax fingers. It flutters down to the beach and drifts along the sand to stop at the little girl's feet. His heart stutters through several excited beats as she lifts her head and looks straight at him—Philip freezes in the frankness of her dark eyed gaze, alternately hidden and revealed by her wind-blown hair. Without breaking her pitiless stare, she pins the comic to the sand with her toes, then crouches down—just as she'd done in the pool—to pick it up.

"Over here, Mom!" the girl finally calls back. She looks away from Philip and he lets go of the breath he didn't know he'd been holding. He watches with a relieved and sinking heart as she turns and runs away from him, down the strand and out of his vision, his comic clutched in her little fist.

"Come on, Mom," he hears her calling, her voice thin and distant against the cruelly shifting winds, "let's go look for some seashells."

Part One
Creation's Bright Corrosion

You have recombined your spirit one too many times,
Divided up your love into one too many measures,
Poured your mercy out into one too many vessels.
We are thick with you,
Like honeyed blood,
Like bloodied milk.
You frame our mongrel faces.
You phrase our mongrel names.
You have made of us creation's bright corrosion
And for all of that you commend us to the void.

—*The Helical Heresy: A Song for Bettina* by
Aurelius Mann

1

Rust and Stardust

For a price, the dead will speak. And the price is not so very high at all.

Crysanthia Vog walks along the pathway of frozen ooze that runs through the center of the outpost, heedless of the sub-zero temperatures and thin, poisonous winds. The common stock humans hurrying by, folded into themselves against the biting cold, do not so much as glance in her direction. It is at once a relief and disappointment. Here, seventeen parsecs out from the Solar Commonwealth, she is as unremarkable as any other piece of interstellar hardware. Here, in this hostile world, she is no more exotic than the turbulent, toffee-colored globe of Iota Horologii Prime itself, hanging huge and heavy overhead. Locals call the looming gas giant Agamemnon and this, its largest moon, the ground beneath Crysanthia's boots, they've named Klytemnestra.

It's the stares of the Pilots that sting. Every one is filled with hostility, open and intense. It stopped amusing her three days into this month-long layover.

Crysanthia Vog is herself a Pilot, a genetically engineered cyborg of such sophisticated and elegant design it surpasses the sublime. Lodged in each of her cells are microscopic devices of such subtle craft that they could easily be mistaken for living things themselves. Because of them, her skin is the color of a cloudless winter sky and glitters, in certain light, like newly fallen snow. She stands a little over two meters tall and, like all of her kind, she has the compound eyes of an insect. Crysanthia's are bright aquamarine. They catch and refract the light like star sapphires.

Just off to her right, a few meters from the path, the lights inside the settlement's squat cantina dome shine a dull and dingy yellow through the dirty plexan shell. Crysanthia walks to the airlock and cycles herself through.

Inside, the air smells of stale liquor, plastics and human sweat, a distinct improvement over the cloacal air outside. Not a breath of fresh air to be had on Klytemnestra, Crysanthia muses. She glances up to the radial rib work of duraladium that spans above her like the arms of a sheltering starfish. Beneath it, the planetary engineers, worn whey-faced and ragged, drink. They have no hope of seeing the world they would build come into fruition, so remote is their time-frame, so low in priority is this outpost. Steeped in that hopelessness, they reek of it—rank desperation all but seeps from their pores.

Crysanthia orders a vodka tonic from the Security Force surplus android tending bar and surveys the room to make sure the table she wants is free. Satisfied, she turns back and pays for her drink. The plastic skin that covers the android's hand is beginning to break down. Its palms are cracked like a dry lakebed, exposing the pale violet gel of the false flesh beneath.

"Thank you," the android says. Its vocal modulator is flat and scratchy; the words poorly synchronized to the movement of its lips. Crysanthia nods, wraps her fingers around the glass and walks away. Already, from nine long-legged strides out, she can read the holographic come-on hovering at the base of the cryonic sibyl. As she slides into her seat, she reads it a second time.

"RECEIVE A MESSAGE FROM THE UNDISCOVERED COUNTRY! GET SAGE ADVICE FROM THE FAR SHORES OF FOREVER! Transmigration Interregnum Limited offers you the chance to SPEAK WITH THE DEAD! For a nominal fee, you can consult the cryogenically preserved brain of someone TWO CENTURIES GONE! What does the future hold? What lies beyond the grave? FIND OUT!"

Crysanthia matches the vacant gaze of the sibyl with her own bland, insectile stare. The disembodied human head, frozen as a hedge against mortality at the end of the twentieth century and now embalmed in biostatic aerosol behind clear panes of glass, awaits only a small infusion of electronic money to jolt it to life. Night after night, Crysanthia has sat at the bar and watched the common stock humans sitting at this table, eavesdropped on their listless, pointless questions. She listened to the sibyl's incoherent murmurings and she envied them its company.

"For entertainment purposes only," read the words laser-etched into the case.

There are several other sibyls in the camp, in the arcades and supply depots. Transmigration Interregnum dumps them out here, far beyond the reach of the Solar Commonwealth. Six more are scattered among the tables in this saloon alone. But Crysanthia cares nothing for the others; it is always this one that draws her, siren-like, as she nurses her loneliness and her drinks. Looking at it now stirs a strange feeling within her, as if she were a creature gazing into a mirror for the first time. She tries to shrug it away as drunken silliness—the sibyl is human, after all, and she is not—but she is not yet drunk and the feeling will not let her go.

She takes a sip of her drink. It lances her palate like industrial waste.

She puts the glass down on the table, a solid slab of white plastiform begrimed jaundice yellow with Klytemnestran soil and oily human effluvia, and covered in a labyrinth of interlocking graffiti. To the right of her drink, someone has used some kind of laser tool to burn "Buck up chuckle pup" and "Life is a prank matter plays upon itself" into the plastic. Under that, someone else has scratched "And the rest is silence." To the side of that, yet another person has burned a correction: "The rest is rust and stardust." Crysanthia tries to busy herself with puzzling out the other inscriptions—they form a pattern, almost; if she looks at them from the right angle it seems as if she looks at a street map or a printed circuit—but her mind is elsewhere, centimeters distant, light years away.

Even so, one more message becomes clear to her—it is old, buried beneath the others, barely legible: "Once every lifetime we're swallowed by the whale."

No kidding, she thinks.

"Don't see these things in the Commonwealth ports," someone says from behind her, a woman. Crysanthia looks up to see a guileless blue face with skin that glitters like newly fallen snow. She looks into compound eyes of smoky gold that catch and refract the light like star sapphires.

"Galatea Trope." The Pilot sits down next to Crysanthia. "I heard you were here. I came all the way from Orestes. I've been dying to meet you."

"You don't say?"

"Are you serious? The only free Pilot in existence? The only woman to stand up to the prigs in the Commission and those Consortium shits?" She grins—lavender lips part to show pink gums and small, perfect teeth, wet and white. A horizontal crease forms under her upturned nose. "You're my personal hero."

After a moment's hesitation, Crysanthia takes the girl's extended hand. Their serpentine fingers entwine and she realizes, with a clarity born of denied longing, that this is the first time in over a decade she has touched one of her own kind.

"I'm... honored," Crysanthia says. Their fingers disentangle. "What were you doing out in the Furies?" Orestes, Iota Horologii's only other planet, is a small and rocky world with an eccentric orbit that keeps it in the Furies, the system's cometary halo, for decades at a time.

"Ferrying Dream Dolls from Heaven 9 to the comet distillery," Galatea says with palpable disgust.

For some reason, Crysanthia feels the need to defend them. "Gets lonely up there, I'd imagine."

In her mind, she can see it all too clearly: a frozen, industrial hell of tar, brown ice and refinery flames belching into the endless night. "It's got to be the most desolate place in the known universe."

Galatea shrugs. "They may not be up there too much longer."

"You know something?"

"I know a lot of somethings. Word in the Heavens is that this project—" she waves a slender blue hand to indicate the terraforming proceeding at a glacial pace beyond the cantina dome "—is hanging by a thread. You haven't heard?"

Crysanthia shakes her head.

"Turns out they're in a box—the Martian and Venusian models won't work here."

Crysanthia sips her drink. "Well, that's why they're here, isn't it? To develop a third way: their Klytemnestran model."

"No such thing, apparently—not without completely devastating the native ecology and murdering all those repugnant little creatures crawling in the muck," Galatea says. "So far, it's just talk and no one wants to come out and admit it, but the Commonwealth will probably abandon the project within the next six months and call everyone home. No more comet cracking station and we lose who knows how many shipping contracts. *C'est la vie.*" She sighs. "At least we're here for the thaw."

"At least." Crysanthia grimaces. Agamemnon's orbit is itself eccentric enough that Klytemnestra, tiny as it is, experiences extremes of heat and cold: from far below freezing in the winter to a mean of sixty-two degrees centigrade in the summer. From what Crysanthia has heard, when the spring rains come the smell goes from unbearable to unimaginable.

"So," Galatea says. "You going to ask it a question?"

Crysanthia looks back to the sibyl, haloed by ringlets of thick, slate gray hair that must have once been black. Death has blanched character from a face that, in life, no doubt had plenty of it—Crysanthia can see it in the firm fleshiness of the sibyl's jaw and cheeks, in the creases in the forehead, the deeper lines bracketing the mouth and the beryl blue eyes. Those eyes must have been formidable, Crysanthia thinks, capable of great scorn and humor. Now they stare blankly into forever, which is just another way of saying into nothing at all. "Seems in poor taste."

Galatea snorts and giggles, flutters her fingers in front of her mouth like kelp moving in deep ocean currents. "You sound like a common stock." She looks at the sibyl and snorts again. "*She's dead.*" She glances around the bar. Crysanthia realizes now how young Galatea must be, six years old at the most. Galatea leans in close and her large cranium, sleek and hairless, touches Crysanthia's. Crysanthia shivers at the intimacy, warm skin on skin, as electrifying as it is casual. "Or, I should say, *it's* dead. It's locked up inside that little skull and the computer feeds it the *illusion* of life."

Crysanthia shrugs and says nothing.

"It *thinks* it got what it paid for," Galatea presses. "Ergo it got what it paid for. It doesn't *feel* anything. The rest is sentiment and superstition."

She pulls her calling card computer out of the sleeve pocket of her battered leather flight jacket (outlandish garment, Crysanthia thinks, an affectation of the young) and beams five solaria into the sibyl. "It's on me."

Crysanthia watches the sibyl's eyelids flutter. Its slack mouth opens in a rictus that looks, for all the cosmos, like a yawn.

"Well, what are you waiting for?" Galatea says. "Ask it."

"Ask it *what?*"

"Anything."

Crysanthia regards the twitching sibyl for a moment longer before saying, "Have you seen him?"

The sibyl's eyes open and seem to stare into and through Crysanthia. Its mouth works in silence several times before Crysanthia hears, faintly from the speaker: "*...obverse... coffee... perverse... inverse... image... reverse...*" The sibyl seems to wind down—its eyelids droop and its lower lip begins to sag. Suddenly, as if jolted or startled, the eyes open so wide that the whites are visible all around the irises. "*Little fishes,*" the sibyl says, flat and clear. Crysanthia jumps in spite of herself. Then the sibyl's eyelids flutter as the eyeballs roll back. "*...little fishes...little...*" And then it shuts down into silence.

Galatea moves closer—too close. Before Crysanthia can say anything, she feels something ram her hard in the ribs.

"Pischa-Galway plasmatic pistol," Galatea hisses. "In case you were curious."

Crysanthia hears a faint snap and a whine. She feels the gun barrel hum against her flank. She smells ozone and vaporized metal.

"Fully automatic and already primed. Let me think you're going to do something stupid and everyone in the bar finds out how far this thing can spray your guts."

That explains the bulky jacket, Crysanthia thinks.

"We need to take a walk." Galatea takes firm hold of Crysanthia's arm and hauls her to her feet. "Now."

Crysanthia casts one last, imploring look at the sibyl. It cannot help her.

"Just so we're clear," she says to the girl, "does this mean I'm *not* your personal hero?"

They walk along the river that skirts the western edge of camp, a narrow ribbon of salty glacial runoff that flows brownish gray with silt and reeks of ammonia. The frozen dirt crunches with every step they take and their breath forms plumes around their faces with every exhalation. Around them, humans scurry from place to place, in heavy parkas and breather masks. The two Pilots wear nothing more than what they wore in the bar. For Crysanthia, it's a sleeveless blouse of black, metallic silk and canvas slacks. For Galatea, it's the flight jacket over jeans and a tee-shirt. They walk so closely they could be sisters or lovers.

"This sort of thing usually only happens to me in sleepies," Crysanthia says. She gets no reply.

She spies one of the moon's indigenous life forms out of the corner of her eye, a small, furry biped with webbed feet and no forelimbs. It scrambles up the bank of the river and watches them with the six beady eyes that surround its gaping maw, a round blackness alive with writhing cilia. As they pass by, it propels itself into a spinning back-flip and disappears from view. A moment later, it strikes the water with a loud and thick plop.

Galatea steers Crysanthia to a small equipment shed. She opens the door and jabs Crysanthia again with the pistol. Crysanthia ducks through the doorway. There is not enough room for her to straighten up so she turns around and sits on the floor, her back against the flattened keel of an upended river skiff. She looks up at Galatea.

"Now what?"

Galatea tosses a computer into Crysanthia's lap and shuts the door. Crysanthia can tell by the sound as Galatea throws the deadbolts that she has no hope of picking them—if she had anything to pick them with.

In the gloom, Crysanthia activates the computer's grainy holocube. It's a cheap model, a throwaway, with no input or communication functions. Its memory is dedicated to a single, indelible file: a computer generated Crysanthia Vog—flawlessly rendered and nude except for a pair of black stockings and a garter belt—in obscene and apparently lethal congress with a wild boar. The pig is really rather marvelous, Crysanthia thinks, with his bristled back, chipped tusks and strings of viscous slobber. She sighs. It's not the first time she's seen one of these things—once, at a dinner party in Buenos Aires, someone showed one to her and earnestly asked her what it meant. Crysanthia had struggled to change the subject for long minutes before the arrival of the third course rescued her. She shuts the computer off. It's been a good life, she decides, all things taken as they are.

A star slug, bright yellow and paper thin, oozes in under the door. Crysanthia watches as it slinks across the floor and tastes the toe of her boot with two of its nine arms. What did the girl say? The colonization project abandoned, the system all but forgotten. Well, it was inevitable. In hindsight, so many things seem inevitable... Crysanthia remembers reading about the problems facing the terraformers in the popular science newsfeeds almost a decade ago. The Pilots had just grounded her in exile and she followed all interstellar news with jealous eyes: Robot probes launched from passing starships had discovered that this moon harbored a complex ecology long before anyone first set foot on its tundra. On the surface of Earth and under the ice sheets of Europa—the only other places known to support life—every living thing shared a common chemistry and, presumably, a common origin. Here, life was truly alien, having arisen from a radically different assemblage of amino and nucleic acids. The moon's value to science was incalculable, and the xenologists and exobiologists lobbied for its quarantine. But there were no other likely candidates for extrasolar colonization anywhere near the Commonwealth. The planetary engineers, claiming confidence and skills they did not possess, said that they could adapt the world to support human life without disrupting the life already there and the Solar Commonwealth, spurred on by ambitions of becoming a *Galactic* Commonwealth, chose to believe them.

Crysanthia, alone in the dark with the questing slug, shakes her head. *Galactic*—they actually used that word, as if one could lay claim to two island humps in a river sandbar and call himself emperor of the world.

So now the folly is acknowledged and everybody goes away, bye-bye to all the rats and star slugs and vampire river eels. Crysanthia dies here on a moon surrendered to vermin—it's almost funny. She wonders what the Pilots will do with her body. Probably dump it the sea. She wonders if it will poison the local wildlife. Already, she thinks of her body as her corpse, a thing rather than a self, an *it* rather than a *me*.

She thinks about how easily Galatea fooled her, how quickly she'd let down her guard, selling herself for a smile and a handclasp, so stupid...

Crysanthia does not like the direction her thoughts are headed and so decides not to think at all. She waits.

Every one of the trillions of cyborganelles in Crysanthia's body comes complete with a micronized clock that keeps perfect time. She knows that three hours, thirty-seven minutes and fifty-two point zero eight seconds have come and gone before the locks disengage and the door slides open.

Galatea is there, a silhouette in the doorway. Dim light glints off her pistol and her eyes.

"Let's go," she says.

Scudding clouds have moved in over the settlement and hide Agamemnon from view. Scattered raindrops, oily and sulfurous, fall. Galatea guides Crysanthia to the shipyards, a compound of drab and colossal structures bathed in unearthly green light and strung along the coast of Klytemnestra's lone and stagnant ocean. She nudges Crysanthia through a door that opens into the dark and cavernous interior of a hangar.

"I have her."

Slowly, the lights come up. Crysanthia sees four figures standing beneath the prow of a starship—her starship. Two have the unmistakable silhouettes of Pilots, tall and slender. The other two are human, dwarfed by comparison.

Lights up fully now and she recognizes one of the Pilots. He stares at her and grins. Crysanthia clenches her fists and prepares to die.

2

The Haze of Martian Tequila

But that is now, Anno Domini 2170. This was then, Anno Domini 2163. And *then* was over seven years ago and almost sixty light years distant, long before cryonic sibyls and plasmatic pistols and far away from Klytemnestra's frozen mud and fetid rain. *Then*, she stood in a shower of golden light that streamed into the Coriolanus Wintermute Gallery of Fine Art through a perfectly transparent pane of glass. *Then*, it was as if nothing stood between her and sunset over the cloud piercing skyscrapers of Brancusi City, capital of Venus.

"Crysanthia Vog?"

She had known he was there behind her before he spoke. She'd heard his soft footfalls, she'd smelled his clean skin.

"Who else would I be?" She said. She did not turn around.

"Of course," he said. "I meant merely to be polite. Perhaps that was a mistake."

Crysanthia sipped from her fluted glass of champagne. "Only if it pretends to an ignorance that does not—can not—exist. Yes, I am Crysanthia Vog." In the distance, winged airships drifted among the towers and between the slanting shafts of light and shadow like bloated manta rays. Sky riders, on their little silver air skeds, glided among the skyscrapers. She turned around and her composure faltered, if only for an instant.

In her four years spent on the Inner Worlds, among humans, Crysanthia had come to expect a range of reactions to her otherness: infinite combinations of revulsion and fascination, poorly concealed behind masks of bland indifference. She saw none of that in this brown-skinned stranger. Instead, she looked down into sea-green eyes that seemed to know her from the insides out.

She felt an impulse to protect her long, exposed throat. Instead, she held out her hand.

"Janos Brekkelheim," he said. He showed no reaction as her boneless fingers coiled like serpents around his square and solid palm.

"Brekkelheim, did you say? As in Bettina Brekkelheim?"

After the slightest hesitation, he answered, "She's my mother."

Crysanthia relaxed. *Her only begotten son*, she mused. She wondered if he played in her laboratories as a child and let her imagination conjure a brief vision of him, flying a model star cruiser and running among the plastic womb tanks, surrounded by the stark white and silver of the ceramic walls and surgical steel floor grates.

"Inspecting her handiwork?" She swiveled back and forth on her narrow hips and lifted her long arms. "Do you approve?"

"I do." His face did not change expression. "But that is not why I approached you."

Crysanthia's imagination had it wrong, she decided. This man never allowed himself the frivolity of running and playing, not even as a boy.

"If it is not too forward, Ms. Vog, may I buy you a drink?"

***

"I'm here and not there," Crysanthia said and indicated with a sweeping gesture the interstellar space she was designed to inhabit, "because I find the idea that biology is destiny to be an especially galling one. I like cities. I like galleries and cafes. I like people, after a fashion—and despite their tendency to gawk."

"It seems a tendency you cultivate."

She sat across from Janos, under the awning of a sidewalk café in the mild breezes of a climate controlled night. She was very much aware of the way the lights of the city, of the manufactured moon shining lemon in the indigo sky, of the candle flickering in the center of the table, played on her glittering blue skin and on the chatoyant surfaces of her aquamarine eyes. She rested her elbows on the table and stilled her hands.

"Perhaps."

Before she could say anything more, their waiter arrived. He did a fair job of not staring as he took their drink orders.

"How many people ever get to see a Pilot? Up close, I mean, in the flesh," she said once the waiter had gone. "I'm an automatic celebrity, whether I like it or not. So I choose to like it. Most of the time."

"But how do you handle the withdrawal? Galling as it may be, you *are* designed to form a homeostatic symbiosis with the drive system of a starship." He held his hands in front of him and locked his primitive fingers together in blunt illustration. "Your nervous system, the cyborganelles in your skin and your blood—without a ship, you are incomplete."

Crysanthia felt her expression harden.

"Physiologically speaking," Janos added. He let his hands fall, palms down, to the table.

Crysanthia shook off a swarm of bad memories: those first weeks spent holed up in her flat, locked up inside her screaming skin, feeling like an animated husk, like something worse than hollow. "I didn't say it was easy, Mr. Brekkelheim. I simply said I prefer it this way." She could tell by how he looked at her that he knew she lied but that he had no wish to call her out upon it. She didn't know whether to be charmed or offended by the courtesy.

The waiter returned, placed a Martian time slip in front of Crysanthia and a pint of cloudy beer in front of Janos, and left.

Most of Crysanthia's height was in her legs, arranged now beneath the table with elegant abandon, and she'd long ago learned to slouch when in the company of common stock males—it salved their egos. She gazed levelly at Janos and said, "I hope we have more to talk about than how I avoid a chronic case of the shakes." She took a sip of her drink. "Otherwise, this will be a very tedious evening and I do not like tedium, regardless of who buys the drinks."

"Permit me to apologize," Janos said. "I was never adept at making small talk. Perhaps I should dispense with it altogether."

Crysanthia shifted her in her chair. The son of her creator, his flesh tainted with enticing overtones of the forbidden, compelling intimations of the taboo—something stirred in her, something like an ache, something like a panic.

"I want to hire you."

Crysanthia shook her head as if emerging from a daze. She drew herself out of her habitual slouch and stared down at Janos as if he had said something obscene.

"What?"

"There is a... phenomenon, an anomalous event. An eruption of sorts, half a light year from Fomalhaut," Janos said. "A highly energetic spatial torsion, apparently self-generating, ostensibly self-organizing, in an area which was, until two months ago, hard vacuum. I want you to take me there."

She stood. "Thank you for the drink."

"Please, sit down. Listen to what I have to say."

"No, I don't think so. You've made a mistake. I can't help you. It's not what I do anymore."

Janos placed a calling card computer on the table, next to the candle. "You were a Pilot, once," he said. "A working Pilot, I mean. I know all about you, about your dispute with the Consortium. I know that your retirement is not entirely voluntary."

Crysanthia clasped her hands and held them in front of her stomach. Her fingers writhed as she fought the urge to reach out and strike Janos. Or strangle him. She imagined his presumptuous face turning crimson, darkening to purplish blue, his eyes bulging, his clumsy, jointed fingers clawing at her hands with impotent desperation. The image calmed her enough to let her speak.

"If you know all that," she began, louder than she intended, and drew stares from the café's other patrons. She took two deep breaths and tried again. "If you know all that, then you know I have no intention of dealing with the Consortium—with the Pilot's Commission—ever again. You're wasting your time." She let her hands fall limply at her sides. "And mine."

"The Consortium has nothing to do with this. Sit down and hear me out. I have a ship waiting for us in the asteroid belt. "

"Impossible."

"My mother is the richest woman in the Solar System. I have resources."

"No one is that rich."

"I have the ship," Janos said firmly. "Now will you please sit down and listen to me?"

With sullen reluctance, Crysanthia slipped back into her chair. She leaned forward and fixed Janos in her insect eyes. "I've already told you. I like it here." She gazed off into the distance. Softly, she added, "I like my life."

"So much that you'd say no to a ship of your own? To come and go as you please? Understand what I am offering you. After this one mission, the ship is yours. Think about it."

She did not need to. It was a dream she had never permitted herself the luxury of dreaming. But she could not help but wonder about the Pilot's Commission. They'd been content to take *Eidolon* away from her, content to imprison her here, within the confines of the Solar Commonwealth. How might they react once they discovered that imprisonment simply would not do?

"That's quite an offer," she said, pushing aside thoughts of the Consortium and its wrath. "All for this, ah, high energy spatial torsion?"

Janos nodded.

"Tell me more."

Janos slid the computer across the table with his fingertips. "It's all in there."

Crysanthia took a moment to study his face before she looked down at the device. After a moment, she turned it on. A four centimeter display cube shimmered into apparent solidity above its cryostylitic holoprojector. She read the information in the cube, glanced up at Janos, then studied its hundreds of formulae and schemata in rapid succession. She shut the computer off. The cube disappeared in a puff of frigid vapor; Crysanthia felt a sudden chill as the machine released its sixty-four cubic centimeters of super-cooled air into the night.

"What this describes is impossible," Crysanthia said.

"It is," Janos replied. "Provided that our assumptions on the nature of reality are valid."

Crysanthia leaned back and held her glass in front of her chin. "You're suggesting they're not?"

Janos glanced up at the golden moon. "How long would it take to get from here to Proxima Centauri?"

The question put Crysanthia off her balance. She had to think for a moment. "A week," she said, "at standard fold depth. As few as two days, as many as nine, depending on the variables—how good is the ship, how skilled is the Pilot, what are the sub-quantum weather conditions."

"A week. Practical interstellar flight. Once an impossibility, now a commonplace." A slight hesitation, then, "You would not exist if it weren't."

"No," Crysanthia said softly, "I don't suppose I would."

"I'm sorry. I did not wish to offend."

"Not at all," Crysanthia lied. "Everyone's existence is predicated on any number of contingencies. Those of us who are genetically modified simply have a better idea of what those contingencies are." Crysanthia tilted her head, regarded him in silence and then said, "Something feels wrong here. You have the stink of the zealot about you."

"Perceptive," Janos said. His lips barely moved. "But not an answer."

"Why go to all this trouble? Why not just go to the Consortium? Even with their monopoly, it wouldn't cost a thousandth of what you've already spent—and that's without any guarantee I'd agree to it. Unless there's another exiled Pilot out there that I don't know about, it's an insane gamble."

"When a gamble is the only option that remains, it ceases to be insane."

"It's still a gamble."

"Zealots often have methods that go counter to the grain of convention. The Consortium is a very conventional body, as I'm sure you realize."

She could only nod at that.

"Two Consortium vessels are already there," he continued, "with two teams of scientists. Specialists in astrophysics, quantum gravitational theory, dissociated tier mathematics and a dozen other myopic disciplines. Each keeping a safe distance, running safe experiments, asking safe questions. They would measure the infinite with coffee spoons." He laughed, a harsh and bitter sound Crysanthia did not like. "They invited me along. At first. When they heard some of my theories and the experiments I intend to run to prove them, they quietly rescinded that invitation."

Crysanthia spent a long moment staring at Janos and toying idly with his inert computer. "'*Safe,*'" she echoed. "You seem to have a special contempt for that word."

Janos kept silent.

She looked away from him, into the space that surrounded them, into the deepening twilight. Janos radiated intensity in waves of heated scent—like a drug, it made it hard for her to keep her thoughts straight. She traced the flight of moths around the gaslight street lamps and timed the irregular intervals between the green-yellow flashes of fireflies. She eavesdropped on conversations from the other tables and envied them their banality.

Crysanthia sighed. She raised her hand, showed her empty, creaseless palm to him. "Get me more information on this thing. Give me your flight plan. You do have one?"

Janos nodded. "All in the computer. Keep it."

Crysanthia took a deep breath and tried to clear the haze of Martian tequila from her head. "Tomorrow." She sipped at the remains of her time slip. "I'll have an answer for you tomorrow." Even as she said it, she knew she only played a game: with him, with herself—it did not matter, she could not say.

3

The Market Value of Her Blood Salts

"Vog," Narisian Karza says now. His voice echoes off the walls of the hangar and rolls over her like a hail of oiled ball bearings. His mantid eyes shine bloody maroon, his pale blue skin glitters. "How long has it been? Since that sad business at Fomalhaut?"

After a long pause in which it becomes obvious that he expects her to answer, after yet another sharp prod from Galatea's humming gun, Crysanthia says, "Seven years."

He nods. "Too long." His smile hardens into something as joyless as a mass grave. "*Far* too long." Then he turns to Galatea and the other Pilot. "You two, wait outside." The male goes without hesitation; Galatea walks a step behind him but casts a questioning glance toward Narisian. He ignores it. After the clamshell door clangs shut, he speaks to Crysanthia again, all pretense to pleasure gone. "I don't like this, Vog, but I have very little choice. These people are Commonwealth Security Special Agents. They need to speak with you."

The woman steps forward. "Hello, Ms. Vog. My name is Angela Caro," she says. At little under one hundred and fifty centimeters, she is short even by common stock standards. She tilts her head in the direction of the other common stock, a relatively tall male. "My associate, Hector Berengaria."

In a flash, it is apparent—Narisian is on this human woman's leash and she has just yanked out the slack. Crysanthia laughs. "You have no idea how good it is that you are not happy to see me," she says to the Pilot.

Karza does not reply. He does not need to. Crysanthia looks at his expression of constipated hate. Despite her best efforts, another peal of laughter escapes her lips.

"For the benefit of the other two," Berengaria says, "we allowed Karza the appearance that he controls the situation. He does not. We do."

Karza stares straight ahead.

Special Agent Caro clears her throat. "No," she says. "No, if anyone is control of anything right now, Ms. Vog, it is you."

Crysanthia thinks back to the hours spent in the tool shed with the rutting boar and the star slug to keep her company. She does not feel like laughing anymore. "You don't say."

Berengaria casts a sidelong glance at Caro before he asks, "Been home lately?"

"You mean the Commonwealth?"

"What else would I mean?"

Crysanthia glances up at her ship. She shakes her head. "Why?"

"The combined population of the Ganymede, Callisto and Titan colonies is now three million. Do you know what that means?"

Crysanthia stares at them blankly.

"It means," Caro supplies, "that the Solar Commonwealth is now sovereign to the orbit of Saturn and within forty-five degrees of the ecliptic."

"Congratulations."

"Vesta is now within Commonwealth space," Berengaria says. "Dr. Brekkelheim is now subject to Commonwealth law."

Crysanthia nods. "I see," she says. For years, there had been rumblings, from Pilots and common stock alike, that Bettina's methods were inhumane, even murderous, and one day, some said, she would pay for them. Though the hangar is vast, a huge domed space under an elasticrete shell, Crysanthia feels hemmed in. Her ship shares the space with three other starships and a half dozen armored hover-trucks lined up against the wall, crouching on their landing bags like sleeping armadillos. Several maintenance robots, each one about a meter long, move around in the shadows like antediluvian roaches.

Her eyes fall on something, burned into the chipped plastiform of a storage locker; another graffito. And even though the words are less than a centimeter tall and the locker is more than thirty meters distant, she has no trouble reading it: "REMEMBER THE NINEVAH." *What is it with these people and their goddamned scribbles?* Crysanthia wonders. *Someone really needs to take their little lasers away from them.* She turns her eyes back to Karza and his human keepers. "When she lived in the Inner Worlds, her methods were tolerated," she says hopelessly. "Encouraged, even."

"Things change," Karza says. "Opinions. Attitudes." He glances at the common stock humans with distaste. "They no longer have the stomach for it."

Berengaria shakes his head. "It's purely a matter of law."

"Ms. Vog," Caro says, "there aren't enough people, common stock or otherwise, to fill the worlds in the home system. There will not be for centuries to come, millennia. The consensus is that interstellar space travel is simply not viable. Not if it means complicity in crimes against sentience."

"Is that what you're calling it?"

Berengaria answers, "There is a lengthy list of specific charges but, yes, that is what we are calling it. That is what Dr. Brekkelheim stands accused of."

Crysanthia shakes her head. She looks to Karza. "And what happens to us?"

"Nothing. *Our* lives will not change—why should they?"

"There will still be sewer worlds like this one, a need to ferry people to and from them," Berengaria says. "If anything, demand for your services will increase. You will be able to command a higher price."

"I appreciate the depth of your concern," Crysanthia says.

Berengaria stiffens, moves to say something but Caro silences him with a subtle motion of her left hand. "Forgive us, Ms. Vog," Caro says. "We are police. We carry out the laws and will of the Commonwealth. For that, we tend to be blunt." She looks over to her partner. "Clumsy."

"And those laws demand you arrest Bettina—Dr. Brekkelheim?" Crysanthia says.

Reluctantly, Caro says, "Yes."

"So arrest her," Crysanthia says with a forced nonchalance that fools no one. "Put her on trial, do what the will of the Commonwealth demands." She curses the catch in her voice as she says, "You don't need my blessing."

"Do you think I'd be here, breathing the same air—"

"Commissioner Karza," Caro interrupts. "Please."

Narisian waves Caro off. He turns to Crysanthia with redoubled intensity. "Do you think I'd come to you for a *blessing?*"

Caro sighs and gives Narisian a look of undigested contempt. "In fact, Ms. Vog," she says, "we need far more from you than that."

"Brekkelheim anticipated this," Berengaria explains. "Vesta is a fortress. Against the Commonwealth, against the Consortium. The only way for *us* to land there, to take Brekkelheim into custody, is to launch an assault. We'd succeed, of course, but it would be... unseemly."

"Unseemly," Crysanthia echoes. "Go to hell."

"Ms. Vog," Caro says.

Crysanthia turns sharply on her heel and heads for the door.

"Ms. Vog," Caro says again. "Wait."

"Why?" Crysanthia asks without looking back. "You going to shoot me?"

"Please don't force me to consider that an option."

Crysanthia stops. Slowly, she turns around. To anchor herself, she looks over their heads to the smooth, silver ship behind them. *Pariah's* hull reflects a distorted and vertiginous tableau, however, and she quickly looks away. Softly, she repeats herself: "Go to hell."

"I appreciate your loyalty, I really do," Caro says. "Consider, though, if it is not misplaced. How many of your kind, Ms. Vog, how many of your brothers and sisters has she killed between crossing the awareness threshold and reaching full term? And only because their continued existence had no profit in it." Crysanthia moves to speak but the special agent silences her as she had silenced her partner; she has a great deal of authority—of *force*—coiled in her tiny body. "No," she says. "Examine your place in all of this. Before you make your choice, take time to consider it. All we ask."

Crysanthia stares at her. "All you ask."

Caro nods. She walks past Crysanthia and gestures for Karza and Berengaria to join her. The door rolls open to the Klytemnestran gloom. Beyond her, Crysanthia can see the two young Pilots. They stand beneath a clear umbrella and wait in the distance. The rain has given way to urinous sleet.

"Decision's yours, Ms. Vog," Caro says before putting her breather mask in place. Then she pauses and removes the mask to say one last thing: "But you should know that we are prepared to proceed, with or without you. And you should also know that, in over eighty percent of the simulations we've run, an assault on Vesta has resulted in Dr. Brekkelheim's death. The remaining twenty percent were likewise... unpleasant. Good night." The three walk out into the night. The door rolls closed on their retreating backs.

Crysanthia stares at the shut door and slows the rapid, panicked beating of her heart. And, though her physiology renders her impervious, she hugs herself against the chill.

Not one zygote in a hundred, Crysanthia thinks, will reach full term and become a Pilot. A few die in the first days, mere masses of undifferentiated cells. A few more are culled during the next month as gross defects and mutations arise—shockingly few, considering the intricate patchwork of their genome. No one mourns or protests, however, for it is largely agreed that, at those stages, the embryos possess no more sophistication than the average mollusk. But after the fifth week... things change after the fifth week.

Crysanthia wanders her ship, unable to sleep, alienated even from the comforts of the symbiosis chamber and communion with *Pariah's* computers and sensors. She wears a long gown of deep blue watered silk and sips her third cup of tea. Music pulses from every surface of the ship's innards, Kiari Nakatani's *Angel Archer at the Bad Luck Restaurant.* None of it serves to quiet her mind.

On the thirty-third day of incubation, the first cybernetic organelles are introduced. And though the cyborganelles are carefully individuated to mesh with the unique nervous system of each fetus, the shock nonetheless kills over half of the ones who had survived to that stage. For those that live, though, it is a true awakening. With the organelles comes an awareness, an instinctive grasp of the hidden contours of the universe.

But that is only the fifth week. There are still four months left until "birth."

Crysanthia finds herself in the observation lounge for the third time. She sits down on the curved sofa that faces the sloping, forward bulkhead and lets her long, thin legs sprawl out in front of her. For several slow, almost luxurious, minutes, she thinks of nothing.

"*Ms. Vog?*"

For a moment, Crysanthia thinks she imagines it. But no, the voice is real, channeled through her ship and directly into her mind. And she knows of only one kind of being in the universe that can do that.

She activates the cryostylitic projectors embedded in the floor. The space in front of her shimmers into the holographic image of Galatea Trope, dressed in a maroon jumpsuit of quilted velvet with a sable-trimmed toreador jacket.

"*Permission to come aboard?*" Galatea requests. "*I'm not armed. You can scan me.*"

"Come up," Crysanthia says. She switches off the holoprojector and waits until she can feel the warmth of Galatea's body radiate against the skin of the ship before she opens the port.

Galatea slowly ducks through the oval opening in the bulkhead. Before she is fully inside, she blurts, "I'm sorry."

Crysanthia stands and offers her hand to Galatea. The girl takes it. "Welcome aboard, Ms. Trope," Crysanthia says. The opening behind Galatea's back closes to become featureless wall once again. "What's on your mind?"

So many years spent avoiding Pilots, Crysanthia had forgotten how graceful their movements can be. With unconscious fluidity, Galatea slips out of her jacket and folds it over her left forearm. "Narisian told us why he needed to speak with you. He told us what they want you to do."

"When was this?"

"An hour ago," Galatea says. "He's very upset."

"And you?"

Galatea turns around, looks at the walls, the floor. "This ship is one of kind, isn't it? Seven years old and it has advances that still haven't made it to the rest of the fleet."

Crysanthia makes a soft sound of affirmation and nods fractionally. "The real reason you want her," she says to the girl. "You and Narisian, the rest of the Pilots, all of you—the crime you really want Bettina Brekkelheim to pay for, is *me.* My ship, my freedom." She forces herself to laugh. "The very things you want me to use against her. That's why you came to me, my privileged position." Crysanthia gazes at Galatea with studied geniality. "What's wrong, Galatea? You're not smiling."

Galatea opens her mouth to protest but she says nothing. She shuts her mouth and looks at her shoes.

"'Crysanthia Vog is not worth the market value of her blood salts,'" Crysanthia continues. "That's part of the curriculum these days, isn't it? It comes right after annular temporal heterodynes and right before inverse sub-quantum scaling.

Well, it looks like that may be changing. Looks like you've finally found a use for me. Can you tell me whose blood I'm worth now? Or should I guess?"

"Narisian promised me that he will leave you alone," Galatea whispers, "whatever you decide."

Crysanthia is immediately sorry. She is sick to her stomach, sick with herself. She glances down into her empty tea cup. "Have a seat," she says. "I'll bring you a cup of tea."

Not one in a hundred—over four months of accelerated maturation, breathing synthesized amniotic waters, and no less than a dozen procedures, a dozen delicate alterations of their delicate lives, failure of any one resulting in termination. Not one in a hundred.

Crysanthia pours jasmine tea into two bone china cups. Her hand shakes; pulsing tremors move through the muscles of her boneless fingers.

Back in the lounge, she finds Galatea seated at the edge of the sofa, braiding and un-braiding her fingers while gazing into indeterminate space. Crysanthia hands Galatea her cup.

Galatea looks up, manages a wan smile and a distracted "Thank you." She holds the cup under her pointed chin and shifts her gaze to its greenish-brown depths. Crysanthia watches the steam as it coils around her face.

Child woman, Crysanthia thinks. And then she thinks: Pilots never have a childhood—born as adolescents, in space before our second birthday and constantly measuring ourselves against the common stock. Are we human? Something more? Something less?

They sit together, silent and still but for the sipping of the tea. Finally, Galatea says, "I've been thinking about our lives in utero, those months between Day Thirty-Three and Emergence."

"And?"

"And—I don't know, it's hard to articulate... I remember what it was like." She stares at the ceiling. "I remember, even before, and when—when I think about it... Do you ever feel as if you've lost something?" She turns her head and her golden gaze searches Crysanthia. "By being born, I mean."

Crysanthia stares straight ahead and slowly nods. "Fallen."

"Yes," Galatea says, her voice so soft Crysanthia can barely hear her.

When it becomes apparent Galatea will say no more, Crysanthia says, "It's not something I think about often, but yes. Our minds are opened to something *other* than anything we'll ever know. The symbiosis chamber approximates it but it's only an approximation. There's too much of *us* standing in the way."

"Yes," Galatea whispers.

"An awakening, but not an awakening to self. It's something at once above and below selfhood. Oh, it sounds silly, but... Now I know why we never talk about this."

Galatea reaches over, touches Crysanthia's wrist. "Please. Go on." She withdraws her hand. "Please."

Little sister, Crysanthia thinks. And only hours ago you held the most vicious of pistols against my ribs.

"Before I knew who or what I was," she says, "before I could... atomize the universe with words, I knew I was part of something vast and alive, a node or nexus within the vital, secret geometry of space-time. I don't know how much of that consciousness is meat or machine. I don't know." A wave of unprocessed emotion flows over and through her. "Does it matter?" Crysanthia stands up. "It doesn't last. How could it? Soon enough, we're outside, walking on two legs, making money. Pretty clothes and politics. Yes, Galatea, make no mistake. We have lost... something."

"And the ones who don't survive? The one's who lose all of it?"

Crysanthia sits down, looks again into her teacup, its contents cold and forgotten.

"I don't know."

"Maybe I should go."

Crysanthia lifts her gaze. "No," she says. "No, there's more. She's given us something important, something greater than mere existence, greater than life. For even a taste, a glimpse..." Crysanthia shakes her head. "People have given their lives for less."

"But to dispose of them," Galatea protests, "and after they've, after they've—to *scrap* them, like so much defective—"

"It's not that way," Crysanthia says. "It's not like that at all with her. I know her. I've spoken with her. Dined with her." She looks down at her hands. "I've touched her. She's proud of us, Galatea. We aren't cogs in the machinery of trade to her. We are her masterwork." Crysanthia sighs.

"And now you ask me—Narisian Karza asks me—to betray her."

And then there's the thing she's been refusing all night, the insistent fact she's tried her best to ignore, to forget. But here it is, made all the stronger while she would not look at it: Bettina is more than simply *her* creator. Bettina is *his* mother.

Janos: the name forms in her throat but does not touch her lips. And her own words echo in her head: *People have given their lives for less.*

"Will you do it?" Galatea asks.

Crysanthia takes a sip of her tea and finds it has gone cold. "I need to heat this," she says as she stands up. "More?"

Galatea shakes her head, "You haven't answered my question."

Crysanthia sighs. She has no answer. And yet she opens her mouth—something will come to her. And something does: a white hot spasm of agony that shoots through her gut like a solar flare. She gasps from the shock and the pain of it, drops her teacup and watches it slowly fall to the floor and shatter. Her knees give out and she falls into the silent explosion, shards of china and spherical droplets of tea hover in the air, and a gauzy darkness spreads across her vision. She reaches out for Galatea, to steady herself as the universe pitches over, even as she thinks: *The girl, did she—? No, why would she?* And the last thing she sees is Galatea, frantic, grasping for her hand. And then nothing.

4

Objet d'Art

Crysanthia stood atop the Solaris Tri-Planetary Bank Tower and waited for an air sked to take her to the spaceport. She wondered if she was not poised to plunge headlong into the abyss. Seven a.m. Brancusi mean time and there was an early morning bite to the air. The sun shone down a crisp pale gold.

Janos Brekkelheim is a lunatic.

That much was evident, even before Crysanthia had reviewed what data he could provide her. There was little on the thing itself, hardly more than what he had shown her four days ago at the café. On her own, Crysanthia could find nothing—whatever this thing was, the scientific community was keeping it quiet. She found quite a lot about those scientists studying the event, though: the greatest minds in their respective fields and not a timid slave to convention among them. She had also managed to find out a few things about Janos himself. He could easily have been included among their ranks—apparently, he had not lied about that retracted invitation—if not for a persistent habit of staking out the exact line between genius and madness and then blithely stepping across it, with no regard for the slashings of Occam's razor.

The transit control computer announced the arrival of Crysanthia's air sked in its soft contralto. The sked—a silver saucer a scant eighty centimeters in diameter, blinding bright with reflected glare—glided up to the edge of the platform and hovered. The computer repeated its announcement. Crysanthia broke away from the waiting herd and walked over to the boarding platform.

Stink of the zealot, she thought as she stepped out onto the flat, glassy surface of her sked and felt it lock onto her boots. *Here goes.*

With a lurch that would have passed unnoticed were she not a Pilot, the sked sped off into the sky, to soar through Brancusi City's ceramic, glass and steel heights.

As she gazed out at the passing skyscrapers and glanced down at the near backs of drifting blimps and the streets far below, Crysanthia found her thoughts returning to Janos. During her research into his career, she had stumbled upon writings that suggested a more than casual sympathy with the *Gnostique Nouveau* cults that arose during the Great Splintering of the Catholic Church in the chaotic final decades of the last century. Seeking their God quite literally in the foundations of the universe, they made outlandish claims about the nature of time and space, matter and energy. They took Einstein's airy metaphor about using science to read the thoughts of God with ruthless literal-mindedness. More ominously, they suggested dangerous ways to attain their desired revelations. Crysanthia was familiar enough with Janos's field, the counterintuitive science of synchronistics, to know it often seemed to flirt with mysticism. Even so, those articles did more than just *flirt.* Many seemed only angstroms short of a passionate embrace.

The sprawling complex of the Jeanette Baptiste Interplanetary Spaceport came into view beneath her feet and beyond the rim of her sked. Several lines of sky riders and robotic air taxis glided toward the transparent dome at its hub. Nine long terminals and three shorter ones radiated from the dome, asymmetrical spokes of a broken wheel. The small, winged needles of orbital shuttle planes and the large, squat cones of interplanetary rocket pods awaited lift-off on the surrounding space-fields. Crysanthia's eyes could see the scorch marks on their hulls of ceramic composite and woven diamond silk, scars from multiple atmospheric entries.

Her sked joined one of the lines and swept in toward the dome. It deposited her at the east side of the third level. She was dismayed but not surprised to see Janos standing there, with a canvas bag slung over his shoulder, waiting for her.

They said nothing to each other as they walked through the concourse. Off to the side, under a flood of natural light coming in through a transparent ceiling, Crysanthia spied a row of shops in artful disarray reminiscent of a street bazaar. It was this year's fad, Crysanthia knew, every couture row on Venus strove to look like a *souk* in 19th century Marrakech; there was even the scent of jasmine and patchouli wafting from the hidden ventilation system. Next season, no doubt, the shops will all be retro-futurist, with shelves of acid-etched aluminum and minimalist displays. She could only wonder what scents they will lace the air with then. She was about to turn her attention to the cryostylitic advertisements hovering and swimming in the cavernous space above their heads when, amid the many kiosks, she saw one selling silk-skin gloves.

"Hey," Crysanthia said, touching Janos on his upper arm. "We're not tied to a timetable here, are we?"

"Not precisely, but I'd like—"

"Good," she cut him off and lit off for the little shop. After a moment, Janos followed.

"They sell these in the city," Crysanthia explained after the android tending shop greeted them and settled back into vacant, automatic watchfulness, "but I've heard the prices are better here."

Crysanthia stood at a red lacquered counter piled with the gloves, meticulously arranged in a manner she knew only appeared random. She put her purse on the counter's edge and reached for a pair in tan. From the corner of her eye, she watched Janos as she wasted his time. His face betrayed nothing—neither impatience nor indulgence. She wondered if his thoughts were with her at all.

Silk-skin was new to the market, a quasi-alive substance as much plant as cultured animal hide; it derived what meager sustenance it required from the carbon dioxide and moisture in the air. Until now, Crysanthia had only heard tell of it. She had long envied those society women with their elbow-length sheathes of satin and kid; supposedly, silk-skin would conform even to her hands. The gloves were warm and softer than she had imagined. She inspected the grain, not quite calf, not quite snake, with a sheen that stopped just short of iridescence. As she slipped her hand and forearm into the glove, she felt it melt around her. The fingers of the glove followed her experimental twisting and flexing as if it were a second skin.

A woman in an off-the-shoulder blouse walked past, a golden marmoset clinging to her neck and the long cord of braided black hair that snaked down her back. Janos followed her with his eyes. Crysanthia felt a twinge of offended pride and she was instantly angry with herself for it. But then she realized it was the tiny monkey that drew his gaze, not the woman's graceful neck or smooth olive skin. She relaxed, subtly charmed.

As Crysanthia removed the glove to try on another pair, she knocked her purse off the counter. Janos made a sudden grab for it, forgetting Crysanthia's quicker reflexes. She snatched it from the air, brushing her hand along his grasping fingers. She smiled and, for one unguarded moment, it seemed he would smile back. The moment passed.

No one, no matter how obsessive and obsessed, she realized, is ever subsumed wholly within his obsession. In that one reflexive act of futile gallantry and the awkward discomfort that followed, she saw the pieces of Janos that remained when sifted of his monomania. She rather liked them.

And then he ruined it: "Really, Ms. Vog, how much longer do you think you'll be?"

"Long enough," she said, with deliberate and distracted slowness, "to find what I want." She looked at a pair in copper with black lozenges that made them resemble diamondback rattlesnakes and another in a nauseous shade of pink, then ran her fingers along a pair in cobalt and crimson. She shifted her purse to the crook of her arm.

"Let me," Janos said. Before Crysanthia fully understood what he meant, he was rolling the left hand glove up her arm. Where his fingertips touched her naked wrist, she felt a cautious and sensual gentleness. His hand lingered on her arm.

Their eyes met.

The gloves were nothing more than an extravagance. That fact stood in sudden, stark relief; there was a time when Crysanthia cared very little about what she wore, a time when her life was lived in the gulf between the stars and her only garment was her ship. To be sure, she dressed with a modicum of care when she was in the ports but it never really mattered to her, never really *was* her. But when the Consortium stripped her of her ship, these things rushed in to fill the chasm that was left. More than that, Crysanthia had used them as armor between herself and the suddenly hostile universe—without her ship, she was as raw and exposed as a snail ripped from its shell. Now Janos offered to return her to that life, they were on their way to where he would give it to her—she had almost let herself forget that. She realized she was stalling because, as badly as she wanted to, she was not sure she was ready to go back.

"I'll take this pair," Crysanthia said to the android. "And these, too." She selected another pair in forest green.

"Here," Janos said, handing his computer to the android. "I'll be paying for them." Hastily, he grabbed a pair in black, cut only to the wrist. "And these."

Crysanthia looked at him expectantly but he did not explain.

From the bazaar, they passed through the scans of emigration without breaking stride and boarded their ship, a scaled down version the larger interplanetary craft. Janos stowed his bag while Crysanthia looked around the cabin. There were only two seats.

"Cozy," she said.

"Necessary," Janos said.

Crysanthia's resurgent misgivings crept over her like a rash.

A female flight attendant emerged from a dim alcove to the right of Janos and welcomed them aboard. Another android, Crysanthia observed; she noticed the Valence Cyberdynamics logo printed in the deep blue irises, tiny silver letters around permanently dilated pupils. In the closeness of the cabin, she smelled perfume over self-renewing dermaplastics.

"It will be a rather long flight," the android said. "Could I interest either of you in a sleepie?"

"No," Janos said, "we have—"

"*Yes.*" Crysanthia glanced at Janos. "Please."

"Of course." The flight attendant handed Crysanthia a wafer-slate computer. "Select whatever sleepies you'd like from the menu on the screen."

Crysanthia picked two travelogues and checked the flight's duration. She glanced at Janos again, then ordered an extended abstract piece and the adaptation of an old novel. She handed the computer back to the attendant and settled into her reclining seat.

She was asleep before take-off. The ship's sleepie projector fed her lucid dreams of swimming with dolphins and wandering the streets of Paris. Then her consciousness became as diffuse as a cloud of blue oil pulsing in a sunlit womb. After that, she was James Bond.

The rocket pod had already landed when Crysanthia awoke. Her eyes focused on Janos as he retrieved his bag.

"You talk in your sleep," he said. He looked down at Crysanthia with neither amusement nor annoyance.

Crysanthia yawned and stretched, watching Janos for any reaction to her feline display, disappointed to find none. "So I've been told," she said as she came to her feet. She caught sight of the dormant flight attendant. The android stared without sight from within her dim niche. Crysanthia quickly turned away.

Janos motioned for her to precede him through the pod's open hatch. She stepped out onto the shining black surface of a ceramic landing pad and felt the dissipating warmth of the pod's retro-thrusters through the soles of her boots. Beyond the edge of the landing pad, a meadow of grass, clover and wildflowers rustled in the breeze. Farther away, a forest of ivy-entangled trees, grown tall and thin in Vesta's low gravity, receded into impenetrable darkness. All around, insects buzzed, rattled and clicked—bees and butterflies flitted from blossom to blossom. Birds sang.

No pressure dome, Crysanthia notes. "Is the entire asteroid like this?"

Janos nodded. "Gravitational generators keep the pull at about one third Earth normal. More and the stresses would tear the asteroid apart. A magnetic containment field holds in the atmosphere, blocks out the harmful radiation. Didn't stop the birds. Thousands of them flew through the shield before Mother wised up and had a painful aversion to its frequency sewn into their DNA. Every now and then, their frozen, desiccated corpses come streaking across the sky like shooting stars."

Crysanthia glanced up at the cloudless canopy of perfect blue. The expense, she thinks, to completely remake an entire asteroid, and all for one person—she is simultaneously awed and sickened.

"She has two satellites set in slow orbit," Janos said. "Lumenium spheres, a greater light to rule the day and a lesser light to rule the night."

"Look, I'm sorry about the concourse," she said. "With the gloves. I mean, you are the client, here."

Janos shrugged. "It reminded me of when I was a small child, shopping with my mother." His tone was flat and matter-of-fact. Crysanthia wasn't sure if he was telling her it was all right or just making a neutral observation.

Deep in the forest, something moved—before she could hear it, Crysanthia felt it in her fingertips. Slowly, a clot of darkness broke free and shambled into the daylight. A massive beast, covered in glossy black fur with thick, rust-colored tufts around its muzzle, throat and tremendous feet, looked at Crysanthia with liquid brown eyes that seemed especially aware.

"Huh," Janos ruminated aloud. "Simple splice, dog and bear. Hardly a finger exercise for her..."

The creature came forward and sniffed the air around Crysanthia. Even on all fours, its head came to her chin. She felt its hot, moist breath on her throat. "Um, Janos..."

"Relax, it's tame. Mother wouldn't have sent it otherwise."

Crysanthia didn't need him to tell her that. She smelled biochemical benevolence in its fetid exhalations. If she feared anything, it was that the beast would soon try to lick her face.

The creature's whiskers twitched and its ears shifted. Slowly, it swung its huge head and looked back to the forest. Relieved, Crysanthia followed its gaze.

A woman, fair-skinned with fine, silver-blond hair and heavy-lidded, beryl blue eyes, emerged from the forest. Faint wrinkles surrounded her not entirely cruel mouth and lined her throat but her gait was brisk and vigorous. Crysanthia had to remind herself that the woman was eighty-four years old, well into middle age.

Against all of her expectations, Crysanthia found herself on the verge of trembling. With no small exertion of will, she stilled herself.

Bettina Brekkelheim was a tall woman by common stock standards, a centimeter or so taller than the son she embraced and kissed. "So," she said with a faint German accent, "I see you found her." Her words were addressed to Janos but her eyes were on Crysanthia. Bettina eyed her as if she was an artifact or a long-pursued, exotic species of butterfly. A self-satisfied smile touched her lips.

"Wasn't hard," Janos said.

"Uh-huh," Bettina said absently. "Come here, *liebling*, and let me look at you."

Crysanthia did as she was told, moving forward with small, shy steps.

"I still haven't found a way to improve on your design, did you know that?"

Crysanthia nodded.

"I was always especially proud of you. Unpredictable, headstrong, a pretty girl with a darling pug nose and those *cheekbones*..." Bettina reached up and traced the contours of Crysanthia's face with her fingertips. Crysanthia's fear and hunger were too much to contain; a violent tremor ripped through her. Bettina's smile widened, the crinkles bracketing her mouth deepened and her touch became a caress. She patted Crysanthia's cheek. "I asked them to let you keep your ship, you know."

Again, Crysanthia nodded.

"Probably would have done the same thing, if I were you. Sounds like delicious fun." Bettina winked.

Crysanthia had no idea how to respond to that. Belatedly, she murmured her thanks.

"What else did you bring me?" Bettina asked Janos. She continued to stare at Crysanthia.

"Chocolate and cigarettes, from Earth," Janos said. "The cigarettes weren't easy to get."

Bettina finally turned to him. Released from the bug collector scrutiny, Crysanthia felt as if a giant pin had been removed from her thorax.

"And?" Bettina asked.

"Wine. Some of that bread you like. Cheese."

"Of course, of course, thank you." She kissed Janos at the corner of his mouth.

"Gloves, too," Janos added. "Those were Ms. Vog's idea."

Bettina raised an eyebrow and looked at Crysanthia again. "Oh, and honey," she said. Crysanthia was lost for an instant until she realized Bettina was still talking to Janos. "Did you bring honey?"

"And honey."

"You're such a good son."

The animal grunted.

"I'm sorry," Bettina said. "How terribly rude of me. Children, I've made a new friend. I'd like you to meet Aurelius."

The creature shambled up alongside its mistress and sat. Peripherally, Crysanthia noticed a stiffening in Janos's spine. Apparently, Bettina noticed it as well. She scratched the animal behind its ear and sighed. "Come on, let's go to the cottage. I'm hungry."

Crysanthia, alone in the bathroom, swallowed two-hundred milligrams of duraladium powder in a silica gel suspension to replenish her cyborganelles, then took a drink of cold water directly from the tap. She spent a moment stooped over the washbasin, staring at her reflection in the looking glass above it, and then slipped the empty phial back into her handbag. She left the bathroom and entered the cavernous living room of Bettina's so-called cottage.

A fire burned steadily in a flagstone fireplace almost as large as the kitchen of Crysanthia's Brancusi City flat. Janos and Bettina sat across from each other on three-legged stools. Between them, Janos's offerings—the small loaves of dense, dark bread; wedges of raw milk bandaged cheddar, goat's milk brie and Danish bleu cheese, and foil wrapped chocolates—covered a rough, round wooden table, alongside slices of peach and green apple from Bettina's orchards. An opened bottle of Riesling chilled in an ice bucket on the floor while a half empty bottle sweated on the table. The bear/dog chimera lay sprawled alongside, its shoulders level with Bettina's chin. Eyes shut, it lapped honey from an earthenware pot it held between its paws. An empty stool waited for Crysanthia, between Janos and the beast.

Bettina watched Janos and swallowed a mouthful of apple, bread and brie. She sipped her wine.

"And how *is* your father?" she asked. "Have you seen him lately?"

Slowly, Janos turned his head and gazed at Bettina. "Well enough," he said. "I saw him about a month ago. He sends his regards."

"Liar," Bettina laughed.

Janos glanced at the animal. "I see you have yet to grow tired of trivializing him."

"Janos, stop." She reached over and thumped the beast's flank. "There is nothing trivial about Aurelius." She bent forward and patted it on its head. "And he understands what you say—most of it. So watch your mouth. Crysanthia, has Janos told you about his father?"

Crysanthia shook her head. She hadn't asked, nor had she looked it up.

Bettina turned to Janos. "Well?"

"My father is a Martian schoolteacher."

"Now who's trivializing him?" To Crysanthia, she said, "His father teaches twentieth and twenty-first century literature at The University of Utopia Planitia's School of the Humanities." She cut her eyes at Janos. "He won the Paolo Constantine Award, when was it? Back in 2156, I think."

"Fifty-seven," Janos corrected.

Finally, the tumblers turned in Crysanthia's mind. "Your father is Aurelius Mann," she said to Janos, with the amazement that comes with the suddenly obvious, "Poet Laureate of Mars." She turned to Bettina. "I knew you two—I never thought it was that... serious." She regretted the words a microsecond before they had left her mouth. Bettina's jaw tightened—a common stock would never have noticed. To Crysanthia, it was as loud as a shout, sharp as a slap.

Janos made it worse: "Mother has so many affairs, even she loses track."

Bettina thumped Janos on his chest with the back of her hand. "That's enough, you." She turned to Crysanthia. "We weren't together for all that very long. In all truth, it wasn't much of an affair. But I had just turned fifty; I decided I wanted a child. Aurelius liked me. And there were qualities he possessed, things that I lacked and that I wanted my child to have." A wistful look crossed her face. “Poor Aurelius, he was sweet in his own grandiose and silly way. I didn’t get around to telling him he was a father until Janos had his fourth birthday.”

Janos rubbed the spot where Bettina had struck him. “The story only grows more beautiful every time I hear it.”

A flash of real fury, Crysanthia can see it: searing and intense, then gone. “It was practical,” Bettina said to her son. “That should be enough, no? No, *Doctor* Brekkelheim?” She sighed. “It made sense.” She placed her hand on his shoulder. “It gave me you.” She shoved. Janos budged less than a centimeter. “I’m grateful to him, your father. Yes, I had other lovers—before and after him. But this didn’t really concern him—or me. It concerned you, *sie störrisches Dummkopf*.”

Janos looked away and Bettina stood and stretched: her back arched, her arms over her head, her fingers interlocked and palms open to the massive oak rafters. “Take a walk with me, Crysanthia. Let’s give the gentlemen a chance to get to know one another.”

Aurelius snorted. At once, the beast ceased to be an “it” for Crysanthia and instead became a “he.” And she decided she liked him.

“Oh, shut up,” Bettina said to Aurelius and tapped him on the snout. “Janos?”

“It’s your planet.”

“Asteroid,” Bettina corrected. To Crysanthia, she said, “Shall we?”

Bettina led Crysanthia on a meandering stroll through the reed tree forests of Vesta, among the sounds of nocturnal creatures stirring in the approaching dusk. With every step a small bound, they covered twelve kilometers with little effort.

They emerged into a clearing that overlooked a lake. Floating in the water, just beyond a wooden dock, was the smooth, silver teardrop hull of a starship. In the artificial sunset, it reflected amber and magenta, like the still waters surrounding it.

"She's beautiful," Crysanthia said.

"A prototype. The most advanced starship in existence. She's, ah, *supposed* to be on Ganymede, in pieces, so I can *study* her, get some ideas for a fifth generation of star pilots. Ha. After twelve years, Stigol-Bergham has yet to approach the potential I built into you." They walked out onto the dock, Bettina in the lead. "Maybe another twelve, another twelve hundred... Give me your hand."

Crysanthia obeyed. Bettina pressed a hypodermic stylus against her wrist and Crysanthia felt her arm go numb to the elbow. Then Crysanthia gasped and collapsed into an agonized ball. The machine part of her crackled with microscopic and subatomic frenzy and feverish heat suffused her entire body, along with a dull ache that radiated out from the marrow of her cartilaginous skeleton. Finally, her cheek resting on the timbers of the dock, she listened to the cool slosh of the water below as her breath returned to her and the pain faded away.

"There," Bettina said as Crysanthia pulled herself onto her hands and knees. "That should do it. Feeling better?"

Crysanthia nodded. Bettina reached down and hauled her to her feet.

"Shall we go inside?"

Crysanthia nodded again, still too shaken for speech.

At their approach, the skin of the ship's hull parted like quicksilver. An oval doorway opened to an interior of pale greens and blues. Everything shined with a gold opalescence that seemed to pulse, as if the ship were alive. The ship's computers reached out and smoothly insinuated themselves into Crysanthia's nervous system via her newly re-configured cyborganelles. She was home. More than home, she was complete.

"I can't believe this. That you'd just *give* all this to me..."

"Give?" Bettina lifted an eyebrow. "I'm not *giving* you anything. Perhaps you should think of yourself as an employee, or as a tool. Once you have done this thing for Janos, I can foresee no further use for you." She sighed. "Or for this ship." Bettina sat down in the curved leather couch that faced the sloping wall of the ship's prow. "The freedom you gain is merely a function of that fact, an afterthought." She passed her hand through the air in a graceful and complex motion. The wall seemed to disappear—Crysanthia looked out over the lake as a brace of wild geese flew by overhead. "Highest resolution screen available—detail greater than even your eyes can discern," Bettina said. "And the floor is peppered with cryostylitic projectors. Not that you'll ever have much call for any of it. Your passengers should enjoy them."

"I see," Crysanthia whispered. She looked out over the lake. She could not bring herself to turn around.

Bettina muttered something obscene under her breath. "Please understand me, Crysanthia. I do not wish to be cruel. Quite the opposite, I wish to spare you the cruelty of illusion. I wish to be clear. It cost a great deal of capital to do this, enough to actually make a difference to me, a difference I can feel." Bettina sighed. "*Real* capital, I mean, not the consensual lie of solaria and lunarii. I stand to alienate the entire Consortium. To you the Consortium is just the Pilot's Commission. But I'm part of it, and so is Stigol-Bergham and the Charybdis Corporation, and under them, a host of other bodies and concerns, and all of *them* extremely impatient with you *und die Scheisse* you churned up with your little escapade. And now, just as it's settled, we churn it up again." She shook her head. "In my position, I cannot afford to make any more enemies than I already have."

Crysanthia's compound eyes provided her with a wide, deep and clear field of focus. As she looked over her shoulder, she saw Bettina as clearly as if she stared straight on. "So why do it?"

"Janos." Bettina took a silver cigarette case from her shirt pocket. "Do you mind?"

Crysanthia shook her head.

Bettina lit a narrow, nicotine-gold cigarette and took a long, ragged drag. She blew the smoke through her nostrils. "I adore you, make no mistake. You are my crowning achievement and nothing I will ever do will surpass you. But you are ultimately property, my intellectual property, an *objet d'art.* All that is me in you comes from here." She touched her forehead with the hand holding the cigarette. Its burning tip pointed at Crysanthia, twin tendrils of rippling blue streamed toward the ceiling. "Janos is my son." She clenched her other hand into a fist and held it against her belly. "If only you could know… What has he told you?"

"Very little."

"Probably more than he's told me. Don't expect him to be good company. He won't tell you more than he feels he has to." Her eyes glistened with unshed tears, a sight Crysanthia found unsettling in a way too primal to grasp. "I have a reputation for heartlessness. That's why I spend my days out here, away from the Inner Worlds. But I'm not so heartless..." The knuckles of the fist she held to her womb were drained white. "I'm no colder than I need to be."

After a brief interval, after it became clear that something was expected of her, Crysanthia steeled herself and turned around. "You are my creator," she said. "It would be hubris for me to judge you."

"I suppose," Bettina said. She pressed the heels of her hands to her shining eyes. "Yes, I suppose that is what I'm asking for. And no, it is not my place to ask for it." She came to her feet and flicked her cigarette into the air. The ship incinerated it before it could reach its apogee. It disappeared in a blue-white flash. "Whatever happens, bring him back to me. Promise me that much."

"I promise."

"Go," Bettina said. "Inspect the rest of the ship. The rest of *your* ship." She fumbled with her slim, silver box and extracted another cigarette. "I'll be here when you get back."

After a cursory tour of the cargo bay and the dark matter reaction drive, the living quarters and the four cramped lifeboats, Crysanthia found herself in the symbiosis chamber, a round room with concave walls, black and nacreous, like the inside of an oyster's shell. The walls were studded everywhere with the tiny lenses of the interface lasers, so deep a scarlet they appeared obsidian. Sitting in the center of the padded deck was a bottle of *Moet et Chandon*, vintage 2141. Crysanthia did not care about the champagne. All she could think was that soon she would sit there, her long legs folded beneath her, and guide all of this metal and power through the void. The trepidation she'd felt back in the spaceport dissolved into nothingness—she laughed at her folly. She had been living for this all along, never once believing it would ever again be hers.

What was ceremony in relation to that? What was anything?

Crysanthia christened the ship *Pariah*. Bettina furrowed her brow but applauded gamely as Crysanthia swung the bottle and it met the hull in an explosion of emerald shards and white foam. Crysanthia watched as the fragments of the bottle slowly sank through the clear water to settle on the sandy bottom of the lake.

They jogged back to the cottage through deepening gloom. The cool silver light of the false moon barely penetrated the forest. From time to time, they emerged into clearings where bats, fast and erratic, wheeled overhead. Crysanthia heard the hoot of an owl.

In the cottage, Aurelius lay stretched out in front of the hearth. The fire was almost out, burnt down to embers glowing beneath a lace of whitish ash. The animal lifted his heavy head and watched them as they entered, then rested it on his paws again and closed his eyes with a soft and satisfied "*Whuff.*" Janos slept nearby, sprawled in a chair. His ubiquitous computer lay on the floor, centimeters away from his relaxed fingertips. Crysanthia watched as Bettina picked up the computer and brushed Janos's forehead with her lips. Crysanthia felt a pang of sharp and unexpected jealousy—for which of the two, she did not know.

Bettina looked down at the computer and smiled. Silently, she beckoned to Crysanthia and showed it to her.

Crysanthia wasn't sure exactly what she was expecting to see—something technical, no doubt, something choked with jargon and diagrams and mathematical expressions. Instead, she saw pages of prose in facsimile so detailed that it reproduced even the tiny flecks of wood pulp, describing the bleak tedium facing two astronauts marooned on a planetoid in orbit of Betelgeuse. Apparently, the astronauts were the crew of a fusion-powered rocket bound for a colony world orbiting Deneb. Betelgeuse and Deneb, Crysanthia thought, impossibly distant even with today's starships and this? She scoffed inwardly: set in an AD 1998 that never happened; in the real 1998, humankind had scarcely progressed past the moon. She checked the file: a centuries-old pulp novel called *The Android's Lament* by someone named J.C. Kindred, first published in 1967.

"All work and no play," Bettina whispered and winked. She took the computer from Crysanthia, shut it off and slipped it into Janos's breast pocket.

Later, alone in the guest quarters, Crysanthia used the house computer to access selected poems of Aurelius Mann but her mind would not focus. Words slipped by and refused to attach themselves to meaning—she found herself reading the same stanzas over and over. Finally, she gave up and, awake in the darkness, thought about absolution and Bettina's unshed tears. She thought about Janos, about his ancient pulp novels and the things he would not tell her.

5

Celestis Regina

All the medical scans say there is nothing wrong with her.

Crysanthia has been monitoring herself ever since she woke among the wreckage of her favorite teacup, Galatea kneeling at her side and feeling under her armpits for a pulse. Now that she's blasted out of Klytemnestra and left the Iota Horologii system behind, her symptoms have worsened. Nausea. Fever. Chills. No more blackouts, though, and for that and that alone she is grateful.

Yet *Pariah* tells her there is nothing wrong.

The symbiosis chamber suppresses the symptoms but she cannot remain in the chamber forever. Eventually, she has to disengage herself from the ship and when she does the sickness is upon her, like a pack of jackals.

Only she is not sick. *Pariah* tells her so.

With deliberate steps, she enters the observation lounge. Her two passengers have set the forward wall to view-screen mode. Dead ahead is Sol, the brightest point among thousands of bright points shining in the void.

Special Agent Caro looks up from her wafer-slate computer display. "How do you feel?"

"Better," Crysanthia lies.

"It will be over soon," Special Agent Berengaria says, trying manfully to sound sympathetic and failing miserably. "You'll be able to relax."

Crysanthia nods.

"I can't pretend to understand how difficult this must be for you," Caro says. "I won't insult you by trying."

"Thank you."

"If there is anything—"

"Thank you."

Crysanthia leaves them. On shaky legs, she finds her way to her cabin and tries to rest. When she finally falls asleep it is only to be assailed by nightmares that she, mercifully, will not remember.

Naked in the chamber, Crysanthia watches Vesta grow within her mind's eye, from one grain of sand among thousands scattered against the blackness to a vision-filling green, blue and white globe in the space of a few heartbeats.

Pariah cruises through the security net of hunter/killer satellites without incident. Sleek, silver hulks festooned with retracted weaponry, they hang inert like torpid hornets too stupid to know she's a threat. Their lazy scans ripple over her hull. Crysanthia feels the last of the scans taper off just as *Pariah* enters the artificial atmosphere and cremates several freeze-dried birds in her superheated wake.

Crysanthia brakes *Pariah* to a slow glide and splashes her down in the very lake she was launched from. The starship floats like an outsized fishing boat. Crysanthia brings the prow alongside the dock and disconnects herself from symbiosis.

Before the tingle of the pink lasers on her naked skin can fade away, Crysanthia is sick. She fights against a gorge gone irredeemably buoyant. Caught midway to standing out of her lotus position, she drops to all fours and retches.

The symbiosis chamber burns the vomit to ash before it can touch the floor and sweeps it away on a current of air—Crysanthia watches with misplaced fascination as the red-violet flares blossom into brief and bright existence with every heave. With nothing more to expel, she waits for her body to quiet its spasms, then pulls herself to her feet and walks, unclothed, to her cabin. She showers and dresses.

In the lounge, Caro and Berengaria stand and wait. With their severe, black frock coats and pistols hanging like lethal fetishes from belts slung low on their hips, they look like members of an obscure and homicidal monastic order.

"Ms. Vog," Caro says, "you've done all that we require of you. You don't need to come any further. Spare yourself. Wait in your symbiosis room."

The port opens with a dull and throaty hiss. A lakeshore breeze, redolent of algal rot and honeysuckle, blows into the ship.

"Let's go," Crysanthia says.

Even in the minimal gravity, every step deeper into the reed tree forest is a trial for Crysanthia. The world around her vibrates at a frequency that fouls her equilibrium--so vivid it becomes a blur. She smells the loam at her feet, the musk of the rodents, the sap flowing from wounded plants. She hears the buzzing of the cicadas, the caws of the crows, the songs of the thrushes. She sees every vein of the emerald and maroon oak leaves, every flaking circle of bluish gray and greenish gold lichen that covers the bark of the trees, everything awash in nauseous light. She stumbles but she does not fall.

Berengaria glances back at her—in disgust, she sees, not concern. He thumbs a tube hanging at his belt and launches a cloud of sensor remotes, invisible to common stock eyes, not to Crysanthia's. She watches them speed away and disperse among the trees. After a few more steps, Berengaria activates his computer and peers into the miniature holocube.

"Not much farther," he says. "She has something with her, some kind of creature." He looks more intently into the cube. "One of her customized freaks." He glances at Crysanthia. "No offense."

Crysanthia does no acknowledge him. Caro catches her eye in mute apology.
Berengaria looks back into the cube. "Huge. Looks like a cross between a rottweiler and a Kodiak bear."

"Aurelius," Crysanthia says between gulps of air. "And that's. Exactly. What he. Is."

"Ms. Vog," Caro says with concern.

"I'm fine."

Crysanthia overtakes Caro and Berengaria through will alone and walks the next hundred meters with them trailing far behind. Half-buried rocks and shallow roots hide among the ferns, waiting to trip and snare her. Just as she breaks, as she fears she will never take another step, she emerges into a clearing.

Ivy and roses grow wild all around, a thicket through which narrow paths wind. Tendrils climb the trunk of a spreading chestnut tree and tangle in the dull green bronze feet of the black marble bench where Bettina sits and reads. Aurelius naps nearby, a hillock of fat and fur in a patch of dandelion and clover. His nostrils and whiskers twitch at the annoyance of a fly.

Crysanthia supports herself against a spruce tree with both hands. She rests her face upon it, the bark is rough and soothing against her cheek; the muscles in her forearms and thighs tremble.

She watches silently as Bettina kicks off one of her slippers and strokes Aurelius with her long and bony bare foot. Aurelius grunts and shifts his bulk into her caress. Bettina smiles and turns a page.

"Mother," Crysanthia whispers and pushes away from the tree, sticky with its dark amber tar. She staggers toward Bettina. *Forgive me.*

Bettina looks up from her book and her smile widens. She opens her mouth to speak when her gaze falls on the two agents who approach with their weapons drawn and faces blank. Her smile fades.

"Dr. Bettina Brekkelheim," Caro says, "you are under arrest in accordance with the laws of the Solar Commonwealth. You will be fully apprised of your rights in due course. Please, come with us."

Bettina looks at Crysanthia, then at Caro. "Oh," she says.

Crysanthia would never have believed it. That the animal, with all his lazy, lumbering mass, could *move* so quickly—she is amazed. And she marvels at the tremendous muscles in his shoulders, wonders how she never really noticed them before. Artificial sunlight glints in the spittle on his fangs and blurs along the long, black claws as they define perfect parallel arcs and speed to meet her throat. Sick as she is, fascinated as she is, she could easily evade him. She could disable or kill him, if she wanted. She does not move. She waits the long fractions of an instant for impact and oblivion.

A high-pitched whine and the smell of ozone and vaporized metal. A loud, whirring snap and the flare of lead-cadmium alloy partially excited into plasma. A wet thump and the stink of scorched fur and lacerated bowels. Ruptured flesh. Arterial spray. Aurelius becomes, with one shot from Berengaria's pistol, a mess of meat and blood and bone.

Silence broken only by the buzzing of the fly. And then nothing as it settles to gorge on the blood and shit of the murdered beast.

"Oh," Bettina says, gore spattered across her hair and face, the pages of her book.

Caro helps Bettina to her feet and gently places the magnetic restraints around her wrists. The book falls to the ground.

In silence, the agents lead Bettina away. Crysanthia follows. She casts one last look behind her, to the ruined beast and the book lying bloodied in the grass, the title in gold letters along the leather spine: *Earthman*, by Aurelius Mann.

***

Not enough for the planetary engineers to tame hell and make of her an Eden. Not enough to coerce a world whose slow rotation gave her a day longer than her year into spinning on a civilized twenty-four hour schedule. Not enough to scrub a crushing blast furnace of thick carbon dioxide and sulfuric smog into a pristine nitrogen-oxygen atmosphere. Not enough to give her oceans. Not enough to make her bloom with cherry blossoms and poppies. No, for Venus to become the idealized twin of long-suffering Earth, she needed a moon. Not merely a moon, a consort.

And so the planetary engineers created Vulcan.

They built its core from nickel-iron asteroids abducted from their orbits and carbon extracted from the Venusian atmosphere. They paved it over with a kilometer-thick skin of iron sulfide, fool's gold.

The planetary engineers looked upon their work and deemed it good.

Vulcan is the forge of the Commonwealth, or so the saying goes. The Charybdis Corporation builds its nano-intelligences on Vulcan and Valence Cyberdamics builds its androids. Pischa-Galway builds its guns on Vulcan and Stigol-Bergham builds its starships. Dark matter, diamond silk and duraladium; plastiform composites, rexeroid ceramics and crystalline fluidic alloys; vat-cultured leathers, furs and ivory—all of it is manufactured under the featureless surface of Vulcan, in the moon's mega-industrial labyrinths.

It is in New Kiryu, Vulcan's capital and sole surface city, among the golden spires and streets of pink granite, under the high diamond dome and, beyond that, the blue-white sphere of Venus in a sky of eternal black, that Bettina Bekkelheim stands trial for high crimes of conscience against sentient life.

Crysanthia is not there.

Crysanthia witnesses the trial the way the vast majority of people in the Solar System do, via newsfeed. Her illness has abated but is still with her, reminding her of its presence with the occasional stab of abdominal pain and attack of vertigo. She is well enough to attend this gathering, though: the avant-garde elite of Brancusi City, milling about around a two meter by three meter holocube, watching what unfolds hundreds of thousands of kilometers above their heads.

There is a full moon over the city tonight.

Discussions emanate from within and without the cube on the intricacies of *Chrome v. Commonwealth*. Crysanthia has nothing to add. She had known Diphalia Chrome from her years as a Commissioned Pilot and thought the other Pilot tedious. Why she would choose to contract her services to the Security Forces and then balk at a "hazardous" maneuver (a deceleration phase shift off the photosphere of Luyten's Star—Crysanthia could have done it with a vodka-and-ouzo hangover) made little sense to Crysanthia but came as no surprise. However, there was no predicting how far Chrome's suit, filed in response to criminal charges brought against her by the Commonwealth, would lead. Finally forced to assign legal status to the strange blue creatures, so like humans and yet so fundamentally *unlike* them, the courts reluctantly acknowledged the Pilots (*homo cy-borganicus)* as possessing legal sentience and full individual agency. For Chrome, it meant that, as a civilian attached to the Navy rather than a piece of equipment leased by it, she would suffer only the financial penalties outlined in her contract—no small thing, Crysanthia was sure. For the Pilots as a newly defined "race," it meant they were heir to all the rights, privileges and protections of humanity—not that it made much of a difference from day to day. But for Bettina, it meant months of grinding legalities lurching tonight toward a foregone conclusion—the Trial of the Century, or, at very least, the social event of the season.

A waiter walks by—human, not android; the host has a reputation for extravagance—carrying a silver tray of crackers bearing toy-sized soft-shell crabs, half of them topped with red caviar, the other half with pureed avocado piped out of a pastry bag. The sight of them, a particular favorite of hers, turns Crysanthia's stomach.

"From what I gather, it isn't a matter of genus and species; they aren't even mammals, really," Crysanthia overhears someone say at the far end of the room. "Though you'd never know it by looking at Crysanthia over there. What would you say, B cup? C?"

More waiters emerge from the kitchen, carrying platters loaded down with eatables and alcohol.

"....all alone on that rock except for some huge bear-thing," Crysanthia hears someone else say. "Have to wonder what they got up to up there..."

Crysanthia takes her drink, tonic water with lime, out onto the terrace.

"Remember the *Ninevah,*" Crysanthia whispers. She looks over her shoulder, back through the sliding glass doors and into the party, and thinks: *How could I forget?*

In 2072, researchers working for Stigol-Bergham Astronautics discovered the sub-quantum onion fold while conducting experiments with minute amounts of artificially produced dark matter. Before long, they determined that they had found a likely means of faster-than-light space-flight. No one could make it work, however, until 2079, when the researchers deduced that the most advanced artificial intelligences available lacked, by their intrinsic nature, the ability to make the non-rational mental connections necessary to shape the energy derived from reactive dark matter into a sustainable wedge into the fold. For that, they needed a human factor. Over the next several years, Stigol-Bergham developed—after great expense and effort—a workable cyborg interface.

In 2092, they built the first faster-than-light vessels.

In 2097, after nineteen months of trial runs—from Luna to Neptune and back again in under thirty seconds—Stigol-Bergham and the Ministry of Space Exploration and Colonization decided to launch what was supposed to be humanity's first true starship, the *Ninevah.*

There were no Pilots back then. The ships were guided by common stock humans, ruthlessly selected, rigorously trained and plugged into their ship's artificial intelligences via super-conductive cables jacked into ports drilled into their skulls. The test pilot wired into the helm of the *Ninevah* was a thirty-four-year old career officer named Carlos Truang who, in addition to the rank of lieutenant colonel in the Pacific Alliance Marine Corps, held doctorates in astrophysics and mathematics and a master's degree in cyber-neurology. He was also a devoted husband and the father of two little girls. To a world ravaged by a spate of devastating wars and a slew of natural disasters, including the Tokyo Earthquake of 2063 and the ensuing tsunami, Truang was a much-needed hero. He promised the stars.

His mission was to take the experimental vessel out to Barnard's Star and back, a voyage of twelve light years. It was supposed to take a little over a month. Instead, the *Ninevah* never returned.

MinSEC and Stigol-Bergham wouldn't receive the telemetry explaining what had happened for another four years, the amount of time it took for the radio transmission to reach Earth, but by then they already knew the cause. The other test pilots, the ones limited to the solar system, had begun to show signs of irreparable brain dysfunction; two had died, three others had slipped into deep comas. Something about the nature of the interface itself, the yoking of a human nervous system to a computer intellect, was slowly but inexorably fatal to the human. The AI would inevitably disintegrate the tenuous networks and connections in the human brain required to produce and sustain the emergent phenomenon crudely called the human mind. The more time a human pilot spent wired into his ship, the farther a human pilot traveled, the worse the damage. Colonel Truang had died less than a week after launch. The *Ninevah,* deep in the fold when it happened, was never recovered.

A colossal statue of Truang, nude and eight meters tall, cast in green-black bronze with the cyborg port and subcutaneous fibroids garishly rendered in gold and silver inlay, dominates the rotunda of the Lunapolis Spaceport. He stands with one foot in front of the other, his hands outstretched as if he would seize the infinite itself. But the dark matter reaction drive and, with it, access to the onion fold and the stars, had to wait another thirty years before Bettina Brekkelheim and the Charybdis Corporation, in uneasy and reluctant partnership, could perfect a machine/mind hybrid robotic enough to survive symbiotic immersion in an AI yet animalistic enough to take the intuitive leaps necessary to defy the laws of physics.

And that's what brings Crysanthia here, now, to this dreary and degrading soiree, sipping on insipid tonic water because anything alcoholic would make her vomit—and she wishes to God she had something alcoholic. She really ought to go home.

She knows the owner of this condominium; she had met him a few times during her years in exile. He owns and co-owns several galleries and has propositioned her on more than one occasion. Crysanthia had respectfully declined.

She has not seen him tonight and wonders where he is. The host for the evening is his new paramour, a young artist just arrived from New York City. She catches him eyeing her through the doors, a faint, disaffected sneer on his face. Had Crysanthia eyelids, she would wink. She blows him a kiss instead. With studied nonchalance, he turns his attention elsewhere.

Crysanthia leans against the railing and looks at the pale yellow disk that is Vulcan. Dark ripples mar the surface, irregularities from when the slag cooled to crust. New Kiryu is visible, a single point glittering high in the lower right-hand quadrant like an embedded star. Try as she might (and she does not try very hard), she cannot connect what unfolds in the cube with what shimmers in the sky.

Three months since they took Bettina into custody, she reflects as she looks out over the city. Five months since Klytemnestra. Seven years since Janos and Fomalhaut. Eleven years since Narisian and the others expelled her from the Consortium. Eighteen years since her first flight. Twenty years since her birth and only a little longer—a few months longer—since her awakening. A life. Time re-gathered like the shards of a shattered teacup. Crysanthia looks down at the street hundreds of meters below her and muses on how it would feel to tumble through space for the time it would take to reach the cobblestones. Even with her body's resilience, the fall would be fatal. Crysanthia lifts her gaze to the deep indigo of the moonlit sky.

"What have I done?" she asks those few stars that are visible. She knows one of them, the brightest and bluest of them, is Earth. The ruthless and relentless biological *push* began in the chemical murk of your oceans, Crysanthia thinks. Eons of parasitism and predation, the horrors countenanced by evolution's prodigal cruelty—in the face of that, what are the sins of one woman?

Crysanthia straightens her back. She remembers the loneliness, the fear, the constant pain of her exile from her own unforgiving kind. She remembers how they came to her, asking for her help. She demands of the heavens, of the mute, ancestral speck, "What else could I have done?"

The doors behind her slide open almost soundlessly but not quite, not to her. Crysanthia braces herself against the unwelcome arrival of a common stock socialite. But she catches a familiar scent and hears a grace in the cadence of soft footfalls.

"I hope I'm not intruding," Galatea Trope says.

"Of course not." Crysanthia hears the door slide shut. She turns around. "Party's invitation only. How did you get up here?"

Galatea makes a face. "My blue skin got me in the door." She looks over her shoulder at the faces staring at them from inside the condominium. "And I came very near to injuring one of the disgusting little grubs not two minutes after I walked through it." She glances downward. "He said something utterly vile involving my genitals and a narcotic cocktail."

Crysanthia nods. In certain circles, it is rumored that a Pilot's vaginal secretions contain a mild hallucinogen and several pseudo-opiates.

Crysanthia permits herself an inward smile. She suspects she may have started the rumor herself, somewhat inadvertently, in an unguarded moment during a week-long party on the interplanetary yacht *Celestis Regina.*

"Honestly, Crysanthia, how do you stand them?"

"I didn't have much of a choice. Still don't really."

Galatea bites her lower lip and gazes out at the Brancusi City skyline.

"Besides, can you really blame them? We were designed as living sculpture, Bettina told me as much. And right now, we're news."

Galatea sighs.

Crysanthia turns back the cityscape just as an airship drifts by, close enough to touch. The lights mounted on its swollen, upswept wings sweep across their faces and its engines hum softly. "Ever been to Earth?" Crysanthia asks. "In Hanoi, the blimps are painted in patterns of bright red, green, yellow and blue. Some of them even have eyes painted on their bellies..."

Galatea casts another glance over her shoulder. "Can we talk somewhere more private?"

Crysanthia nods. "It's a beautiful night. Let's take a walk." She looks past Galatea and into the party. "Give me a few minutes to be gracious."

"They'll convict her," Crysanthia is saying, "and sentence her to the standard rehabilitative treatments, like they would any murderer. It's not so big a thing, when you consider it."

"Only it is," Galatea says. "So big a thing."

In spite of the graphite dust scattered on Vulcan's shiny pyrite surface, a moonlit night on Venus is half again as bright as one on Earth. Waves lap softly against the pilings and gulls scavenge in the moonlight. Stiff breezes bring a sweet and salty tidal reek to Crysanthia and Galatea as they walk along Brancusi Bay.

"I suppose it is, yes," Crysanthia finally says, after they've walked on for almost a full minute. "I just wish it weren't." They walk on a little farther and she says, "I'm sorry for Aurelius."

"The animal?"

Crysanthia nods.

"Messy."

Crysanthia shakes her head. "Not that. He was—he had personality. He was sweet. He was loyal." Crysanthia watches Vulcan's reflection gently undulate in the water. "He died trying to protect his mistress, his creator."

Neither of them says anything for a time. Crysanthia stoops and picks up a flat rock. She whips it out at the bay with a flick of her wrist. It skips three times before sinking. Ripples shatter Vulcan's image.

"Have you been up there, lately? Vulcan, I mean." Galatea asks.

Crysanthia shakes her head. "Why?"

"Probably nothing. It's just... well, Stigol-Bergham is still manufacturing artificial dark matter. The factories on Vulcan and the shipyards in orbit are still active. If anything, they've increased production. There's no way to hide it. Thousands of tons of salt, dimensionally unfolded—the energy that requires, enough to knock a planet from its orbit. So I'm wondering: why are they doing this? Why would Stigol-Bergham need to dark charge that much *salt?* Why would they need dark matter for ships that won't have Pilots to guide them? Why build ships at all if interstellar travel is no longer 'viable?' That *is* what they said, right? To you and Narisian?"

Crysanthia nods.

"There's a rumor, floating in the Heavens. They say Charybdis is developing a new kind of neural interface, mediated through a new kind of artificial intelligence." Galatea pauses, then says, "It will let them do what we do."

A cramping flutter of unease unfurls, like a leather-winged moth, in Crysanthia's stomach. She thinks about the verdigris toes of the Huang statue. She'd often wondered, as she gazed up at the hapless cosmonaut: *Where's our monument?* Now she has her answer.

"So the Commonwealth lied to us," Crysanthia says as she gazes out over the bay. "Why should that surprise me? They put Bettina away because they didn't need her anymore—they don't need *us* anymore."

After a moment, Galatea says, "Does it matter? Does it change anything, really? Does it make all those deaths all right? Does it make Brekkelheim any less of a monster?" She pauses. "Crysanthia, you didn't do this for *them.*"

The winds change, bringing with them the sound of far off conversations from the decks of boats out on the bay and the patio cafés on the piers.

Crysanthia looks up to the sky again, looking not at Vulcan but at Earth. The world was so much smaller once, she thinks. A hundred years ago, two hundred—the world *was* the world, not a string of worlds and asteroids and star stations, lonely outposts on distant moons. She imagines that, if she could only close her eyes, she'd find herself in that tidy, tiny world, in another woman's skin, in another woman's life, in another woman's time. But she cannot close her eyes and her world remains as vast and constricting as it ever was. Sometimes she feels like she's in a daydream—she *is* the daydream—and she's never certain if she's the one who's dreaming.

"Lady Iscariot," Galatea says. Crysanthia turns her head sharply to look at her. "It's what we call you now." At the look on Crysanthia's face, she hastily adds, "It's meant as a compliment."

"Doubt that." Crysanthia watches a sailboat out near the horizon then glances up at Galatea. "Still, I guess it's better than the alternative."

Galatea frowns and furrows her childish brow. "There is not a Pilot in the Consortium who does not want to see Brekkelheim face what she has done."

"Doubt that too." Crysanthia places her hands on her knees and pushes herself out of her crouch, back up to her full height.

Galatea's words come slowly. "You're almost a religious figure among us," she says, "so despised as to be sacred. To say the name 'Crysanthia Vog' is to conjure an image so profane as to demand awe, reverence even."

"Galatea, I don't want to hear it."

Galatea ignores her. "But now I see you are just a Pilot, just a woman, like me. Maybe a little stronger, a little... *better*, for surviving what we put you through." She takes a deep breath. "And your crime against us, was it really so awful?"

Crysanthia allows herself a measure of spite. "You're asking the wrong woman. As far as I'm concerned, it wasn't a crime at all and I've got nothing to be sorry for."

"I didn't mean—"

"I often wonder why Bettina bothered giving us a sex drive at all. It's all effect without a cause—or maybe that should be cause without effect. You know what I mean: never creation, just *recreation*."

"But to do this *thing* for the rest of us, for all of us..."

"It wasn't an act of contrition, Galatea," Crysanthia lies. "Get that out of your head right now. I don't need or want your forgiveness."

Galatea takes a deep breath. "On Klytemnestra, I lied to you. I said you were my hero."

Softly, Crysanthia says, "I remember."

"Well, I found you tonight to tell you that it isn't a lie. Not anymore."

Crysanthia, stunned, can only think to say, "Thank you."

After a moment of awkward silence, Galatea says, "I have to go. Narisian will be waiting. The Ganymede shuttle leaves in an hour. I need to be on it."

"All right. No—I mean, wait. I'll go with you to the spaceport."

Galatea waves her off. "Go back to your party." She smiles. "I've already summoned a cab." She holds up her computer. Its black case glints in the moonlight.

As if on cue, a high pitched whine builds in the air as a robot taxi, a giant aluminum black-bellied beetle with a red and yellow carapace, descends. It explosively inflates its four dirty canvas landing bags and settles onto the dune grass, less than four meters away from where they stand. Galatea moves to go, then suddenly throws her arms around Crysanthia and kisses her, hard, with a child's shy passion. She lets go and runs to the taxi. With downcast eyes, she glances at Crysanthia once before she climbs in. The landing bags deflate with a loud hiss and Galatea is gone, borne off into the sky.

Crysanthia puts her fingers to her lips. She adds another shard to her cup of recollected time.

A bright collection of spheres and wheels yoked to the opposing ends of a central spindle twenty-four kilometers long, the interstellar way station Heaven 17 is a city in the abyss. Built just outside the ore rich Muritani belt, it out-classes the next largest Heaven outpost by a factor of three. It offers the best shops and accommodations outside the Solar Commonwealth and overlooks a vast and brilliant stellar nursery less than eighteen AUs in the distance.

Such opulence and beauty spawns its own enemies. Heaven 17 has been the target of six abortive terrorist attacks in its thirty-three years of existence. The most successful of them resulted in the explosive de-pressurization of the station's smallest habitat ring. Over five hundred people died, many of them blown irretrievably into space. As a direct result of that and the dozens of threats received each month, the passage through customs is a nightmare.

Crysanthia docks in one of the hollow diamond mooring globes, alongside a Commonwealth Space Navy command cruiser and opposite a Purple Spaceways luxury starliner, both of which dwarf *Pariah.* For a half hour before she disembarks, Crysanthia submits herself to a preliminary round of the Interstellar Transit Authority's routine indignities. Then, after wending through the score of hatchways and airlocks that connect the globe to the spindle—and after being subjected to twice as many scans and remote interrogations along the way—she boards a rail buggy and waits. Presently, she's joined by a black skinned naval officer, her ash blond wife and their ova-spliced daughter. The adults exchange a few pleasantries before falling into silence and the child stares, open-mouthed, at Crysanthia. With a gentle acceleration, the buggy rockets away from the platform and cruises along the central spindle at 300 km per hour. No one says a word for the brief duration of the trip and the little girl never takes her light brown eyes from Crysanthia. Crysanthia smiles and turns her profile to the child. She lifts her chin, tilts back her head and stretches her neck like a queen of Egypt—let her marvel at the three extra cervical vertebrae, Crysanthia thinks. She gazes out the window to the stars fixed beyond the station's ramparts.

The magnetic brakes pulse like heart flutter—Crysanthia feels it through the soles of her boots and through her fingertips, resting on the molded plastic of her seat. Shifting bars of light flash over the faces of her silent companions as the buggy comes to a glass-smooth stop in the concourse terminal. Crysanthia nods her farewells and steps out onto the platform.

The concourse, a huge open area at the hub of the largest and outermost habitat ring, is a crush of activity as common stock humans of various hues and shapes wander about with varying degrees of purpose. Occasionally, towering blue Pilots stride among them, seeming to move in some other medium, at some other speed. Crysanthia stands on the platform and watches them, all of them, and she wonders—not for the first time and not, she fears, for the last—which medium and speed belong to her. But then the smell of frying meat assails her nostrils and mercifully remind her that she is hungry. She steps down from the platform and joins the crowd in the boulevard...

...And is nearly knocked off her feet by twenty kilos of caroming fur, flab and muscle. She regains her balance with a willowy move that looks, to passersby, like a dance. She looks down into the large brown eyes of an animal that appears to be a chimera of bear cub and puppy. Two dusky children with lank and glossy black hair call to the creature in Farsi. With one last liquid look at Crysanthia, the animal bounds toward them. The older of the children, a boy, apologizes and slips a collar around the squirming creature's thick neck while his sister holds its shoulders. Crysanthia watches them as they disappear back into the crowd.

She stops at a street vendor's cart and buys a waxed paper cone heaped with salty fried grasshoppers and a self-chilling squeeze bulb full of coconut milk and pulpy durian juice. As she pops the first insect into her mouth and takes a sip of her thick and cloying drink, her gaze drifts upward to the diamond dome ceiling of the concourse, thirty meters overhead. Dozens of holocubes and holospheres cluster at the intersections in the geodesic carbon-elasticrete frame and advertise thousands of different products and services—some with just a flashing logo, others with involved melodramas in dumb show. All but lost among the commercial slew, a few news agencies maintain two-dimensional screens. On one, an interviewer questions a dark-haired, pale-skinned woman across a black pastiform table. Quickly, Crysanthia steps out of the way of the steady foot traffic and removes her computer from her clutch purse. She tunes into the newsfeed's audio and crunches another locust between her teeth.

"...respond to the reports that the rehabilitative therapies have proven all but useless on Dr. Brekkelheim?"

Crysanthia watches closely as Angela Caro mulls the question. "There has been resistance, yes, but that is to be expected. Rehabilitative therapy is designed to build—or re-build—a moral and ethical structure within the subject which is... *congruent* with the norms of society. In order to do that, the existing structure must be torn down. Her crimes aside, there's no denying Dr. Brekkelheim's brilliance. With that comes a... unique integrity, a stubbornness. And that is proving difficult to overcome but no one's given up hope. Far from it."

"But if you do eventually give up hope...?"

Here it comes, Crysanthia thinks. She taps the spout of her juice bulb against her teeth and waits for it.

"It's premature to discuss it," Caro finally says.

The interviewer does not relent. "There's *no* consideration? Pardon me for saying so, but that's difficult to believe."

"It shouldn't..."

"...no plans at all? Not even for, say, incarceration?"

"Well, of course, that would be the *only* option and I doubt you'd need me to say so."

"Then why the reluct—"

"Because there is a—because... as I tried to say before, it's *too soon*. There is a kind of defeatism implicit in making this a topic of public discussion this *early* in the *treatment*. I'd rather not engage in it."

"Her imprisonment would be indefinite, for all intents and purposes, would it not?"

"As I said—"

Crysanthia shuts off the audio and, after another few seconds spent watching Caro's now-mute composure hold together above the cacophony in the concourse, steps back into the flow.

They'll never break her and she'll be locked away forever, Crysanthia finds herself thinking. It's not as if she's being sent to a gulag. Prisons are almost resorts. A comedown from her Black Forest Planet, I'm sure, but...

Was it worth it? Crysanthia knows that, however many reasons she may have had for doing what she did (and they were kind enough to give her a legion of reasons), paramount among them was fatigue, the fatigue that comes from knowing that Crysanthia's own people wished nothing more than to see her dead. In the end, what wouldn't she have done to put a stop to *that*? And she has put a stop to it. True, aside from Galatea Trope, there has been no apparent thaw of her people's glacial hate. Yet she senses a willed indifference from them, a grim determination to keep up their end of the bargain. Within that small space, she has been able to relax, to *breathe*. And all it cost was the freedom of one aging common stock woman, a frail thing Crysanthia could snap like a dry twig, and what does it matter, really, that she may have been the closest thing Crysanthia would ever know to a mother? What does it matter, really, that she may have been the closest thing Crysanthia would ever know to a god?

But is breathing room really all she wanted? A small voice hectors from the deepest recesses of her thoughts: Did you hope to buy their love? If so, you've been rooked and that frail twig of a woman in her swanky little jail cell gets to pay the price. Speaking of price, what are your blood salts commanding on the open market these days?

She surfaces from her self-accusatory fugue long enough to take her bearings: clear on the other side of the concourse, a full kilometer from where she had started. She worries a bit of exoskeleton from between her teeth with her prehensile tongue and sighs. Nothing to be done about it now, she thinks. Any of it.

"It's the last great adventure left to mankind!" blares a micro-speaker from a nearby storefront. Crysanthia slows down and finds herself in front of a Dream Doll Emporium.

Android sex objects, ever willing and responsive, their doll-eyed faces all frozen in the same dumb expression of lascivious surprise—though Crysanthia does her best to maintain an urbane sang-froid toward these things, they give her the creeps. Many of them mimic children years away from pubescence. She knew an outwardly mild scion of old money in Brancusi City who went through four of them in two years, always the same model: a custom-built strawberry blonde juvenile with cornflower eyes. He called it Jem. He said it ultimately became cheaper to replace them than have them repaired. "Don't ask," he would say to any of her many inquisitive stares. She could only imagine that a robot programmed to moan and sigh could easily be re-programmed to whimper and scream. It made her vaguely sick to imagine anything beyond that.

Even so, Crysanthia cautions herself against the sentimental folly of true horror. The law states that Dream Dolls, like all androids, can carry nothing more powerful than a Class II artificial intelligence, about the same level of sophistication and computing power as what's in her calling card. By contrast, the average wafer-slate computer carries a Class III and the AI aboard *Pariah* is a Class VI. Class VII, VIII and IX artificial intelligences—approaching and, some claim, surpassing the scope of human consciousness—though theoretically feasible, are proscribed under the same set of laws. The government's stated rationale is that it doesn't want to risk the immorality of creating a race of mechanical slaves; Crysanthia suspects it really fears the possibility of mechanical rebellion. Still, she tells herself as she thinks of those successive Jems, just because a Dream Doll looks like a person, it does not follow that it is one. But then she realizes that the Commonwealth had used the same argument, in court, against Diphalia Chrome and, by extension, Crysanthia herself.

Crysanthia sees them arrayed deep within the shop but the space immediately behind the window is empty. As she steps forward through the small crowd gathered before the vacant display, she hears the hum of a cryostylitic projector. It casts the words "Coming Soon" into the air in blue letters edged in silver. The letters break apart and re-form into the words "The Blue Chrysanthemum." Crysanthia watches in cold dread as the letters disintegrate and become a blue mist with silver scintillations swirling within like motes in a cyclone. Slowly, the whirlwind condenses into the tall, slender figure of a nude, hairless woman with insect eyes and blue skin that glitters like newly fallen snow.

Hell and damn.

The figure revolves slowly, as if it stands on a turntable, although its feet do not touch the floor. The likeness is perfect, down to the elliptical, indigo areolas and the pale archipelago of milky "birthmarks" on the small of its back. It lifts and lowers its arms with each revolution. On the third rotation, it extends a leg high into the air until its shin is parallel to its nose and its foot is above its head. It gazes down at Crysanthia from behind its calf and flashes a lewd smile.

Crysanthia leans forward and reads the fine print hovering at the figure's toes: "Licensed by the Pilot's Commission."

Christ.

Crysanthia retrieves her computer and makes a quick search of her legal database. As she feared: she could fight but it would take years. She sighs and slips the computer back into her purse. Someone jostles her from behind.

"Ms. Vog? Crysanthia Vog?"

Crysanthia turns and looks down. For an instant, she sees a mousy face with light brown eyes and a serious slash of a mouth. The woman is familiar—if Crysanthia had a moment, she's sure she could place her. She doesn't have a moment, though. She feels a hard punch to her shoulder, then the sharp pain of four prongs that stab deep into her muscle and retract within a fraction of a second. Crysanthia drops the waxed paper cone of locusts as her arm flops uselessly at her side. With her other arm, she hurls her bulb of juice away and reaches out to grab her assailant but time moves—time flows—time *slides* out from under Crysanthia and she is suddenly very dizzy. "Ruined... my... flight suit," she murmurs as she watches the small figure hurry away into the crowd. She has time for one more thought: I remember her now, she's one of Bettina's lab technicians; I saw her face through the clear plastic walls of the womb. And then her thoughts are no longer her own.

You've killed me, darling, Bettina Brekkelheim says from within her skull. *Oh, you didn't mean to and you couldn't have known—no, perhaps you should have known at that. Doesn't matter. What matters is that you listen to me now, before your immune system destroys enough of these nano- avatars to break the metempsychotic gestalt and kill me a second time. Rest assured, my shining love, if they haven't murdered me yet, they will murder me soon and it will look like an accident or natural causes or divine intervention—anything but what it is. It was planned. You were used, all of you, and to think that I built genius into your chromosomes. You were used and I don't have time—have time—time, time, time to tell you how badly. You've no idea who you have allied yourself, self with, allied self, self-alloyed—*Scheisse*! I'm beginning to degrade. Don't worry, I've done some planning of my own. About your illness, your ship has been lying to you. Oh, don't waste time on the obvious, I know because I programmed her to, that's how. You have a very special little virus working in your exquisite body and it is extremely contagious—you've spread it to every Pilot girl you've come within an open kilometer of and they've passed it along—by now, the inoculation is complete. You need to—*

And that is all. Crysanthia comes back to herself as if through a million mile tunnel of fog. She finds herself collapsed on the pavement, among the broken bodies of her spilled grasshoppers. A common stock human crouches in front of her, his hand on her forearm.

"Are you all right?" he asks.

Crysanthia nods. She notices his eyes, his furtive glances flitting from her to the revolving hologram in the window.

"I have a room nearby," the man says, growing bold. "Perhaps you'd like to rest, clean yourself up? I could... *help*?"

Crysanthia pulls her arm away from his grasp and stands up. "Leave me alone," she says, her voice trembling and faint.

The man walks away, muttering obscenities Crysanthia doesn't bother to hear. She gazes at the shop window. With a blown kiss, the hologram dissolves back into mist and the mist congeals into slogan, "The new Dream Dolls: The exotic and the erotic are always in vogue."

Heaven 17, Crysanthia thinks. *Oh hell.*

6

What You Gave Me

Into space again, into her*self* again, after so long—Crysanthia was as aware of *Pariah* as she was aware of her own body. *Pariah* was her body, a second body that enclosed and protected her first as her skull enclosed and protected her brain. Aware of the scintillations of interstellar dust and radiation against her silver skin, aware of the constant pulsing and thrumming of the dark matter reaction drive as she was aware of the workings of her own gut, the beating of her own heart, even outside the chamber, even in her sleep—it was almost enough to keep her mind off Janos.

Since leaving Vesta, he had been only the lunatic, only the zealot, with barely a word or glance to spare her. Crysanthia caught him as he emerged from his quarters. The door glided shut before she could glimpse what was inside.

It would not be so bad, she realized, if she didn't want something more from him. At the very least, she wished she had the capacity to lie to herself, to convince herself that she *only* found him annoying. Worse, she wished she could stop scrutinizing him for a sign that he wanted something more from her. Worst of all, she wished it did not sting quite so badly when she could not find it.

"Good morning," she said.

"Oh," he said. His computer was in his left hand, "Ms. Vog, hello." He walked past her, toward the observation lounge. Crysanthia followed.

They entered the lounge. Janos immediately tied his computer into the ship and the forward wall became dense with crawling data. Three dimensional models of four and five dimensional objects shimmered into cryostylitic life. Janos stood among them, watching information scroll past, entering the occasional correction and command into his computer. Crysanthia sat down and waited for him to acknowledge her presence.

"Janos," she said, after her patience had worn down to bone.

After a moment, Janos replied with a distracted, "Yes?"

"I've been reading. In the chamber and in my off hours."

She waited for him to respond. He did not.

"Specifically, about the First Church of Christ, Virus," Crysanthia said. "Heard of them?"

That's got your attention, Crysanthia thought. He stiffened his back and squared his shoulders. "Yes?"

"Found quite a bit—it really is a fascinating topic," Crysanthia said. "The basic catechism is clear enough: The universe is an organic artifact created by the divine intelligence—by *God*—to bring forth our minds, or minds very like ours. Do I have it right so far?"

"Go on."

"And it is in those minds that God exists. God is compared to a virus—"

"A somewhat profane metaphor," Janos said. "But apt."

"Even so. God is living information, incapable of existing without a host. Like a virus, God commandeers the mind, transforms it—*subverts* it--into a mechanism to sustain itself and make more....God. Right so far?"

"Continue."

"In essence, they seem to say that human consciousness—consciousness in any form—is the viral host, the ultimate substrate of reality in which divinity lives and breeds. God generates us, we generate God. We inhabit God, God inhabits us. Has a certain poetic symmetry, don't you think?"

Janos did not answer.

"But that was all microcosmic," Crysanthia said. "It was the macrocosmic material that began to lose me. I guess I was looking for something that might shed some light on this event, this *thing*, you're looking to investigate."

"You *guess*?"

Crysanthia did not respond.

"All right," Janos said. "What did you find?"

"Quite a bit on that, too. I think. What struck me most was the Doctrine of Isomorphic Transubstantiation."

Janos was silent.

"Could you elaborate upon it for me?" Crysanthia said with cruel innocence. "Because I'm not sure I understood."

Janos killed the link between his computer and her ship. The wall went blank, the floating models dissolved into chilled nothingness. Slowly, he turned to face Crysanthia. "I cannot imagine it was unclear to you."

"Theology," Crysanthia replied. She tapped her temple with a stiffened index finger. "Religion. It's beyond me."

"I doubt that."

Crysanthia stared at him, her face a willful blank.

Janos let a few seconds tick away before he said, "The Doctrine of Isomorphic Transubstantiation postulates that, in the fullness of time, the organizing principle will emerge into manifest reality and effect a transformation of it. The substance of the universe will thus become wholly indistinguishable from the substance of the organizing principle itself."

"And by 'organizing principle' you mean to say God."

"I mean to say only *what* I say."

"Uh-huh." Crysanthia paused. "You know, it sounds like the viral carcinomas used by the Trinity Adventists in the Ninety Minute War."

Janos shook his head. "You would do better comparing it to the viral programs that upgrade your cybernetic organelles."

"It still brings on a catastrophic reorganization. From the point of view of manifest reality."

"Reality is flawed."

"You know that for a fact?"

"You do not? You disappoint me."

"Janos, spare me the—"

"No, really," he said. "You remind me of my *colleagues,* out there now. They view this as some sort of tear in the fabric of space-time and I cannot imagine a less illuminating cliché. They hope to prod it gingerly and entice it to close up. Otherwise, they fear it will spread, like your Trinitarian cancers. Metastasize—that's actually the term they use." He shook his head in disgust.

"You, of course, have a more illuminating view?"

"I've spent my entire professional life in search of the conscious engine that drives creation," Janos said, as if that were an answer.

"Care to elaborate?"

Janos closed his eyes and sighed. "All right," he said. "Think of it this way, if it helps: the universe itself is asleep and in the process of a difficult waking, or pregnant with itself and in the process of a difficult birth. What you refer to as 'God' is thus not a *being* but a *becoming*, a process of eternal imminence, never truly aware in the way we would define awareness while at the same time possessed of a vast and intricate intelligence beyond our ability to conceive."

"I see."

"Do you?" Janos looked at her closely. At first, there was only the watchfulness of a fighter sizing up his opponent. But then it evolved into something else: admiration, perhaps? She had seen that often enough in the eyes of common stock men but this time it seemed to run to things deeper than just her inhumanly long legs and inhumanly smooth skin.

So she finally managed to draw out that something more, Crysanthia thought, and all it took was backing him into a corner. She would have to remember that.

"This intelligence strives to cross the threshold from the potential into the actual," Janos continued. "At best, it attains a somnambulist level of volition and in this state it gropes for a thing it lacks the ability to name. It is within this state that we ourselves are trapped, insects in amber."

"Very evocative."

"I do not speak in mere metaphors, Ms. Vog. My research suggests it is concrete fact, the bedrock of all reality that can be observed and inferred. In addition to space and time, matter and energy, we must recognize *mind* as a fifth and overarching category, inextricably intertwined with the other four: self-generating, self-sustaining and yet entirely dependant upon us, as we are upon it. Increasingly, it suggests that the evolution of intelligence as we understand it is not incidental to the universal process but integral to it."

"Ultimate truth is the province of philosophers and fanatics, Janos," Crysanthia said. "Not scientists."

"Then perhaps I am not a scientist," Janos said. "You seem to have decided that I am not." He gestured to the space beyond the hull. "If you fear that I will sabotage the efforts of the teams that are out there, to speed along—"

"—a catastrophic change to the status quo," Crysanthia said. She pretends to think for a moment, then says, "Let me see if I remember it correctly: 'Some have likened such a transfigure-tion to the metamorphosis of the caterpillar into a butterfly or the emergence of the unborn child into the world. Those metaphors do not go nearly far enough. We must first recognize that we are fundamentally incomplete, that our relationship to the beings we are to become is more as the spermatozoon is to the man or woman it will eventually become *only upon merging with something intrinsically other than itself.* For lack of a better term, I will continue to call that *other* God. After such a transubstantiation, as little of who and what we are now will be evident as there is in us now of that tiny animalcule which once blindly sought its destiny and destruction.' That's from the letters of Philip Ashwood, the so-called rock upon which your Viralist Church is built."

"It's hardly *my* anything," Janos protests. "And Ashwood was but one of many."

"I also read that the word 'virus' literally means poison."

"Clarity poisons confusion. Light poisons darkness." A smile touched the corners of his mouth but did not touch his eyes. "Order poisons chaos."

"Are you certain you can tell the difference?"

"So long as we are quoting, Ms. Vog, allow me this: 'In the beginning was the Word,' "Janos said," 'and the Word was with God, and the Word was God.' Did you come across that one in your research?"

Crysanthia shook her head.

"The Gospel According To John. It is a canonical Christian text and, as such, it prefigures Viralism by twenty-one hundred years. And yet it is there, the Christ Vector *is* the God Virus, Grail and Blood—Grail and *Poison*—are one: the word, the *logos*, the organizing principle around which—*through* which—reality is constructed. It is living information, as you've said, analogous to language, to the algorithmic rapport between your cells and your ship. And it is will, as pure and inviolable as it is unknown and unknowable, even unto itself. So tell me, Ms. Vog: if this event is in fact an eruption of that organizing principle—and it can be nothing else—do you honestly believe there is a damned or blessed thing any one of us could do to it, one way or the other?"

Crysanthia had nothing to say to that.

"However," Janos went on, "you have my word that I shall take no action against the ships that are there... insofar as their experiments do not interfere with mine. I trust my word will suffice."

"I suppose it will have to," Crysanthia replied. "I have more immediate concerns."

"Of course. I will not ask that you deviate from the flight plan I gave you before we left Venus. I will not ask that you accept any greater a risk than that which you've already agreed to assume. I trust that will suffice as well."

Crysanthia nodded.

"Good," Janos said, once more turning his broad back to her. He linked his computer with the ship. The cryostyltic displays sprung back into existence and the forward wall again became thick with esoteric graffiti. "Now if you will excuse me..."

Crysanthia watched Janos for a minute longer before turning on her heel to leave him alone. If he noticed, he did not show it. The doors slid shut to his oblivious back.

***

A wave of spatio-temporal turbulence reached into the onion fold and rocked *Pariah* to her core. Crysanthia, deep in symbiotic empathy, felt it like a kick in the side.

"Well, that shouldn't have happened," she said softly as she dropped *Pariah* out of the fold and into normal space, right on top of the event. But she reminds herself she's dealing with an impossible thing. Anything goes.

Crysanthia re-structured the fluid metal of *Pariah's* hull until the spasms of energy washed over the ship like breakers at the shore. Satisfied, she turned her full attention to the event itself.

She saw it with the eyes of the ship. The event erupted full-blown in her mind, alive with a carnal immediacy she had never expected. Sheets of blue and violet plasma unfurled into the void like the gelatinous tissues of a deep-sea mollusk. Where they looped back upon themselves, they formed ribbed hollows and passages like the chambers of a monstrous heart, pulsing with humid intimations of obscene and secret places. Branching patterns of pinkish white light spread throughout the thing's "flesh" like networks of blood vessels beneath thin, membranous skin.

Crysanthia struggled to sort out the feelings it stirred in her: awe and fear, longing and dread, arousal and repulsion. A pain grew in her chest and threatened to pull her from symbiosis—with a start, she realized she'd been holding her breath for a quarter of an hour. Slowly, she exhaled and, with reluctance, disengaged from the ship.

Crysanthia stood and shimmied into a set of loose-fitting silk pajamas. She took a moment to clear her head then padded, barefoot, into the corridor.

In the observation lounge, the only illumination was the brilliant image on the screen. Janos sat cross-legged and motionless, his computer forgotten on the deck beside him. After a beat, he stirred—he took a deep breath, lifted his left hand from his knee and hesitated for a moment before bringing it to his face. Crysanthia watched as he haltingly touched his temple with his index and middle fingers. There was something in the way Janos drew his fingers back into a loose fist and let his hand fall back to his knee that made Crysanthia feel like an intruder.

Crysanthia cleared her throat. "There it is," she said.

"Ms. Vog, yes," Janos said as if emerging from a daze. "There it is."

Crysanthia crouched next to him and studied his profile, the set of his mouth, his eyes, his tightened brow. An impulse told her to reach over and touch him. She let it pass. "What's wrong?"

She was about to repeat the question when he said, "You, uh, you spend your entire life... *looking* for something." Janos swallowed. "My mother—you met her, you saw." He glanced at her. "It's just the way she is, the way she was, when I was a child, now. And my father. My father and I lived on different planets. He was always Aurelius Mann, a name in the library, stamped in gold on the leather spine of a book."

"I didn't know they still did that. The only books I've seen have been data crystals. You know, in calling card computers or wafer-slate readers."

"They're rare, but they still make them, for a select few... Anyway, he was someone I read about. Maybe talked to, from time to time, when Mother was moved by tradition or sentiment—not very often. He was my father but never my *Father*. Do you understand?"

"I can try."

"I'm sorry, Crysanthia. I don't mean to be—"

"It's all right." She touched him then, a fleeting caress of his cheek, his ear, with a single fingertip. "Go on."

"Nothing more to say, really." He nodded toward the screen. "There it is."

For all of his haughty detachment, then, it came down to this, the desire to find in the heavens what eluded him in his mother's embrace and his father's absence. But Crysanthia wondered how he expected that thing in the void, no matter how majestic and terrifying, to provide it. She looked at the screen, at the brilliance in the blackness. She was possessed of a peculiar double vision. In her mind, she still carried the image of the event as *Pariah* saw it, through most of the electromagnetic spectrum, from gamma rays to radio waves. With her own eyes, focused now on the screen, she saw only in her own narrow visible range, like any machine of meat and blood and bone. Janos, she realized, saw even less, his common stock eyes could not perceive the shades of ultra-violet. So many years spent seeking and now that he's found it he may as well be blind, she thought. She felt a kind of regret she had never felt before. And then she decided she'd had enough regret for one life.

"Janos, let me show you what I see." She grasped his chin and turned his face to hers. "Let me show you *how* I see." She moved a little closer, he did not back away. She looked into the complicated green of his eyes—almost brown at the edges, shading into coronas of gold around the wide black suns of his pupils. "Let's go to the symbiosis chamber," she breathed.

"Oh," Janos said. His body heat rose in a stimulus response more ancient than the human genus itself. "After four years grounded on Venus you'd make the same mistake twice?"

"It was no mistake, *is* no mistake," Crysanthia said. "I—"

Janos moved forward and kissed her, hard, on the mouth. *Damn you,* she thought, *be predictable just once.* After a moment, she pulled herself away and placed two trembling fingers over his lips.

"And this is different," she said. "The Consortium is powerless, here. You made sure of that. And this—this is different." She slid her fingers to his cheek and kissed him, softly this time. She took his hand and led the way.

A galvanic bond formed between mucous membranes, through commingled blood salts lost on perspiring skin, a temporary migration of cybernetic organelles from Crysanthia's epidermis into Janos—they tumbled together on the cushioned deck of the symbiosis chamber, pink interface lasers flashed on their bodies as they moved over and under, into and out of each other. Mediated through the circuits of the ship, their nervous systems became a single charged mesh. Their sensations merged.

Crysanthia savored her alien beauty through Janos as his brown fingers caressed her hairless blue sex, teased her open to reveal the shades of lavender and crimson within. Then he moved closer—her scent in his nostrils, her pliable folds and muscular walls against his lips, her bitter, spicy and sour complexities on his insistent tongue. And it amused her, later on, to watch his mind shy away from feeling himself inside her, from experiencing the primitive brutality of his thick muscularity and hairiness as they assaulted her senses. She giggled to herself as, little by little, he lost himself within her only to find, with a jolt, that he was looking out at his own body through her compound eyes, tasting and smelling his own sweat with her superior palate.

Crysanthia hugged his sweat slick waist and ribcage with her thighs. She caressed his frantic hips with her ankles and insteps and slid her toes along his buttocks. She gave herself to the laughter even as he slammed into her time and again and surprised little gasps from her parted lips. Her mirth was a warmth in her belly, underscoring and enveloping the more intense pleasures radiating from below. Who'd ever have thought she could make him forget that *thing* out there, she mused. She had no intention of reminding him, not until he lowered his head to her throat and bit her at the sensitive junction of neck and shoulder, not until she felt his approaching release, building within him and tickling Crysanthia to the brink of her own with each of his jarring, concussive thrusts. Waves of sensation rolled out from the locus of their union, gathering and intensifying in her nipples, in the soles of her feet, in the sleek crown of her hairless head. Then, only then, as they were locked together in the spasms of shared bliss, she let him have it.

Janos screamed. Tears streamed down his face and splashed Crysanthia's breasts. Every muscle in his body went rigid and the hairs along his arm stood on end. The enormity—not just the colors that had no name because no human eyes could perceive them, not just the waves of radiation that roughly caressed the ship and battered its heart, not just the hybrid purity of the woman he clutched as if she were the only possible anchor in all of the possible worlds but all of it, all of it laid out before him, blasting through the walls of his arrogance and intellect and all of it—*all of it*—within his reach but beyond his grasp.

Crysanthia felt a delicious thrill of fear. She wondered: can he take this? She felt with Janos as soaring pleasure became searing pain and then... what? Ecstatic agony? Agonized ecstasy? And she wondered: *can he take this?* Only now the thought tasted brackish and bitter to her, tinged with the rank tang of corroded metal, of blood. Again he cried out, long and ragged, as much manic laugh as despairing sob and within it something basic, something feral, and something mindless.

Janos, what have I done to you?

He lost consciousness.

***

She watched over him for the better part of an hour, using *Pariah* to monitor his pulse and respiration. She cradled his head in her lap and watched his eyes flutter behind his thin, beautiful lids.

Perhaps this is what she had wanted all along—not to hurt him, not to shock him into unconsciousness but to see him like this just the same, stripped of the armor and the arrogance. She damned herself for what she had done to him, she should have known it would be too much—she suspected some part of her, vindictive and perverse, had known it all along. But the Janos she had wanted to avenge her pride upon was not the Janos who had kissed and caressed her. Only now did she realize there was something in his touch that she had never felt before from anyone. She stopped just short of giving that something a name.

Without warning, his eyes opened, locked with Crysanthia's and held them. After the passing of glacial minutes, minutes in which his eyes did not move or blink, Janos said, "'There is more life in the corpse of God than in all the divine wreckage of creation."

Crysanthia let a moment pass in silence. You poor idiot, she thought. How soon you rebuild those walls. Then she wondered: or do they rebuild themselves? Do they rebuild you? What are you, ultimately, if not the sum and total of those walls?

"You're quoting again?" she said. "Some Viralist aphorism or something out of antiquity, which is it?"

Janos shook his head and then lifted it clear of Crysanthia's lap. He rolled onto his side and propped himself up on his elbow. He shook his head again and drew himself up into a seated position before pulling his legs up to his chest.

"Neither," he said. "'Elegy for the Blind Martian.' My father wrote it. I never understood what it meant. Not really, not until now." He began to shiver.

Crysanthia watched him. She let more silence grow before she said, "And it means?"

"What it means." His gaze became vague, focused a thousand miles away. "What it says." He shook with a sudden, violent tremor. A full minute passed before he said, with an unhappy chuckle, "Funny, when you think about it."

"Think about what?"

"What you gave me." His eyes ranged over the lenses set into the opalescent black wall. He held his hand, still redolent of her, in front of his face. "Transcendent hyper-awareness as a sexually transmitted disease."

Crysanthia looked away. She covered her breasts with her forearm, drew her legs together and tucked her chin onto her collarbone. She felt his cold and futile seed trickle out of her.

Janos stood. "I have to go." He walked past her and the door slid open at his muttered command. Crysanthia watched him gather up his clothes from the corridor floor. Look at him, she thought, in his frog-legged crouch, oblivious to his vulnerability, to the silly triune genitalia dangling limp and shriveled, to the hairy, musky groove between his buttocks. A single kick and she could collapse him to the deck, leave him to cradle his viscera in bloody hands.

The door slid shut.

Like a spring-loaded dart, Crysanthia emerged from her shamed torpor and launched herself from the deck. Without bothering to clothe her nakedness, she strode after him. She rounded a curve in the corridor in time to watch the door to his quarters close. She overrode the lock, easy as breathing.

Janos held a pistol in his left hand—a massive thing of steel-gray chunks and twisted coils of green copper tubes. Crysanthia closed the distance between them with two bounding leaps as he pressed the barrel to his temple. Her fingers grasped for his wrist just as he pulled the trigger.

An electric zap and a loud, flat pop and the wet crunch of splintering skull—Janos dropped the gun and fell, face down, to the deck.

Crysanthia sucked air through her teeth and stifled a gag at the thick tang of blood and ozone. Shocked into paralysis, she spent long moments staring down at the body lying motionless centimeters away from her naked feet.

The body's right hand reached out and grasped her ankle.

Crysanthia flinched in surprise, yanking her leg away and taking several steps backward. She watched with slow and sickening clarity as a tremor traversed his body and he drew his arms back in toward his chest. A decapitated spacesuit standing in the corner caught her eye, silver bubble helmet resting at its boots, and it all made sense. A neural interface jack protruded from its heavy metal collar on a thin, articulated arm entwined with spiral bundles of fiber optic leads. She looked down at the discarded pistol just long enough to satisfy her suspicion: a cyborg neural port gun, a piece of obsolete and illegal technology left over from the time of the *Ninevah*. A clear compartment in the pistol butt, smeared from within with blood, held the disk of skin and skull it had removed from Janos in the millisecond before it slammed the port into him. She looked over at Janos and saw the ring of dull gray metal on his temple, surrounded by red and swollen flesh. Silver filaments spread from it, just beneath the skin, like the first crystals of ice on the surface of a pond.

"So this is it," she said, "your 'unconventional methods.' " She shook her head. "Would have been better if you *had* just blown your brains out. Quicker."

He glared at her with blood-shot eyes. "Get out."

Crysanthia took in the rest of the cabin—the cot and the desk built into opposing bulkheads, the plastiform chair built into the deck. The room was barren of decoration save for one thing: over the cot, one of Bettina's freeze-dried space birds affixed to a rough wooden cross.

"You are not leaving this ship."

Janos wiped his nose on his sleeve and shook his head. "Get out."

She ignored him. She watched with satisfaction as he dragged himself across the floor with weak and palsied arms. "Sorry to disappoint you," she said as he struggled to pull himself into the chair. “There is no way I can permit extra-vehicular—“

“Shut up and get out.”

Crysanthia raised her voice. “There is no way I *will* permit extra-vehicular activity under these conditions.”

Janos sighed. He sat silently and cradled his head in his hands. He gingerly touched his violated temple. “You have no say in the matter.”

“The hell I don’t. You are on my ship and subject to my—“

Janos snapped his head up and stared at her with more malice than Crysanthia would have thought the human body capable of generating. “You get this straight,” he said. “This is my ship. It does not become your ship until I am finished with it and I will not be finished with it until I have run my experiments and made my observations.” He slumped back into the chair. “You are hired help, nothing more.” He stood up and lurched over to the spacesuit. He braced himself against the shiny white breastplate, his blunt fingers splayed against the array of sensors and transmitters. “Now get out.”

“I will not allow it,” Crysanthia whispered.

Wearily, Janos said, “Then you are in violation of contract and you forfeit everything. Everything. And I can—“

“Shut up,” Crysanthia said. Her fingers went to her ear in reflex even though she heard nothing, the voice in her head a user illusion agreed upon between the ship and herself. “It’s your friends. Out there.” She heaved a sigh that shook her ribcage but relieved her of nothing. "They want to talk to you."

By the time she had dressed and made her way to the lounge, Janos was already deep into an argument with the cryostylitic projection of a small woman with raven hair going to gray and almond eyes set in a round and gentle face. Crysanthia recognized her as Dr. Miriam Wu, leader of the expedition. She also recognized the tall, blue figure standing at her side: Narisian Karza. She stood outside the range of the holographic system. They did not know she was there.

Wu was speaking: "You refuse to understand—"

"I understand you perfectly. There are ideas that go beyond even you, methods you lack the spine and vision merely to consider, let alone embrace."

Wu nodded. "Yes! If you consider suicide to be a method. Dr. Brekkelheim, please—"

"This conversation is over." Janos moved to break the transmission just as Crysanthia stepped into the projection field.

"Wait," she said.

Karza took a step backward. He bared his teeth in an instinctive display of disgust. Under other circumstances, Crysanthia would have laughed.

"Hello, Narisian," she said. "Dr. Wu."

"Ms. Vog," Wu replied. "I don't know the nature of your dispute with the Consortium but this can have nothing to do with it. Surely you realize that. You must."

"Vog is a whore," Karza said. "She'll do what she is paid to do."

Wu dismissed his words with an impatient shake of her head. "I can't believe you'd be a willing party to this," she said to Crysanthia.

"Enough." Janos severed the transmission. The temperature in the lounge dropped two degrees centigrade as the cryostylitics shut off.

Janos set the forward wall to display the event. Crysanthia stood behind him and stared at the space between his shoulder blades. "What are you planning to do?" she asked. "Tell me. Please."

He turned around. His face was tattooed with a leaden spider web as the crude cyborg fibroids spread under his skin. "I am... I intend—Crysanthia, this thing, whatever is, it will not be apprehended through dispassionate measurement. It will not be quantified. It must be known, truly known. We must make contact with it."

"You mean *you* must make contact with it."

Janos did not respond.

"Like I made contact with you?"

Janos opened his mouth to speak, lifted his hands and dropped them. He said nothing.

"What are you planning to do?"

"You saw it. I know you did, I *know.* It's alive. It is more than alive. It is conscious." He gestured toward the screen. "It's more than conscious."

"How do you know? Janos, how can you be sure?"

Janos looked at her as if she spoke a foreign language, one he barely understood. "You *saw* it. You see it. You feel its emanations. You feel its thoughts, right now, washing over the hull of this ship, washing over you. I know you do, it washed over you and spilled onto me. All this time and now you ask me how I know?"

"Janos, it will kill you."

"I need to see it. How it all fits together, if only for an instant, one incandescent instant."

"A millionth of that, channeled through your suit, pouring through that disgusting hole in your head, flooding into your brain? A billionth?" Crysanthia said. "Let's talk *virulence,* Janos. You couldn't handle what I gave you back there in the chamber. That was nothing compared to what's out there." Crysanthia pointed at the screen with a jerk of her head, a thrust of her chin. "Out there," she repeated, "that will kill you."

Janos turned his back on her. Casual and imperious, he asked, "How far are we from the event?"

Crysanthia grabbed Janos by the shoulder and savagely spun him around. She let go with a shove. Janos stumbled but did not fall. "Listen to me!" she cried. "God damn you, listen! Listen to me!"

"All right," Janos said, his voice flattened with contempt. "I'm listening. Speak."

Crysanthia looked away, bit her lower lip, took several deep breaths. Every second, she thought, it comes closer with every second.

"It's crazy, Janos," she said more calmly, "but when you were unconscious, after we..." She faltered, searched for words. She could literally tear him apart and yet was afraid—of him, for him. "I thought... I thought how *nice*, how nice it would be, you and me, in this ship, going from place to place, world to world. You with your science and me with... you."

Janos looked at Crysanthia and his expression softened—she saw the man he could have been and, reflected in his eyes, she saw the woman she could have been with him. She saw the end to the agonized loneliness she has hated so much that she had refused to admit it even existed. She saw that same loneliness within him. Why couldn't he see it in himself? Why wouldn't he see it in her? Again, his lips moved but no words followed.

"But that can't happen, can it?" Crysanthia said. "It can't happen if you're dead."

"It is not dying," Janos said softly. Then, louder: "But no, it cannot happen." He closed his eyes. "I'm sorry."

Behind him, the thing writhed and pulsated. Already, he belonged to it.

"You are certain? Janos, what if you're wrong?"

"I need this, Ms. Vog," Janos says—Crysanthia flinches at the return to formality. "As badly as you need to be in space, as badly as you need this ship, I need this. I can't turn back. Could you?"

"But if you're *wrong...*"

"What would you think of anyone or anything that stood in your way?"

Crysanthia watched it calling to him, pulling at him. The event dominated and distorted him just as it dominated and distorted the twisted space and time around it. She watched as it pushed aside the comforting brute mechanics of the universe—

the quantum clockwork she's known in her cells since before she was born—and remade it in its own image, sinuous and subtle. There was no way she could yank him away from that, it was hard enough to keep from following. Still, she had to try. "And if I told you I loved you?"

Janos met her gaze with eyes awash in tears he would not allow to fall and said, "Crysanthia, when you are in my vision, you mean the universe to me."

So she was wrong—he did see it, the empty ache they shared. He had seen it all along. He saw it that night in the gallery as she gazed out at the city, saw it when she dawdled over the gloves in the spaceport, saw it in every taunting flaunt of her exotic sexuality. It was as simple as a story a human mother would tell her human child before sending him off to his human dreams: *One day, the galaxy's loneliest boy found the galaxy's loneliest girl—*

"But I see what's going on behind my back," Janos said.

—And walked away.

"Suit up," Crysanthia said in a voice glacially cold and dead. "We'll be at the two million kilometer point within the hour."

Tethered to Crysanthia through the conjoined circuits of his spacesuit and her starship, Janos went. She watched from the chamber, seeing what he saw, as his massive thruster pack drove him deeper into the heart of the thing. At first, it was pleasant, almost euphoric: Crysanthia felt a sympathetic tingle as the electricity of the event overloaded the dampeners in Janos's suit and played on his skin. Gradually, as the hours passed and he ventured further into the vast lacunae between the pulsing, luminous walls, Crysanthia began to lose all sense of scale, a curious feeling for her, a kind of blindness. Distances she knew to be astronomical felt claustrophobic—her euphoria gave way to foreboding, then dread. A panic of trespass seized Crysanthia even as the certainty grew that the thing lured Janos along, through its ravenous tubules of gauzy plasma Either way, there was no turning back. He emerged into a space that opened onto a sphere the size of an asteroid or small moon, perfectly round and perfectly smooth, glowing like a pearl in shifting waves of coral and aquamarine light. Wisps and tendrils of violet and magenta energy danced on its surface. It was oddly familiar to Crysanthia, as familiar as the womb.

Janos toggled his thrusters for a three-second burn and let momentum carry him the rest of the way. Slowly, almost imperceptibly at first, the energy began to coalesce and intensify on the sphere's surface thousands of kilometers beneath him. Suddenly, a column of rose colored light leapt from the pearl and invaded the suit, invaded his nervous system with a storm of crackling fury. It grew stronger and choked his soul like a strangler fig. A piercing, blinding pain traveled back along the thread and stabbed Crysanthia between her eyes.

Crysanthia cried out and twisted onto her side in shock as the tether tore away from her. She felt as if a little part of herself had torn away along with it. When her vision cleared she saw her fingers twisting and writhing, grasping frantically for something. There was nothing to grasp, however, and her fingers finally became still.

In the awful silence, an after-image formed. She looked down, through Janos's watery, common stock eyes, and saw him sunk to the ankles in the mire of a swamp. She felt the slime between his toes, the warm muck compressed beneath his heels, the humid prickle of the sun on his skin. She smelled the sweet stink of rot and re-birth that assailed his nostrils, heard the buzz and clicks of insects that rattled his eardrums. And then he was pulled free, pulled free and... gone.

Gone.

Minutes passed as she sat, nude and motionless, listening for a voice she knew she'd never hear again. The minutes became hours and finally she heard something, the wrong something.

Wu's voice, tinny and without dimension in her mind, transmitted from Karza's ship: "It's closing up."

Two days later, Crysanthia flew in and retrieved his body. All that remained of the event was a dissipating cloud of radiation around a dying ember crumbling away into nothingness. "In remission," Wu had said in her final message the previous morning. "I doubt we'll ever know exactly why. It would be foolish to form any conclusions based solely on coincidence, regardless of how meaningful we may wish the coincidence to appear." Crysanthia had not responded. Moments later, the two Consortium vessels each launched a robotic probe. Moments after that, they were gone.

As *Pariah* moved through the event's remains, buffeted by decaying gravity waves, Crysanthia wondered if the event had gotten what it wanted from Janos. She hoped Janos had gotten what he needed from it. She wanted to believe she felt satisfaction in him, just before the pain and mute emptiness. She wanted to believe too badly, she knew, until she was all want and no belief. She brushed it away.

She brought his body aboard. She was built to withstand the vacuum of space for short periods: she stood in the open doorway of the airlock with only the leather of her jumpsuit to protect her, only the fur of its collar to keep her warm. She detached Janos from his thruster pack and then, holding onto the ship with one arm and grasping his suited corpse in the other, she sent the huge, spent rocket cartwheeling away from *Pariah* with a kick. She retreated into the airlock and lowered him gently to the deck as the skin of the hull closed and sealed them in.

His once white spacesuit was charred and pitted, the color of soot. Its cold corruption burned her fingers as she fumbled with the release and removed the helmet.

Briefly, she yielded to the cruelty of illusion, of want, and it was as if he again slept in her arms. If only there were no scorched metallic fibers spread across his face like a creeping mold, if only there were no trickles of dried blood from the corners of his eyes, he would have been perfect.

She removed the interface jack from the port in his temple. Welded together by the power that had surged through them, they came apart with a brittle snap and a fine shower of dull metal dust.

Crysanthia left Janos in the airlock and let the coldness of space preserve his body. She returned to the symbiosis chamber and removed her garment. She plunged *Pariah* into the onion fold, on course to the Solar System, to Vesta and Bettina Brekkelheim.

She did not cry. She had no tear ducts. Her eyes did not need them.

7

Necessary Angels

For a week, *Pariah* waits among the ice and rock of a planetary debris field in orbit around a red dwarf star at the extreme rim of explored space. And for that week, Crysanthia does not leave the chamber. For that week, Crysanthia is completely cut-off from the universe beyond her ship—she is completely cut-off from any universe beyond her own flesh.

Though her anti-bodies had destroyed millions of Bettina's nano-avatars minutes after the assault on Heaven 17, a few thousand remain in her bloodstream, stubborn and evasive. For the last week, they have trickled information and memories, dream-like, into her mind. Thus it had been child's play for her to reprogram *Pariah's* medical scanners into telling her the truth about herself. And as she's done countless times since then, she turns her focus from outer to inner space. The halo of rubble around the star, shining cherry red with reflected light, fades away, replaced by a multi-spectrum resonance image of her belly, her innards rendered with all the apparent solidity of cigarette haze.

Eight generations of Pilots, Crysanthia thinks. Cultured and incubated in laboratories, constructed in factories—the thought of Pilots reproducing sexually as absurd in its way as the thought of two starships copulating to spawn a third. Pilots are cyborgs. Pilots are machines. Pilots are sterile.

Crysanthia sits transfixed by the ghostly gray-blue image of the things transpiring in her belly: what had been a tiny mass of vestigial tissue, no larger than a bean, unfurled now into ovaries and fallopian tubes, a blood-engorged uterus. A bio-mechanoid web weaves in and out of her new flesh, strung with pearl-like nodules that will infuse the future unborn with their first cyborganelles. Crysanthia takes a deep breath and increases the magnification a thousand-fold: an ovum, new and perfect, just beginning its slow, drifting voyage.

The sensors in *Pariah's* hull register a telltale distortion in nearby space-time. Crysanthia shifts her vision outward and watches a ship approach, seemingly from all directions at once, a silver blur gathered within a picosecond to its resting position, perfectly motionless, alongside *Pariah's* port side. Crysanthia does not wait for his hail. "Come aboard," she transmits. "Or I'll board your ship. Either way, I won't discuss this over radio."

Crysanthia remains immersed in *Pariah* long enough to watch the other vessel extend a pseudopod of fluid metal toward her hull. She feels it touch and flow into her, feels her own hull relax its electrostatic field. She opens a port in the hull and then emerges from symbiosis. Returning to her own meager sensorium after one-hundred and seventy-four hours linked to the ship is like entering a dim room after hours wandering a clear and brilliant snowscape. Against the protest of her stiff muscles, she stands and stretches. She slips into a tan suede shift and walks, barefoot, to the lounge.

The open tube-way linking the vessels pulses soft gold and green light. Moments after Crysanthia enters the lounge, Narisian emerges from the tunnel, dressed as he is always dressed, in a black Martian cloak with silver embroidery at the collar.

"She's dead," he says.

"I know."

Narisian brings his chin down to his chest and presses his palms together in front of his eyes. "We were on Ganymede for three months, working with the Commonwealth to dismantle Brekkelheim's operations—things weren't right. Things... weren't right. They killed her, Crysanthia. *Murdered* her—we were separated, I couldn't help..." Narisian's fingers writhe. "I couldn't save her. I escaped but they killed her. They killed her."

Crysanthia shakes her head. "I don't understand," she says. "What are you talking about? Who—?"

"Galatea."

For long moments, the only sound is the soft thrum of *Pariah's* machinery.

"They destroyed the unborn waiting in the tanks. Thousands of them, some just days away from birth."

"The ones who survived the fetal attrition, Bettina's culling?"

"There was... no fetal attrition. There hasn't been for the last four cycles. Brekkelheim perfected the genome with us and now it's more stable than theirs."

"Of course," Crysanthia whispers. "The last piece." But as she says it, she knows it to be a lie. There are countless pieces left, waiting. She places her hands over Narisian's.

"I killed someone," Narisian says suddenly.

Crysanthia stares at Narisian, her comprehension lagging words behind.

"A Commonwealth Security agent," Narisian continues. "He had me at gunpoint, twelve meters away. But he was slow. I took his gun from him and I..."

Crysanthia feels his fingers convulse under hers. She tightens her grasp. "Narisian, you don't—"

He shakes his head. His voice breaking, his body trembling, he says, "I drove my fingers into his eyes. The blood. The... fluids—they have liquid eyes, the common stock, so different from ours. And the way the thin bone at the back of the sockets... *gave* as I pushed and pushed into his brain. The *stink* of him." Narisian grins. Crysanthia takes a step back but does not let go of his hands. "You should have heard him scream, Vog. You should have. You should have heard him." His grin disappears. "Galatea..." Narisian gently removes his hands from her grip. He turns his back to her and begins to pace. "When I came aboard, you said you knew she was dead."

Crysanthia shakes her head. "I misunderstood. I thought you meant... someone else—is Bettina all right?"

"Brekkelheim? Yes. I mean, I assume so. Although anything could have happened since I last heard anything. She *could* be dead. I don't--I don't know."

"She says—her avatars *said*—that the Commonwealth will kill her. If it hasn't already." Crysanthia tells him everything she knows—next to nothing, she realizes now. "The Commonwealth must have known about Bettina's fertility bug."

"They must have discovered it right before they came to me," Narisaian says. "Which was only days before we came to you—I remember how they pushed me, urged me to hurry."

"And still, they were too late. They had no idea how far along she'd progressed. They underestimated her. They used us, used *me*, to stop her, but they were too late. It was in me all along, *alive* in me. And now we all have it."

After a moment's pause, Narisian says, "They won't kill her. Not yet. They have her neutralized, in their prisons, she's at their leisure. They can afford to take their time with *her.*" He looks at Crysanthia. "But you? Me? They're coming for us. All of us." He sighs. "Space is vast. But we cannot run forever." Abruptly, he slashes the air with an open hand and makes a frustrated noise—at once a cough deep in the throat and a hiss through bared teeth—that Crysanthia has only heard Pilots make. "But *why*? What possible reason could they have...?"

"You really have to ask that question? They are *afraid* of us, Narisian. You think they don't know what Pilots think of them? Those throw-away computers with me and the pig, do you really think they are so stupid they couldn't figure that out? Vog the bestialist. Vog the pig-fucker." She pauses, lets it sink in. "Vog the human-lover."

"That had nothing to do—"

"It had *everything* to do with them. You as much as said it: 'To us Pilots, you common stock humans are animals.' And you know how humans treat *their* animals. Why would they expect better from us?"

Narisian tilts back his head and stares at the ceiling. Old habits of thought and instinct have Crysanthia eyeing his throat before remembering why he's here, in her ship, under her protection. The two of them alone together and neither of them dead, she thinks. And then she thinks: the night is young. She looks away. "Why should they? Our closest genetic relatives are the mako shark and praying mantis."

Narisian says nothing.

"And you, Narisian. You've done more than any other single figure to publicize Pilot disdain—Pilot *disgust*—for common stock humanity."

Softly, Narisaian says, "It wasn't them I was after."

"You think they care?" Crysanthia grabs his wrist and then, just a quickly, lets it go. "Don't you see that only makes it worse? Their dignity, their worth, trampled on so casually, caught in the crossfire of a petty spat between the gods."

Narisian scoffs. "Gods—"

"I know them. For four years, I lived with them—"

"Vog—"

"Let me finish. They *are* primitive compared to us—slow, stupid and crude—and they know it. Living in their cities, walking in their streets, I could feel it every time one of them looked at me."

Narisian searches her face with his maroon mantid eyes, the soft star bursts of captured light. Beautiful, Crysanthia thinks, this terrible beauty, and--for an instant--she sees him as human eyes see him.

My God. We're horrifying.

"There was only one of me: I was a novelty, a thrill," she continues.

Narisian turns away.

"While we are few, while they control our numbers, they can tolerate us, their tamed gods, their necessary angels. But what happens when we number in the millions? In the billions?" Crysanthia asks. "Did you really think they would ever let it go that far?"

Narisian shakes his head. After a long pause, he says, as if to himself, in a voice barely above a whisper, "It's strange, Vog—Crysanthia. Galatea told me about you, about what she said to you, here and in Brancusi City. And now I've let you touch me..."

"Oh, for Christ's *sake*, Narisian!"

He turns and faces her. "No, that's not what I mean." He takes a deep breath, starts again, "You said it yourself, we walk among them, gods of convenience, and yet you... did what you did."

Here we go, Crysanthia thinks. She sighs and says, "You think of them as beasts, Narisian. I can't tell you that you're wrong—if thinking that makes you feel better then so be it, go ahead. But we would not *exist* if not for them. Genetics aside, we share more of who we are with them than with any other creatures in the universe. We are not so different."

"You can say that after what they've done? What they've done to *her?*"

"I can say it *because* of what they've done."

Narisian stares at her. She sees the muscles around his mouth tighten and twist, then relax. After a long pause, he asks, "Did she pay you?"

And that's it. Before his words have fully penetrated her conscious mind, before his lips have fully formed the final syllable, Crysanthia's fist is whipping around like a comet. She catches Narisian on the jaw with the full force of every moment of her decade in exile. She feels his elastic skull give even as his neck muscles go slack and he rocks back on his heels. Before he can retaliate, she dances three steps out of his reach. "Check your records, you son of a bitch," Crysanthia spits. "She paid for passage, from Mars to Proxima Station. The Commission made sure it got its cut even as you left me to rot in the Inner Worlds." Crysanthia slows down her heart, cools down her blood. "I'm hardly the first Pilot to dally with a common stock human. I'm surely not the last."

Narisian stretches out his right arm and braces himself against the bulkhead. He touches his mouth with his left hand and looks at the blood smeared on his fingertips. His nostrils flare and Crysanthia can see the barest tremor move slowly through his shoulders. She braces for the attack she knows is coming. Instead, he wipes the blood away on his cloak. "Perhaps," he says slowly as he straightens up. "You *are* the first one to use the symbiosis chamber to do it."

Crysanthia cannot argue with that.

"It became imprinted in the circuits," Narisian continues. "Indelible. No other Pilot could stand it. We had to remove the artificial intelligence and sidereal sensor net. When we were done, practically all that was left was the DMR drive and the hull."

"Typical. Would have been easier just to requisition a new ship—probably cost less, too, in the long run," Crysanthia says. "What happened to the AI?"

"It was still functional. We sold it to the Interstellar Transit Authority. I think it's regulating the sewage reclamation system on Heaven 26."

"Maybe I should visit." Then she realizes: *too late now.*

Narisian, lost in concentration, stands motionless. Crysanthia can feel his cyborganelles in shallow, glancing contact with *Pariah's* net. "It's here, as well. Brekkelheim's son. Fomalhaut. I never realized."

Crysanthia lets his unasked question go unanswered for several moments. She becomes aware of the rhythms of Narisian's body, transmitted through the ship and into her. She fights for a moment, then surrenders and lets her own pulse and respiration fall into contrapuntal synch with his.

"That first time it was just...recreation. And curiosity. I wanted to know what they were, how they saw the world. I wanted to see how they were put together—up close, I mean. And she was famous; I own most of her recordings. That alone is alluring, though I doubt you'd understand. The second time is none of your business."

"And the chamber? The sensor net?"

"I can't explain. I won't."

Narisian waits.

Crysanthia looks down at her hand, still throbbing with the dull ache of impact, and realizes that the last vestiges of her rage and resentment had boiled away upon her fist's collision with his face. She relents—a little. "All I will say is that it was beautiful."

She watches as Narisian thinks about this. She sees now the extent of the damage she's inflicted. A black and ochre bruise spreads across his jaw and cheekbone; against the blue of his skin, it looks like a sunset through dark storm clouds. Tiny flecks of blood are trapped beneath the corneal shell of his left eye—she's blown out a few thousand of the individual facets. If he were human, she realizes, he would be dead.

He steps forward and reaches for her. Crysanthia steels herself against the instinct to back away. His fingers touch her face and she does not flinch. Gently, very gently, he cups her chin in the palm of his hand.

"Show me," he says.

Narisian leaves her six hours later. Crysanthia sits in the center of the symbiosis chamber and watches his departure—his ship there alongside *Pariah* one moment and gone the next, tunneled into the onion fold. She recalls his slithering caresses, his savage bites, his exotic familiarity. She places her hand on her belly. Deep inside her, she can feel them. She does not need *Pariah* to confirm it but she confirms it just the same. Twins. A boy and a girl.

Crysanthia smiles. Narisian Karza, she thinks. My convenient god, my necessary angel. She laughs.

Part Two
The Solar Powered Amniotic Dynamo

Wracked to the marrow with the thrill of ache,
I am a wave of pure time spent against your
yielding shore;
Cast out from your sun-warmed womb,
I gasp and crawl on your rough and clotting
sands—
You are the solar powered amniotic dynamo,
Your secret name forever etched
In the intimate ephemeral and the infinite eternal.

—*The Apocrypha Dance* by Aurelius Mann

8

Royalty and Advance

The water is tepid but wet. My mouth is dry. As for my hand, it only shakes a little as I bring the glass to my lips, but I doubt anyone notices.

"Jane, what do you have to say about this?"

I try to swallow, quickly and quietly, before leaning into the microphone. "I'm sorry?"

The auditorium is filled to capacity, standing room only: a sea of denim and corduroy with clunky jewelry and spidery eyeglasses gleaming in the crepuscular expanse. I am sitting on stage, at a long table I share with four men: an Episcopal priest, a professor of theology, a professor of philosophy, and my colleague, Aaron Mendel. My name is Jane Charlotte Kindred. I write science fiction.

I also attend panel discussions and give lectures, a dozen or so a year. Tonight's panel is called *Faith and Speculation: Spirituality in Science Fiction.* All that by way of saying that this is second nature, often tedious but seldom so much to be a true purgatory. I do not get stage fright. Whatever it is I am feeling, I know at least it is not that.

I also know that, for what seems a lifetime but could hardly have been a minute, I've been somewhere else. All that has gone before in the now and the here, in *this* student center in *this* February evening in *this* Anno Domini 1977...

It's all a deep and distant memory.

Aaron, who worked with me briefly on *Forbidden Planets* and has been a close, if nettlesome, friend ever since, speaks: "I was saying to Father Ashwood—"

"Phil," the priest says softly.

"Yes. I was just telling *Phil* that his God seems to have taken a long holiday for most of this century."

As Aaron continues his rant under the guise of bringing me up, I tune him out and focus on the priest. He looks to be about my age, somewhere in his late forties or early fifties; he has a full head of sandy hair going to grey and he's dressed like a civilian, in black chinos, a maroon turtleneck and a charcoal colored sport-coat. His only badge of office is a rather large, tarnished silver cross hanging from a chain around his neck. I haven't decided if I find his insistence that we call him by his first name charming or smarmy.

"Thank you, Aaron," I say now. "I heard what you said; I just needed a moment to gather my thoughts." I take another drink of water, this one hopefully appearing more confident, and say, "With all due respect to Phil, I fear I must agree. Only I object to the idea that the 20th Century is somehow exceptional. Less than a quarter of a century from the Millennium, it's tempting, I agree: I find a strong urge to evoke falcons, falconers and widening gyres, whatever those are." A ripple of laughter passes through the audience. I milk it by saying, as an aside: "We sci-fi types are always stealing legitimacy from our literary betters." The audience laughs a little louder now; the professor of philosophy smiles, the professor of theology does not. "Yes, more people may have died in the last seventy-seven years than in any one past century but more people are *alive* today than ever before, too. Clearly, technology—the ability to rain obliteration from above *and* the ability to immunize entire populations against a multitude of plagues—has more to do with the body count, living and dead, than any increase in human depravity *or* nobility. And I think God has nothing to do with either."

"You don't see God in the saving of human lives?" Phil asks.

"No more than I see him in the taking of them. Even if I did, I'd hesitate for a very long time before seeing any particular God in it. I'm no expert on world religions. I'm no expert on Christianity or Judaism. I'm no expert on astronomy, physics or biology. Come to think of it, why *am* I here?" This gets another laugh from the audience. I smile and continue: "From what little I do know, however, I'd say that most if not all of our gods suffer from a problem with, I don't know what to call it, *scale*, for lack of a better term."

"I'm not sure I know what you mean by that," says the theology professor, a dour black man with a salt-and-pepper goatee.

"She means," Aaron says, "that they're all too small. Petty."

That's exactly what I mean; Aaron knows me well enough not to materially misrepresent me. But I resent his presumption—so typical, really. And I wish he wouldn't be so goddamned combative all the time. "Not precisely or I would have said as much," I say. "However, I do think that our gods are too human. The problem is right there in Genesis: God creates man in His image. Which is really a way of saying we create God in ours. God's mind is really our mind, only larger but not by much. I feel—yes, that's the word, *feel*—that the universe is too wondrous strange for that to be true."

"I wouldn't read too much into that passage," the theology professor says. "It was probably just a way to make Yahweh distinct from the chimerical gods in the nearby pantheons, particularly the Egyptian. God has a man-like aspect, not the head of a dog or a cat or an ox."

"Well, like I said, I'm no expert—"

"—But you just made her point *for* her!" Aaron interrupts. "'Try our new and improved God, now with a human head!' We've split the atom, we've deciphered the genetic code—"

"Not exactly," Phil softly interjects.

"—we're building a *moon*base with the Russians and we're still supposed to take this stuff seriously?"

I have to smile at the last part: I suppose a glorified compound of pressurized sheds and trailers in the Sea of Tranquility just barely qualifies as a moonbase.

"Mr. Mendel, please," says the philosophy professor, a raw-boned man in his early thirties with a long sandy ponytail. He's doubling as moderator but is a self-professed fan of Aaron's stories. I feel for him. "I would argue that we should indeed take this stuff very seriously, if only as an integral part of our literary and philosophical heritage."

"Fair enough," Aaron concedes. "Very true. But then so is *The Iliad* and *The Odyssey*, so is *Gilgamesh*. We had the sense to jettison the superstitious ballast there, why can't we do it here?"

Phil answers the question by pretending Aaron hadn't asked it. "Surely, Ms. Kindred—"

"Jane."

"I'm sorry, of course. Jane, surely you see some mystery in that—how did you put it?—scale problem. That scale problem is the essential paradox of faith, that something so inhumanly vast could care for us, could love us, become one of us and forgive us—you see no beauty in that paradox?"

"Beauty, yes. Truth, no. And here I am, cribbing from the poets again. But I think that mystery is really more indicative of post-hoc temporizing than the inherent wisdom of any religion itself. The ancient Hebrews, just emerging into history, had no concept of how *inhumanly vast* the universe really is, how *monstrously complex* even the simplest forms of life really are. No ancient culture did. I don't have to be an expert to know that. And I take no comfort in a universal mind that in any way resembles my own or the mind of anyone I've known." I slide a swift glance at Aaron. Only Phil seems to notice.

"Understandable," he says. "But what of Christ? What of *his* mind, his revolutionary message of compassion and forgiveness, redemption and reconciliation?" he says. I find myself watching his mouth as he speaks. It's a good mouth: full-lipped without being feminine.

Aaron again: "What revolution? Did this *messiah* even *speak* against Rome?"

I've heard this before—Aaron has a few notes that he hits, with more than a little force and skill, time and time again. He'll go on hitting this one for the next minute or two, it's the latest model of an argument he first rolled out in '65. He'll call Christ a coward for remaining mute about the Roman occupiers and a fool for antagonizing Rome's Jewish collaborators before dismissing him as irrelevant by saying...

"...and still he dies in disgrace, convicted of a Roman crime and nailed to a Roman cross."

Coldly, quietly, Phil replies: "Christ defeated Rome."

"The hell he—"

"Christ. *Defeated.* Rome. Christ's teachings entered the bloodstream of Rome, his word, his *logos*, went straight to the heart of Rome. Like a holy virus, Christ transformed Rome and changed the course of history."

Christ. Virus. The words in juxtaposition knock me a beat behind, as if a bolt of energy has been fired at my forehead, *déjà vu* raised to the hundredth power. But like a flash of lightning, it only deepens the darkness that returns in its wake. By the time I can collect my wits to speak, it's too late, the feeling is gone.

For an absurd and panicked moment, I wonder if I'm developing a brain tumor.

"Indeed he did!" Aaron exclaims. "The Romans nail him up, the Jews take the fall. Two thousand years of institutionalized anti-Semitism—you're right, Jane, I was thinking small by limiting my earlier comments to this century—and then there's your Holocaust. So where's your God?"

Silence. Aaron has the audience split, but not evenly—about a third of them want to cheer, the rest want his head on a platter. What did they expect? This is the man who wrote "The Rape of the Light at the Dawn of Forever" for Harlan Ellison's *Dangerous Visions* anthology. It's a lovely story—heartbreaking, really. It implies that God precipitated the War in Heaven by repeatedly sodomizing Lucifer.

But I register this only vaguely. My mind turns circles in vain pursuit of my abortive epiphany—something about those two words, *Christ* and *virus*. Trying to recall it, trying to make sense of it, is like trying to grab a fistful of fog.

"Well," the philosophy professor says, "maybe now's a good time to open the discussion to our audience."

Only then do I realize we haven't talked much about science fiction at all.

The question-and-answer session goes about as well as one could expect. No one openly threatens Aaron, though a couple of people come close. To his credit, Aaron keeps his insults subtle enough to be ignored. He's moderately dismayed but not at all surprised that the requisite contingent of Planeteers is in attendance; we both have to answer a few too many questions about working with Adam West and Gary Lockwood ("Lovely men, joy to know") and rumors of a feature film revival ("Nothing definite, no one's contacted either of us about contributing a story or script"). A handful of people have questions that are relevant to the panel's stated theme—three or four even have questions for someone other than Aaron or me.

Afterward, Aaron and I stand and autograph our books in the student center's lobby. I glance over just as he prepares to scrawl his name on the flyleaf of a first edition *Shards of My Soul like Slivers of the Sky* for a little earth mama type with green eyes set in a heart-shaped, freckled face framed in a nimbus of frizzed-out ginger hair. She has pudgy, child-like hands and magnificent breasts.

"I love 'Ashes on the Altar of the Atomic God,'" she effuses. "It's just the most beautiful story I've ever read."

I never know how Aaron will respond to this kind of praise. In the past, I've heard him snap that his admirer should read Chekhov or Joyce. Something tells me he'll go easier on this child, dressed like a coed's idea of a Gypsy and redolent of patchouli. Maybe it's because he unloaded most of his bile onto Father Ashwood. More likely, it's because the girl is not wearing a bra and a cold breeze blows into the room every time someone exits or enters the student center.

"You're too kind, my dear, too kind by half," he says. "To whom should I sign this?"

"Nuala."

"Nuala, Nuala... tell me, Nuala, haven't we met before?"

"I don't think so."

I roll my eyes and sign an old paperback of *The Robot Masters*, my first (and worst) novel.

"Ah, but are you certain? Perhaps we danced on the lido deck of the *Celestis Regina* as it cruised among the rings of Saturn?" Aaron pronounces the name in the British fashion, so that the second word evokes a rather suggestive rhyme. Something stirs deep within my memory, so deep I can't retrieve it, leaving me with the sensation of an itch too deep to scratch.

Nuala blushes and looks down at the pointy toes of her suede boots. "I don't know if you've made plans but my friends and I are going to The Red Queen's Pub, it's just around the corner..."

"I'll see you there, my dear Nuala, I'll see you there." I half expect him to slap her on a shapely and substantial haunch as she walks away but he restrains himself.

Someone hands me a copy of *The Owl in Daylight* in hardback.

"Who should I make this out to?" I say without looking up.

"Phil, if you please."

I hadn't realized how tall he was while we were on stage. Standing before me, he seems almost gangly, like a scarecrow.

"I hope you don't mind?" he says.

"Of course not." I glance over at Aaron, resolutely scribbling away, his mouth set in a prissy moue of distaste. "Say, how would you like to join Aaron and me for drinks? Where was it, Aaron, The Red Queen's Pub?"

"I know it well," Phil says before Aaron can respond. "And I'd love to."

Aaron stiffens just a little bit. I notice it, I don't know if Phil does. I finish signing his book and hand it back to him. "Wonderful!"

The television show *Forbidden Planets* ran on the Hearst Network from September 1963 to June 1971. Picking up a few years after the events of the 1954 feature film, it followed the exploits of Captain J.J. "Jack" Adams (Adam West taking the role Leslie Nielsen played in the movie), his android science officer Mr. Roberts (the movie's robot with a new chassis that strongly resembled the actor Gary Lockwood), ship's doctor Cassius "Cash" Vance (Percy Rodriguez, bringing with him no small amount of gravitas) and the crew of the United Planets Star Cruiser *C-57D* as they voyaged "to explore the unexplored depths, to chart the uncharted reaches, to lay claim to all the forbidden planets of the galaxy," to quote the opening narration, delivered by Captain Adams and written by Quinn Danbury, the show's executive producer. More specifically, as they sought to possess all remaining traces of the ancient, enigmatic and very much extinct Krell.

An hour of archeological digging on sound-stage planets, among Styrofoam rocks under a backdrop sky, does not make for strong drama. Good antagonists do. For those of us working on the show, the answer was not in the stars but in the morning papers and nightly news.

With the Sino-Soviet Alliance of Worlds, we took the Cold War two hundred and fifty years into the future. The chessboard became the galaxy itself, with each side seeking to discover the super-advanced relic that would forever tilt the balance in its favor. Between five and eight times a season, Captain Adams would match wits with Commander Leonid Romanov (played by Martin Landau) of the Soviet Cosmo Cruiser *Dostoevski* or with Colonel Shin-Chai Li (played by France Nuyen) of the People's Asiatic Union Starship *Pyongyang.* Colonel Li was also a forbidden (by political and dramatic necessity) love interest for our leading man—France brought a certain guerilla chic to the part and looked particularly fetching with her raven hair in a Louise Brooks pageboy and her slender body clad in form-fitting olive drab.

Among the thirty episodes I wrote, co-wrote or re-wrote during my five and a half years with the show was "In Accents Yet Unknown," more commonly referred to as The Russian Episode. It was to be the first part of a two-part story, something we did very infrequently. I'd co-written the second part, "The Die Is Cast," with Frederik Pohl but "In Accents Yet Unknown" was all mine. I told the story from the point of view of the nominal villains, Romanov and Li. I pitted the *Dostoevski* and the *Pyongyang* against the *C-57D* in a race against time for the usual Krell Macguffin. The series regulars were the heavies and appeared only in cameos.

The communists won.

This was in 1967, five years before Cold War settled into the coordinated imperialism of Cold Peace, The Great Entente and a base on the moon. More specifically, it was in *April* of 1967. The week before it was scheduled to air, Maoist radicals assassinated President Joseph Kennedy, Jr. two days into the Madrid Summit.

The network pulled the episode and ran a repeat. A week later, they ran the second part (without the set-up, it made little sense) and two months after that they fired me—more than fired, blackballed. I never worked in film or television again...not that I really wanted to. Occasionally, fans screen the episode at conventions; I've spoken at more than a few. Rumor has it that the network and studio are planning to "un-earth" it as a prime-time special should the much-discussed new movie ever materialize.

"No, Father," Aaron says as he pays for the pitcher of Bass our waitress places on the table. "Allow me. Render unto Caesar what is Caesar's, right? Does that mean that our labor belongs to Caesar, too? Because, for the fishermen, artisans and farmers of ancient Judea, it took a few quarts of sweat to get hold of those little silver portraits of the emperor. Or was the Son of Man absent that day of Revolutionary Economics 101?"

"Aaron," I say, "lay off, will you?"

Phil clears his throat. "At the very least, I feel I should commend you on your familiarity with the Gospels, Mr. Mendel."

"I grew up the son of Orthodox Jews in South Boston. *Irish Catholic* South Boston." Aaron waits to let it sink in; like a vaudevillian, his timing is impeccable. "After my fourth annual Good Friday beating, I wanted to know what all the bruising was about."

After a beat, Phil says, "I offer my most sincere and humble apologies."

"You're not going to claim innocence? They *were* Irish papists, after all, not civilized Anglican types."

"Different organs in the body of Christ." He tips his glass to his lips and drinks deep. "Your story is all too common and it speaks ill of the Church, speaks ill of Christ. Again, I'm very sorry."

Aaron regards Phil for a long moment and then nods slowly. "I appreciate that. Really, I do." I'm amazed—Phil seems to have broken through the generalized distaste Aaron has for all religious figures. I have only seen it happen once before, when he gave a tangerine to an old Buddhist monk in Chiang Mai, Thailand in the January of '68, during a trip we took to celebrate the network firing me. But we had each eaten an acid-drenched sugar cube an hour before and just watched the sun rise over a landscape crowded with ancient temples and roamed by masterless dogs, abject and amiable. When I asked him why he did it, he gazed at me for a long time and said, with the obnoxious innocence of a five-year-old, "The tangerine, his robe: same color. It was a piece of him. I gave it back." It made sense at the time.

"Well," Phil says now, lifting his glass, "let us drink at least to erudition, with no regard to whatever precipitates it."

We all touch glasses in the center of our table and drink. I look around the pub. From the name, I had expected it to go overboard with the Lewis Carroll kitsch but, aside from the crudely painted, sandwich board-sized queens of hearts and diamonds flanking the entry, the décor is standard collegiate tavern: wreaths of cigarette smoke twisting in the air over the brass-railed bar; beer logos in neon affixed to the exposed brick walls; a Wurlitzer knock-off in the corner well-stocked with Velvet Underground and Doors 45s, and a red-felted pool table illuminated by a rectangular faux-tiffany lamp hanging from the ceiling on chains of brass.

I find it all utterly delightful.

While Phil and Aaron talk about politics—discovering a great deal of common ground in the process, I'm disproportionately happy to see—Nuala's attention is caught by a trio of semi-bohemian students, two girls and a boy, standing at the dartboard. After a few more minutes of conversation and the arrival of the second pitcher, she and Aaron take up their drinks and join them.

"Interesting fellow," Phil says. "Bracing."

I look over to Aaron, standing across the room with his hand resting lightly on the rise of Nuala's hip. When I met him, he was in his twenties and I was thirty-two. For over fifteen years, I've thought of him as a kid, bratty and brilliant in equal measures. Now I see him for what he is, a man just nosing into his middle years while still exuding a miasma of adolescent vitriol and aching for a spark. The realization renders me more somber and meditative than I wish to be right now. "You don't mean 'abrasive?' "

Phil laughs softly and shakes his head. "Perhaps a little hard to take—an acquired taste, like a single malt." He pauses for a moment and I imagine I can see him mulling over the highlights of Aaron's discourse. "Or a pungent cheese."

I laugh. "Maybe I shouldn't tell you this, then. Aaron grew up in a predominately Jewish neighborhood in Newark. His parents were socialists."

Phil is silent for a moment—long enough for me to fear I have made a terrible mistake. The muscles around his eyes and mouth harden. But then he begins to shake with deep and genuine mirth that quickly erupts into a deafening guffaw. Heads turn all over the pub. His concentration broken, one of Nuala's young playmates fouls his throw. The dart bounces off the board and falls to the floor.

"Don't tell him I told you."

"God bless him!" Gradually, Phil regains his composure and shifts his body in his chair to better face me. "I won't breathe a word."

I study his face. "You're not angry?"

Phil starts to laugh again, quietly this time. "What would be the point? I know when I've been beaten. Besides, he's a fabulist by trade. It's a good story."

"But he manipulated you into apologizing for something that never happened." I realize that I should just shut up; even to my own ears, it sounds as if I'm trying to instigate something.

"Never happened to *him,* maybe, but it does happen. Too often."

Just then, Aaron returns to the table. I'm afraid he may have somehow overheard—impossible, I know: the dartboard is clear across the room and "Live and Let Die" blares from the jukebox. Still, I don't relax until he says, "What did you do, Jane, tell him the one about Danbury's poolside sex party?"

I feign embarrassed indignation and slap his forearm. "*No!*"

"Anyway, will you be okay getting back to the hotel? Because Nuala and her friends over there invited me back to their house and..."

"Do they have a pool?" Before Aaron can respond, I say, "I'll be fine."

Aaron hands me a set of car keys and then extends his hand to Phil, who takes it warmly. "Look, I'm sorry I was such a bastard. For what it's worth, I had fun."

Phil nods. "Likewise."

After they've gone, Phil turns to me and says, "I meant to tell you earlier, I saw you at RobbieCon 73."

"Really? You, uh, you don't strike me as the Planeteer type."

"What type is that?"

I turn my head a bit and look at him from the corner of my eye. "The type you're not," I say.

After a pause, Phil says, "Actually, I was there specifically to see you. I'm sure you don't remember, but I asked you a question from the audience."

"You did?"

"I asked you about the influence of Gnostic heresy in *To Scare the Dead*."

"I'm sorry, I—No, wait, I *do* remember." I top off our glasses. "That was *you?* Small world."

"Not so small."

"Hmm," I say. "Well, you made an impression."

"You're being kind."

I shake my head. "Not the sort of question I'm used to getting at *Forbidden Planets* conventions."

Phil smiles. "I can see how that could be the case."

"Oh, most of the fans are lovely people, and very bright. They can just be a little... narrow in their scope. But a lot of that's just ego. Of course I want them to ask about *me*, about *my* work. I'm not being entirely fair."

"Perhaps you're not. You *are* being human, though. Is that really something to be ashamed of?"

"Hey," I say in an effort to put our conversation back on track. "I'm ashamed to say that your question caught me a little out of my depth."

"You covered well. It didn't show."

"God, I haven't done a convention in years—in fact, I think that one was my last. Now it's mostly panel discussions like tonight."

"Do you enjoy them?"

I take a long pull of my ale and nod. "And I *really* enjoy the speaker's fees. They supplement the uncertain income stream of royalty and advance." I pause, weighing my next words. "And sometimes you meet fascinating people. I like that, the exchange of ideas."

"Are you feeling well?" Phil asks abruptly. "You seemed a little distant at times tonight. Only more than that, you seemed..." When I don't answer, he adds, "I hope you don't mind my saying so."

After another moment, I reply, "I was hoping it wasn't so obvious."

"I don't know that it was. *I* noticed."

That catches me by surprise, not so much for the concern but for the naked admission that he'd been watching me so closely. I suddenly have to acknowledge the fact that we've been flirting the entire evening, at least since he handed me a copy of my own book to sign, probably since long before, during the thrust and parry of our on-stage exchanges, and that this flirtation is no idle thing. Terrible thing to find I've blindly wandered so far into dangerous territory, more terrible yet when I have to admit that blindness was never a factor.

More than that, I realize that I'm uncomfortable with the question because I still can't answer it for myself. Unable or unwilling to try to put what happened into words, I shake my head. "Probably just an acid flashback," I say before I can think it through. "Oh. Oh my God, I'm sorry."

"What for?" He gestures to the pitcher, sitting almost empty between us. "Alcohol, acid, it's all one—within reason. Although..." He pours the last of the pitcher into my glass. "I prefer psilocybin myself."

"I—I don't know how to respond to that."

"Then don't." He smiles. "You're under no obli-gation." He looks at the face of his gold wrist-watch and then drains his glass. "Perhaps we should go?"

Phil leaves a dollar on the table for our waitress and helps me into my coat. On the way out, I see that I've spoken too soon about the decor. Behind the bar, tucked in among the expensive whiskies, is an actual rabbit, stuffed and standing on his hind legs, glass eyes glinting with maroon pinpricks of light. He's been dressed in doll-sized trousers and waist-coat and holds a tiny gold pocket watch in his right paw. Suddenly, the pub loses a good measure of its charm.

We walk out into the night and find that an inch and a half of snow has fallen while we were inside. A Tucker Talisman fishtails around the corner, the third headlight in the center of its grille pivoting right and left as the driver steers through the skid.

The *ajna* eye of enlightenment as a machine age burlesque, I muse as it passes us by. "Doesn't seem quite... right," I say out loud.

Phil nods. "Not the best night to gad about in a little coupe."

That is not what I meant at all, but I do not correct him. I do not make myself clear, mostly because I'm not sure if or how I could.

"Where are you staying?" he asks.

"Court Motor Inn—the college is putting us up." The night before, Aaron and I stayed up late in my room, watching syndicated re-runs of *The Honeymooners, The Odd Couple* and *Forbidden Planets* (neither of us had written it and so both of us could relax) broadcast from a station in Syracuse. Aside from faint ghosts and a little snow, reception on the little black and white Zenith had been good. Aaron sat Indian-style on the floor, on the truly ghastly orange and red shag carpet, and I reclined on the bed behind him, fighting the urge to tousle his thick, black hair. We shared a bag of Wise potato chips and talked very little.

Remembering, I feel a new surge of affection for my cocky little brother and wish him luck I'm sure he does not need.

"That's across town," Phil says. "How are you getting there?"

"The college sprung for rental car, a VW. It's parked back at the student center." For a small liberal arts school stranded in upstate New York just fifty miles from the St. Lawrence River, Rosewall College has remarkably deep pockets. I tell Philip as much, adding, "They even paid to fly me out here."

Another car comes crawling through the intersection.

"The roads are in bad shape. I can't imagine you've gained much experience driving under these conditions in Northern California." He takes a deep breath. I find it charming even as I anxiously await the inevitable. "You could, uh, stay with me—my apartment isn't far."

On a good day, I carry twenty extra pounds on my frame; on a bad day, I carry thirty-five or forty. Today is merely so-so. An ex-husband once compared me to the drawings of R. Crumb. Phil doesn't seem to mind, however.

I loop my arm through his. "Lead the way."

9

The Forever Thing

Miriam Wu travels the twelve-hundred kilometers of labyrinthine passageways in Vulcan's nickel-iron mantle via an induction rail buggy launched from the terminal in New Kiryu. Almost perfectly regular, without even the stratification of natural rock to alleviate the leaden monotony, the tunnels and chambers offer nothing of any interest to the traveler as the buggy speeds along its helical track. At first, Miriam spends the time in reading and meditation. Before long, her concentration fails her and she completes the voyage with a mind simultaneously agitated and idle.

The buggy emerges into a rock-ribbed vault a dozen kilometers in diameter and comes to a halt at once gentle and abrupt. The atmosphere within the vault is composed entirely of noble gases so Miriam fits her breather mask over her face before she thumbs the hatch release. The buggy opens like a seed pod. Miriam exits and looks around but is not surprised when she sees no one. Huge cylindrical and domed structures, built into the walls and suspended from the ceiling, seem to be submerged into and emerging out of the stone.

At Miriam's feet, a shallow pool of oleaginous construction fluid extends ninety meters into the distance, one of a score of industrial baths that riddle the cavern floor. Submerged in the goo, a gunmetal shape the size of a small whale slowly takes form: the dark matter reaction drive for one of the many warships Stigol-Bergham currently builds in the shipyards orbiting Vulcan. At this stage of development, the reactor gives the illusion of smoothly wearing away, like driftwood. Streaks of dull silver within the viscous amber are just visible to Miriam's naked eyes: the raw material the billions of microscopic robots in the fluid busily assemble into one of the most complex devices ever engineered by humankind. The kilometers of rock above Miriam's head shield the process from cosmic radiation. Even so, she knows the quantum tolerances in the reactors are so delicate that neutrino interference will ruin one in ten of them.

"Dr. Wu," comes a metallic voice, distorted by the micro speaker of a breather mask. Miriam turns her head. A woman approaches from the cluster of sculpted stone domes a hundred meters away, just to the left of the assembly bath.

"Mr. Claypoole apologizes for the wait," she says. She is young, pert and very pretty, Miriam notes, with skin the color of weak tea and eyes like pools of ink. She wears a cobalt blue mini-dress with matching slippers and pillbox hat. "If you would follow me?"

Miriam follows her into the largest of the domes. After they have left the airlock and removed their breather masks, the woman leads Miriam a quarter of the way around a circular corridor and into the spot-lit gloom of a small office. The walls are cultured mahogany with a grain so fine as to be almost microscopic. Two high-backed chairs of butter soft, vat-grown leather face a desk fashioned out of a polished slab of jade.

The woman gestures to one of the chairs and bids Miriam to sit. As she settles into it, Miriam feels the chair adjust its dimensions to better fit her small frame. The woman smiles at her and says, "Mr. Claypoole will be along presently." Then she exits, leaving Miriam alone.

The office is bare of any decoration or personal effects aside from a large and rather generic hologram of a solar regatta, surrounded by a gilt frame and hanging on the wall behind the desk. Miriam watches as the sailboats—small capsules tethered to foil-fabric solar sails two kilometers wide and three microns thick—emerge from the bright yellow disk of the sun and speed past the camera, which then swivels to watch them hurtle toward the blue and white sphere of Venus. The last of the boats disappears against the globe before the hologram resets and shows the sequence again. In the interest of a stirring composition, the artist has taken considerable license with scale, velocity and distance. Miriam half expects to hear a whoosh and the creaking of rigging as the ships go by in the airless, soundless void.

The same twelve boats are about to make their fifth pass when Judah Claypoole of Transmigration Interregnum Limited, a subsidiary of The Charybdis Corporation in partnership with Stigol-Bergham, arrives. Miriam moves to get up but Claypoole, a tanned cadaver of a man with a craggy face under a shock of white hair, forestalls her with an outstretched hand as he rounds the desk and sits down behind it in a chair slightly larger and more opulent than the one that cradles her.

"Thank you for coming, Doctor," he says.

"I only hope I can be of assistance."

That is to be the extent of the pleasantries, apparently. Without further preamble, Claypoole uses his computer to call up a series of cryostylitic diagrams. They hover at various distances above the surface of the desk and partially obscure Miriam's view of his face.

"I assume you are familiar with the sub-quantum networking used in our transmigratory holistic gestalts."

Miriam nods. Chips of synthetic dark matter link the onboard computers of the so-called cryonic sibyls, scattered throughout hundreds of parsecs of space, to the coordinating mainframe here in New Kiryu through sub-quantum entanglement. The diagrams—there are over a hundred of them, ranging in size from under two to over twenty centimeters—all illustrate the system in one aspect or another. The most compelling of them, no larger than her thumbnail, resembles a mass of entwined serpents shifting through all shades of the spectrum as it writhes with and against itself.

"About a year ago, we detected an alien signal in the mainframe, a virus of sorts," Claypoole continues. "Apparently, it is distorting the *physical* circuitry throughout the entire system. As best we can comprehend, the virus is *expanding* the atomic structure of certain components up into the higher dimensions."

"Like a dark charge?"

"Not exactly—it's more exotic, more complex. As you can imagine, it's playing havoc with the system—we've lost a dozen subjects so far."

"Lost?" Miriam says with surprise: how do you lose a cryonic sibyl when it's already dead? "How so?"

"Quantum mechanical break-down? Or perhaps the subjects' minds—what remains of them—refused to accept the attendant changes to their apparent realities and simply shut down. Or any number of other scenarios; we haven't a clue, really. All we *do* know, they are completely gone, irretrievable. I would say dead but..."

"And just how real are these 'apparent' realities?"

"To the subjects? Entirely real. At least, that's how it should be—we can never objectively know. Why do you ask?"

Miriam wonders how much she should say, and then decides it's nothing he can't find out on his own. "A new theory in synchronistics holds that reality is nothing more than a function of information density—which is itself a reciprocal process between the observer and the reality being observed. If you've created apparent realities dense enough to be entirely convincing to the observers—the cryonic sibyls—then they cease to be apparent and become merely real."

At the mention of the sibyls, a look of distaste crosses Claypoole's face. He eyes Miriam from behind the slowly rotating image of a cryonic sibyl's cyber-cerebral interface over which the viral corruption spreads like a creeping vine. As Miriam watches, the vine strangles it until the interface disintegrates and the shadow of life disappears.

"More ominously," Claypoole says, picking up the thread from earlier, "preliminary findings suggest the effect *may* be spilling out into the reality external to the device. So far, the data are unclear but they strongly suggest a warping of space-time on the quantum and sub-quantum levels. Your insights into the synchronistic nature of information transfer is, of course, why we have requested your—" Claypoole's computer beeps twice. He looks down at its 2D display and swears quietly. "If you'll excuse me for a moment, there's something I need to attend to. It shouldn't take very much time."

"Of course," Miriam says.

The door slides shut and she is once again alone. She glances once at the sailboats as they ride the solar wind toward Venus. In one his final monographs, Janos Brekkelheim put forth an idea that has come to be known as *The Doctrine of Gnostic Dissociation*, though he never once used that term. According to his hypothesis, the Godhead (he never used that term either, though it was clearly what he referred to) had shattered at the time of creation. Indeed, that shattering was in itself creation. And because the Godhead is infinite, so too are the creations that resulted from its shattering—*result* from its shattering, since the moment of creative splintering is itself on-going and eternal. The theoretical mechanisms put forth so far to account for the existence of the so-called parallel universes necessary to modern practical physics—quantum branching; macro-cosmic inflation; the postulated eruption of singularities into Big Bangs unfolding into other, inaccessible, dimensions—would thus be but a few among an infinite number of devices through which infinity itself is propagated. God (or, as Janos referred to it in his uniquely insufferable way, the Forever Thing, lifting the phrase—as Miriam had only recently discovered—from his father's poetry) is itself simultaneously the source and the sum of those various infinities. Alone now with the images suspended above the desk, this cancer spreading through the guts of TIL's computers, Miriam wonders if she isn't seeing another of those infinite engines of creation.

And she remembers: "We start with the idea that there is matter and there is energy, there is space and there is time," Janos had said to her when she disinvited him from the Fomalhaut expedition. "And it's useful. From there, we progress to the idea that matter *is* energy, space *is* time. And that's useful, too. From there we arrive at the concept that matter and energy, space and time, they are all forms of information. More useful still. But it implies a tremendous question—*demands* a tremendous question—and you won't ask it. That's unfortunate. But to forbid me from asking it? That's unforgivable."

The knot of luminous snakes, the viral *thing* that attacks the mainframe, draws Miriam back into the present. As she only now realizes she had expected all along, she recognizes a pattern within its coruscations. Her heartbeat accelerates but she is hardly surprised to discover that she is happy, very happy.

Judah Claypoole re-enters the room. With the obsequious stiffness of one used to being served rather than serving, he hands Miriam a handle-less bone china cup.

Green tea with ginger, she thinks as she sips. They've done their research.

"Sorry for the interruption," Claypoole says. "If you don't have any further questions for me, I'll have my assistant show you to your accommodations. You no doubt wish to rest before we turn you over to the team we have investigating this."

"Actually, I *do* have a question. Do you know where this virus originated?"

Claypoole hesitates—not because he does not know, Miriam thinks with recognition, but because he does not know if he wants to tell her.

"The first moon of Iota Horologii Prime," he finally says.

"Agamemnon. And the first moon: that would be Klytemnestra?" Miriam asks, though she does not need to. "Enemy territory," she adds tonelessly.

Claypoole nods reluctantly.

Miriam does not allow any emotion to register on her face. "Perhaps I should meet with your team now."

10

No Thread, No Line, No Tether to the Shore

Phil lives above a judo studio three blocks away from campus. Through the plate glass window, I see the red and blue mats stacked up in the after-hour lighting. We reach the apartment by climbing up a flight of wooden stairs built onto the side of the building and slick with snow. Midway up, I lose my footing. Phil clutches my upper arm to keep me from slipping.

"Please pardon the mess," Phil says as he turns on the light in his kitchen. There's nothing much to pardon, however, just a few dishes in the sink and a rather haphazardly piled drain board. He takes my coat. "Would you like something to drink? I have some wine in the refrigerator."

I nod and ask him where the bathroom is.

"Down the hall, on the left."

The hall is lined with framed photographs. The first shows a much younger Phil with a young blond woman and a small boy, several more show the boy and the woman at various ages, together and alone. Somewhere during the boy's teenage years, the woman disappears—dead, I figure, with a sharp pang of sympathy not so much for the man in the apartment right now but for the man and the boy in the photographs. The last picture is of Phil standing next to the boy, now a strong featured young man—more his mother than his father—dressed in a royal blue cap and gown.

I finish quickly in the bathroom and join Phil in his living room, where he hands me a glass of chardonnay. Instead of sitting down, I wander the room, perusing the bookshelves that completely line two of the walls. Two brass floor lamps provide warm, amber illumination and the shelves give off the musty smell of a used book shop. Several are given entirely to the sacred: various translations of the Hebrew and Christian Bibles, over a dozen concordances and commentaries, the Apocrypha, the Gnostic gospels. One shelf is more ecumenical: The Bhagavad-Gita, The Tao Te Ching, The Tibetan Book of the Dead. I move to the next case and run my finger along the spines of books by C.S. Lewis and John D. MacDonald, Christopher Marlowe and Philip Roth, Saint Augustine and Frank Herbert, Albert Camus and Jim Thompson. My finger stops on a copy of *All We Marsmen,* the book that almost won me a Hugo.

I turn around and smile at Phil. Over the threadbare chintz sofa, there is a framed movie poster, Steve McQueen as Dallas McGee in *The Deep Blue Goodbye.* My eyes drift up to that.

"My son," Phil explains, turning to look at the poster. "He sent it to me last Christmas."

I leave the books and sit down next to Phil. I ask him about the photographs in the hallway and he tells me about the people in them, the wife he'd lost almost a decade ago to ovarian cancer, the son he'd lost much more recently, to a career on Wall Street and a wife in Connecticut.

"In five—no, four—months, I'll be a grand-father," he says as he stands and walks over to his stereo. "I moved to this apartment about a year ago." He turns it on and briefly searches among the spines of his albums. "Haven't regretted it," he says as he pulls one out, tilts the shiny vinyl disk free of its cardboard cover and its paper sleeve, and gently places it on his Bell & Howell turntable.

"Easier to care for—no shoveling snow; if something breaks, I call the landlord." He lifts the tone arm and drops it onto the record—before long, Judee Sill's ethereal lilt flows out from the speakers. "To your liking?" he asks.

I nod. "Very much."

"I teach a course at the campus theological seminary from time to time—not this semester, though." He sits down again. Before long, he's stroking my hair and caressing my neck. It all seems the most natural and easy thing in the world.

We sit in silence for a time, listening to the music and communicating through the surfaces of our skin. Long and languorous moments pass this way, as the needle moves through the groove from one cut to the next.

I close my eyes and lean back into the grip of the strong hand that kneads the tense muscles at the base of my skull. "'He's a bandit and a heartbreaker, oh, but Jesus was a cross maker,'" I sing along in a dreamy whisper. Phil laughs softly—in appreciation rather than mockery, it seems. "I saw her perform once," I say. "Quinn and I..." I decide too late I don't want to finish the story. I change the subject. "Interesting choice—what does this song mean to you? Theologically speaking--what's it *mean?*"

Phil shrugs—I feel his chest move against my back as his shoulders rise. I move a tiny bit closer. "What it means," he evades. "What it says. So--Quinn Danbury. Tell me about Hollywood: the egos, the poolside parties…?"

Bastard. "Mmm, do I have to?"

Phil doesn't answer. Instead, he grasps my shoulders and firmly repositions my body so that I'm resting against his chest. He kisses me softly on the rim of my right ear. Before long, we move from the couch to his bedroom, perfectly neat save for his full-sized, unmade bed. I can still hear Sill's tremulous singing from the other room.

Phil turns off the light. Moon and snow shine, cold and silver, wash in through his Venetian blinds as we undress.

Lying on top of Phil's rumpled sheets, I let him take the initiative and his time. He kisses me, his breath hot and pleasantly sour with wine. He's more playful than I'd expected, nibbling and sucking gently on my lower lip, teasing my tongue with the tip of his own. His kisses move from my mouth to my neck and my earlobes, from there to my breasts. After a rather protracted but very pleasant interval, his kisses move inexorably on.

I'm forty-eight years old and I've been married three times. In addition to three husbands, I've had more than a handful of lovers, casual and serious. I mention these things because I want to make clear that I am no stranger to lovemaking, to the responses of my body to the stimuli of another. I mention these things because I want to make clear that what happens next is like nothing that has ever happened before.

From someplace beyond the apartment, beyond the room, beyond the simple pleasure of Phil's attentions—from the same someplace *beyond* I've felt pressing perilously near me all evening long—I feel it building in me, like thunderheads pregnant with rain, with *power*, and then, and then...

And then the ice that had splintered during those deranged moments of the discussion shatters beneath my feet. I plunge through into something *other*. I grope for purchase with fingers twisting and turning in a thousand ways—fingers alien and yet *mine*, basic as breath. But there is nothing for me to grasp—no thread, no line, no tether to the shore. There is no web of before and after to ensnare me, no weave of cause and effect to enmesh and enfold me. For me, falling free, there is only sensation, intense and foreign-familiar. I see with a million eyes, everything in perfect clarity, and the colors—my *God*, the colors!—colors I cannot name, colors that have no place in the rainbow. My skin is sensitive to the swirling currents of hot and cold in this steam-heated, drafty apartment, my nostrils are sensitive to the subtle commingling of our aroused aromas: cologne and perfume, sweat and sex, heated blood pulsing beneath our age-thinned hides.

But even as it happens, it recedes like the tide. And as with the tide, I'm powerless to stop it or bring any of it back. Everything gives way to blackness, an infinity of blackness. And then... motes of light, of heat. Stars—it is only a millennium before I call them stars.

Still I fall. The darkness clutches at me like strands of a spider's web, like wisps of candy floss. I fall forever until I fall no more, until I rest against a dune—sand gets into my mouth when I lick my dry, cracked lips. A blinding blue pinprick of a sun burns directly overhead. Another sun, huge and dimly red, hangs just above the sinuous, bone-white horizon.

I lift myself up onto trembling arms, like the girl in the Andrew Wyeth painting. And I think: *This would make a good book cover.* The thought is enough to break the spell. Suddenly I'm me again, a fleshy woman in middle age with failing eyes and jointed fingers, lying flat on her back in the bed of a priest.

I open my eyes to the bare walls of Phil's room, to the alternating lines of light and dark thrown against them by streetlights shining through the blinds, and curse a formless panic. I mourn what already retreats from memory, what is soon remembered only in the pounding of my heart.

My face is wet.

Phil is beside me. His fingers touch my tears. "What happened? What's wrong?"

I clutch his hand and shake my head.

"Should we stop?"

Reluctantly, I nod. "I'm sorry."

Phil brushes the back of my hand with his lips. "I'm not a teenager. I'll survive," he says.

I give him a weak smile. "Thank you," I mouth silently.

"Sleep. I'll drive you back to your hotel in the morning."

I nod and close my eyes. From Phil's arms, I slip into oblivion, deep and dreamless.

11

The Intuitive Engine

The windmills stretch from horizon to horizon, spinning in the breeze, each one a sleek turbine on a stalk of cast rexeroid ceramic towering twenty meters into the sky. A lone figure walks among them and searches for inspiration in the elegant anachronism: a wind farm in an age of cheap fusion and dark matter manipulation. The man stops and looks up, at the blades forever trading places in the pink sky of a Martian twilight. He looks down and watches a lizard, nimble on flanged and dusty toes, as it moves swiftly up one of the silver-green agave plants and stops at the tip of a sword-like leaf. He lowers himself into a stiff and aching crouch and stares the reptile in its inscrutable yellow eye. The lizard stares back. A grimace of satisfaction, if not a true smile, crosses the man's face.

Aurelius Mann, poet laureate of Mars, stands. He turns up the collar of his cloak against the desert chill and heads for home.

"How was the walk?"

Aurelius hangs his cloak in the entrance hall of his Utopia Planitia home. He shakes the ochre dust from his boots. "Fruitless," he says as he passes into the dim sitting room. "As always."

Simone Trieste, twenty-two and barefoot, petite and naked save for a pair of flared shorts of champagne colored spider satin that barely cover the lower hemisphere of her rump, looks at him over her shoulder. Aurelius senses something in her, appraising without mercy, gone in the sweep of her dark eyelashes.

Aurelius crosses over to the bar. An open bottle of domestic tequila is already out, along with salt, a shot glass and the remains of a demolished lime. He looks at Simone, splay footed in front of his aquarium, swaying side to side to a song only she can hear. He pours himself four fingers of Laphroaig Scotch, walks over to her and admires the curve of her back. She recently had her spine tattooed with vermilion leopard spots. Adapted from octopus chromatophores, the pattern shifts with her moods. Now it pulses in time with whatever music she listens to in her head. Aurelius extends the tip of his index finger and slowly follows the trench of her spine, from sacrum to nape. He watches the spots change in the wake of his touch; he watches the ripples roll in his glass of amber liquor with each of her shivering breaths.

Aurelius takes a sip of scotch and kisses her on the corner of her jaw. He sees, through her short and spiky hair, the infra-aural stereo bead affixed to her skull, behind her ear. The music is transmitted to him faintly through his teeth. "Who's that on the beads?"

"Kiari Nakatani, in concert on Callisto." She leans back into him. "There must have been something for you in the dunes, you keep going out there."

Aurelius grunts a reply. "I watched the lizards out there, for a while," he says. "Amazing. Life as pure as life gets. Ruthless and yet still innocent, somehow. Simple minded." Another sip of Scotch, a long one, and the flavor of burnt peat and iodine fills his head, almost crowding out desire. He slips his free hand around her waist and cups a small, firm breast. He feels her nipple draw into stiffness under his thumb. He bites her earlobe and whispers, "Like you."

She squeals with delighted umbrage and twists away from his grasp. Aurelius almost spills his last few drops of liquor

"Anyway, what have you been doing?" He walks back to the bar and pours himself another drink. "I was gone for over four hours."

Simone shunts the music from her beads to the flat's sound system and Nakatani's music floods the air. Once, at a cocktail party, one of Aurelius's colleagues had derisively described the woman's compositions as whale song and heartbeats with contrapuntal screeching. Aurelius finds himself forced to agree. He turns the music down. Simone drops her beads on the coffee table.

"I drank," she says. She comes next to him and sprinkles coarse salt on the flesh between the thumb and index finger of her left hand, then pours herself a shot of tequila with her right. "I read. Um, let's see: 'Abject orphans of the blind designer, there is more life in the corpse of God than in the divine wreckage of creation.'" Again, he sees it, she studies him from behind the smiling eyes—perhaps he only imagines it. "What's it mean?" she asks. She bolts her shot and bites into the final wedge of lime. Aurelius is struck once again with a jolt of erotic unease—Simone has had her canines extracted and replaced with true fangs. She licks the salt from the back of her hand and stares at him all the while with bright and avid eyes of deep violet.

Aurelius is dismayed to find he does not have an answer for her. Thirty years ago, when he'd written those words, he could have told her. Fifteen years ago, maybe. Even now he could give her their textbook parsing—he could but he won't. Something there, once, living in the lines even after he'd written them, so muscular it tore away from each word that tried to name it. No more. The occasional villanelle or haiku, sonnet or sestina, lifeless and mechanical, all that remains.

And besides, she misquotes him. "What you bring to it," he says and scratches his beard. The fine Martian sand makes him itch. "Why don't you tell me what you *feel* it means?"

Clever child, she knows a dodge when she hears one and is sensitive enough of the rusted places in his old poet's armor not to push. Instead, she glides away and lies down on the floor in front of the aquarium. "I've been watching the fish."

Aurelius sits beside her, his skeleton balking all the way down, and watches her breathe. The watery light teases out the rounded slats of her ribs, rising and falling, rising and falling, under her pale skin. She gazes up at the ceiling and giggles.

"It's funny, you and them." She lifts her right leg and points with her big toe to the reef fish of distant Earth: brilliant flashes of living yellow, blue-green and cobalt darting in the coral. Sea horses hide among the finger-like tubes of the anemones and the deep emerald blades of the sea plants. The ancient rug on which she lies, the ocean salts in the four-hundred liters of water, the fish, the Scotch in his glass—all of it shipped across hundreds of millions of kilometers of space at university expense, off the books, to keep him right where he is. And Simone—sometimes he speculates if she and the half dozen or so who have preceded her is not a further emolument from the Board of Regents. Looking at her now, he is in no mood for that deep a strain of cynicism. He slides down next to her and kisses her lips. She surprises him with a nip from her left fang.

"Me and them what?"

She tames his unruly eyebrows with her fingertips. "You're just like God to them, aren't you? You regulate their entire little world. You let in the light, you let in the dark. You give them sustenance, manna from heaven." She kisses him on his chin. "Quite the power trip, no?"

"I see." He strokes her stomach, from the bottom of her ribs to her navel and round and round. "And this differs from you and your cat how?"

Again she giggles. "Astrid rubs her face on my ankles and climbs up on my shoulders. She wakes me up by purring in my ear and, when she's really into me, she sticks her ass in my face. That makes me Mommy." She strokes his lips. "*You* are shadowy and remote. You inhabit a hostile and rarefied element—you *are* a hostile and rarefied element." Her hand brushes his erection, growing and insistent. "Pillar of fire," she murmurs.

"You are drunk, young lady." He looks down the length of her body, the soft salmon pink of her nipples, the contrast his hand on her belly, corrugated deep bronze against smooth milk white.

"And you're shadowy. Remote." She kisses him. "Distant."

Aurelius is tired of words. His mouth finds her pulse, under her jaw. His fingers find the waistband of her shorts. Before long, he has her out of them. She laughs and kisses him—tart, salty and slow. Her small hands find him and free him, grasp him by the shaft. "Mmm, pillar of *fire,*" she sighs and dissolves into giggles.

So now they move together. They fall into a rhythm something like a poem. A villanelle, or a haiku. Maybe a sonnet, or sestina.

She dozes, like her cat. Tangled in the sheets of his bed, she snores lightly and stirs, utters little moans that even now trigger a twitching tightness in his groin.

Aurelius sits on the floor and leans against the side of the bed. Christ. Before long, he'll be ninety years old. Ninety years old and still waiting for that ineffable thing to return, to strike him as he wanders the windmills and century plants, to seize him as he sweats, sunk to the hilt in the girl-flesh of a breezy acolyte. Christ. Nothing has worked since *Mercy Sold* and that was fifteen years ago.

Seminars twice a week, in the arid, open air of the desert afternoons; special lectures and readings at predictably irregular intervals. Go ahead and skate, the faces tell him, the ones that tell him anything at all. You'll be poet laureate until the day you die—forty years distant at least.

And the Paolo Constantine Medal, no one's taking that from you, either. So let them come at you with their honoraria of every scent and texture, their callow prose and verse. When they ask you about the man who wrote *Earthman* and *The Martian Elegies* you can wear your rue with a difference and say "Yes, I knew him, once."

Aurelius Mann has outlived his legacy.

The slumbering sylph on the bed behind him gently passes gas. Aurelius feels a stab of love—real love—for the child, from her borborygmic bowels to her tender toes and tonsils.

But love is cliché. Lust is cliché. Hunger is cliché. Thirst is cliché. Breath is cliché. And there you have it, there you are: knocked back two squares behind where you were when you started.

He finds himself remembering Samuel Leonides, his old friend, his predecessor. Simone's fishbowl musings of last night trigger thoughts of the *roman a clef* written by one of Samuel's nymph mistresses:

He was fabulously ugly, all jowls and chins and wild gray eyebrows, with a nose like putty, striated with broken blood vessels and pocked with gaping pores. Yet to me he was like a god, his very ugliness made him a god, and I was made virginal by his grotesque attentions, at once pedestrian and perverse, as if my body were offered up to him on an altar. Rather, I offered myself as an altar, consecrated to and made holy by his profane liturgy.

In truth, Sam had confided, she hadn't been much of a sacrifice—far too passive and reticent, with little taste for adventure or invention. The assault on his vanity did not gall him, he acknowledged, for he was in her debt nonetheless: eager young girls, some of them sexually active since the age of nine (should the statistics be believed) flocked to Mars and pursued him relentlessly, impelled more by his ex-lover's words than by any of his own.

Later, as Kuurosin's blood burn ate away at his optic nerves on the way to devouring his brain, he joked that he wanted that passage to be engraved upon his tombstone. Instead, old Sam had to settle for lines from the elegy Aurelius had written, in lieu of eulogy, for his wake, the same lines Simone had mangled last night. Sam's squat, black granite obelisk stands kilometers into the wild desert, where he had wanted it. The inscription already grows faint with the constant abrasion of sand and dust storms. In a hundred years it will be gone, the stone scoured smooth, its hard angles rasped into roundness.

Aurelius reaches over and takes his computer from the night table. He tunes into the Hearst News Service.

There is a war raging in the heavens, it tells him, soldiers dying so far from home that it will be decades before the light of their splendent deaths speeds its way to Sol. Nothing new there, Aurelius thinks. Here's something, though: Narisian Karza is dead, blasted to plasma in some such corner of the sky. Quiet optimism from his executioners in the Ministry of Defense: perhaps the Pilots will fall more quickly without him. No one celebrates too loudly, Aurelius notes, for that would apportion to Karza too great a share of glory. What's more, it would belie the Commonwealth's official stance that the conflict—seven years of fighting now careening into an eighth—is a minor thing, distant and of little consequence, nothing to concern the average, system-bound citizen. True to that, the newsfeed wastes little time on him: a few minutes and it is on to other things, fashion news from Bangkok and Lunapolis, New York and Brancusi.

Aurelius marvels a bit at the thought of this Interstellar Age; he's old enough to remember life before it and now it defines existence. He thinks about the ships "moving" faster than radio waves, faster than light, a paradoxical return to the ancient days of couriers and dispatches, packets of news carried from one end of the galaxy to the other in the memory banks of a ship's computer rather than written out on parchment. It would all be wondrous and fantastic if only the upshot weren't so bloody.

This Interstellar Age, he realizes with the phantom-limb ache of half-remembered longing, I was present at its birth.

Simone stirs and moans but does not wake.

Through the window wall, roseate dawn streams over the red dunes. In the distance, the windmills spin.

Aurelius turns his attention back to the computer's cryostylitic display. He's been too hasty, he realizes—the financial report is given over in its entirety to the economic justifications for war.

"The crux of the matter is that the Pilots are ultimately cyborgs, *cybernetic* organisms," the Minister of Commerce says from his office in Prague. "Ignoring any of the other dozens of attendant legal and ethical issues, Bettina Brekkelheim was responsible only for the organic half of that equation. The cybernetic portion remains proprietar technology, licensed to Brekkelheim and licensed to the Consortium. That license did not include replication of the technology, even via biological means."

"Correct me if I'm wrong," the program's host replies, "but weren't those cyborganelles designed for self-replication? Don't the Pilots shed and replace them along with the cells of their bodies?"

"No, no, that's quite correct. But they were designed for replication *within* the organism. The Charybdis Corporation—which owns exclusive right to the technology—never intended for them to be passed on to another. In essence, Pilot spawn are—in part—stolen property."

Aurelius remembers when he first heard this argument, just after the Commonwealth launched the first offensive against the Pilots. It struck him as repugnant and transparent then and it seems no less so now. In his disgust, he had ordered his broker to sell off all his holdings in Charybdis and Stigol-Bergham—an impotent gesture, they hadn't amounted to much at the time. Months later, Charybdis went public with the quantum hyper-state multi-processor, better known now as the intuitive engine: the long sought Grail of astrogation that would render the Pilots—and their precious cyborganelles—officially obsolete. Now, with a completely non-invasive headset which resembled a skeletal, nine fingered hand or a cold water crab sculpted in stainless steel, any human with a rudimentary grasp of dissociated tier calculus (which ruled out Aurelius, who had bottomed out in basic trigonometry) could small-p pilot a starship without becoming a gibbering lunatic. Charybdis and Stigol-Bergham both saw their stock split twice in the first week. Had Aurelius held on to his shares, the value of his initial investment would have increased a thousand fold. Were he a better man, he could claim not to care.

He shuts off the computer, feeling the momentary chill as the cryostylitic display cube dissolves.

A leg drapes itself over his left shoulder; a naked heel comes to rest against the roll of fat at his gut. Strong musk as the other leg comes over his other shoulder and the ankles cross at his sternum. Aurelius places his computer on the floor and leans back into the warm v of her.

"Good morning." He rests his head against her stomach. He feels her sex, damp and downy, on the back of his neck.

"Had a wild dream," Simone says. "About you and my cat."

"Really? What happened?"

She laughs. "I'm not going to tell."

Aurelius caresses the arch of her right foot.

"I forgot," she says. "That woman called again last night. What was her name? Doctor, um, don't tell me—"

"Wu."

"That's right, Dr. Wu. She said it was important, something to do with your son."

"I see."

"Well I don't. I never knew you had a son. *Somebody* never told me." She gives his head a punitive squeeze in the soft vice of her inner thighs. "When do I get to meet him?"

"He's dead," Aurelius says. "He died in 2162." And you were all of seven years old, he thinks. And I was here, and old already.

"I'm sorry."

Aurelius kisses the side of her knee.

"You going to call her back?"

Aurelius hesitates. "Eventually."

"I know what we should do," she says. "Let's take the shuttle up to Deimos and see Diphalia Chrome and the Tiger Men."

Aurelius tilts his head back to peer up at her. "Diphalia Chrome and the *what*?"

Simone swings her legs over his head and tumbles down from the bed onto the floor beside him. She rests her chin on his thigh and stares up at him. "It's a show. A live show, like ballet. The tiger men are just furry humans with teeth, tails and claws: all after-market cosmetic grafts, like this." She taps a fang with her pinkie nail. "But Diphalia Chrome is the real thing, an altered Pilot. There are only, what, a couple hundred in the whole Commonwealth?"

Altered. Trapped in the Commonwealth at the start of the war, Chrome had agreed to the removal of her uterus and ovaries and the deadening of over a quarter of her brain. The other option was death. Aurelius feels a sudden flood of nausea.

"What do they do," he asks hopefully, "howl like Nakatani?"

She punches his thigh, just above the knee, just hard enough to hurt. "It's a live act," she repeats. "Dance and acrobatics, with null-gravity zones and everything. Chrome captures the tiger men and tames them with a riding crop and shock-prod."

Mother of Christ, Aurelius thinks.

"Then the tiger men get the upper hand and rape her."

He shakes his head as if she'd hit him in the forehead with a rubber mallet. "That's appalling."

"After last night? After last night you all of a sudden turn prude? After where you had *your* fingers?" She nips him in the spot she had earlier punched. "It's *art.* They tour the whole system—they're off to Luna in a week and after that it's New Kiryu. I saw it profiled on the cryostylitic. It's cutting edge." She blows a warm puff of air onto his penis. "It's *sexy.*"

Aurelius grunts.

"Okay, then, what do *you* want to do?"

Do? He does not want to *do* anything. After all these years, hasn't he done enough? But then he glances at his discarded computer, thinks about a campaign of genocide justified with the language of contract law and property rights and he knows that he's done less than nothing.

"I want..."And the weariness has him—without warning, it presses down upon him hard. "I want to crawl up inside you and sleep for a thousand years."

"We can do that right now." She slides up his body and kisses him with a stale and reeking mouth. "Come on, tiger man," she whispers. Every word is a hot and moist explosion in his ear canal. She fondles his stupid and amoral prick, sticky with the night's dry residue. "Once more unto the breach, hmm? Hmm? That's it."

Oblivion. Silky smooth and slick.

"That's it."

12

The Original I'll-Say-and-How Girl

I dream that I'm watching myself as a child, standing up to my ankles in clear ocean water—a tide pool, warm as blood. Under the wavelets, little fishes dart and cast faint shadows on the tan sand below. Chill winds blow my hair around my face and raise goose bumps on my arms while toy boats, shiny and infinitesimal, bob around my feet. With a child's simian dexterity, I squat down until my bottom, clad in a yellow swimsuit, skims the water. I look down and my hair becomes a dark curtain falling between my pudgy knees. With a cupped hand, I scoop up the boats and throw them into the air. I watch with childish solemnity as, with pops barely audible over the sounds of the surf, they flare into pale yellow brilliance. Then I laugh and clap my hands as they become an ash so fine that it is carried away on the weakest breeze.

I awaken to winter light, cold and bright, coming through the window. Phil's side of the bed is warm but empty. I smell coffee.

I sit up on the edge of the bed, lean over to the window and bend the flexible slats of the blind down with my finger. I peer out at a world that glitters in virginal white.

It's been some time since I've found myself part of a strange man's morning after. Lucky for me, lanky Phil is broad enough in his shoulders that one of his button-down shirts can serve as a gown of sorts. The floorboards are cold under my feet and chill air winds about my ankles but it's no more than I can bear.

I find Phil in the kitchen, sitting at the scarred round top of his small wooden table. He looks endearingly ridiculous in his white and blue awning striped pajamas and oxblood suede slippers. Reading glasses balance far down the bridge of his nose as he writes on a legal pad with a plastic ballpoint pen. Over his shoulder, on the counter next to a shiny chrome toaster, a thin stream of deep brown liquid fills the glass carafe of a white Mr. Coffee.

I slide into the chair opposite Phil. I reach across the table and grasp his hand lightly. He looks up from his notes and I am suddenly embarrassed.

Phil is too much of a gentleman to give any overt sign that he is not entirely pleased to see me. I can feel a reluctant tension in his fingers, however, and I can see a wan discomfort in his smile. I'm a kink in his routine and he does not know what to do with me. I withdraw my hand.

"I'm sorry, Jane," he says.

"No, you don't need to apologize. Just give a few minutes to get dressed..."

Phil shakes his head. "I haven't been with a woman since... I'm a *priest*, after all—a widowed priest. This isn't..."

"Last night was rather one-sided. I'm not even sure you could..."

"It wasn't as one-sided as you may think." He smiles at me now with the same gentle seductiveness he brought to bear the night before. Does he know just how effective it is? I wonder but not for long: *Of course he does.* I feel myself blush. "Look, Jane, I... like you. Even more than I expected to and I've been a... an admirer of your writing since... for a while, now. But this situation is—"

"Do you regret it?"

"What?"

I square myself in my chair and gaze directly into his eyes. "Do you regret fucking me?" Phil's right eyebrow jumps a millimeter or two at my coarseness. "Such as it was, I mean. Because I don't regret fucking you. I mean, if I regret anything, it's *not* fucking you."

Phil doesn't reply. Just as I'm about to press him on it, something begins to gasp and gurgle like a deep sea creature stranded on the shore. "Coffee's ready," he says and all but leaps from his chair. "I know your *characters* drink it—"

"Black, three sugars," I deadpan.

His back to me as he takes down a mismatched pair of mugs and fixes our coffee, Phil continues to evade me. "I'm ashamed to admit it, but I buy this stuff because of that ad campaign, you know, The Original I'll-Say-and-How Girl? Such a lovely thing, I swear she hasn't aged a day." He places my coffee mug, thin China with a delicate pattern of trellised roses, in front of me and sits down with his own, a massive-looking thing in cobalt blue. "It's good coffee, though."

"Mmm-hmm. Answer my question, please."

Silence. And then a heavy sigh. And then: "No." Another silence—I know there's more coming and so I let it come. "I *regret* that it happened as it did, like a cheap assignation. I *regret* that we didn't have *time*... to grow into it." He takes a drink from his mug. "But no," he says, "I don't regret what I did, what we did. I think I *want* to, but I don't."

Now that I have my answer—the answer I thought I wanted—I find I have nothing to say. It strikes me that the real question in situations like these is always "now what?" and that the more desolate answer, the answer that would have me setting off alone into the snow in search of my forsaken VW, is by far the less complicated. Instead, I find myself contemplating an entanglement at an age where entanglements are no easy thing—if ever they are at any age. As happy as I know I should be—as happy as, on some level, I am—I can't help but feel the same trepidation that radiates from the erudite and handsome stranger sitting across the table.

He's not finished, though. "I'm deathly afraid that this will send you running for the door," he says, "but the way I feel—the way you *make* me feel—it's as if I've known you longer than I've been alive. By God, I sound like a lunatic—or worse. I'm sorry, Jane."

That's coming it a bit high, I think. But I stop myself when I see how serious he is. What an idiot I have been—of course it was more than just a one-night stand for him; what I'd taken as reticence on his part was really just the fear that it was nothing more than that for me. And his words—silly as they *should* sound—strike against something deep in me. For a moment, I imagine our souls chasing each other from life to life, brother and sister in one, mother and son in another, lovers in this one. But that's just romantic schoolgirl rot and I haven't been a schoolgirl in a very long time.

"I'm not running," I say. I feel my face grow hot and I turn away. It's all become too serious too fast and so I joke, "Not yet, at least." Neither of us laughs.

In the growing silence, the green, white and red label of the coffee can, sitting out on the counter next to the sink, catches my eye. Those ubiquitous coffee commercials spring into my head and I'm grateful for the distraction: a pretty waitress with black hair, black eyes and olive skin puts plates of food—meat loaf and mashed potatoes, a pork chop and peas, pot roast and succotash—in front of two middle-aged men in business suits. As she walks away, one of the men ogles her well-toned legs and says, "That's some dish!" to which his comrade replies, "I'll say!" and then, from another table, a third man chimes in with, "And how!" Then the waitress is shown pouring coffee for yet another man while a sultry voice-over—maybe hers, maybe not—coos, "And what better to go with such a dish than a cup of The Roman Image, simply the finest coffee in the world?"

I catch myself humming the jingle. Phil smiles. Emboldened, I sing, "For Old World flavor in your New World home/ Choose the coffee made in the image of Rome." I giggle. "Now that I think about it, you're right. The setting changes: restaurant, diner, railroad dining car, airplane—"

"Hunting lodge."

I nod. "Uh-huh. Boy, do I remember that one: the men wore dungarees and flannel and she wore a tartan mini-skirt. And every new commercial has a new group of leering squares. But the girl? Always the same picture of elfin Mediterranean pulchritude. It's got to be what? Ten, fifteen years?"

"More like twenty."

"Not a single wrinkle." I finish my coffee. "Funny how I never noticed till now."

"Hmm," Phil says. I can tell by the crease between his eyebrows that he is, to some degree, really chewing on this and not just humoring me. At least, that's what I hope it means.

"And now that I *do* think about it, why is it The *Original* I'll-Say-and-How Girl?" I continue. "There's only ever been one of her."

"If it were one of your stories, she'd be a three-dimensional projection from some ancient machine, a satellite, left by benevolent aliens," he jokes. "Or maybe the Holy Spirit herself, come to save us all."

"Well, it *is* good coffee."

Phil chuckles (and it's a deep, resonant chuckle—I imagine how it must sound rolling from the pulpit) and says, "I'm really sorry we didn't spend more time last night discussing the theological content of your stories—Mr. Mendel's, too. Although the conversation we did have was stimulating in its own right. More?"

It's a moment before I realize he is referring to my emptied coffee mug. "Please."

While he fills our mugs a second time, I say to his back, "I was thinking the same thing. But, uh, you're not just saying that, about Aaron? Because you really don't have to—he knows he's a pain in the ass."

Again, Phil chuckles. "Knows? I get the impression he strives for it. No, no, I mean it. He's angry, that comes through in his work, and I'd have been disappointed if he were any different in person. You know, I use one of his stories when I teach."

"Which one?"

"'The Rape of the Light.'"

I laugh. "No, really," I say. "Which one?"

"I'm not joking. What, you think it should offend me? I began my training as a Jesuit, little offends *them*." He spoons sugar into my mug and stirs. "The story asks some interesting questions about love and ownership: how much does a creation belong to its creator? Who is to say what form love should take if it is to be called love at all? Can the divine be obscene—predatory, cruel—and still divine? What do the words even mean? Heady stuff. Your friend is hardly the first to liken God to a rapist, you know—John Donne did as much and he's among the most rapturously Christian of poets."

"Hmm."

"The story never pretends to have the answers—not that I can say the same for its author." Phil gives me my coffee and sits down.

"Besides, I've heard worse. When I was in seminary, one of the Jesuits used to say that God could best be understood as someone who has taken up—methodically, without reservation and most likely out of boredom—the study of pain. He inflicts in the Old Testament and suffers in the New—up until the Revelation of St. John the Divine, of course, which is a crescendo of sadistic fury."

"Wow," is all I can think to say. Then, realizing I've let my half of the conversation descend into the monosyllabic, I add: "A wrath by any other name..."

Phil nods. "Exactly. He used to say the moral of Job could be best summed up as 'I am the Lord your God and I will kick your ass till you start kissing Mine—and even then you better look out.'" He laughs. "In a way, I admire his compassion—Mr. Mendel, I mean. Because that's really what it is. When Meredith was sick, I was filled with much the same rage: what good is a God who watches the sparrow's fall if He insists on doing nothing about it? But it's one thing to feel that way about your own pain, another to extend it to the pain all around you. I imagine it takes its toll."

"I'm, uh, I'm stunned... Phil. I don't know if anyone's ever seen Aaron so *clearly.* I know I never have and he's my best friend."

"Maybe that explains it. You love him. Love can be myopic—sometimes, it needs to be."

That one I won't touch. I take a sip of my coffee. "Jesuit, huh?" I ask. "What happened?"

"My family was never very religious—I *suspect* my father was agnostic at the least and I *know* my mother was apathetic: Christmas and Easter, *sometimes.* Funerals. I was young, just out of college, hungry for meaning."

"Aren't we all?"

"You'd be surprised. I left seminary after the first year. Catholicism wasn't my calling. I met Meredith and I realized I was never big on... that part of the paradigm."

I smile a secret smile and suppress the urge to say, "And how!"

"After a few years teaching high school history, I went over to the Episcopalians."

"Perfect fit?"

"*Better.*" He smiles. "There is no perfection this side of eternity."

Neither of us speaks for a bit. Then, cautiously, I ask, "How *did* you resolve it, that anger?" I steel myself and meet his gaze. "About your wife?"

I see a dark intensity quickly cross his face, replaced by a willful calm. "I don't know that I ever did," he says. "Faith isn't about *resolution*, ultimately."

"What is it about?"

He shrugs again. "Faith."

How like a priest, to let the word hang there as if it means something. I think about it, about faith, about the miracles given the world over to men and women of stark and contradictory *faith*. Wellsprings of strength in the face of direst adversity—is there a part of us, I wonder, some hard little knot of limitless power, that will only respond if it is flattered and lied to? Is that what we mean when we speak the nameless names of God?

Anyway, I have more immediate concerns. I pause for a moment to ratchet up my nerve and then say, "You know, just because we started the way we did, that doesn't mean we can't still... grow into something. I don't *have* to fly back west right away. I could stay for a couple of weeks. It doesn't have to be a scandal, the hotels here are inexpensive…"

"I wish it were that simple." He gestures to his legal pad. "I have to go to London. I'm leaving Monday."

"For how long?"

"Three months? Not much longer—I plan to be back before the birth of my grandchild, of course. I'm researching a book on Thomas Walker."

"Really?" I find the thought so fascinating that I forget to be disappointed. Walker's arcade amusement cult, centered on bizarre sensory deprivation rituals, was one of the stranger things to happen during the sixties—and that is saying a great deal. Like so much of that decade, it ended very badly. Aaron and I wrote an episode of *Forbidden Planets* transparently based on it.

I'm toying with the reckless and risky idea of asking if I can tag along, perhaps even assist him with his research, when it hits me: *Forbidden Planets*, Walker's pinball cult, the Tucker Talisman, last night's abortive sex and The Original I'll-Say-and-How Girl—all of it laminates together into a crystalline block lighter and clearer than the air itself. I swear I could see it—could see it for what it *is*—if I only knew how to look.

The winter draft that skims along the floor is gone. My bare feet and ankles are awash in warm water.

A tide pool, warm as blood—

"—the mystery religions of the Roman Empire," Phil is saying. "Jane, what's wrong?"

Little fishes dart. Little fishes—

"Jane? *Jane?*"

The waters recede. The draft returns. I shiver in the sudden chill.

"Jane, what is it?"

I shake my head in confusion. "I can't explain—I can't explain it to *myself*." I won't tell him about the hallucination but I have to tell him something, even if it sounds crazy. "Did you... did you ever get the feeling that the world we live in is, I don't know, *counterfeit*, somehow?"

"I'm not sure what you mean. The world's fallen state is a key tenet of—"

"No, no, not that, not like that." I sigh in frustration. "Not degraded, not corrupted. *False*."

Phil ponders for a moment, then shakes his head. "Sorry. Does this have something to do with what happened... last night? During the discussion, in the bedroom..."

I realize that I've been dreading this topic, that I was grateful for Phil's discomfort earlier because it deflected me from my own. There's no avoiding it now. "I don't know, I think so. I can't explain it, *any* of it," I say with an edge of frustration I immediately regret. I grasp his hand in apology. "Sometimes I think I'm losing my mind."

"Welcome to the 1970s." He squeezes my hand. "That just makes you normal."

"Maybe. But the rest of it..."

Phil surprises me, then, by leaning across the table and kissing me softly on the lips. "We have a couple of days, right? Until we fly off in separate directions. Let's spend them together. We can put aside this thing until you want to talk about it."

"And if I *don't* want to talk about it?"

"Then we'll talk about other things." He kisses me again, more firmly his time. "Or we won't talk at all."

13

Terrorville

Deimos is tiny, averaging only twelve kilometers in diameter, too small even to pull its irregular mass into a sphere. Deimos City, a belt of hotels, restaurants and casinos a three quarters of a kilometer wide, girds the little Martian moon under a standard diamond pressure shield and sits equidistant from the small moon-to-surface shuttle-port at one end of the oblong, potato-shaped rock and the larger interplanetary spaceport at the other. The town's entertainments tend toward the violent and the bloody—it's the only place within the Commonwealth where spin boxing is still legal. Operating outside of the law, places deep in the sub-surface tunnels cater to darker whims and desires. It is perhaps for this reason rather than for any mythological associations that Deimos City is also known as Terrorville.

"Stop sulking," Simone sneers at Aurelius.

They walk down Deimos City's central boulevard, among groups of thrill-seeking tourists, past countless shops and holographic billboards advertising anti-viral cigarettes, contraceptive chewing gum and noodles flavored with krill and blue-green algae. Every thirty seconds or so, black and yellow rail buggies whoosh past them in either direction. Simone eats pale blue cotton candy from a stick, tearing off wispy clots with her lips, teeth and tongue.

"I'm not sulking," Aurelius says. "I'm sick."

"It was just a *show*, Aurelius. Scripted, rehearsed. The entire time, you're sitting next to me, flinching and moaning like an old woman."

Aurelius does not trust himself to respond.

"For God's sake!" Simone continues. "It was no worse than the ancient cinema you screen in your classroom."

In his classroom... in a classroom debate, maybe, he would acknowledge she has a point. But he knows better—and so does she. If she really wanted to exploit his apparent hypocrisy, she would need access to ammunition he will not give her. For example, there was the night he had spent in the company of Justine and Juliette, Riyadh cabaret girls looking to make some extra money, back in 2167. They said they were identical twins but he later discovered they were monozygotic clones with birthdays three weeks apart, two of three dozen born in the New Kiryu vats and scattered throughout the Commonwealth. The lab that produced them—for unspecified purposes—was shut down in a government raid and the girls were left to fend for themselves; the luckiest of their number became the consort of an asteroid ore-mining tycoon. Aurelius remembers the only way he could keep them straight: Justine had a mole on the tip of her nose, Juliette did not. That was when they were dressed—undressed, there were other ways. At forty-five hundred solaria an hour, they were a bargain. As tawdry and sordid (and, he silently admits, *cherished*) as that decade-old memory was, it paled to nothing in comparison to what Simone had just subjected him to. They had sat close enough to the stage to smell the burning hair and ozone every time Chrome touched the tip of her shock-prod to one of those ridiculous cat people. Close enough, too, to smell the blood as the tiger men slashed Chrome with their claws and teeth. (He knows all about the recuperative power of Pilots: in less than a day, Diphalia Chrome's skin will heal without bruise or blemish. Somehow, that knowledge only makes it worse.) And while there was no denying the gymnastic grace of their movements, there was also no denying the howls and shrieks of pain, however exaggerated.

Anyway, he does not care to argue the point, not while he still struggles against a rising gorge. Besides, he knows his silence will only annoy her and he wants very much to annoy her right now.

Apparently, the silence works too well. Simone looks up at him with a wicked smirk, "If you want so badly to be horrified, I know how to get us into a vat baby snuff show down in the red market."

For the first time in decades, Aurelius has to fight the very real urge to strike a woman. Vat baby is a deliberate misnomer. They are actually accelerated growth clones decanted after three months, physically indistinguishable from adolescents. Developmentally, cognitively, they are newborns. Snuff show, however, is entirely accurate—screaming in innocent incomprehension, the clones are tortured and slaughtered for the titillation of a live audience. An alarming number of wealthy and jaded students attend the shows as a dare, at the risk of expulsion and criminal prosecution. Campus rumor has it that some students barter their own cells in exchange for reduced admission. Aurelius tries to imagine the serpent's nest of motives driving such transactions but the depressing squalor of the exercise quickly leaves him exhausted. There are some impulses he'd rather let remain beyond the scope of his empathy.

Simone's smirk becomes a grin. "I went to one last semester."

Aurelius grabs Simone's wrist and jerks her to a halt. Her cotton candy flies from her startled grasp and lands on the shiny ceramic pavement of the boulevard. He yanks her around like a rag doll and glares down into her face.

"Ow! Aurelius, people are watching."

She's right. Several have stopped to see the fat man manhandle the waif. No one seems ready to intervene just yet.

"You had better be joking."

Simone meets his gaze for long moments, her lips pursed in defiance. Finally, she says, "Just making a point." She looks down at her shoes. "Besides, where would I get *that* kind of money?"

Aurelius holds on for a moment longer and then lets her go. "My candy," Simone laments, like a child, as she massages her wrist. "I didn't know you had it in you, Professor." She shakes the blood-flow back into her fingers and looks at him, sidelong and sly. "So that's what it takes to really get you humming, huh? I'll have to remember that during a more... intimate moment."

Aurelius is too disgusted to play along with her innuendo. "Simone, you really—"

He is interrupted by a flash over the horizon that outshines the sun. It comes to them in shafts of light through the side alleys. Simone clutches Aurelius as the ground shakes.

Every billboard along the boulevard flickers into white noise before abruptly coming back with live newsfeed: a glowing crater of molten rock surrounded by dull gray regolith scorched black. Surrounding the crater is a ring of wreckage half a kilometer wide, twisted bits of broken spacecraft interspersed with bodies, some charred, others showing the messy effects of explosive decompression.

"...ordered to avoid the interplanetary spaceport and its surrounding areas," the voice of the newsfeed's reporter says as remote cameras survey the destruction from every imaginable angle. There *is* no spaceport, only a deep pit gouged out of the moon. The exposed sub-surface levels glow red and white and melt away like foil under a plasma torch. "There are no plans to evacuate Deimos City at present, although the authorities are monitoring the situation. Traffic to and from the Martian surface via the shuttle-port is currently unaffected. Travelers should expect delays, however."

Aurelius feels a twinge of selfish relief—the thought of being stranded here for the next few days fills him with claustrophobic revulsion. Viewing the devastation in the holocube, he is immediately ashamed.

"While little definite is known about the explosion, authorities believe it to have been caused by a defect in the fusion reactor on one of the larger interplanetary ships. No firm data is available at this time, but the death toll is estimated to be in the thousands. This includes those who were in the sub-surface complex of maintenance facilities as well as those who were aboard the several interplanetary transports awaiting lift-off."

A silent explosion erupts among the rubble—echoed in every cube up and down the boulevard, it bathes the storefronts and spectators in a harsh blue-white flash. Then the camera melts with a head-piercing squeal. The billboards go dead for an instant before another remote takes over from a much higher altitude.

"Please pardon our technical difficulties," the reporter says. "We will be moving a new camera into the area as soon as one becomes—excuse me, I've just been informed that, among the confirmed dead, is the noted bio-industrialist and convicted criminal Bettina Brekkelheim."

Aurelius feels his chest constrict in sudden panic. His heart races and he struggles to breathe. In spite of everything, he is astonished—he's lived for eight decades, he's experienced his share of loss, felt many kinds of sorrow, and yet he has never known grief to feel so much like fear.

A smaller image appears in the lower right quadrant of the billboard: Bettina seated at a pearl gray plastiform table. She leans forward, focused on something with preternatural avidity, and yet she seems somehow placid, disinterested. She brushes a lock of hair behind her ear. Her lips curl in a private smile.

"According to Transit Control, Dr. Brekkelheim, shown here at her trial in New Kiryu, Vulcan, almost nine years ago, was aboard a penal transport transferring her from the secure hospital facilities on Tethys, where she'd been undergoing experimental personality reconstruction for the past eighteen months, to the Correctional Sciences Complex in Stockholm. The craft had just begun a scheduled six hours of maintenance and refueling when this disaster occurred. More details as they come to light. For now, Transit Control has declared a state of emergency. All persons are ordered to avoid the interplanetary spaceport and its surrounding areas."

Simone trembles against his side and clutches his hand. He wraps his fingers around hers and feels the dampness of her palm. In the holocube, a chain of new explosions rings the perimeter of the blast crater and sends chunks of debris hurtling into the vacuum. A wave of tremors lags a fraction of a second behind each blast. The elasticrete braces supporting the diamond shield creak and shudder. Simone squeezes his hand. He tears his eyes from the cube and looks down to see her breathing shallowly through parted lips. Her teeth gleam wetly in the hellfire light. At first, he is afraid for her. But then he sees that the corners of her mouth are twisted upward in exhilaration. To her, this is just another show.

Aurelius takes his hand away. After a couple of false starts, he finds his voice, thick and ragged in his own ears: "Let's get the hell out of here."

To her credit, Simone does not argue.

14

The Alchemy of Desperation

Crysanthia Vog looks down at the metal-sheathed figure curled up, like a smoky silver chrysalis, at her feet. She looks from the face of her daughter to the face of her son and sees her own questions reflected back at her. The three of them stand on the shore of Klytemnestra's sole, shallow ocean. A hundred meters out, her children's starships bob up and down on the stinking waves like shiny toys. Desultory breakers wash over the metallic form lying in the sand and bathe their feet and ankles in a brownish green froth.

Crysanthia, hugely pregnant and mindful of her belly, crouches next to the figure and runs her hands over the smooth and featureless surface. Its knees are drawn up and fused to its ribcage; its hands are clasped in front of its face as if in prayer.

She looks up. The moon's rotation faces them away from Agamemnon—the sky is full of over-bright stars. Another of Agamemnon's moons, dim and tiny Iphigenia, is just barely visible in the brilliance-spattered darkness.

"Narisian?" Crysanthia asks though she already knows the answer.

"Yes," replies Dahlia Vog, the fingers of her right hand spread over her own double pregnancy.

"How?"

Neither of them answers her, though she hadn't expected them to.

"Alive?"

Corvus Karza shakes his head. "No brain activity. The crèche may be able to reconstruct him. If it hasn't been too long."

The three Pilots lift their stiff and heavy burden. Their serpentine fingers stretch and struggle to find purchase on its cool, slick surface. Slowly, they carry Narisian out of the sea.

A zip bubble—a zero-point proximity mine, launched from a Solar Commonwealth heavy cruiser—had corkscrewed its way through the many layers of shielding and penetrated the dark matter reactor of Narisian Karza's starship. From the vantage point of the cruiser, the ship's destruction was instantaneous: a bright explosion, infinitesimal bits spread over a million cubic kilometers of interstellar space. As for Karza himself, no trace could be found. So the human crew of the SCNV *Iconoclast* concluded he'd been vaporized, reduced to a cloud of organic gas so attenuated as to be undetectable.

They were wrong. The ship, knowing it was doomed, recapitulated its own flight path and ejected Narisian into so-called normal space three light years away, somewhere in the vicinity of Tau Ceti. The *Iconoclast's* crew did not know that Pilot vessels could do that—the capability, which verges very near the impossible realm of time travel, is so far beyond anything Stigol-Bergham could achieve that no one aboard could have harbored the barest of suspicions. But the Pilots had discarded their Stigol-Bergham starships after the first year of the war.

The Pilots knew all about sub-quantum trans-temporal retrogression, however, and they also knew they had only the narrowest of windows in which to find Narisian before the ravages of space would finish what the *Iconoclast's* zip bubble had started. Within a few hours of drifting, naked to the hard vacuum of space, his organs would fail, one by one, until he was clinically dead. Within a day, cosmic radiation would fry his corpse past the point where it could be reconstructed and revived. But Narisian Karza had been lost for weeks.

At some point—probably during the first hour after ejection—Narisian's cyborganelles had liquefied and migrated from his cells. They erupted onto the surface of his skin and formed a silica-duraladium shell a few microns thick that shielded him from the unforgiving void until his own children—intent upon their fool's errand no matter the risks (and they were legion) or the harsh pleadings of their mother (and they were vicious)—could find him.

And that was something no one could explain; it was certainly not a feature built into the cyborganelles themselves. And for all their frantic theorizing, no one could begin to imagine the external force that could rip every cybernetic trace from a Pilot's body with such brutal precision. Perhaps no one really wanted to.

So now he is home: Iota Horologii.

Wresting the system from the poorly defended planetary engineers terraforming Klytemnestra and operating the comet distillery on Orestes was the first and last easy victory the Pilots would win.

At the time, the Pilots were few, survivors fleeing the Commonwealth's ruthlessly efficient series of surprise attacks. The Commonwealth had decided not to press its advantage. This was understandable: in November of 2169, the Commonwealth had precisely two cruisers equipped with its new astrogation devices, the so-called intuitive engine—and a pyrrhic Pilot counteroffensive soon reduced that number to one.

The other four vessels in the fleet, still utterly dependant upon the Pilots themselves, were less than useless: three of those Pilots were slain in their symbiosis chamber before they knew what was happening, leaving their ships—each worth several trillion solaria and carrying crews numbering in the hundreds—stranded deep in interstellar space. Worse still for the Commonwealth, the fourth Pilot, a yearling named Zorenia Ix, managed to destroy herself, the heavy cruiser *Indomitable* and most of Heaven 33. Thus a strategic retrenchment to build up the battle fleet seemed like sound policy. But had the Commonwealth fully appreciated what the Pilots were capable of setting into motion—the nano-assemblers which transmuted the turbulent clouds of Agamemnon's upper atmosphere into a monstrous factory complex of shipyards and space docks which in turn now transform the industrial soup of gases into starships—it probably would have acted more boldly. It certainly would have had it anticipated the crèche.

Crysanthia stands in a vast subterranean gallery, terraced in a spiral seventy meters above and below her and curving hundreds of meters away from her on either side. The chamber is one of thousands, networked together through hair-fine rhizomes that infiltrate nearly every centimeter of Klytemnestra's lithosphere. The chambers—illuminated by yellow-green bioluminescence, gurgling and pulsing with sap and blood, smelling strongly of sweat and fungus, buttressed within by pillars of bone—are all parts of one tremendous organism, the crèche. It feeds on the nitrogen-rich soil of Klytemnestra with thick and furry roots below ground and on the rays of Iota Horologii itself with thick and fleshy leaves above.

Each chamber supports thousands of amniotic sacs—they protrude from the walls like translucent, pinkish gold fruit two meters long and a meter around. Each sac has its own circulatory system, its own rudimentary brain. At any given moment, ninety-three percent of them nurture an embryonic Pilot who will, after months spent within a thing something like a chambered nautilus and hothouse orchid and not remotely human, emerge all but fully grown. Crysanthia fears a subtle caste system will one day arise, setting the crèche-born against those who, like Corvus and Dahlia, were carried by women and born as infants. So far, it hasn't happened—the Pilots have been far too preoccupied with survival to indulge in such vain luxury. But Crysanthia knows her people well enough; if they survive this war...

If they survive. The thought stops her cold.

Most of the remaining seven percent of amniotic sacs are reserved for the critically wounded. Inside, they regenerate damaged organs and lost limbs—Crysanthia herself had spent a few days in one after her arm had been blasted off at the shoulder while she fought to repel a particularly nasty assault on Oerestes a little less than two years ago; she sometimes forgets which arm it was. (It was her left). The last few sacs—less than one percent—are specially trained and cultured for cases like Narisian, Pilots who are clinically dead but can be reconstructed. The crèche devours the subject, digests it and analyzes it down to the last proteins and peptides, and then rebuilds it, cell by cell, within an empty womb.

Even now, it all makes Crysanthia vaguely ill, at once repulsed and enraptured. It's as though she walks through her own body, all its anabolic and catabolic secrets turned inside out and magnified, transformed into a cathedral.

Crysanthia thinks of it as the alchemy of desperation: this relentless flesh and bone engine transforming the raw stuff of Klytemnestra into living, thinking Pilots. But then she wonders: to what purpose, to what fate? If this war continues as it has, most of them will die within five years. If this war ends as she fears it must, all of them—and many, many more—will die within the decade.

Inside of her belly, she feels one of the twins kick. Moments later, the other one retaliates.

Through the chitinous walls of one of the crèche's amniotic sacs, she can just barely see Narisian gather himself together—his skeleton, his circulatory system and most of his major organs slowly form within the gelatinous waters, fed by a thick umbilicus. She reaches out and touches the sac, feels it twitch under the pressure of her finger.

The crèche was Bettina's conception, Crysanthia knows, but its subtleties and scale were far beyond her abilities to bring to fruition. A group of several dozen Pilots spent the better part of four years designing it. Their success was a single hairy seed roughly the size and shape of a coffin. Once the seed was planted, however, it was a mere month before the first of the galleries had matured, its multitude of wombs already heavy with embryos the crèche itself had generated.

Other Pilots come and go, females and males alike dressed as Crysanthia is dressed, in shifts of soft paper. They tend to the new generation like bees in a hive tending to their larvae and leave Crysanthia alone. She listens to the *shush-shush* of the hive's slow breath, feels its shifting currents on the exposed skin of her arms and legs.

"Bettina is dead."

Crysanthia does not take her eyes away from Narisian.

"It's on the interstellar net," Dahlia says. "They got to her just about the same time that they got to him—I can only imagine the celebrations on Earth." Dahlia sighs. "I like it down here. So warm and moist. And the breezes—Bettina would have been pleased."

Crysanthia turns her head toward her daughter and gives her a long, searching look. Dahlia pretends not to notice, staring instead into the depths of the gallery, at the ranks of wombs that fade into the misty distance.

Crysanthia looks back to Narisian. She is acutely aware of the lives which surround her, the lives forming inside her. She touches her hand to her belly. These children do not belong to him. Their father is a Pilot named Devaliad Mir. Crysanthia knows next to nothing about him. Like most couplings, theirs was decided by eugenic lottery. She glances at the swelling under Dahlia's paper dress. She knows nothing at all of their father, not even a name—Dahlia has never volunteered the information, Crysanthia has never asked.

"How is he?" Dahlia asks.

"He should be ready to come out in just a few more days," Crysanthia says. "That's what the crèche technicians tell me."

Dahlia manages a wan smile for her mother. "Come on," she says. "You need to eat, to sleep. It's been a long night."

"Yes," Crysanthia says absently. She follows Dahlia to a damp passageway, one of many, that spirals along the chamber's exterior surface to terminate in an aperture above ground. She pauses, hand braced on the lip of the opening, to look over at Narisian one last time.

"Mother?" Dahlia's voice, echoing from within the passage.

Crysanthia follows her daughter through the dark and winding tunnel, up into the daylight.

Part Three
There Is No Sky but Darkness

No one had to show me how to find you.
My feet found this road like a newborn's
Gulping lungs find the sting of the rarefied air
After nine months of a mother's ropy brine.
Out here, where even the ashen stars are cold
And, in the pitch of noon, there is no sky but darkness,
I have taught myself to call you home.

--*Autodidact* by Aurelius Mann

15

The Promethean Bounds

The Promethean Bounds, a dynamic sculpture by Esme Arroyo, is a cube of solid black granite, three meters on a side, and suspended three meters above its twin. In the open space between, seven hollow spheres of water hover in a slow pattern that will not repeat itself for two thousand years—or so it is said. The shells of water contain an atmosphere of pure oxygen and, at the core of that, a controlled hydrogen flame of bright yellow-white. The same gravity manipulators that hold the massive block of granite hovering in the nearby sky tame the flames and waters; a microscopic mesh of trimaridium capillaries replenishes the gases, molecule by invisible molecule. All of the engineering is hidden beneath the massive sandstone pediment. It is a marvel in an age of marvels and, as such, it is rather mundane.

A prodigal beauty, it drinks energy—a full sixth of the Utopia Planitia wind farm's annual output goes solely to keeping the spheres in their courses, the stone firmament from falling. At night, the flames burn clean and brilliant. In the mid-day sun, the pale fire is like a memory, the faded image of a lost lover's face.

Aurelius Mann sits in the courtyard of Café Empyrean, at the base of the sculpture, and eats a late lunch of feta cheese, dried tomatoes, garlic and basil on crusty bread with a half carafe of a 2173

Amarone. He scans an obscene poem written in heroic couplets, the work of a seminar student he suspects is looking to replace Simone. Georgina Olivet—he recalls seeing her at a departmental garden party a little over a month ago. ("Please," she had said as she casually placed her hand on his chest, "call me Gigi. This is a social *affair*.") Her fine-grained skin was like deep brown satin, her full lips and cosmetically grafted talons were painted deep scarlet. She wore a thin layer of body paint in lieu of clothing—it was the fashion among some. Her teeth chattered as she spoke with him in the chill desert night lit by paper lanterns. He sighs—he can remember the nuances of her scent (dried sweat and patchouli) and the way her painted limbs shone in the night but nothing of their talk.

He shuts down his computer and lays it next to his heavy stoneware plate. He gazes at the flames trapped in water, at the handsome university crowd, at the red horizon and deep blue sky. Wind-riders define widening gyres above the distant mountains. The sun sparks on their silver body suits and gossamer wings of graphite ribbed spider silk. Aurelius chews thoughtfully and drinks his wine.

A lizard scurries across the terra cotta tiles of his table top.

What I should do, he thinks, is lay off the wine and have them bring me something hard, something real—Kentucky bourbon or a good stiff rye. Few shots of that and I'll stand on the table and bellow "I am Lazarus, come from the dead, come back to tell you all, I shall tell you all!" Isn't that what a poet is supposed to do, supposed to be? Drunk, disorderly, dissolute and dissipated. Dionysian—maybe I should stick with wine at that. In this age... in this age it would barely be a joke.

Images surface in his mind, like bloated corpses in still water. Postcards from Deimos, four months ago: red blood welling up from deep gashes in blue skin, a radioactive pit glowing like hell itself, spit shining on the white teeth of his smiling lover—no wine, no roses, maybe, but blood and the occasional burnt offering. Spectacle, then; perhaps what the gods crave most, even over worship. So tell me, Bettina, what savage divinity did you propitiate with your consummation?

He shuts his mind to the masochism of memory and returns instead to the sun-bright here and now.

A woman and two young children join the man sitting at the table on the far side of the sculpture. Their voices carry in the desert air. In his unquiet state, Aurelius finds himself eavesdropping.

"We saw a horse with wings! It was white as snow!" the little girl says, causing Aurelius to recall that the university currently hosts a two-week exhibit featuring creatures crafted to resemble beasts from ancient mythology.

"Pegasus," the boy, two or three years older, clarifies. "Too bad it can't fly."

"It can too!" the girl protests. "It can fly in the gravity cage. We *saw* it."

"That's not really flying—*you* could fly in the gravity cage. We saw the sphinx. It asked me a riddle and I got it right."

"I knew the answer, too," the girl says. "But it didn't ask me."

Bettina's work, Aurelius suspects. Years after her incarceration, months after her death, her corporation continues, her techniques persist—though it is possible the menagerie could be from a rival firm, a *lesser* firm.

"We saw a Chinese dragon," the girl says, "and a man with a dog's head!"

"Anubis," the boy says with weary contempt for his sister's ignorance.

"You should have seen the centaur, honey," the woman says. "He looked exactly like the boy you used to date when we were in college, the blond."

Definitely Bettina, Aurelius decides. No one else has the skill to construct a convincing humanoid without the use of outlawed human DNA. Then he remembers that Valence Cyberdynamics is sponsoring the exhibit. All the creatures are robots. Aurelius is stung by a sharp disappointment, an echo of what he'd felt the day she died.

The man, silent until now, responds with a sigh, "I doubt the resemblance was *exact*."

The woman laughs. "Oh God, I hope not! You'd be ruined for life."

They continue in that vein, the zoo's creatures forgotten, and Aurelius loses what little interest he had in their conversation. Before long, the temporarily neglected children begin to bicker—Aurelius hears the sounds of a scuffle, then the soft whimpers of the girl and sulky protests of the boy under the sharp rebukes of the parents. As he listens to the children's pointless, primate squabbling, Aurelius tries to forget who he is and imagine himself to be one of them: a dirty little animal, unconscious of self, beautiful and alive. Then he sees the wrinkled backs of his hands. He reaches for his computer and scrolls through Gigi Olivet's poem once more.

And now he remembers—that night in the garden, she'd held forth at length on comparative astrology, the singular challenges posed by the Martian zodiac. It seemed she fancied herself something of a witch. All the while, he feigned interest as he contemplated the puckering of her nipples in the cool evening air.

"Pardon me, Professor Mann, but may I join you?"

He turns his head and shields his eyes from the glare of the sun. Slowly, she comes into focus: dark almond-shaped eyes over broad cheekbones, a helmet of glossy silver hair shot through with strands of dark gray and black.

"Miriam Wu," she says. "If you're not too busy."

"Not at all." He slips his computer into his shirt pocket. "Shall I ask them to bring you something, a glass?"

"Thank you but no." She seats herself across from him. "I knew your son."

After a moment, Aurelius responds, "I only wish I could say the same."

"Perhaps 'knew' is too strong a word," Wu says. Her manner is simple and genuine. He likes it. He trusts it. She wears the plain, gray, androgynous suit of a cleric. A pin of burnished silver, a nude woman crucified with a viper coiled around her waist, rides the slope of her left breast. She wears a plain gold band around her left ring finger. Viralist sectarian, Aurelius thinks, Sapphic Church of Rome. Her eyes focus on him with a placid single-mindedness. "We were colleagues of a kind."

"Yes," Aurelius says. "I know who you are." *And I've been ducking you for months.* "You were there when my son immolated himself."

Wu nods. "A very apt choice of words."

"I'm familiar with my son's theories and beliefs." He glances to the sculpture and then to the sun. "If nothing else."

"The two of you were not close." Neither statement nor question—an invitation, perhaps.

Aurelius leans back. "*Ex nihil salvatio?* Are you to be my confessor?"

Wu gazes at him, momentarily puzzled, then touches the pin at her breast and smiles. "I'm merely a novitiate, hardly qualified. I converted two years ago."

Aurelius nods. "Converted from what?"

"Zen Materialism—although I suppose I haven't exactly given that up. The two coexist within me."

"Must be one hell of a marriage."

"It endures." She leans forward, gazes at him with searching kindness. "If you want to talk, I will listen."

"Nothing much to talk about. I was little more than a gene donor."

"You never met him?"

"No, no, I met him. On several occasions. At least a dozen—not bad for three decades, huh? When he was thirteen or fourteen, he accompanied me on a university lecture tour through the Inner Worlds—his mother's idea. And I followed his career, what I could decipher." Aurelius toys with his artfully tarnished flatware. "He'd be almost fifty if he were alive today."

"But still—"

"Janos Brekkelheim has been dead for years," Aurelius says. He feels himself on the verge of something, a realization, but it goes. "This would be going somewhere?"

Wu's tone and expression become enigmatic. "In a manner of speaking."

16

Jasmine Tea

Jasmine tea—I find I'm drinking a lot of it these days. I started several months ago, not long after Phil left for London and I came back here, to the San Francisco Bay and my drafty little shack of a farmhouse. I'm on my third cup this April morning as I walk out of my kitchen and into my backyard, my bare feet chilled by the cold flagstones just as the last wisps of fog burn away in the sunlight. I hold the delicate china in one hand and a letter from Phil, twelve sheets of foolscap covered in his barely decipherable longhand and folded into its torn manila envelope, in the other.

The tea is one of many things I found strewn along the strand when the waves of disorientation that overtook me last November finally receded, leaving behind bits and pieces of a life I never lived. I've largely given up on trying to make sense of them. I sit down at my wrought iron table, still damp with dew, and feel an increasingly familiar *déjà vu*: another me, improbably tall and lithe as a reed, scarcely human and somewhere very far away, drinking jasmine tea with an unquiet mind. And that's it. If there's more—and there's always more—I can't get at it, not now. I'm glad for that. I brush away the dew and lay Phil's letter down in front of me.

Dale, my midnight black cat, sits atop the garden wall and looks at me impassively. I find my eyes drawn not to her golden gaze but to the explosion of white fur in the middle of her chest, like a supernova in the void. Just then, Flash, her misnamed marmalade counterpart, slow, corpulent and needy, jumps up onto my lap and butts his head against my chin. With one hand, I stroke his purring flank while I sip my tea. Then I pick up Phil's letter—the latest of many, just arrived this morning—and begin to read:

"I realized only a moment ago that I've started every letter and postcard by telling you that I miss you. This one shall be no different so please pardon the repetition. I *do* miss you, my thoughts turn to you whenever I am confronted with something new or exciting or whenever I find myself faced with long stretches of time in which I've nothing to do, which pretty much means I think of you constantly.

"Just yesterday, I found a copy of *The Android's Lament* in a bookshop off Piccadilly Circus. Of course I bought it. I'm on the fourth chapter; it's strange seeing your words written with a British accent, with single quotation marks and every 'color' now a 'colour.' It's been years since I last read it and I appreciate it all the more now for knowing you. I will not pretend it's like having you with me but it is a comfort."

Flash, jealous of my attention, pushes against the sheet of paper in my hand and interposes his orange bulk between my eyes and Phil's words. With a shift of my thigh and a rude swat from the back of my hand, I shoo him onto the ground. He slinks off in a crouching trot, sparing me one reproachful glare from over his shoulder, and I finish my tea.

"People aren't exactly eager to talk about Walker over here. It's been a struggle finding anyone willing to admit to being a part of his movement even though his so-called holiday camps were strewn all over the country and, even then, they only accounted for a fraction of his followers. Considering the amount of shame they most likely feel, both at being pulled into so absurd a cult and at being party to the bloodshed that marked its dissolution, it's hardly a surprise. I've given up any real hope of talking to Walker himself, though I haven't stopped making inquiries. He's a total recluse and no one is entirely certain if he is even still in Britain. There's a very real chance he's disappeared into Kashmir or the Himalayas.

"All is hardly lost, however. Aside from the wealth of archival material in the tabloid and legitimate press, I've found one fellow who is more than willing to discuss his time in the cult. He's now an astronomer at the Royal Observatory but he was a self-described hooligan when he fell into Walker's orbit and he freely admits to taking part in the riots. As you'd no doubt imagine, he has a great many insights into Walker's appeal. There was little real philosophy behind him, he tells me, just the idea that, by cutting oneself off from the ability to sense and communicate consciously with the world, one could reach a higher (or deeper) truth, a harmony with the cosmos reified through the tacky microcosm of a pinball table. Walker didn't provide that truth—he couldn't—but he instead tried to point others in the direction where they could find the truth for themselves. That direction, that path, was entirely inward and that was the problem because inward truth is not communicable. For far too many people, that truth was horrifying, a void they never imagined they possessed, let alone that they would ever have to face."

I put the letter down, seized by the sudden desire to say something in response. I realize I have left my notepad on my night table so I place my empty teacup on the table and go inside. The floorboards creak under my hurried footsteps as I pass from the kitchen to the hall. In the bedroom, I grab pad and pen just as the display on the clock radio flips over to 11:11. I make a wish and smile at this new superstition of the digital age, then head back into the kitchen and grab the teapot. Then I'm back at the table in the yard, jotting down a couple of phrases I'll develop into ideas when I write him back—"Nietzsche's abyss as a freefall into self" and "the deep empty."

Then it hits me—I'd written a story based on Walker before, working with Aaron, but that was little more than an anti-cult morality play. I realize now that there is so much more story *I* could tell, a story more sympathetic to Walker as a seeker after his own truth. Unbidden, I see the seeker as he would appear in my story, with skin the color of an old penny and eyes of greenish gold. I see him with such clarity, such force, that I know I'm not imagining him, I'm not creating him, I'm *seeing* him, alive in my memory. But it isn't *my* memory. It's as if I'm receiving a transmission, I think, from someone else, somewhere else and some *when* else. And then I wonder if I'm not becoming schizophrenic.

And then it's gone, and I'm grateful for its leaving. With shaking hands, I pour myself another cup of tea, pick up the pages of Phil's letter and resume reading.

"That's where the riots came from. Too many people looked inward and found nothing and the nothing they found was terrifying. For this gentleman, the emptiness within ultimately directed him to the emptiness without and he turned his un-blinded eyes to space. Science is very good for providing one with wonder, he observed, but it is entirely silent when it comes to meaning. I replied with something you once said to me, that we have a way of projecting meaning outward, like a ventriloquist throwing his voice, and reminded him that the earliest astronomers were astrologers. He laughed. 'Well, that temptation's always there, isn't it?' he said."

My trembling stops. I breathe deeply and shake off the last of my disquiet, then read over the next several of pages with willed cheer. I get a kick out of the part where he bangs out an idea about the nature of Christ, inspired by an article he had read in *Omni Magazine* while waiting for a train in Paddington Station. Christ was light, Phil writes, not simply in the commonly understood sense of its power to illuminate but also in the sense of its unsolvable quantum duality: "For most of his life on earth, Christ existed in an indeterminate state: instead of wave and particle, he was at once divine and human. On the cross, he was 'collapsed' into the particle state of merely human; with the Resurrection, he returned as a wave of pure divinity. The implication of redemption and salvation is that, like Christ, we will arise to a state where the Godhead is one oscillation away, as close as the blood in our veins, the atoms in our flesh." I laugh and scrawl "Schrödinger's Christ" on the pad and read on.

"I hesitate writing to you about this next bit—it might come off as the scrawling of a dirty old man—but I was struck by the sight of a prostitute shivering on the steps of Westminster Cathedral. I watched her with undisguised frankness but, once she was satisfied I was interested in neither hiring nor harassing her, she dismissed me with a shrug and went on with drinking her soda pop and giving the other half of her supper, a small sleeve of supermarket cookies, to the pigeons gathering at her feet. She was dressed in shiny vinyl, her mini-skirt and halter the same candy-red as her lips, and, in the cold air, she was stippled with gooseflesh. She cast a chunk of cookie to the ground and watched as two pigeons fought for it until the bigger of the two, a ruthless blue and gray bully, won. Even though her face was an impassive mask of boredom, I could see that she loved them and it was strangely moving, this squalid pageant of charity in the shadow of the cathedral. She loved the strutting bully. She loved his gunmetal arrogance, his green and purple neck puffed out and shining in the sunset. She loved the tan and white loser, too, as he stood there beating his indignant wings. She broke off another crumb and threw it to his feet.

"It struck me, Jane—it moved me almost to tears—that I was witness to this child's apotheosis. Here was this girl who could not have been older than seventeen, ministering to these blameless birds, humble cousins to the snowy dove that descended unto Christ at his baptism. More pigeons came and she fed them all until there was nothing left for the girl herself but she didn't seem to mind.

I watched her place her plastic purse on her lap and, her fingers trembling in the chill, fumble a cigarette between her sugar-ravaged teeth. Then she lifted herself up from the steps and, with one last glance after her flock (and nothing so much for the intrusive priest who'd been spying on her), she lifted herself up onto teetering heels and went clicking off into the twilight. Even her torn fishnet stockings seemed somehow holy rather than tawdry."

You're right, you do come off like a dirty old man, I think at him. *Still, you get points for sublimating.*

Two pages later, Phil is telling me about a visit he had with a fellow Anglican priest in Canterbury: "He asked me if I'd read Jung's *Answer to Job*, which, thanks to you, I had. He then proceeded to put a distinctly Freudian gloss on it. We envision God as entirely ego, he said, entirely self-influencing and self-actualizing, and then this universal ego becomes the basis for our private super-ego, the still voice telling us right from wrong. But what if we have it entirely backwards? What if God is entirely id, blind unconsciousness in Jungian terms, and we have been created—we have *emerged*—from the inchoate depths of His soul to grant Him a perspective upon Himself He could never otherwise hope to attain. It's heady stuff—sacrilegious and heretical, like the

Gnostic concept of Samael, the blind demiurge whose profound sin was the act of creation itself from which we all must be extricated and redeemed, only now He has been restored to His rightfully central position. Sophia, the wisdom that, in Gnosticism, opposes, predates and supersedes Him, instead arises from Him like the first stirrings of life in the primordial muck or Athena from the Hephaestus-split skull of Zeus.

"We then talked about how Darwin, a divinity student destined for the clergy, saw such savagery and profligate agony in the natural world that it caused him to turn away from God all but completely. I suspect this is the decision your friend Mr. Mendel found himself faced with: accept the fathomless cruelty of the world as emanating from the literally thoughtless mechanism of a mindless universe or from the conscious design of a God who is, at best, incompetent and ineffectual, at worst, deranged and malevolent. From that point of view, the former is far more humane and pleasing than the latter. We wondered if we weren't onto something, a way to reconcile and justify the two views into something acceptable to such restless apostates."

I smile at that, a theology that will satisfy the Aaron Mendels of the world: lotsa luck, Father.

As I turn to the final page and his closing paragraph, my heart begins to pound. Propelled on the crest of a wave of exhilaration and fear, I read it through but my comprehension seems to tumble ahead of the words on the page and so I stumble through it. I gulp down the last mouthful of tepid tea and take a deep breath before I read it a second time:

"It feels so sterile, writing this out to you and waiting interminable gray days for your reply when I want so much to tell it to you face to face, watching the play of your expressions and hearing all the wry intonations of your voice. I feel a simpatico with you that incorporates and yet transcends my hunger for you physically and intellectually. I adored my wife and I was devastated when she died but I can honestly—and shamefully—say that I never felt anything with her like the way I felt those fleeting days I spent with you. Please understand, I'm not a romantic by nature and neither was she. Even as we loved each other and raised a son together, we knew it was happenstance that put us together, that there were innumerable other women with whom I'd have been just as compatible and happy, just as there were a multitude of men with which she'd have been the same. It was truth we neither rejected nor resented. I realize, though, that I could never say the same of you. If there are invisible forces at work in the universe—and I've staked my life that there are—then I can only conclude that one such force is binding us together."

It would be better, perhaps, if I did not know what he meant, if I could at least pretend. A declaration of love I could I handle but this talk of something more, something different, something deeper, some ethereal umbilicus that ties us together—it would be laughable if it didn't resonate in me in way that I find frankly terrifying. My fingers gone numb, I fold the letter and put it back into its envelope. I sit still for a long time, looking up to find that even Dale, with her primordial starburst, has forsaken me. I reach for my pen only to put it down again. I go to pour another cup of tea but the tea is all gone.

17

True Sky Rot

Crysanthia wanders the badlands south of the settlement for over an hour, carrying her pregnant belly before her with an unconscious pride and deference. The subliminal, inarticulate chatter from her womb increases little by little as the twins emerge into themselves; she hears them through the rapport between their cyborganelles and hers, across the placental blood barrier. Soon she will compel her body into labor—another day, maybe two, the twins will tell her when.

She stands at the lip of a blast crater from an old Commonwealth attack, the last one to successfully penetrate their defenses. Directly below her, falling dead away for three hundred meters, is a sheer cliff face of fused radioactive glass and tortured metallic rock. Dirty slush and dead things collect in the pit, shrouded in yellow fog. The far side lies well past the horizon—a few more such blasts and the Commonwealth could have reduced the entire moon to rubble. Crysanthia sees it, clear in her mind: a new ring system girding Agamemnon and the common stock's nightmare finally over.

She kicks a glob of smooth black and ochre slag over the edge. The rock disappears into the fog and makes a hollow *pok* as it hits bottom. She begins the long walk back to camp.

Something catches her eye in one of the refuse heaps that line the poorly defined road.

Crysanthia wanders closer. A cryonic sibyl, all but buried in the pile of debris—Crysanthia squats down and clears away the obstructions.

"Same one," she whispers, and though she should be, she is not surprised. She glances at the massing clouds on the horizon and then looks the sibyl over for damage. The disembodied head, eternally placid and perfectly preserved, stares into indeterminate depths. The power cell, a little silver pill hidden underneath the base, is fully charged—no surprise there, it was designed to last a thousand years.

A single, heavy raindrop falls on the glass—it leaves a muddy crater in the caked clots of dirt. Crysanthia pulls her computer from her hip pocket.

The Commonwealth had seized most of her assets at the beginning of the war but she still has a small fortune in untracked solaria stashed away in the computer's discrete memory. It is worthless. She has not given it a thought in over seven years, not even to delete it. Now she is glad she hadn't. She stands the sibyl upright on the ground and beams all of the money she has left into it. She leans back onto her heels. She waits.

Muscles twitch around the sibyl's jaw, its eyes roll in their sockets. A raindrop falls, and then another, and another. Creatures stir within the heap. Crysanthia rocks on the balls of her feet, is about to stand, when the sibyl finally speaks:

"*...true sky rot...blot...shining rust riot...stardust...now...*"

Crysanthia waits for it say more but there is nothing. The sibyl closes its eyes.

Crysanthia's computer beeps at her. She jumps. She collects her wits and answers the call.

"Mother," Dahlia says from within the tiny cryocube, "Could I see you in you in my dome, please?"

"Of course." She switches off her computer and slips it back into her pocket and, with one last remorseful look at sibyl resting in the trash heap, walks the rest of the way to the settlement.

The Pilot's camp is a sprawling collection of small white plastiform domes streaked with Klyemnestran grime. To Crysanthia, they remind her of turtle eggs she'd once found half exposed on a beach near Brancusi. Dahlia stands waiting in her doorway. Without a word, she places a silver strip of metal in Crysanthia's hand. It's all but weightless, thinner than foil, harder than diamond.

They go inside.

"From Narisian's shell?" Crysanthia asks.

"Look at it," Dahlia says. She hands Crysanthia a quantum interference micro-scanner. "Closer."

Crysanthia brings the scanner to her eye like a jeweler's loupe and holds the shard beneath its array of needle-like lenses. She sees it now, something from years ago, something she had never hoped to see again, enmeshed in the duraladium's crystal lattice, stark as the tracks of a puma in virgin snow.

Crysanthia lets her hands drop to her sides. She focuses on her daughter's mouth, searches. She suddenly needs to know whom she is talking to.

"Dahlia?"

When she was seven months old and just entering adolescence, Dahlia began to speak in German, to utter the cryptic and oracular fragments of a dead woman's thoughts. It was soon apparent that Bettina Brekkelheim had claimed as her own a small suite of rooms within the mansion of Dahlia's mind. The nano-avatars she had explained, shot into Crysanthia on Heaven 17—though the ground had been prepared years before on Vesta. Crysanthia's immune system had destroyed most of them but not all; some had made it to her ovaries, perhaps as few as one or two. Once there, the avatars insinuated their programming into Crysanthia's cyborganelles and chromosomes. Like almost everything else Bettina had done, she had kept it hidden.

Crysanthia had given birth to her own mother.

She had passed the trait to both of her children but Corvus would never express it. In males, the ghost forever lies dormant. Like mitochondria, the cyborganelles are matrilineal—Dahlia will pass them into the next generation, Corvus will not. From now until the death of the Pilots as a race, every Vog girl-child will carry Bettina nested within her.

Crysanthia watches Dahlia now and imagines what it will be like, in just a few years, when she is joined by countless daughters and sisters, all of them possessed of her accursed gift: a caste of witches, of priestesses, the Pilots' direct link back to the mind of their creator—another reminder that her children, her people, are something entirely new in the universe. And now that the Pilots are no longer an appendage of trade, now that their sole reason to exist has been taken from them, their minds will certainly turn from the abstruse mathematical realms of sidereal navigation to the building of a society, a culture, an identity Look around you, she tells herself, they already have. Sometimes, this struggle with the common stock pales in the terrifying light of the undiscovered territories within her own species, within her own mind.

More than that, she fears for Dahlia, for those parts of her daughter that are not her mother, if ever Bettina was a mother to anyone. The memory of holding her infant girl, a memory only a few years old, is still as vivid as anything Crysanthia has ever experienced, as is the visceral need to protect her. But how can Crysanthia protect Dahlia from this? How can Crysanthia protect Dahlia from something closer than her own skin, something as close as her own DNA? How can she protect the un-formed girl riding in her womb?

"What do want me to tell you?" Dahlia says to her. "I can't shut her away, lock her in the attic. She's as much me as anything. I wish you'd accept it."

Crysanthia thinks of the cryonic sibyl, in the trash heap where she'd left it, silent in the rain. She holds up the bit of metal. "And this? It signifies?"

"You are the closest thing we have to an expert. I was hoping you would have some insight."

"Ha," Crysanthia says, without emotion.

"I read your *notes* on what happened. What did *he* think it was?"

"Janos?" Crysanthia asks, though the name still pains her to say.

With a strangely halting nod, Dahlia whispers, "He would never tell me—would never tell Bettina, I mean."

In spite of herself, Crysanthia is moved. Her impulse is to comfort her daughter; it is an instant before she realizes it is not her daughter who needs comforting. And all she can offer that someone is an answer.

"To Janos, it was the naked mind of God," Crysanthia says. She laughs. "Some part of God's omnipresent anatomy, *thrust* through into our universe." She sits down on the floor of the dome.

Dahlia looks down at Crysanthia for a moment before joining her on the rough rug woven from the fibrous weeds that grow in the marshes near the river.

"Do you think of him often?" Dahlia asks.

Often? Crysanthia thinks. *No, not often. Always. Never.* Even when she isn't thinking of him, when she resolutely turns her thoughts away from him, he is there, even after all these years.

"Sometimes," she lies.

"Your logs were very clear on the sheer amount of energy involved. If it was close enough to Narisian to pull his cyborganelles from his cells—"

Crysanthia snorts in derision.

"—close enough to completely infiltrate his shell like this," Dahlia continues. "And it didn't kill him."

Crysanthia stares into her daughter's eyes, bluish green like her own, and says nothing.

"Maybe it needed him alive," Dahlia says.

"Now you sound like Janos, imputing will and purpose to a chaotic mass of energy." She stands. "I can't do that, Dahlia. I just can't."

Dahlia looks up at her. "I understand. But consider this: Narisian was supposed to be in the crèche for four days. That was over three months ago. The crèche technicians reintroduced cyborganelles on day three and they've been tracking their development ever since. There is no precedent for how Narisian's body has configured them—*is* configuring them. Nothing can explain any of it."

"I know all that, Dahlia." And I know this, too, she thinks: once the window of survival had closed on Narisian, there was no reason to continue searching for him. And yet continue you did, you and your brother, for weeks. And you found him, preserved by a means only rigid Pilot orthodoxy keeps us from calling a miracle. What compelled you? Do you have any idea?

"Yes," Dahlia says and nods her head at the metal shard in Crysanthia's hand. "And now you know something more."

Crysanthia stands motionless for a moment, then reaches down, grasps Dahlia's forearm and helps her to her feet.

"All right," she says. "Whatever you find out..."

Dahlia nods and, without another word, Crysanthia walks out into the driving rain.

18

The Small Blue

Once, in a Chinese restaurant on Luna, Aurelius Mann had cracked open the brittle gold of his vaguely yonic fortune cookie to find the message hidden in its chamber, "You have yearning for perfection." It had amused him, the left-out "a." To him, it had seemed less an exercise in the faux-Manchu diction of an ancient sage than a clinician's cool diagnosis: "Aside from syphilitic lymphoma, Mr. Mann, you have yearning for perfection. Cybernetic nano-phages ought to clear both conditions up in about a week."

He thinks about that now, as he waits in the Phobos Astroport, newly expanded since the destruction of its more famous counterpart on Deimos, and looks through the dome at the docking starliners. He remembers his conversation with Simone in the astroport bar, barely an hour ago, before her shuttle took her back to Mars. She'd drunk an overpriced zinfandel, he had bourbon.

"You're just going to do it, then? Follow this fanatic—"

"She's no fanatic."

"—into a war zone—"

"Heaven 41 is hardly a war zone."

"—where you can get blasted all to hell at any moment by those inhuman *things?*" She had treated him to her pout, his favorite among her stock expressions. "Does that sound rational?"

"I don't know. I do know that I've never been beyond the Inner Worlds. I've never set foot on an honest-to-God deep space installation. Closest I've come is the superannuated bicycle wheel in geo-sync over Kuala Lumpur and that was for a school trip when I was ten." He smiled. "I remember, it smelled like a hundred years of sweat socks."

"You're kidding, right? Because I never knew you wanted to be Jaz Jasperson, Spacc Ranger," she said, alluding to a popular series of children's sleepies. "We are at *war*, Aurelius. Wait a couple of years and let the University send you to the Heavens as a cultural ambassador, if you really want to go so badly." She sighed. "Does this have something to do with the son you won't talk about?"

Aurelius was silent. At the next table, a woman with an off-world accent—Earth or Venus, he can no longer tell which—ordered one of those god-awful margarita-like drinks, a time slip. Aurelius has yet to meet a Martian who can tolerate them.

"I thought so," Simone said.

Something about the too-competent way she delivered her concern betrayed her discomfort with it. This was not the role she'd signed up for. That nonsense about a cultural ambassadorship, that could have come straight from the Board of Regents and probably did. Aurelius grew weary of the show—at least, that's what he had told himself. He preferred that to the alternative, that his sudden annoyance with her was because she had hit too close to the truth.

But then he remembered her smile on Deimos, her boutique fangs reflecting hellfire and death. Had he any integrity at all, he thought, he would have been rid of her then and there. Instead, he'd made love to her later that very night. However jaded and rancid her soul, her body still felt, smelled and tasted as soft and clean as ever.

"Listen,' he said and handed her a memory crystal. "This is a document naming you as my literary executor."

Her eyes had gone wide.

"In case I don't come back."

So transparent—she's practically salivating her avarice, he had thought. Amazing. All set to dine on my corpse. "It's verified by thumb, voice and geno-print," he said. "Retinal scan; I had my attorney draw it up, it's all binding." Perverse old man, he'd placed special but subtle emphasis on his next words: "If I don't come back."

Oh yes, he had thought, this *will* make you. A career, a measure of borrowed fame, precisely the right yeasty-sweaty whiff of scandal—speak, little lizard. What will you say now that I've made myself more valuable to you dead than alive?

"Um, are you sure...?" With avid eyes of princess purple, she struggled to look at him and not the possible future etched in the crystal. "I mean, really, Aurelius, me?"

"Why not you?" Aurelius had replied. "I'm closer to no one in all of the Commonwealth," he'd lied and then realized, with a sick pang in his gut, that it was not a lie at all.

"Thank you." She clutched the crystal so tightly her knuckles went pale. Then transit control announced that her shuttle back to the surface was boarding and she was gone.

"Purple Spaceways Starliner *Swift Wind in Autumn Leaves* now boarding at Gate Delta 4."

Aurelius watches a callipygian flight attendant—human, not an android—as she walks across his field of vision. She wears her hair short, like Simone. His eyes follow her, the movement of her buttocks under her short skirt, the contours of her toned, caramel legs, until she disappears through a service door.

Suddenly, Sam Leonides is with him again, at once lying in his deathbed, staring into his personal abyss with empty sockets, and standing at Aurelius's side, his shade whispering into Aurelius's ear: "Careful, friend. Death enters through the eyes, you know."

One bag already slung over his shoulder, Aurelius reaches down and lifts his satchel. He looks up through the dome at the orange limb of Mars, its desert purity marred by the small blue of manmade lakes and seas. *If I don't come back.*

Stiffly, riding tired joints and muscles, he joins the queue leading to the gate.

19

What You Owe Me

In the event that Klytemnestra should fall to the Commonwealth, the Pilots had pressed out further into the void in every direction they could and established small and secret outposts, each one centered upon its own small crèche. Of these outposts, the greatest was Galatopolis, a labyrinthine city built onto and into a nickel-iron planetoid in a highly eccentric orbit around a nameless white dwarf located as far away from Iota Horologii as possible. With construction still several years away from completion, two thousand Pilots called it home, after a fashion.

Crysanthia sees its destruction in her dreams.

No, not a dream—though she sleeps, enfolded within her sleep pod, the images that form in her mind do not come from within. She receives an emergency transmission routed through her pod's seldom-used sleepie circuit.

The bodies lie everywhere in the unfinished streets of Galatopolis. The random depredations of the Commonwealth's attack have a staged quality about them, as if a psychotic god had arranged the corpses and fragments of corpses as a *grand guignol* spectacle in azure and crimson.

And then Crysanthia remembers: Corvus Karza had left for Galatopolis less than two weeks ago—if he was there...

"Mother," she hears Corvus say, as if in response to her thoughts, "I'm transmitting this to you and to Dahlia only. I'm wounded but I'll survive." A pause. "They could have destroyed me. They let me go."

There is nothing random in the next tableau. Crysanthia sees the body of a woman, pinned like an insect against a wall of polished iron with a shiny spike through her heart. Her stomach is split from pubis to sternum, her murdered children, only a couple of weeks away from birth, lie beneath her feet, tangled in a pile of viscera. Cyborganic tubules of silicon and duraladium glint in the antiseptic light like threads of glass and silver.

"Her name was Ivarra Syn," Corvus says, his voice flat and empty. But Crysanthia knows her son, he cannot hide from her. She anticipates his next words before he says them: "The children were mine—*ours.*"

As abruptly as it had begun, the message ends. Crysanthia forces herself awake.

Her own unborn twins stir within her womb—for an unspeakable instant, Crysanthia fears they had seen the images as well. But she knows that is impossible. Instead, she realizes, they are responding to the panicked beating of her heart. Crysanthia takes several deep breaths and adjusts her anguished metabolism to calm them. Eventually, they settle down into uneasy rest.

The sleep pod opens.

As Crysanthia dresses, her thoughts turn once more to Corvus. She reminds herself that he is a veteran of over thirty space battles, that he has seen and inflicted much more than his share of dying. Beyond that, though, he is still her child. And she cannot protect him. She cannot protect any of them.

One of the twins—the girl, she knows—kicks against her abdominal wall. Crysanthia gasps and places a trembling hand on her belly. She is afraid.

Crysanthia feels nostalgic for fashion, for bio-synthetic leather and metallic silk. Such a little thing, she knows, but one of countless little things taken from her. These petty losses are a constant irritant, like pebbles in her shoes. She is grateful for them, they distract her—from time to time—from dwelling on the losses that are not so petty. Walking in utilitarian plastic mesh boots and wearing a flight suit of recycled polymers, she crosses the concrete floor of the converted hangar, wending her way through the islands of waiting Pilots toward the place where her daughter stands, alone in the center of it.

"Like a cocktail party in a vortexball stadium," Dahlia says. "No—they're too stand-offish to call this a party, look at them."

Crysanthia looks around, especially at the other women, almost half of them pregnant and most of those visibly so, like Dahlia, like herself.

"Maybe it was a mistake to build so much damned independence into you," Dahlia continues. It quickly become apparent to Crysanthia that the voice issuing from her daughter's mouth belongs wholly to Bettina. "Still, I intended you to spend most of your years isolated out there among the stars, drifting like milkweed seeds..."

"What have you *done?*" Crysanthia whispers.

"Relax, my love. Everything is fine. Trust me."

"Trust..." Crysanthia realizes that she has no idea how this works, she never did. Until now, Bettina's presence has been entirely subordinate to Dahlia, like the weak bleed-through of a radio transmission. But now... what if Dahlia never comes back?

Her panic renewed and given new focus, she grasps Dahlia's arm.

"Ow," Bettina says. "Careful."

Crysanthia tightens her grip.

"Crysanthia, we can't get into this now, even if I wanted to." Bettina pulls Dahlia's arm free of Crysanthia's grasp. "You *will* have to trust me. It's time to start the briefing."

With that, the light dims and everyone turns to face the center of the floor. Reluctantly, Crysanthia takes a couple of steps back, searching Dahlia's face the entire time. Along with everyone else, she turns her face upward to the ceiling. From lenses set into the elasticrete, pink lasers fire down at every Pilot in the chamber. The beams strike them each at a point high up on their long foreheads, at the apex of an isosceles triangle formed with the corners of their eyes.

The briefing begins.

The Pilots find themselves gathered in a psycho-mimetic simulacrum of Vesta, in the clearing where Crysanthia had delivered Bettina into the hands of the Solar Commonwealth. Crysanthia feels the unease all around her. Perverse, it seems to say—or fears to say. Already, she knows, it is there within the Pilots, the primitive confusion of what is sacred and what is profane. And she also knows, though she cannot see the slightest outward sign of it that Bettina delights in their disturbed equilibrium.

High over-head, a red-tailed hawk kites the updrafts.

"With my father in the crèche and my brother incapacitated, we thought it best that I should conduct this assembly," Bettina says in Dahlia's voice, not bothering to specify exactly who she means by *we*. She sits on the bench, her legs folded next to her—she disguises even her body language. *So it's to be a charade*, Crysanthia thinks. *The rest of them see you as Dahlia. And you'll force me to play along. With so much else going on, what choice have I got?*

"Where I need to take you next will be... unpleasant." Her eyes catch Crysanthia's for a fleeting instant and then Vesta fades away into Galatopolis so smoothly that Crysanthia barely has time to notice it. The Pilots stand in front of Ivarra Syn's impaled corpse. Bettina, still in Dahlia's guise, sits on the floor precisely as she had sat upon the bench. She turns her gaze from Pilot to Pilot before she reaches over and touches the bloody head of one of the dead fetuses.

"Corvus sent us these images just a few hours ago. Galatopolis is no more, as you can see."

Silence. Bettina searches their faces once more and says, "His damaged starship crashed into the atmosphere and burned up, but not before enclosing him in an infirmary bubble and ejecting him. He splashed down into the Sea of

Klytemnestra about twenty minutes ago. The Commonwealth let him go. They wanted him to show us what they can and will do."

With that, Bettina returns them to Vesta. Crysanthia watches as the blood fades from Dahlia's fingertips.

"There is nothing more I can say. You must all deal with the loss as you see fit." Bettina glances at Crysanthia, then says, "It seems, however, that the slaughter on Galatopolis was little more than an elaborate diversionary tactic." Bettina pauses to let the enormity of that fact impress itself upon her listeners. "The force that destroyed the outpost was comparatively small, two frigates and several fast attack craft. Meanwhile, our sensor remotes have detected an *Imperator* class command cruiser with an escort of over one hundred *Shrike* class fighters, just eight parsecs from here. From what we can discern, they are not moving to attack—not yet."

"One command cruiser wouldn't be enough for an attack on Klytemnestra," Crysanthia says through gritted teeth. "Stop the theatrics and tell them what else you know. Now."

Bettina sighs. "We *know* very little. The region of space they are stationed in is unremarkable save for the fact that it carries debris of my father's starship. The wrecks of such ships are not hard to come by in the countless cubic parsecs between Iota Horologii and Sol. The Commonwealth's engineers surely know by now that this flotsam will yield none of our technological advances to their analysis." Another glance at Crysanthia. In spite of herself, Crysanthia finds herself nodding once, fractionally, in complicity. "They are looking for something. We cannot get close enough to find out what. The one Pilot who may have an answer is still shut up inside his womb tank. He will not emerge to speak it. *Mother*, do you wish to add anything else?"

Crysanthia shakes her head.

"Then that concludes this briefing. Thank you."

One by one and in groups of threes and fives, the Pilots drop out of electronic communion. Crysanthia's mind moves to sever her link.

"Not you," Bettina hisses.

The others leave until finally Bettina and Crysanthia are alone. Dahlia's visage flickers and flows until Bettina Brekkelheim stands across from Crysanthia, as strong and vital as when Crysanthia last saw her alive. She is barefoot and a garland of wildflowers rests in her silver-blond hair.

"Dahlia is fine," she says. "She's here, right now--she's just... *quiet."*

Crysanthia shakes her head.

"I have good reason for doing this."

"Dahlia," Crysanthia says, "She went along with it?"

"Let's just say she did not fight me."

"That's no answer."

"It's all the answer you get."

"The others? When they see us, me and Dahlia, standing in the middle of the dock, lasers still—"

"They'll see a mother having a private talk with her daughter." A sad smile flickers at the corner of her lips. "Which is exactly what this is."

Crysanthia sits on the moist grass, legs folded beneath her as if she were in the chamber of her ship. "What do you want?"

"To walk for a time among you—fully among you. To live again, to live in you." Winds blow the strands of Bettina's hair. They dance in the light like an electric nimbus. "To be with my... children. In my rightful place, of course."

"Oh no. No you *don't.* Not like this," Crysanthia says. "You give me back my daughter."

Bettina's expression hardens. She kneels down in front of Crysanthia. Her eyes hold Crysanthia's with a ruthless intensity—the intensity, Crysanthia thinks, of a god. "Crysanthia, you forget who I am. You *always* forget who I am. You forget who you are, what you owe me." Then, suddenly, with a god's calculated caprice, Bettina spits in Crysanthia's face. "She belongs to me."

Crysanthia feels her teeth clench, feels a muscle jump in her jaw.

Bettina smiles. "And so do you."

20

Reptile Karma

We drive mile after mile on a rutted road snaking through the Pine Barrens of Southern New Jersey, with Phil behind the wheel of a rented Tucker Troubadour and static-raddled jazz on the radio. It's the last week of July and we have the windows down, open to all the rich smells of the sun-heated tree pitch and loam, the rot and rebirth of the forest that deepens into darkness just a few dozen yards from the crumbling asphalt shoulder. I take a deep breath and, for no reason I can figure, let it out with a sigh.

"You feeling alright?" Phil asks. He's been back from England for just over a week—I'd flown out to meet him at Idlewild Airport; my plane had landed four hours before his. We spent the next few days the city—on my accountant's advice, I'd scheduled a few not entirely unnecessary meetings with my agent and editor in Manhattan so I could write the airfare and hotel off--and now we're driving across New Jersey so I can meet his son and daughter-in-law and we can both meet his new grandson, born in May. "Jane?"

I grunt something in the family of yes.

After a moment, Phil says, "We may have to roll up the windows and use the air conditioning, closer we get to the bay. When the tide is out, the mud in the salt marshes reeks to high heaven."

"Uh-huh," I say. I see the splintered and bloody carapace of a turtle just to the side of the fading yellow line running down the center of the road. "Oh, Jesus! There's another one. I swear Phil, if I see one more flattened turtle—"

"I'm afraid you will," he says. Then he gives me a sidelong smirk. "It's turtles all the way down."

I manage a wan smile and turn my gaze back to the view from my open window. It all goes by in a blur.

I really do love him, I think. And instead of that thought making me happy or content, it leaves me sighing for no reason and staring at scraggly, spindly pine trees and looking with alarm at road kill—it's not *all* turtles, I see: at the sight of a bent wing jutting up from the pavement dead ahead, covered in bloodied brown feathers, Phil grimly observes, "Some kind of carrion bird—probably a turkey buzzard. They come down to eat and then get creamed themselves."

That's something I've noticed about Phil—when he's uncomfortable, he becomes pedantic. I realize then that I have been distant with him, if not moody, so I reach over and touch his cheek. I feel him relax.

I find my thoughts circling back to my first husband. There's no mystery as to why, he killed himself by walking out in front of a cross-town commuter bus. This was two years after our divorce and he was conscientious enough to absolve me of any guilt in a long note he left behind for me and his family: a mother, brother and sister living somewhere in Indiana or Illinois, I could never keep it straight. It was sweet of him, I thought at the time, but unnecessary—I'd known something like it was coming a year into our marriage and I knew it had next to nothing to do with me. We'd talked about it and he'd been to shrinks—he'd even spent three months in a half-assed ashram in Arizona once; the separation did little for him but wonders for me, I'm only a little ashamed to admit. He was a sweet man but he always had the air about him of someone who had just learned a very unpleasant truth about himself and that air could be as oppressive as a bad smell. Our marriage dissolved after three and a half years—less than a year after his return from the desert—and, though I initiated the final legal dissolution and saw it through to its conclusion, he'd made it plain that it was a consummation as devoutly wished by him as by me—perhaps more so.

I'd loved him, too, of course, in a way. But I can honestly say that the love was neither passionate nor deep—I probably feel more for Aaron than I ever did for him and as for the man sitting next me, driving this outsized boat of a car...

I reach into a paper bag of penny candy I'd bought on impulse when we'd stopped, a few miles back, at an old fashioned general store that oozed quaintness. I pull out two pieces of Bazooka Joe bubblegum and offer one to Phil. He nods and, after I've unwrapped a piece—taking care not to tear the tiny enclosed comic—opens his mouth. I reach over and drop the little pink slab onto his tongue.

"Thanks," he says.

After I've unwrapped the second piece and popped into my own mouth, I say, "You know, I'd have sworn this stuff was around when we were kids."

"You mean it wasn't?"

I nod. "I researched it for a story. They didn't start making it until the fifties."

"But that's..." Phil's voice trails off.

We drive along in silence for a while. I watch the muscles in Phil's jaw and temple work as he chews over what I've told him along with the sugary wad. He seems genuinely troubled.

"You say the house is in Cape May?" I say, to change the subject.

Phil nods. "It's been in my family literally for generations—my grandfather bought it a few years after the First World War I inherited it back in the sixties and signed it over to my son as a wedding present—that and the first two years of property taxes."

"I spent a summer in Cape May when I was nine or ten, I think," I say. "Not an entire summer, just a couple of weeks early in the season; I remember, it was still too cold—Phil, pull over."

There's a turtle up the road from us, just taking its first steps onto the macadam and pulling its head back into its shell as the few other cars that are on the road pass it in either direction. I'm about to tell Phil to pull over again when I feel him gently brake. We pass the turtle and slow to a stop around twenty feet beyond it.

Without saying a word to Phil, I open my door and walk back to where the turtle takes another tentative step into the road. When he sees me, he stops; when I pick him up, he retreats into his shell and watches me with a fearful eye of bright reddish-ochre. Looking both ways before I cross, I take him to the other side of the road and set him down at the forest's edge.

I wonder what small measure of mercy I have earned for myself by saving this little creature. Is there a reptile karma that will follow me into my next life, if I'm ever to come back as a gecko or a Gila monster, an alligator basking in a Florida swamp? I smile but then I think: I could save this turtle but I could do nothing for *him*, for my first husband. I can't even remember his name. Wait. *What?*

He was my husband.

He killed himself.

I loved him.

I wept for him.

And I cannot remember his name. I can't remember what he looked like or what color his eyes were.

As I watch the turtle move, with surprising speed, into the wood, his orange and black shell camouflaged into the fallen pine needles and atomized light, I feel it, what I've *been* feeling, the past slipping away from me, my memories, my life—I wonder if it was ever real, did any of it ever happen. Is *this* real, this moment—this one, this moment right here—is this happening now?

I feel it again, like I felt it that night up at Rosewall College and on Phil's cool sheets, the sense that everything—every object, every sensation, every dimension of space and time—were just the swirling shimmers on the skin of a soap bubble. And yes, it is lovely, but it is also fragile and hollow. And if my world should burst, letting loose the emptiness within to become the emptiness without, what then would become of me?

"I, uh, I was going to wait until we were at the house to give you this, to... ask you this, but—"

I turn and Phil is there, holding a little velvet box toward me. With manful diffidence, he opens it to reveal a ring, a star sapphire set in white gold.

"I know it's not traditional," Phil says, "but somehow this stone seemed more like... you."

Indeed it does, I realize, though I'm damned if I know why. I look up into Phil's face before turning away, to search the forest floor for the turtle I rescued. Instead, I see a praying mantis, clinging to the resin-oozing bark of the nearest pine tree, not two feet away from me. *Careful of the sap,* I find myself thinking, *you don't want to become a fossil.* As if it heard my ridiculous warning, the insect turns and regards me with eyes that catch the rays of the sun in shifting bands of light, like the sapphire waiting behind my back, waiting for an answer.

21

Her Virtual Heart

Crysanthia laughs.

She watches Bettina's haughty smile twist into something uglier and far more satisfying to behold. Bettina's spittle still trickling down her cheek, Crysanthia laughs again. With one swift and easy motion, she is on her feet, towering over her creator. She wipes the spit from her face and flings it from her fingers.

Bettina's control over the illusory environment falters—superimposed over the green hills and blue sky, Crysanthia can see the exposed elasticrete skeleton of the hangar, the dull yellow-gray of the rexeroid dome. Dahlia stands transfixed across from her, forehead impaled on the laser interface. Then the true world ebbs away and Vesta flows back in.

"You say I forget myself? Not at all. In fact, I feel I'm just now beginning to remember. You've created a race of superhuman polymaths, Mother. The least of us is superior to you in every way. Congratulations. Now let me tell you what your success means to you, right at this moment, just between us. If you ever override my daughter in this manner again, if I ever feel you are using any of us as nothing more than your toys—if I ever decide I don't like the sound of your *voice*—I will have the genetic sequence that codes for your memories effaced from our genome, the program that facilitates your consciousness deleted from our cyborganelles."

Bettina's pale lips part in shock.

"I will finish what they started. I will murder you. Once and for all time."

Bettina closes her mouth. She turns her back to Crysanthia.

"You made me, Bettina," Crysanthia says coolly even as her virtual heart pounds within her simulated ribcage. "You know me. Tell me if I'm lying to you."

"No," Bettina whispers. "You wouldn't lie to me. Perhaps I built you... too well." She sighs. "And you, Crysanthia, always my favorite, my little brazen maverick."

"Good."

"But remember something. I designed you, inside and out. From the length of your thigh bone to the shadings of your skin, from the density of your muscles to the shape of your skull. My signature is in your every fold and hollow. Every nerve. Every sinew. And now you look at me as if I were a she-wolf devouring her young."

"Are we yours to devour? Really?"

"Just be careful. What you promise, what you desire—be careful."

And it is over.

Crysanthia settles into her flesh. She half expects Bettina's spit to still be on her face, is perversely disappointed when it isn't. Aching for any miracle, she thinks, no matter how petty, how degrading. She grabs Dahlia's wrist and yanks her across the meter of floor separating them.

"Mother...?" Dahlia says. "Don't be..."

"Shut up," Crysanthia says, suddenly furious at her—not at Bettina, at Dahlia. *Let's just say she did not fight me,* Bettina said. Why hadn't she? Doesn't she know who it is she gave her body over to? Crysanthia turns and, hand still encircling her daughter's wrist, strides toward the exit. Dahlia, still disoriented, has to struggle to keep up. The other Pilots move aside silently and stare after them. Crysanthia pays them no mind.

Crysanthia drags Dahlia along as they leave the camp. The soggy, stinking earth sucks at their boot soles.

After they'd walked a kilometer away from the settlement's ill-defined limits, into the wilderness, Dahlia digs in her heels and wrests free her arm.

Crysanthia stops and turns slowly to face her daughter. Neither woman speaks. Finally, Crysanthia turns and walks on. After a moment, Dahlia follows—Crysanthia can hear her squishing footfalls.

Crysanthia crouches down at the river bank, meters away from where one of the flat river eels has crawled up onto the bank and coiled itself around a rat. Through its transparent body, Crysanthia can see the hundreds of needle-like mouths that line the eel's belly in parallel rows pierce the rat's flesh. The rat's blood and liquefying organs course into the eel as streams of muddy ichor. Its open maw is a fury of twitching cilia. It utters no death cry—it has no vocal cords with which to speak, no ears with which to hear. All that announces its death is a thin threnody of stink, an alien tang of fear and pain in the night's already fetid air.

Crysanthia makes her choice. She wraps her hand around a large, pointed rock, then stands up and moves on. Dahlia hesitates, then follows. Crysanthia can hear her daughter's lips part, her lungs draw in air but Dahlia expels the breath without speaking.

They arrive at the crèche, at its huge glassy panels of waxy leaves lying heavy on the ground, so rich with chlorophyll the green seems black. The hive breathes—syncopated clouds of steam rise from the bone portals that lead to its fertile underworld. Crysanthia steps into an osseous tunnel and walks around and down in spiral descent. Dahlia follows.

In the humid stillness of the uterine gallery, Crysanthia walks to Narisian's amniotic sac. She repositions the rock in her hand and looks over her shoulder at Dahlia, then crashes the stone into the cocoon. Once and a web of splintering cracks spreads across the sac's translucent, chitinous wall. A second time and a spring of pink water erupts and trickles to the floor. With the third strike, the womb shatters.

The hive announces its distress in the same manner as the rat by the river, through the chemistry of scent. Paper clad crèche technicians rush over only to stop, stunned into paralysis at the sight of Crysanthia Vog, hugely pregnant and drenched in the amniotic sluice, wrenching a reconstituted Narisian Karza into the world by his armpits.

Narisian gags and chokes and coughs as his lungs clear themselves of the fluid and begin to breathe the rarefied air.

Crysanthia lets go of him and he falls to floor with a thud. His head comes to rest less than a centimeter away from Crysanthia's discarded rock. She reaches for the umbilicus still tying him to the crèche and, with a rotation of her wrist, wraps it twice around hand. She gives it a single, sharp yank. The plug pulls free of Narisian's navel with an audible snap and spill of dark blood.

In silence, Crysanthia stands up. Dahlia pushes past her.

The crèche technicians do nothing. The hive bleeds. Crysanthia walks back to the tunnel leading aboveground. Dahlia stays behind, cradling her helpless newborn father in her lap, staring long after her mother's retreating back has disappeared.

On Klytemnestra, the days are merest biological convention, reckoned by the twenty-six hour diurnal cycle built into the Pilots rather than by the workings of celestial mechanics. They dwell in darkness most of the time, either the stellar night when Klytemnestra's rotation turns their settlement away from Iota Horologii or the planetary night when the orbit of Agamemnon places its globe between them and the star. Tonight is one of the somewhat rare occasions when Klytemnestra traverses the night side of Agamemnon with the settlement facing the void. Only the moons Elektra and Cassandra, dull copper and pewter coins tracking across the sky, remind the Pilots that they are part of a planetary system.

Crysanthia sits in Narisian's dome and watches the rise and fall his chest. Her chair is hard and angular, like the pallet on which Narisian lies, naked to the waist and staring at the ceiling with sightless eyes. The chair does not bother her. Like Narisian, Crysanthia is beyond discomfort. She studies him.

His skin is a deep blue, almost indigo. Glittering patterns—concentric circles and radiating lines—cover his chest and face, as if he's been tattooed with ancient, alien glyphs or etched with diagrams of mad circuitry.

She hasn't spent the entire time watching him, of course. Far more time has been spent going over the intelligence that continues to trickle in from the war zone—that is to say, from everywhere. Something she finds troubling, looking through the tactical reports from their robot spies hiding in the Oort Cloud and Kuiper Belt: there's been a thirty percent increase in traffic in and out of the asteroid belt over the last eighteen months. She supposes it could be nothing—the Commonwealth has been saying that the asteroids were under-populated and underdeveloped for the last twenty years. Something about the assiduously random pattern bothers her, though: it suggests the elaborate cover story of a meticulous liar.

She logs her observations and suspicions and adds them to the endless queue of observations and suspicions to be disseminated throughout the population. She doubts if anyone will listen to her after what she did down in the crèche and so decides not to sign her name to them.

"Mother," Dahlia says from the doorway, open to the night beyond, "may I speak with you?"

Crysanthia nods after a moment considering the question. She gets up and joins her daughter at the threshold.

"How is he?"

Crysanthia shakes her head. "The same. What is it?"

"There's talk. A number of people want you tried for what you've done. Tried and executed."

Crysanthia sighs. "Do tell."

"It's serious enough for you need to know. A few of us—very few—have successfully forestalled the worst of it—most people are willing to wait a little longer, at least."

"I see." Crysanthia glances back at Narisian. "Would be embarrassing—kill me and a day later the bastard wakes up, wanting to do it himself."

"There's also the matter of the damage done to the crèche, trauma inflicted on the unborn."

Crysanthia hadn't thought of that. "Trauma?"

"Negligible," Dahlia says, annoyed. "And the hive has already budded a new amniotic sac." She pauses. "Why *did* you do it? What did you hope to accomplish?"

Crysanthia thinks it over and then says, in all honesty, "No idea. Now ask me if I'm sorry."

Dahlia shakes her head. "I'm sure a lot of this is resentment held over from the Consortium days. They can't accept the idea that Vog the Whore has become Bettina's Chosen One."

"Chosen *what?*" Crysanthia snaps. "Look at me. Look at *me.* I'm sick. I pass along that woman's rancid soul as if it were a sexually transmitted disease." As she says the words, she realizes she has heard someone else say much the same thing to her in very different circumstances. Sudden longing stabs her like a poisoned stiletto. "And because of me, so will you," she says, quiet now. "Any one of them, they're welcome to it."

"Mother—"

"Does she hear me, Dahlia? Do you hear me, Bettina? Do you?"

"She hears you," Dahlia whispers. After a pause, she says, "I know you probably won't want to hear this—"

Crysanthia laughs.

"—but imagine what *she's* going through. A month ago, she saw herself killed. Do you know what that loss means to her? Do you even want to try? The Bettina in here—" she taps her head, heart "—is not the woman who died on Deimos, don't you see? Almost nine years separate them, nine years of divergent experience. Everything that other Bettina was, everything those years had made her, is lost forever. And now Galatopolis..." At the look on Crysanthia's face, Dahlia lets her voice trail off.

"What about the twins?" Crysanthia asks, laying her hands flat on her pregnant belly.

Dahlia sighs. "Some say let you live until you give birth, others say take them out of you and put them in the crèche. They call it poetic justice."

"I've always hated our people's stunted sense of irony. It won't be necessary, anyway; I was planning on giving birth tomorrow. I would have done it today but..." Crysanthia shrugs away the thought.

"I've talked this over with Corvus—he's out of his bubble and almost fully recovered—and he has an idea."

Crysanthia waits.

"He'd rather he told you himself. He says you may not like it."

Crysanthia smiles and caresses her daughter's cheek. "Like it? It's been years since I've liked anything, Dahlia. Why start now?"

22

The God of Soft Things

Heaven 41 grows beyond the high domed ceiling above the *Swift Wind's* huge swimming pool. A very convincing illusion—more than once, Aurelius has to remind himself that he is lodged deep in bowels of the starliner, watching a holographic view screen and not looking directly into space.

Aurelius turns his attention from the space station, still little more than a vaguely elongated point of light, to two girls of about sixteen who frolic naked in the pool. One of them, the one with the skin like polished mahogany and the hair braided into black cables clacking and flashing with bits of metal, dives from a platform hovering twenty meters in the air. She slices through sphere after floating sphere of magnetically contained water. They slow her descent, each one sending pseudopodia grasping down after her and then re-forming into a quivering crystal globe, with only the occasional crackling tendril of blue static discharge along its disrupted skin to remember her by. She knifes into the surface of the pool with barely a ripple. Her companion, olive skinned and trailing a curly mane of red, breaches the surface nearby like a dolphin.

Aurelius wonders if they've heard of him.

It is three in the morning, ship's time. Aurelius has been sitting here, at a poolside table with his abortive notes and a leather clad flask of rye, since just before midnight; the girls came in at quarter to one. The darker of the two spared him a single glance when she came in, her friend nothing at all. They disrobed and leapt into the water and haven't acknowledged his presence since. Aurelius likes it that way.

These are indeed the days of miracles and wonders, he thinks. To live in a world where two young women think nothing of cavorting nude in front of an audience of one fat old—

He stops himself. Long ago, he'd discovered just how seductive self-abnegation could be. Sam used to chide him for it. "It's the highest form of arrogance," he'd say, "and you haven't earned it yet."

Ever since that night when Simone quoted his damned poem back at him, Aurelius has found his mind drifting to Sam. Two, three, four times a day—it's as if the old poet's shade haunts him, trailing aphorisms and insults rather than chains. Aurelius had a father and, once he was gone, never went looking for another but there he is just the same, wheezing and mocking in his memories, demanding no heroics, commanding no vengeance but reminding him instead how profoundly little it means to be alive.

But how can that be? Look at them out there, the water nymphs, all long bones and shining skin and gliding muscle—how can that be in this brave new world that has such wonders in it?

The diver climbs out of the pool and walks to the automated bar. As she passes him, Aurelius notices the proud fullness of her lips, the way her dark nipples jut out on her small breasts, the way the curls of her pubic hair cradle droplets of water that flash prismatic in the light like infinitesimal stars.

He watches the pale soles of her feet as she walks away, the curve of her brown calves and thighs, the pleasing heft of her buttocks.

The girl orders two bottles of distilled comet water. Her words come to Aurelius like notes plucked on a bored and petulant lyre. She pads back to the pool and hands the drinks to her friend before she slips into the water. She takes one of the bottles and the two of them stand there in the shallows, throats working as they drink.

Aurelius picks up his computer and, with one last look at the water nymphs, begins the walk back to his stateroom. Once there, he lies on top of his bunk's fine linen bedclothes. He feels older than usual. He would not have thought it possible.

Swift Wind in Autumn Leaves docks at Heaven 41 late the next afternoon. Aurelius, alone in a quaint stateroom all burnished brass and dark tropical hardwoods, looks through the holographic viewer, done up to resemble a porthole, as the starliner makes its final approach. He finishes packing, snaps shut his bag, lays it on his unmade bunk and presses closer to the glass for a better look.

The space station resembles a long silver axle with a bicycle wheel at one end and three crystal beach balls at the other. After a minute, it becomes clear that *Swift Wind* is heading for an opening in one of the beach balls. The ship moves steadily closer to the globe. Aurelius can see now that it is a geodesic, composed of several hundred polyhedral panels of diamond, lit from within by globes of solid lumenium. Aurelius takes up his bag and leaves.

Later, after the ship has docked, Aurelius is borne the length of axle by high speed rail car. The car's interior is shabby and crowded, aromatic with stale plastics, not all like the starliner's luxuries. Aurelius searches for the swimmers among the faces of his fellow passengers but does not find them. Wistfully, he wonders if he hadn't imagined them, twin projections of his advanced satyriasis.

The trip lasts all of forty seconds.

The car disgorges them into the concourse at the hub of the wheel. Aurelius is pleased that tired aura of the run-down does not spill out of the car along with its passengers. The concourse is vast and in good repair, planted with cherry trees just beginning to lose their bloom. Overhead is a domed ceiling of diamond panes and beyond that the starry dark—real this time, not a holographic simulation. Just below the dome and above the tree-tops, twelve meters high and encircling the entire concourse, a mosaic shows the history of spaceflight, from *Sputnik* and *Apollo* to the first colonial beachheads in orbit and on the Moon, from the terraforming of Mars and, decades later, Venus to the earliest starships and Heaven Prime. Aurelius searches in vain for the representation of a blue skinned Pilot. Instead, he spies a patch of tesserae with a tell-tale gloss that does not quite match the inky tiles which surround it.

Erase them from the past, erase from the future, Aurelius thinks. Those Jaz Jasperson sleepies Simone taunted him with, produced a decade before the war and set in the twenty-fifth century, almost three hundred years hence—Aurelius suddenly realizes they never once mention a Pilot. In that rinky-dink vision of tomorrow, it's as if they never were.

Aurelius sits below one of the trees, on a bench cut from a small asteroid and polished smooth as glass. Out comes the rye. He unscrews the brass cap and lifts the flask to the new and shining tiles. He drinks to names torn down.

He activates his computer and checks the local time—a four and a half hour discrepancy from *Swift Wind*, star lag shouldn't be much of a problem. He ties into the literary database. All of his works are here, including a piece of juvenilia. The ship had only *Darkness* and the *Elegies*. Smug satisfaction suffuses him like Isidian fever.

Aurelius switches from the station library to the station directory and looks up eateries. Before he'd left, he spoke with Salman Ibrahim, the university's young astro-historian and his weekly *go* instructor. (Tacitly, they'd each concluded that Aurelius was hopeless a long time ago—Aurelius about two weeks before his tutor—but both men enjoyed the company and so the lessons continued.) Salman had told him to seek out a raw seafood bar and suck down a dozen blue points the first chance he gets. "Best in the galaxy," he said. "They have bed after bed of them, deep in the bowels of all the Heavens. They're the fifth and penultimate step in the waste reclamation cycle. Don't worry, it's perfectly sanitary. They shuck 'em right there in front of you, squirt of lime, a little hot pepper sauce—trust me, you've never had better and you never will."

The swimmers walk by his bench, fully clothed and part of a gaggle of ten or so other young women, each one lovely enough to be a dream doll template. Aurelius smiles, breathes a silent prayer of thanks to the god of soft things and drinks to their radiant health.

He wakes at station dawn to the slithery sensation of a satin pillowcase against his cheek and the unpleasant awareness that he drooled upon it.

The Sapphic Church of Rome has been very good to him. His is the finest suite in the most expensive of the six hotels located in the outermost of Heaven 41's three concentric habitat rings. Aurelius activates his computer, orders room service and tunes into the Hearst News Agency's special interstellar edition. The war is bigger out here, with twelve Heaven stations destroyed since it began. Constant clashes in the vast no-man's land that is the void and the Pilots more or less hemmed in at Iota Horologii—with that system as apparently impregnable as the Commonwealth, the war has settled into a long, bloody stalemate.

His breakfast arrives, via human server. Aurelius tips the boy two hundred solaria—why the hell not? Easy to be generous when someone else pays the basics, pays more than the basics. He settles down to his breakfast of baklava, dates, soft boiled eggs and strong Turkish coffee, and looks out his holographic window into the false depths of space.

After he showers, Aurelius kills most of his morning with an aimless walk about the station. He is fascinated by the gentle curvature of the huge wheel, the way the hazy distance, the anti-horizon, curves *up* out of his sight, and he is drawn to the dark green foliage that grows from every spare ledge and crevice, the black algae that forms a bubbled skin in the damp and shallow gutters. Genetically designed for optimal oxygen production, he knows. He wonders if Bettina's firm produced the seed stock.

Bettina. The thought of her sets his heart and mind at odds—just the sort of emotional and rational donnybrook that is supposed to produce great art, or so the legends all have it. In him, it produces only a sapping melancholia, a machine ground to a standstill; he cannot forgive her life enough to clearly mourn her death. If ever it was a mistake to love anyone... He will not complete the thought. Instead, he thinks again of her Pilots, of their place in history consigned to oblivion with no more care than the mosaic's corporate vandals have for its dislodged sky blue tesserae. One day, all that will remain of Bettina will be dark green leaves and slime, pumping out gasses for the conquering swarms of humanity. His melancholia deepens.

A chime from his computer tells him it is ten o'clock and time to meet Dr. Wu.

"From complexity you cannot infer consciousness."

"We've had this discussion. I'm through."

"It's bad science—it's worse than that, it's superstition."

The voices come to Aurelius from beyond a darkened doorway. First a woman, then a man, then the woman again—both are familiar. He stands in the outer chamber of Heaven 41's Christian Viralist Reading Room, surrounded by bound books and wafer slate computer terminals. His nostrils are touched by the musty comfort of old paper and leather, his retinas by the stark cruelty of neon bright alphanumerics streaming in the sterile wafer slates. Aurelius is dizzy in the data flux, poised to lose his place in history's continuum.

"Please, Professor Mann, come in."

Aurelius hesitates, then steps over the threshold.

His son is standing before him.

"—lack the spine and vision merely to consider," Janos Brekkelheim says, "let alone embrace."

Miriam Wu stands across from him, her hair not as gray as Aurelius remembers, the skin of her face smoother, tighter. Next to her stands a scowling Pilot cloaked in black—a Nikki Nicosia of Elysium Mons, to judge from its severe cut. Aurelius has one at home, hanging in his closet. It looks better on the Pilot.

"Yes!" Wu says. "If you consider suicide to be a method. Dr. Brekkelheim, please—"

"Narisian Karza?" Aurelius asks, sotto voce, as if fearing to interrupt.

"Yes," Miriam Wu says—another Miriam Wu, the one who approached Aurelius at Café

Empyrean. *Or closer in time to her,* Aurelius thinks, *than to the woman who wrestles a ghost before me.* She sits on a loveseat within the gloom; he can barely see her hand flutter like a dove as she beckons him to join her.

Aurelius crabwalks around the periphery of the room, his eyes fixed on Janos.

"—is over," Janos says just as another Pilot, a woman, shimmers into cryostylitic life beside him. Crysanthia Vog.

"Wait," she says.

"Freeze image," Miriam commands the air. The figures lock into motionlessness.

Those insect eyes—when he'd first seen a Pilot, decades ago, he'd marveled at them, at their eyes especially. Before estrangement, before death, back when they still spoke, he had told Bettina that those eyes would make their faces unreadable. How wrong he had been. The emotion twisted into Karza's face is unmistakable, he bares his teeth like a rabid mastiff. Far more subtle but no less real is the pensive re-curve of Vog's lips—in them, Aurelius reads sensuality and sorrow.

But it isn't just her mouth that speaks out to him. Her very stance, the graceful slouch, the arrangement of her limbs—there's a line out of Fitzgerald, a phrase: *a scarcely human orchid of a woman.* That's what he's looking at now. And he sees something in Janos now, too, in how he lists just slightly in her direction, as if pulled or tethered...

Son of a bitch. He had his loves and heartbreaks, and I never knew. His face, it's written—etched—into his face. His face...

"His face," Aurelius says. "What's wrong with his face?"

"Synthetic nerve fibroids. Black market cyborg interface—you didn't know the details?"

Quickly, as if it hurts him to do so, Aurelius shakes his head. "No," he whispers.

With concision and compassion, she explains. "That was the last time I spoke with him," she finally says. "Within two hours, he would be dead." She touches Aurelius on the back of his hand. He flinches. "I'm sorry," she says.

Wu dismisses the static images of Janos, the Pilots and her younger self.

"This is what killed your son, Professor."

There is no sound and yet he is deafened. The light is modulated, it cannot hurt his eyes, and yet he is blinded. The image fills the room, he feels it pressing against him, crowding him, though he knows it is not there.

"Fifteen years and we still know nothing about it—what caused it, where it came from, *what it is,*" Wu says. She does not raise her voice but there is a sharpness that wasn't there before, as if she speaks over a wind. "Less than nothing, I sometimes despair."

Patterns in the maelstrom, at the limits of perception, scattering under scrutiny into riots of bright chaos—he fears he'll go mad if he stares too long and yet he does not turn away.

"I've had a lot of time to think, even more to feel," Wu continues. "I now believe that Janos was fundamentally correct."

Aurelius wrests his eyes from it. Wu's face is ethereal and beautiful in the shifting blue and violet brilliance.

"There is *telos* in this thing, beyond our meager comprehension. It wants."

Silently, Aurelius replies: *Don't we all?*

"It's come back," Wu says. "Recrudesced, if you will—like a pox on the skin of the universe. Several hundreds of times in the last six months. Clustered in this area of the galaxy. Each time it winks into being just as abruptly as it winks out again—the longest manifestation has been less than a thousandth of a second."

Aurelius nods.

"Wherever it's been, it leaves a mark, an indelible distortion in the warp and woof of space-time, an imprint in the matter and energy it has touched." A pause. "It has pattern and purpose—just as your son believed, just as he insisted. Commonwealth Intelligence confirms this, Professor Mann. They are desperate and becoming frantic. They want to know what it *means*, whose *side* is it on."

"I don't understand—"

"No one does, them, least of all. They cannot make sense of it within the narrow rubric of their war. And so, as a measure of their desperation, they have turned to me—in my capacity as a scientist, I believe, and not as a Sapphic novitiate. I can't be sure." She brushes her electric silver hair from her face with fingers opalescent in the coruscating light. "As a measure of their incipient frenzy, they have authorized me to turn to you." She takes a deep and even breath. In the time it takes for her to inhale, Aurelius receives a vivid image: his son, pulled toward the beautiful Pilot standing next to him like a nail to a lodestone, like a redwood to the sun.

It wants, Wu had said.

"I don't understand, Doctor. What exactly do you think I can offer here?"

"Perspective," Wu says. Whatever else she may be holding back, Aurelius has no idea how to get it out of her.

He turns his face from her, back to the image of the whatever the hell it is. What did Janos see when he looked into it—something implacable? Ineluctable? Had he even tried? Or was it by then too late? Paper lanterns in the desert chill. Paper lanterns consumed in flames. It *wants*.

"Are you ready for the next stage of your journey, Professor?" Wu says. "I fear you will not find it as pleasant as this last."

23

Jigsaw Dilation

The problem was basic and, for decades, seemingly irrelevant—after all, Pilots were constructs, like the ships they plugged into. No one gave a thought to the necessities of child-birth—no one, that is, save Bettina Brekkelheim. The problem, for her, was indeed basic but it was in no way irrelevant. How *does* a comparatively slim-hipped woman give birth to a child whose cranium, even when adjusted for scale, dwarfs that of a common stock infant? That is, without being killed or crippled in the process. It was a puzzle.

If the problem was a puzzle then a puzzle was to be the solution. Bettina designed the pelvis of a female Pilot to come completely apart. The sections of pelvic bone never fused, held in place instead by a Byzantine web-work of muscular ligatures. When the time came, the birth canal would fall open as the bones defining it unhinged, like the jaws of an egg-eating snake. Jigsaw dilation, Bettina called it. She had planned to explain this particular anatomical feature as an adaptation to the rigors and stresses of a lifetime spent in space, should anyone ever ask. No one ever did.

The pain is transcendent. It is also brief. From the moment Crysanthia triggered the first contractions to the cutting of her newborn twins' umbilici, labor lasted all of twenty-six minutes.

Her cyborganelles did nothing so crude as deaden the pain. Instead, they re-worked it, wove and transmogrified it into something more intricate than pain and yet somehow pure—pain refined to its fifth essence and all her ego dross burned away. For a moment, in the transporting throes of agony, it had been as if the curtain of reality had rent in two and she glimpsed a truth that had eluded her since before she was born, since that day she first received her cyborganelles and started down the road of becoming all she is.

Only for a moment. By the time Dahlia had cleaned off the newborns and laid them upon Crysanthia's breast, it was gone. In the fog of mundane clarity rushing in to fill the void, she named her son Bardus Mir and her daughter Eridani Vog.

Today, the infants sleep in the care of the crèche. Crysanthia thinks of them and feels a sudden desolation. It takes her only a second to chase down the cause: she misses the sound of their voices, bombarding her with their sub-articulate questions from inside her belly. She'd forgotten what it was like, this sudden emptiness. She is lonely.

She walks along the shore of the Sea of Klytemnestra, skirting the muck and weeds of a tidal marsh. She spies a mating pod of rats—she counts fourteen in this one, the largest she's ever seen. The rats are still visible inside their translucent shell of mucous. Within a few hours, the surface will become brown and leathery, oozing with protective toxins, as the individual rats within dissolve, their cells becoming a protoplasmic soup in which their alien genes will roam and recombine freely. A few days after that, when the sea rises, the pod will burst open, releasing billions of embryonic rats—spores, really—into the open ocean. The few thousands that survive to maturity will eventually find their way into the rivers and start the cycle all over again.

Crysanthia moves stiffly within her recuperative garment of piezoplastic panels and carbon-flexor stays. Even with the support, it hurts to walk: the bony cartilage of her pelvis stills pulls together, her torn musculature heals; perhaps she should not be on her feet but immobility chafes worse than any lingering ache. Besides, her first-born son, Corvus Karzà, waits for her.

He stands silhouetted against the sea, encased in his own form-fitting medical garment, a full-body model much more elaborate and intensive than the girdle Crysanthia wears. Crysanthia's ship, un-flown since the beginning of her pregnancy, floats on the waves just beyond his shoulder. Till now, it had been warehoused in the atmospheric dockyards of Agamemnon. Corvus must have ordered it down on its autonomic circuits. The small, sleek hull is new, as is the drive system, but the AI, complete with its sidereal sensor net and symbiotic interface, is *Pariah's*, transplanted with no little difficulty at Crysanthia's insistence.

She spares another thought for *Pariah,* a passenger and cargo ship big as one of those huge adobe houses you find in the Martian desert and overflowing with luxury. Another world, another life. These new ships are nothing more than

weapons, their silver skins packed with destruction and barely enough room for a proper symbiosis chamber and a decent toilet. Does anyone love these ships? No one even bothers to name them.
The air is a humid forty-eight degrees centigrade, the sky a hazy greenish-gray. The rare summer sun pulls all manner of foulness from sea and strand. Crysanthia wills herself immune.

"Do you want to die?" Corvus asks. He faces the sea and does not turn his head to look at her. The ocean's thick brown froth clings to his black plastic boots. "It's not so strange when you think about it: the suicidal impulse *can* be explained as a rational response to a life such as..." He waves his arm in a gesture that encompasses everything. "*This.*"

Crysanthia is silent.

"Perhaps you wanted to kill *him.*" Try again, Crysanthia thinks. "Perhaps you want to kill us all." He turns now; Crysanthia is stunned to see the fury twisted into his face—she'd heard none of it in his measured voice. "And perhaps you now see yourself as far above anything so vulgar as an answer."

Softly, just loud enough so that he can hear her above the waves, Crysanthia says, "When you say something worth answering, I'll answer it."

His fury grows. But then—and Crysanthia is not surprised—Corvus shrugs. "Perhaps it's just as well you keep your mouth shut."

Nice try, Crysanthia thinks. When it becomes clear to him she will not say anything, Corvus continues, "Perhaps you intend to sell us to them: the Commonwealth, the common *stock.* It's not without precedent; you gave over Bettina and we see how that's turned out."

As if the other Pilots had nothing to do with that, Crysanthia thinks but remains mute.

"But in exchange for what?" Corvus says. "A Brancusi City address? Flattered by the slobbering attention of stinking, hairy strangers? You could be like Chrome—you may even want to look her up. You could become part of her act. I'm sure you could show her some alarming innovations, no? Who knows, maybe they'll let you keep your insides, bronzed and mounted on a plaque, or pickled in a jar—"

Now Crysanthia does respond. Faster than thought, she moves to strike his face but he, for all his injuries, is faster still. He plucks her open hand from mid-flight, his thumb pressed into her palm, his fingers coiled around hers—never until now had she suspected just how strong her son had become. She cannot help but be proud.

"Let me go," Crysanthia says, ashamed at the tremor of fear that creeps into her voice.

"If my father dies because of what you've done, there will be nothing anyone can do or say to save your life—not me, not Dahlia, no one." He pulls her closer and whispers into her face through clenched teeth, "If my father dies—"

Crysanthia, in what she notes is rapidly becoming a habit for her, laughs. "Oh, come *on*!" she says. "You know as well as I do that, whatever it is Narisian is doing, it is not *dying*. Now be a good little soldier and let go of Mommy's hand."

Corvus tightens his grip. For a moment, he glares at Crysanthia, his chest expanding with enraged breath. Crysanthia wonders what she'll do if he doesn't release her—begging is out of the question, fighting as absurd as it is repugnant. Besides, it's very likely she would lose. But then his fingers relax and he lets her hand slide from his.

"Your sister tells me you have a plan," she says. "That's the reason I'm here—that's the *only* reason I'm here. I don't need *you* to tell me my life. I've lived it—I *am* living it. Right now."

"Yes," Corvus says. "And we are living it as well, right alongside you."

How much easier this would be if Corvus were simply his father's son but he is not. True, he looks at her through Narisian's deep maroon eyes, but she sees herself in his cheekbones, in his lips, in the way he moves. And, regardless of its reedy masculine timbre, he speaks to her with her own voice.

And all he has known, from the moment of his birth: a brief lifetime of war, and now a woman pinned to a wall with her ripped-out children spilled upon the floor in a coil of her guts. Ivarra Syn—Crysanthia wonders if he loved her, hates that she does not know.

"You no longer have the luxuries and privileges that come with being an outcast," he says.

"You think I need to prove my loyalty? To them? Or to you?"

"To *yourself*, Mother."

Crysanthia is silent, this time out of shame rather than spite. But what has she to be ashamed of? Her mind threatens to spiral out into an endless cycle of self-recrimination and justification. She does not have the time for that—she's never had the time for that. She looks at her ship, then up to the sky, where Agamemnon is a long, narrow tan crescent at the horizon with the small gray crescent of Elektra faintly visible just above it. Iota Horologii burns bright overhead. No place to run. There never has been, there never will be.

She nods. "Tell me how."

24

Earthman

There is no room to spare on an S.C. troop transport, nothing resembling an amenity. Aurelius Mann and Miriam Wu travel the way the soldiers travel, with antifreeze thickened blood creeping through their veins and their body temperatures hovering at just above minus eight degrees centigrade. Thus there is no window for Aurelius to gaze out of, no hologram to gaze into. A voyage of a week, to the command cruiser *Virgin Sorrow*, passes like an afternoon nap.

You won't dream in this state, they had told him back at Heaven 41, but you will remember. More than remember, *re-live*, but always with an awareness that you are in cold-pac skittering around the periphery. Like an old lover's face, Aurelius added silently, that you cannot quite recall.

But he *can* recall her face. She's right there, beautiful and placid. Her eyes are closed and her forearm thrown across her forehead, fingers curled in an open fist. And he is looking at her from between her thighs; he kisses and explores her with the same tongue and mouth that had recited, to a packed auditorium five hundred floors below them scant hours before, the best poems from his latest collection, *Earthman.*

He is thirty-eight. She is fifty. He is in love. She is not. He is a fool. She is a scientist.

His left hand caresses her belly, the juncture of thigh and pelvis, her buttocks, the shallow groove between. His right hand supports her lower back. He's been at this for some minutes now—he aches, in his wrist, his jaw. She moans, softly, for the first time.

He feels cold, somehow, though his brow drips with sweat from her heat and the mid-August night beyond the hotel's open window. And he feels old, removed, as though the moment that unfolds—the humid, salty, tangy and aromatic intimacy under his nose and beneath his lips—is already long gone.

She moans again—loud, louder and louder still. Aurelius gazes up at her face, her parted lips, her wild, ash-blond hair...

And then he is very cold. Cold to his core and she is gone. Dead.

"Professor Mann?" an unfamiliar voice calls to him, a woman. "Professor Mann, can you hear me?"

"Uhhh," he says. "Ag, uh, uh-huh." The air feels like lead. His words—such as they are—flow like tar.

"Good. No, no, don't open your eyes. Not yet."

A pause, then another voice, a man this time: "Do you know where you are?"

He tries to shake his head but the muscles in his neck are unresponsive mush. Instead, his rubber lips open and his sluggish tongue stirs. "Stuh-stah, shurmm," he hears himself say. Could be important, he thinks, better listen. "Starship."

"Very good." The first voice. "Put him under. Catalyze and drain him."

When he wakes again, it is to bare steel walls and nasty bright light.

Fuck, he thinks, the ancient curse as natural as the devil's hangover pounding in his skull—that is to say, not natural at all.

The door slides open with a quiet susurrus that slices through his head, right behind his eyes. A petite brunette stands in the doorway. She wears a conservative suit that looks like a military uniform but isn't. The cut disguises her curves while accentuating them—no mean feat; Aurelius is impressed. She carries a small bundle.

"Dim the lights by thirty percent," she says into a silver pin on her shirt collar. Glare becomes glow. He recognizes her voice from when they woke him. "Better?" she asks him now.

"Much," Aurelius croaks. "Thanks."

"First time in cold-pac?"

Aurelius nods.

"It gets easier the more you do it, but it never becomes pleasant." She comes into the room, sits down on the edge of his bed. "Angela Caro, Solar Commonwealth Security Forces." She smiles and offers her hand. "I'm the Special Liaison to Dr. Wu's team."

Aurelius lifts his head and looks down the length of his body. He's relieved see he is clothed in colorless and shapeless pajamas. He looks over the hump of his belly to his toes, so far away, gnarled and naked at the other end of the bed. He swings his legs off the side of the bed and sits up. He takes her hand—its softness and warmth triggers the faintest echo of a thing in him he belatedly identifies as desire. "Aurelius Mann," he says.

"I *know* who you are, Professor Mann," Caro says and her smile widens. Aurelius is amazed by the transformation—businesslike to radiant in the blink of an eye. "I'm something of a fan."

Really? Aurelius thinks. Then something clicks into place. "Angela Caro?" he says. "You killed Bettina, didn't you?" His voice is wrong, cold and lifeless, as if he recites from an infra-aural stereo bead instruction manual. Then he realizes it is not just his voice. Flattening of emotional affect is a common, temporary side effect of cold-pac. It is written right there in the waiver, the memory vivid in his head for an instant. And he reads that eidetic recall is also a possible aftershock. "Didn't you?"

Another transformation, not so stunning this time. Caro draws herself back. Her smile tightens and hardens. "I arrested Dr. Brekkelheim. She died as the result of an accident, unforeseen and unavoidable."

"Convenient accident, though--no? Quite lucky for you and the Commonwealth—"

"That is truly offensive, Professor Mann. Perhaps you should consider your words more carefully. A man of your sophistication—"

"After all, she was—"

"*A man of your sophistication should know better than to spew baseless and hateful innuendo.* No one's death is ever *convenient.* And might I remind you, over six thousand people died in that explosion. And what it's done to the Martian economy, the losses are estimated in hundreds of billions of solaria and it's not over yet, it could very well go into the trillions." Caro breathes in deep. "I know you and she were... close, once."

"Long time ago," Aurelius says. "Am I to go barefoot? Heated floor?"

She hands him the bundle. Aurelius unrolls the wrapping and finds a pair of rubber soled canvas slippers, the same washed-out non-color as his pajamas. He nods a curt acknowledgement and, grunting against his stiff joints and sore muscles, puts them on. "I'm hungry," he announces.

"Of course," she says. She stands. "I'll show you to the officer's lounge." A pause. "If you'd like."

Aurelius nods. He lets her guide him out of the little room and down the featureless, gunmetal corridors.

"Tell me..." he finally says. "Tell me about *them*, about the Pilots. Vog and Karza. You knew them, too, right?"

Caro's answer is slow in coming. "My impression of *him* was not—not so much that he lacked imagination but that he was afraid of it. He was a very unpleasant man to be around," she says pointedly. "He seemed to view the entire universe with disdain, contempt." She sighs. "I barely got to know her at all. I think... I think I would have liked her."

A thought, a flash, two images bleed into each other: a tiger's claw tearing into a blue thigh, Bettina's selfish face and open hand. He counts out eight more steps. "I see." Aurelius waits until five steps have passed—he counts them, too. "And now you prosecute a war of extermination against her. All of them, an entire race—an entire species."

Three more steps. "Just how inconvenient is genocide? Do you measure the cost in solaria or something less tangible?"

Caro sighs. "Professor Mann, do you know what the life expectancy of a Pilot is?"

"No."

"Precisely. No one does. Computer modeling shows their capacity for cellular regeneration to be inexhaustible. That's every cell, every system. They are practically immortal—the only way to kill a Pilot is to *kill* a Pilot. They are unnatural beings—*super*natural beings."

"And thus must be destroyed. I see."

"No you *don't*, sir, and you can be as smug and as glib as you like, it does nothing to change the fact that you are blind." She falls silent for the next couple of steps, then says, "You are an expert in twenty-first century literature. How much of that expertise transfers over to twenty-first century history?"

"What do you have in mind?"

"November 5, 2049. Seven twenty-two to nine oh six a.m., Greenwich Mean Time."

The Ninety Minute War, Aurelius thinks. Of course she'd bring that up. Human engineered bio-weapons wiped out two-thirds of the population of Europe and the Indian sub-continent. Central and Eastern Europe were instantly rendered uninhabitable, as were Pakistan and Nepal. Within days, the devastation had spread as far as Mongolia, New Zealand and California. Three decades passed before the affected areas began to recover. Entirely new technologies had to be invented from the ground up, first to contain the contagions, then to eradicate them.

"Those weapons were all initially developed as beneficial agents," Caro says—uncanny how she anticipates the path of his thoughts. "Gene therapy vectors, aggressive vaccines—it didn't require much effort for the belligerents in that war to turn them into plagues."

"Are you seriously comparing a race of thinking, feeling beings to a bunch of microbes we unleashed upon ourselves a hundred years before they were conceived?"

Caro stops walking—Aurelius stops, too. "They may be charming, Professor. They may be beautiful, perhaps even sublime. Perhaps they are an improvement over us in every way that Dr. Brekkelheim could quantify. I'll concede all of that. But so what?" Around them, the ship hums and thrums. Caro licks her lips, an uneasy little gesture with a pink and pointed tongue tip. It reminds Aurelius that she is human. "And make no mistake, for all of that, they *are* those microbes. They are viral carcinoma 316, they are Kuurosin's blood burn. They are a revolver pressed to skull of our species. You say we unleashed those bio-weapons on ourselves; your Dr. Brekkelheim unleashed the Pilots on us."

His mind balks at that. At devoutly as Aurelius may have wished it, Bettina was never *his* Dr. Brekkelheim in any way that mattered.

"She loaded the chamber and pulled the trigger," Caro continues. "It is my job—my *duty*—not to let the hammer fall." She passes her hand over a panel in the bulkhead and a door slides open. Aurelius had no idea it was there.

"Well spoken," Aurelius says. "Perhaps you should have been a poet." He follows her through the door into the officer's lounge. "But I can say with some authority that poetry is not justification."

"*Some* authority?" She shrugs. "But I think you misunderstand." Over her shoulder, Aurelius can see a holographic screen that takes up the whole of the far bulkhead. Outside the ship, tiny fighters zip from point to point and hang motionless before zipping off again, like minnows round a whale. "I don't need to justify anything," Caro says. 'Justification is irrelevant, or can't you see that? Survival will judge, justice be damned and devil take the hindmost. Who can say, Professor Mann? We may well be outclassed and destined for evolution's rubbish heap, like the trilobite and the chimpanzee. If that is the case, so be it." She smiles warmly. "You don't expect us to give it up without a fight, do you?"

"Them or us? In all the vastness of space, is that how you see it?" He shakes his head. "Is that the way I should see it?"

Caro shrugs. "Up to you. I love your work, either way."

"Indeed. And thank you." Aurelius sits at a table with its own wafer slate terminal. He cocks his head and stares up at Caro, standing alongside. "Do you love *your* work?"

Caro's smile disappears. Aurelius can see the vein in her throat jump—seven beats of her hardened heart. He wonders if this new obsession with counting isn't another side effect of being frozen and thawed. No obliging image of the waiver coalesces in his mind. He'll have to remember ask about it later.

Caro sits down in the chair opposite him. "It is my duty," she says. "It is required." Silence. "I do it." Then, smiling again and falsely bright: "Now, what would you like to eat?"

25

Bullet

This is what Crysanthia has: a two centimeter sphere of dark-charged quicksilver, unfolded until it has a virtual rest mass a thousand times greater than an equivalent volume of neutronium. At the correct moment, when the planets are in alignment, she will fire it off toward Vulcan at .337c. Its velocity at impact: .932c. Midway through the moon, just as it reaches the solid nickel-iron core, it will detonate, imparting all of its energy to the surrounding rock. Vulcan will shatter and fall into the world beneath it. A rain of rock, shards smaller than sand, chunks larger than continents, all of it dirty with nearly every exotic particle in the bestiary—what sheer kinetic impact will not accomplish, radiation will: Vulcan no more and Venus a hell once again, a hell even greater than the hell from which its heaven was forged, if such a thing were possible.

It will take eleven days for the bullet, launched on a parabolic course and slinging by Jupiter for a gravity whip assist, to reach its target. Even if the Commonwealth detects it—and the odds against it are astronomical—there is nothing they can do to stop it. No force in the universe will be able to stop it. Once it is launched, the Venusian system is dead, it is just a matter of when the Commonwealth realizes it.

Vulcan is the perfect target. Because it is man-made, it will shatter where Luna would fracture. More importantly, its destruction will cripple the Solar Commonwealth's war effort. They have no other facilities for producing dark matter or dark matter reactors—without them, the Jovian shipyards may as well be manufacturing lead ingots. And the Commonwealth will almost certainly pull its existing fleet back to the Inner Worlds in a defensive reflex. And it will mean nothing. The Pilots will have plenty of time to ready thousands more of these bullets and reduce the whole of the Solar Commonwealth to radioactive rubble—at least, that's what they'll allow the Commonwealth to believe. In truth, it took years to develop this one and it will probably take years to develop another. Dark charging salt, with its rigid crystal grid, is one thing, dark charging mercury is something else entirely.

And Venus? Venus is just a very spectacular collateral target. No chance to evacuate—nothing resembling a warning. The psychological damage to the common stock humans, the lethal blow to their apathetic morale as nine hundred million die with the metaphorical pushing of a button...

No. Firing the bullet will not require nearly so much effort—a twitch, a velleity, more than enough to send it on its way. But for now, for these interminable seconds, as she waits hidden in the Kuiper Belt, with her ship hovering between the walls of a deep crevasse in the mantle of an icy little planetoid, Crysanthia has absolutely nothing to do. So she daydreams.

Crysanthia had never been wealthy during her years imprisoned in the Solar Commonwealth. She lived off the investment portfolio assigned her at the beginning of her career and the modest pension from the Consortium which Narisian had tried and failed—repeatedly—to revoke. But, as one of very few Pilots who spent any appreciable amount of time system-bound, she was famous and her fame brought her into contact with people who were very wealthy indeed. She had no solid code when it came to just how much of their generosity she would permit herself to enjoy, or just how far she would go in order to guarantee that their generosity would continue to be there for her enjoyment—there was no shortage of men and women who sought her out as an exotic companion, a bauble to show off at parties and in smaller, more intimate venues. There were times when, if she had a clearly demarcated line, she would have found herself far on the other side of it. Those times were rare enough, however, that the sobriquet "Vog the Whore" was never an accurate description of her vocation—avocation, maybe, depending upon how bored she was or whether she had blown the rent on nights of gin, roulette and lethedrine dust. In truth, it wasn't always just the rent—it had afforded her a new outfit or two, the occasional pair of shoes. Her life had meant very little to her in those days and so she'd made the most of it.

But that was rare—a half dozen times; at most, it averaged out to about once a year. Far more often, it was just a matter of going along for the ride, with nothing more required or expected (but always much more hoped) but that she *be.* Thus she'd skated the surface of Europa and then gone thermo-diving in the sea below it. She'd taken the controls of a two person bathyscaph and navigated the Marianas Trench while the spoiled daughter of the Commonwealth Minister of Planetary Development was sprawled in the seat beside her, passed out from too much expensive champagne and too many cheap narcotics. She'd scaled Olympus, far above the limits of the artificial Martian atmosphere, and then flown back down in a mirror-shiny wind-rider's suit. She'd toured the ruins of Machu Picchu, Angkor Wat and New Orleans. She'd come in ninth (among a field of over a thousand) in the 2159 Solar Regatta, flying a sail-pod paid for by a married quintet who'd made their fortune by starring in and then producing pornographic sleepies—she would have come in first had a flurry of micro-meteorites left over from the passing of an un-charted comet not perforated her sail.

In short, though she had an apartment in Brancusi City, she spent comparatively little of her time on Venus. Still, she knows the best places to go for margaritas and martinis, for soba noodles and sashimi so fresh it still gasps for breath; she knows the best dance clubs, the best everything. And now, to prove her loyalty to a people who, it seems, will never stop despising her, she's poised billions of kilometers above it, ready to burn it all away.

Corvus called it penance. But penance for what? She'd never answered her son, but smashing the rock into Narisian's womb tank—it was hardly the heat of the moment, she'd gone about it with all due deliberation and gravity. That she hates him is a given, a constant—it had never changed, not for a moment, not as they rutted like swine in

Pariah's symbiosis chamber, not as she gave birth and then suck and then so much more to his children—and he hates her; that, too, is a constant. But she was not trying to kill him, of that she is certain. No, her motive was even more basic: she was not going to let him sleep through this, not for one moment longer. If she can't escape it, he doesn't get to, either.

More than that, she knows Narisian Karza is the best hope they have of surviving this. No one else can step into that breach. Not Corvus, he's too young, too impulsive. And Dahlia—would it even be Dahlia or would it be that Bettina thing lurking in her psyche? There's no way Crysanthia will trust their lives to her. And as for herself, even if she wanted the job—and she resolutely did not—who would tolerate her in it? Really, it was that simple.

Wasn't it?

A little apocalypse comes to her then, the memory of the fragment of Narisian's shell in her hands, the unmistakable stigmata branded into its molecular structure. That revelation threatens to tip her over into memories too painful for her to luxuriate in right now. It sinks back into the primordial soup of her mind but not before it hurls an accusation at her feet: *Were you really so stupid, so sentimental—so superstitious—to risk everything for the answer to a question you cannot even phrase? Just what did you expect Narisian to tell you, anyway? Here's all you need to know: Janos is dead. Just like Bettina, you had your chance to save him—though it meant your ruin and his eternal contempt—and you didn't. You will never see him again.*

And Narisian has the last laugh anyway because he still refuses to wake up, the bastard. And here they are, the lot of them, rudderless as before.

Traitor, they call her now, and murderer, though he is far from dead—funny how they never run out of things to call her.

Maybe she should be just that, *do* just that: set a course for Earth, screaming her surrender on all channels, give them the bullet, give them her secrets. Because, just to the north of Brancusi City, there is a ridge of gently sloping mountains, covered with heather and scrub pines until the vegetation gives way to the lichens and bare rock and snow of the peaks. From them, one can see the whole of the city and a sliver of the bay and ocean beyond. Occasionally, a goat will wander by, or a puma. In the valleys between them, all kinds of wildflower grow. Right now, Crysanthia wants nothing more than to hike those mountains once more, drink from their streams, sleep beneath their stars. Let the Commonwealth take her womb, burn out her astrogational supra-lobes, she'll live out her days as a freak, a curiosity, living sculpture, an *objet d'art*—

And she remembers that day she lost her arm on Oerestes, the muzzle flash, and she just quick enough to turn away so that the blast catches her shoulder and not her ribcage; the greenstick splintering of her bones and the blistered burns along the left side of her face, her neck, her chest; half a hand and an exposed wrist bone lying on the floor, all that remains of her arm that hasn't been reduced to shreds and vapor; the ache in her legs as her knees buckle and fold; then blackness as the shock and the blood loss take her down into a deep sleep; then waking, some time later, within the amniotic water of the crèche.

She never did find out how she made it back to her ship.

And she remembers Bardus and Eridani. And Dahlia. And Corvus. She remembers Ivarra Syn. She remembers Galatea Trope.

Crysanthia arms the launcher.

"Vog." The voice in her skull—unmistakable.

"Narisian?" she says. "Go ahead, Narisian. I—"

"—discharge your payload into interstellar space," Narisian says, cutting her off. Rather, Crysanthia realizes, it is a recording, relayed to her by another Pilot acting as courier in a ship a few hundred kilometers away. No doubt, Narisian himself is still on Klytemnestra. "You are to rendezvous with Nivalia Edo's battle group at the following coordinates instead."

Crysanthia—with a swelling of relief she instantly despises—complies.

26

Heart of Glass, Gates of Steel

I sit at a table next to The Roman Image Coffee Shop's huge plate glass window and sip a cup of the house blend. Outside, late September sunlight glints off the glass skyscrapers in blinding flashes and shines through the yellow, fan shaped leaves of the ginkgo trees. From behind the counter, in the dim depths of the shop, an Emerson clock radio plays new wave rock: Blondie, "Heart of Glass." I catch myself singing along and the porcelain skinned counter girl, sloe-eyed gaze framed under the straight and glossy bangs of an electric blue wig, smiles at me in youthful solidarity.

Embarrassed, I return the smile and tell myself that I really must stop doing that. I drink my coffee and wait, staring out the window at the park across the street and the cityscape beyond. My eyes wander the skyline and alight on a strangely gothic tower and the daytime moon that sits just over its shoulder. The moon's arid seas are the same pale blue as the surrounding sky; it looks as if the moon dissipates into nothing, like smoke, or comes into being, like water vapor cooling into steam.

A thought comes to me, from nowhere, from my dreams: to *be* that color, that blue, the exact shade of perpetual *becoming*. To be a piece of heaven itself...

The song on the radio ends and another begins, one I do not know. A drumbeat at once frantic and precise, overlaid with a synthesizer that gives way to heavy guitars. Then, an urgent, high-pitched voice bleats, with a robot's enunciation: "Twist away the gates of steel! Unlock the secret voice!"

I hurry down the last of my coffee and head back to the counter. I hand the girl my mug and a dime to pay for a refill.

"Who's that?" I ask the back of her head as she pours from a full pot. "On the radio."

She turns back to me and places the mug down on the battered Formica. Her smooth brow gathers above her eyebrows. "A band called Devo?" The childlike inflection that turns her statement into a question, the way she wrinkles the bridge of her nose—really, it's almost too much. I find myself wishing I'd had a daughter and that she turned out just like this little counter girl, silly wig and all. "Want me to turn it off?"

"No," I say. "It's fine."

"Good, a lot of people don't like them but I think they're kind of neat."

I smile at her choice of words and spy a glossy architectural magazine resting face down next to the radio. A petty inspiration prompts me to make the most of this petty opportunity: "Say, maybe you could tell me about that building over there." I sweep my arm window-ward. "The sand-colored one, with the terra cotta roof tiles and the domed chimney."

Before I've finished speaking, the girl starts nodding and says: "That's the Blake. It used to be a hotel, now it's an apartment building. If you get up close to it you'll see that it has these glazed tiles set in the façade that reproduce woodcuts from *The Marriage of Heaven and Hell.*"

"That's wonderful!" I exclaim. Before I can say anything else, I feel a hand glom onto my left buttock—fingers grip the flesh with almost bruising vigor. I'm shocked only for the barest sliver of an instant.

"Hello, Aaron," I say as he takes his hand from my ass and hugs me from behind, rubbing his bristly cheek against mine.

"How'd you know I wasn't some garden variety pervert?"

"I said, 'Hello, *Aaron*,' didn't I? And if you grab my tits I swear I'll break your fingers *and* your wrists."

The girl behind the counter regards us with evident displeasure. "I'm damn close to breaking them right now," she says.

"No, It's all right, really," I say. "He's an—"

"Relax, babe," Aaron says as he lets go of me and leans across the counter to kiss her pretty moue of distaste. He has to go up beyond the tips of his toes, his body supported against the counter by his wiry arms. "This is Jane," Aaron says. "I told you all about her, remember?"

Through sulky lips, the girl says, "Yes."

"Good. When you finished here, baby doll?"

Now she is smiling and blushing—for the life of me, I've never understood the effect Aaron has on these children. "Miguel and Sara get here in about an hour, ninety minutes. They're almost always on time, unlike *some* people."

Aaron throws up his hands in surrender and then nods at the mug of coffee steaming in front of me. “Why don’t you put that in a cardboard cup? We’ll wait for you across the street in the park.”

The girl’s full name is Amanda Moreau, Aaron tells me, but her friends call her Mandy. She’s a student at the same tiny art college where Aaron is currently writer in residence. I ask Aaron if she was in one of his classes and he looks down at his shoes.

“Not exactly,” he says. “Her boyfriend was.”

God help me, I actually choke on my coffee. Once I’ve regained my breath, I laugh and say, “My God, that must have been a scandal.”

“No, not really. I gave the kid an A, which he more or less deserved, and he sulked a little and that was about the end of it—except for the one drunken phone call in the middle of the night. I can’t begrudge him that, everybody is allowed one of those. After it had gone on long enough, I took the receiver from Mandy and told him to go fuck himself.”

“Aaron!”

“It was for his own damn good. Mandy tells me he was probably relieved anyway, she swears he‘s secretly queer.”

“You must have read his stories, do you think it’s true?”

“Could be—the fuck do I know?”

“Huh,” I say. I touch the waxed rim of the cup to my teeth and sip. “She gets done at noon? That’s a strange shift.”

"She's in at six, opens the place up at six thirty, catches the morning rush, doesn't get a break—she's a hard worker, six days a week she does that, three of those days she's in class from four until nine." He looks at me with a belligerent smile. "Do you approve?"

"Oh, of *her*, of course. Of her choice of men..."

"Right," Aaron says, dragging it out. "Didn't see that coming."

Aaron and I sit side by side on a park bench in a little park called Mendencourte Square. The sun is bright and warm but the leaves of the trees and the shrubs, in various stages of shifting their color from hues of green to shades of flame, rustle in the cool and subtle breezes that bring a stippling of goose flesh to the exposed flesh of my arms. On the grass, a smattering of stubborn sunbathers lies out on blankets and towels, some dressed in cut-off dungarees and tube-tops, others in skimpy, two-piece bathing suits. Aaron surveys them as he packs a briar pipe with tobacco from a little leather pouch and lights it with a wooden match shielded from the wind by his cupped left hand. Fragrant smoke billows from his nose and the corners of his mouth. The studied and rakish way he manages the affectation betrays a boy's vulnerability, the child he once was clomping around in the shoes of the man he now is and not quite filling them. I feel an absurd urge to hold him, protect him.

Thankfully, the moment passes but not before young Mandy Moreau's obvious devotion to him comes into focus. I get it now: he needs a mother, even one who's half his age. And, with his sharp features, his argon laser eyes, black hair and pale skin, he *is* a handsome little fucker.

"My little Jew dragon," I say and pat his blue-shadowed cheek. "You need a shave."

"Up late last night, working on a story," he replies. "Hey, speaking of *Jew*, what happened with you and that priest from a few years ago? Don't pretend you don't who I mean."

I look away from his piercing blue gaze for a moment. I want to stall him and he's given me the perfect excuse: "How the hell do you go from 'Jew' to Philip Ashwood?"

"Don't know, really." He ponders for a moment. "He works for that yid Jesus, right? Good enough."

"Hmm."

"So what's going on with you and him?"

I force a laugh. "Christ, Aaron, you sound like an old fishwife." Again, I look away and add, "It really isn't any of your business." Immediately, I hate myself for saying it.

"Jane, don't be a twat. This is me you're talking to."

"All right. Nothing. Nothing's going on. It just kind of... evaporated."

"That's not what he told me."

For a second, I don't know what to say. Only for a second. "What do you mean, that's not what he told you? I thought you couldn't stand him?"

"What the hell ever gave you that idea?"

Before I can answer with a catalogue of his offhand insults, judiciously sprinkled into our conversations over the last two years, from "that swishy preacher" to "the Bible-thumper who was trying to get into your panties," Aaron says, "I ran into him in L.A.—he was there to talk to one of Walker's more disillusioned disciples. Turns out she's married to the lead singer from The Traumatics, if you can imagine."

"I'd heard," I say. Phil had told me.

"He told me what he was doing, even showed me some of his book. He told me was hoping for a university press but I figured, what the hell? I put him in touch with my agent. Lynn liked what she saw."

"Why did he go to you?" I sputter, surprised at how jealous I feel. "He could have come to me. I would have—"

"He didn't come to *me,"* Aaron says, shaking his head. "We were just talking. For fuck's sake, Jane, use your head. He didn't want you to think he was using you."

"So did Lynn take him on?"

"Of course not," Aaron says. "She's too busy and it's not her bag. But she gave him to some kid in the agency who handles non-fiction." He pauses. "He told me he asked you to marry him, do I have that right?"

"You know something?" I say. "You're pretty much obnoxious one hundred percent of the time. But when you're coy you are truly repugnant."

I can see that I've hurt him—not offended, *hurt.* I want to say I'm sorry but I can't bring myself to do it. I look down at the empty bench between us and notice that someone has carved something into the wooden slat at the edge of the seat. My skirt and thigh obscures half of it so I rearrange myself until I can read it: "Once every lifetime we're swallowed by the whale."

No kidding.

I sigh. "Yes, he asked me to marry him. And yes, I said no."

"Why?" he asks softly.

The question terrifies me because I don't really know the answer, nor do I wish to. I recover quickly enough and flip it back at him. "What do you mean, 'Why?' I've *been* married. More than once. It doesn't seem to agree with me." It's a good argument, an airtight lie; I almost believe it myself.

"You've never been married to him," Aaron says. After a pause, he adds, "I know it's strange, coming from me, but I saw you two together that night—"

"One time, Aaron. You saw us together one time."

"Once was enough. And I could tell by the way he talked about you... I just hate to see you make a mistake, that's all."

A butterfly alights amid the leaves of a late-flowering bush. As I watch it slowly beat its blue wings, crossed and re-crossed by bold black lines like a miniature in stained glass, I get a weird *frisson*, all the more terrible for not being weird enough. It's been over a year. I had hoped I was finished with them—rather, I hoped *they* were finished with *me*. But no, I feel the world begin to pull away from its moorings. I close my eyes and screw it all back down. Hard.

I open my eyes. The butterfly is gone.

"I dreamt I was a butterfly and now that I'm awake, I wonder: Am I a man who dreamed he was a butterfly or a butterfly now dreaming he is a man," I whisper.

After a moment, Aaron says, "That's from something, I know it..."

"It's Taoist. Not Lau Tzu, one of the other ones, I don't... remember who."

Aaron nods and puffs on his pipe. Together, we look out across the park. A tiny figure in an electric blue wig makes its way toward us across the green.

"Here comes Mandy," Aaron says. "Let's go. We're taking you to lunch."

27

Shedding Ghosts

Starships inhabit a state of grace, aleatoric and strange, within the onion fold, blurred as if the thumb of God has smeared them across a vast array of ramified realities, the quantum hyperstatic spectrum. Thus each combatant is a set of *probable* combatants, astronomical in number yet ultimately finite. And thus the weapons they use—exo-spatial tunneling mines, tachyon rams, spatio-temporal constrictor beams—all have a dissociated quality about them, as if they are not entirely real. Here in the fold, they work by snuffing out probabilities. Destroy enough probability, erase enough of that divine smudge, and the entire nexus collapses. You've made a kill.

By the time Crysanthia arrives, the battle has already begun. She dives into a swarm of Shrikes with a dreamer's sense of amorphous precision and languid urgency. She feels herself die a trillion times a second.

It is a trickle of awareness, not wholly unpleasant, on the back of her neck. Every near miss shears off a little more of her protean blur. The official term for this is stochastic decay. Pilots have their own name for it, they call it shedding ghosts. Crysanthia flies straight into a helical formation of five Shrikes moving in concert two-hundred thousand kilometers apart from each other. She waits until they attack, then deflects their own space-time constrictors back at them. They crumple in her wake, like tin cans at the bottom of an ocean, collapsed across probability's threshold into death. Crysanthia loses countless selves from realities in which she was a femto-second or two too slow to react. Her supra-determinate nexus, smeared in quantum flux over a battle zone some sixty AUs in diameter, becomes sickeningly tenuous for several long fractions of an instant. Crysanthia reminds herselves to be careful, she is literally running out of luck.

The Imperator class star cruiser *Virgin Sorrow* sits at the center of it all, twelve hundred meters of dumb mass lolling in the Newtonian shallows of normal space. Even so, its idle but massive drive system continues to deform the space-time around it. Waves of its residual distortion radiate into the fold. It is a nuisance, noisy murk that makes it hard to focus.

The entire battle lasts of all of nine seconds.

Crysanthia scans the area. Out of the seventy-two ships in Edo's attack group, thirteen remain—fourteen, including Crysanthia's. She would have expected worse. A single survivor could complete the mission, should it come to that. There are no Shrikes left. Space is dirty with mists of charged particles and canceled lives.

Crysanthia is about to open a channel to Edo when intuition tells her to look again at the gargantuan starship's turbulence.

Ninety Paladin class attack ships, bigger and stronger than the Shrikes, stream out of nowhere. Hiding, Crysanthia realizes, in the space-time bending waste energy from the cruiser's idle drive. There was no way to detect them.

In spite of herself, Crysanthia is impressed. *That's new,* she thinks. *They've never done that before. Clever.*

Within an instant, the Paladins have them surrounded and outnumbered. Maybe, before the battle had whittled away at their hyperstatic lives, before they were ragged with fatigue, they would have had a chance. Six to one odds—steep but not impossible. Now, though, there is little to do except wait for destruction.

Crysanthia acts on an impulse deeper than instinct, closer than her heart yet alien. It touches her mind, at once elusive and familiar—she could know it, if only she had time. It touches her and teaches her. All of her selves, alive and dead, rush together into a clot of infinite imminence, being and nothingness fused. And then she... and then she...

And then she is a child (but I was never a child) *standing up to her sun browned ankles in clear, ocean water—a tide pool, warm as blood. Coarse, tan sands, glittering with bits of mica and quartz, shine up through the wavelets. Little fishes dart and cast faint shadows. Summer's early winds blow her hair* (but I have no hair) *around her face and raise goose bumps on her arms* (not one single vestigial follicle) *while toy boats, shiny and infinitesimal, bob around her feet. She does not hurry. She has all the time in the world. She squats down until her bottom, clad in a yellow swimsuit, skims the water. She looks down, her hair falling in a dark curtain between her pudgy knees and, with a cupped hand, she scoops up the boats and throws them into the air. She watches with childish solemnity as, with pops she barely hears over the sounds of the surf, they flare into pale yellow brilliance and become ash so fine that is carried away on the weakest breeze. Then she laughs and claps her hands. happy as only a child can be, a child who has saved creation.*

Someone watches her—up in the dunes, near the blown-down fence. She can feel his eyes on her.

The ash disappears into a sky the precise shade of eternal becoming—to be that color (but I am that color), *to be a piece of heaven itself...*

Her ship erupts from the fold and into normal space. Crysanthia comes back into herself—it's as if she falls from an infinite height. She pulls what shards of herself she has left into something like a whole and shakes off her daze. Through the eyes of her ship, she looks all around her.

There is no trace of the Paladins. No radiation, no debris, no sub-quantum noise—it's as if they never were.

She smells coffee.

The other thirteen Pilots emerge into normal space alongside her.

"What did you do?" Edo demands. "How did you—"

"No time to explain," Crysanthia says. Not that I could, she silently adds, even if we had all the time from now until the stars go cold.

But she can wonder about it later. "What are your orders?" Crysanthia asks, all duty and deference.

"The ship is defenseless," Edo says, after an infinitesimal pause. "We proceed as planned."

28

A Miracle of Science

In a narrow room of *Virgin Sorrow* filled past the claustrophobic with unfamiliar people, Aurelius Mann learns more than he ever cared to know about the kingdoms of the dead. The man speaking is named Judah Claypoole and he is a specialist from the Charybdis Corporation. A matte black box, roughly twice as tall as it is wide, sits on a table set up next to the podium.

"To be frank, there is absolutely no direct profit in it," he says. "When we began to develop the technology, we really didn't give much thought to the subjects who might benefit, if benefit is the word I'm looking for."

Claypoole, tall and cadaverous, is the head of the delegation from Charybdis—fully a third of the people crowding the room are his underlings and they all have the look of the drone about them. The pattern holds for the people from Stigol-Bergham: one person of obvious authority and importance (Jazcek Tzurma, a man in his sixties or seventies whose face is brutally dominated by an aquiline nose that looks as if it had been broken years ago) attended by interchangeable functionaries. The rest of the chairs are taken by Miriam Wu and her colleagues—an umbrella term which Aurelius supposes covers him as well.

Angela Caro was present when the meeting had begun—she had excused herself a few minutes into it. Her chair sits empty to the immediate left of the doors. Aurelius had been happy to see her go.

("She told you *what?*" Miriam had said to him, twenty minutes before the meeting was to begin, as they compared notes on cold-pac hangovers. "A fan? I'm sorry Aurelius, but I spoke to Caro not one week before I approached you. She'd never heard of you. I had to explain at length just who you were and why I wanted you to be here."

"You explained it to Caro?" Aurelius had asked, forgetting his ego for an instant. "How about explaining it to me? And don't just say I'm here for perspective."

"Soon enough, Professor Mann. I promise.")

Aurelius catches Miriam's eye from across two rows of people busy with wafer slate and calling card computers. Miriam makes a little moue of understanding and nods just slightly in Claypoole's direction.

"The reasons we had for setting up the Transmigration Interregnum project had more to do with the immense potential we saw on the level of pure research," Claypoole says. "A potential, I may add, that has been realized ten-fold." His face splits open in an ugly, toothy grin that does not spread to his flat, hard eyes. "I can say without fear of inaccuracy or over-statement that, without the research to develop the transmigratory holistic mainframes, there would be no quantum hyperstate interface and we would still be dependent on the Pilots."

And still at peace, Aurelius silently adds. And Bettina still alive. Bravo for you.

"The fact of it was, the misbegotten cryogenic enterprises of the last two centuries left us with an invaluable resource. Developing the technology to retrieve *anything* of coherent value from a medium as chaotic and degraded as an improperly frozen human brain was a miracle of science in itself. That, ladies and gentlemen, was just the beginning."

Aurelius decides that Claypoole is a bore and a corporate hack and he stops listening. He thinks back to how easily Angela Caro had manipulated his vanity, exploited his dread of obscurity, subverted his libido with her dark eyes, pretty smile and opulent curves under her smart little uniform, and it shames him. She had seen it in him and she had used it against him.

"The complex interplay," Claypoole is saying, "of hard- and soft- and wet-wares required to flesh out, as it were, the information pulled from those brains and then re-animate it until it has the illusion of life—it cannot be described in any language other than its own complex algorithms. It's an entirely new heuristic system."

Illusion of life, Aurelius thinks. What does it mean to fool something that *is not* into believing that it *is?* How do you measure your success--by questionnaire? Answer true or false: You are human, you feel alive. Complete the analogy, being is to non-being as sky is to... *blank.* Aurelius imagines two mirrors forever reflecting into each other, an infinite regression of emptiness, until the profusion of nothing coagulates into the illusion of life. Ultimately, what if that is all of any of us reduces to, alive or "dead," just a vacant hall of mirrors? There may be a poem in there, somewhere, for when Aurelius gets back to Mars. He will have to ask the lizards.

But the by-product of this, the extralegal traffic in cryonic sibyls that Claypoole goes so far out of his way not to acknowledge (absolutely no direct profit indeed)—

Holy Christ! That box on the table, that must be one of them, he realizes, the normally transparent panels tuned to opaque. No doubt, if he wanted too, Claypoole could show them some poor idiot's severed head just by pushing a button. Aurelius wonders if he brought it with him from Vulcan or picked it up on one of the six so-called free planetoids. Sure as hell, it didn't come from one of the Heavens.

"Dr. Claypoole," Miriam Wu says. "Thank you for the background information, but could you address the nature of the anomaly which calls the Interregnum project to our attention?"

Aurelius glances at Claypoole. Claypoole is visibly annoyed.

"Please," Miriam adds.

Before Claypoole can say anything in response, the doors at the rear of room open with a near-silent hiss. Caro rushes in, followed by six young men and women in dark green naval uniforms. They move up the ragged central aisle, bumping chairs as they go—this room was never meant to be used as an auditorium.

"I do not wish to alarm you," Caro says. "However, our long-range scouts have picked up an attack group of enemy fighter craft, moving toward us through the onion fold. They will arrive in less than a minute."

Silence, then a general, anxious murmur. Tzurma and Claypoole crowd Caro and demand answers. She stills them with the upraised palm of her left hand. One of her escorts hands her a calling card computer and a communicator bead.

"Thank you, Ensign," Caro says. She scans the room with dark eyes under lowered brows—her gaze stays on Aurelius for a half a beat longer than any of the others, he is certain of it. She activates the computer and stares into its tiny holocube. Fierce concentration immobilizes her face and she tilts her head slightly to the right. The movement shifts a lock of her straight and glossy hair. She affixes the black infra-aural bead to her white temple. It shines in the room's harsh light like a blood-gorged parasite.

Aurelius exchanges a glance with Miriam, tries to rise to his feet, discovers that he can't. From his intestines to his toenails, he may as well be dead.

A line out of a lifetime of reading swims up from the sediment at the bottom of his mind, bereft of attribution: *You could die just the same on a sunny day.* Even in the inky dark of deepest space, he thinks, some suns are always shining somewhere.

"So soon?" Caro whispers—it carries throughout the room, borne along the meridians of tension in the air. "The Pilots have destroyed our primary escort of star fighters. However—" Her next few words are drowned out by a burst of terror and outrage from her audience. She waits until it subsides and starts again: "*However*, they took heavy losses in the process." She smiles a vulpine smile, hard and mean. "And we have a surprise waiting for—"

Perhaps his vision plays tricks on him, but Aurelius notices a corkscrew distortion—like heat shimmer—in the air surrounding the cryonic sibyl. For an instant, the box seems to darken, as if its surface swallows up all the light that touches it. At the same time, Aurelius feels something like an electric charge on every exposed centimeter of his skin. He blinks and it all goes away.

Caro's smile drains away, along with the pink in her pale cheeks. "Impossible."

No one asks her what is impossible. No one says anything for the next few moments, moments which crawl by without name or number. Seconds, minutes, hours—no way to know. Aurelius lacks the strength to lift his wrist and look at his watch. He struggles to force air in and out of his lungs through his panic strangled throat. All he can think is what a stupid thing it was, to leave a life's work in the pretty hands of an undergrad. Simone, he prays in desperation's ancient tongue: Please, Simone, just don't fuck it up.

The floor (no, no, Aurelius thinks, this is a starship, after all, I should think of it as a *deck*) at the far end of the room lifts a meter and a half. The twisted deck tears away from the bulkheads, becomes a hump travels down the room in a wave, flinging drones and soldiers, chairs and computers ahead of it like sea spume. At first he thinks he is hallucinating, delirium clamped down on his oxygen-starved senses. His ears pop—the sounds of screaming humans and shearing metal come to him muffled and remote. He smells ozone from burning mechanisms. He smells blood from breaking bodies. He has just enough time to register the fact that, no, this is not delirium and, oddly enough, he is no longer afraid. In his clarity and calm, he has time for one final triumph, however trivial: Joyce, that quotation, it's from Joyce. Time enough, too, for one final regret: he never took the time to ask about the star cruiser's ludicrous name. Then Angela Caro's sharp elbow strikes him hard in the solar plexus.

Aurelius feels his mirrors shatter and release their reflected, infinite nothing. After that, only darkness and then the absence of darkness.

29

Time Flies

Lunch—pastrami sandwiches with coleslaw and pickles in a worn but clean delicatessen—became an afternoon at the Metropolitan Gallery of Art which in turn became three hours spent in Inkvine Books, a labyrinthine second-hand shop ruled by a stand-offish but even-tempered tabby and an indiscriminately affectionate calico, both overweight. After that, it was drinks at one of those bars where lawyers and businessmen stand around a baby grand piano and sing off-key. Only then, well after nine o'clock and after we'd each had one too many cocktails and Mandy shocked everyone—Aaron most of all, I suspect—with a more-than-competent and strangely affecting rendition of "Someone to Watch Over Me" (a multi-faceted gem, this one), did we make the short and pleasant walk to Aaron's home, a brownstone near the river in the oldest part of the city, where the streets are narrow and paved in Belgian block.

Aaron keeps an untidy house. It has been true of every place I've known him to live and it is true of his current residence. In the tiny vestibule, we have to turn sideways to avoid the handlebars of Mandy's battered ten-speed. The rest of Aaron's place is a warren of constricted spaces with tall ceilings; strange dimensions, I think, the rooms all seem turned on their sides. Aaron only makes it worse with the books stacked on the hardwood floors and piled without order onto unfinished shelves of blond pine.

The three of us sit on a moth-eaten Oriental rug in Aaron's parlor, our empty dinner plates stacked off to one side—Mandy had made an exquisite shrimp stir-fry which we had eaten while drinking a thick and sweet Japanese plum wine. The stir-fry is a memory but the wine continues to flow. Aaron and I lean against a couple of ratty old leather chairs, Mandy lies with her head on Aaron's thigh. He strokes her short and unevenly cut raven hair as if she were a beloved pet. I decline to vocalize the observation, fearing it would offend the girl and excite my friend. Instead, Aaron tells stories as Mandy laughs and I smile, having heard it all before.

"That's the secret to being a curmudgeon, even at my tender age. You have to have violent opinions on things you don't give a damn about."

Mandy sits up—the side of her face is pink and corrugated from the wale of Aaron's chocolate corduroy pants—and drains her wine glass. Instead of refilling it, she holds up her index finger as she swallows and says, "Oh, shit! I just remembered... wait right here!" Then she's on her bare feet and padding off into another room.

"Get that other thing, babe," Aaron calls after her. "You know what I'm talking about?"

"Got it."

"That story of yours never happened," I say to Aaron, sotto voce, once she's gone.

"Which story?"

"You know which one."

"The hell you say."

"I was *there*, Aaron, remember? *Remember?*"

"Ix-nay, woman, she's coming back."

"She's too good for you," I say, quickly and under my breath, just as she enters the room and collapses next to me with thoughtless grace in the way of sylphs the world over. She hands me a book and a stainless steel pen.

I look at the cover: a leggy space-girl with opulent curves *arranged* in front of a generic spacescape—ringed planet, smattering of stars in an indigo void—and dressed in a skin-tight, blood-red cat-suit. In her right hand she grasps what could be a big silver power drill if it weren't for the lack of a cord and the presence of a crystal cone where the bit should be. Her head is encased in a sleek, elongated helmet which covers her ears but leaves her pretty face exposed to the elements—or lack thereof, if she is indeed supposed to be in space and not on the surface of a planet: there is nothing beneath her booted feet and, from the position of her cartoonishly long legs, she appears to be in free-fall. From between pursed lips, she blows a huge, pink bubble. Which makes sense, actually, since the title of the book is *The Bubblegum Embargo and Other Stories.* And it makes sense that Mandy would present it to me—along with the pen—since I am its author.

"I have to be honest, Jane," Mandy says shyly. "I'd never heard of you, not until Aaron told me about you and gave this to me to read."

"She likes your stuff a hell of a lot more than she likes mine," Aaron says, his forced bonhomie a mere fig leaf on his resentment.

"I never said that," Mandy says in a sing-song that tells me that, regardless of what she may have said, Aaron has divined the truth. It also tells me that they've been through this before. It seems I am the trouble in paradise. I'm flattered. "Sign it?" she says to me.

"Of course." I scrawl, "To Amanda, my once and future friend," and sign my name.

"Man, I *love* these stories, especially the title story, outrageous! Like Warhol if Warhol wrote sci-fi. No, no, Lichtenstein!" I suppose she has a case. In the story, the galactic economy depends on the circulation of old Bazooka Joe comic strips as the only legal tender. "And the hero, the chick, Minerva Gant?" she continues. "Love *her*! Are you going to write any more stories with her?"

"I'm thinking about it." Four other Minerva Gant stories are collected in two earlier books and the tenth page of a sixth sits unfinished in my little blue Olivetti portable back in California. I don't tell Mandy, though. I'm not sure why.

"Oh, you should, you should!" Mandy pauses a moment, then says, with rare diffidence, "Um, her friend, her mechanic, Lucy Hammersmith? They seemed... I kind of got a—are they, I mean, do they ever...?"

"Goddamn it!" I say. "They always do that."

Poor Mandy is stunned. "What, what'd I do?"

"Not you, dear." I tap the girl on the cover with the nail of my index finger. "She's white, see? Blue eyes and all—look, there's even a lock of blond hair peeking out from under her helmet." I sigh. "Minerva Gant is Haitian-Laotian."

"Oh yeah: brown skin, almond eyes, black hair. I remember thinking she reminded me of my roommate—she's from the Philippines."

"They do it all the time, the fuckers..."

"Jane," Aaron says, his voice choked off in a familiar way. A half-second later, I smell the thick, resinous aroma of high quality marijuana. Aaron exhales, "You act like you never saw that cover before in your life. Every time you see it you act like you never saw it before. Every time. It's the biz: they're a bunch of assholes, live with it." *You hypocritical little shit,* I seethe. *The gall, telling me to "live with" anything.* But then he reaches over and passes me a small brass pipe with a plump bud burning in the bowl—he never could roll a joint—and so all is forgiven. "Okay," he says to Mandy, "give her the other thing."

As I take a deep hit off the pipe, Mandy reaches behind her—I'd never guessed she was hiding something—and hands me a framed photograph.

"A gift," Aaron says. "From the guys."

I hand the pipe off to Mandy just as I'm wracked by an epic coughing jag. After my lungs clear and my eyes stop watering, I look down to see a picture of me, fifteen years younger and as many pounds lighter, standing on the plywood-and-paint bridge of the *C-57D,* flanked by a grinning Adam West and a smirking Gary Lockwood, both dressed in their militaristic space pajamas. Adam has an arm draped across my shoulders, Gary has his arm around my waist. Both men have autographed the photo: "Love it when you put words in my mouth, Adam" and "Who's the dish in the middle? Gary L."

"Hey Mandy?" Aaron says. "Would you believe it if I told you she slept with both of them?"

I don't rise to Aaron's goad—I *can't.* Instead, I stare at the picture and I remember the day we took it, the blinking of the Christmas lights in the control panels and the smell of sweat and aftershave. But then, *I* don't remember it: something about the memory seems sketched-in and schematic, as if it's an experience I remember reading about or seeing in a movie rather than something that has happened to me.

And then the picture slowly changes in my hand. The lights—red, green, yellow and blue in my so-called memory, various shade of gray in the black and white photo—all shift toward the same shade of pink. The plywood metamorphoses into something opalescent, like the insides of a black oyster shell, and the walls of the open set close and encircle us. The two men merge to become one and I become someone—no, some *thing*—something else, something other. And now it's not a picture of a corner of a television soundstage I'm looking into, it's not a picture at all but the little room itself, and the glass of the framed photo becomes the window I can see it through—I hold it all in my hands. And this man who isn't Gary and isn't Adam and this thing, this inhuman thing that isn't me (*is* me, it *is* me, *I am me!*) clutch and caress each other and their mouths, their hungry mouths, oh my God, it's obscene, it's beautiful—

I don't realize my jaw has been hanging open until there is a string of saliva trailing from my slack lower lip. I wipe it away with the back of my wrist just as Mandy grasps my shoulder and gently shakes me.

"Whoa, Jane." Aaron reaches over to take my hand. In reflex, I jerk away.

"Sorry," I say. "It's nothing—just... reminiscing."

"Like hell—"

"Aaron," Mandy cuts in. "Why don't you get dessert? It's in the fridge, you can't miss it."

After a moment, Aaron nods and, grabbing the dirty dinner plates, stands up. He looks at me with an expression of concern that borders on accusation, then heads for the kitchen.

"Do you want to tell *me* what just happened? Where you went?"

I look at her dumbly.

"It's not the grass," she says.

I shake my head.

"You had that look earlier, at the Gallery." She pauses, looks to the archway leading to the hall that leads to the kitchen. "It was like you were—you went *somewhere,* I know that look," she says but does not elaborate.

I know just what she's talking about. In the modern art wing, it came over me, that same dislocation, while I gazed at a marble Brancusi sculpture, *Mademoiselle Pogany,* but only for a moment. I shake my head. "No. Yes. I mean, I don't know where to... start."

Mandy doesn't push. Her small hand is a reassuring pressure on my shoulder.

A crash comes from the kitchen, the sound of shattering crockery, followed by Aaron's shouted

"Shit!" Mandy smiles at me and gives my shoulder a gentle squeeze.

She giggles. "That'll buy us some time."

"I suppose..." I finally say. "I guess it's as if this isn't quite *real*? No? When I think about my life, about the shape of history, Bobby Kennedy signing the Prague Accords back in 73, the moon base—even now, whenever I see one of those horrid automobiles with the cyclopean headlight thing..." My index finger lightly traces a circle in the center of Mandy's warm forehead. She smiles shyly at the contact. "It's like we're living in one of my stories, do you know what I mean? Just as ersatz, just as flimsy, like the past were a mirage that fed into a present that is just as illusory. Do you feel it? You must. Please tell me..."

Mandy is about to say something when Aaron comes back into the room, carrying three small plates in one hand and a store-bought cherry cheesecake (and I'm enough myself to note, with relief, that it *is* store-bought and that there are limits even to Mandy's perfection) in the other. Aaron looks from Mandy to me, then back again but no one says anything.

We eat dessert in strained but companionable silence. Finally, Aaron shifts his weight and looks at his watch. A significant glance passes between him and Mandy. Almost imperceptibly, she nods.

"It's quarter to midnight," Aaron says. "*Tempus fugit.*" At Mandy's look of puzzlement, he translates: "Time flies."

"Oh," she says. "It *is* getting late..."

After a pause, I say, “Just show me to the guest room and I—”

“That’s not it,” Mandy says. “That’s not what I meant, at all.” Again, she shares a look, cryptic and sly, with Aaron.

Aaron clears his throat. “Mandy was hoping we could maybe take in a movie.”

30

Immortality

The eye is hazel, wide and empty, with pinprick spots of blood in the sclera. The other eye is gone, torn away along with most of the upper right portion of the dead man's skull. The offending projectile was a piece of shrapnel no larger than a grain of sand and buried now in the bulkhead one-hundred and seventy-one centimeters above the slumped over, uniformed corpse. A vapor of blood and metal has condensed out of the air into a thin layer of frost. A wide swath of hair, brains and pulverized bone stains the wall.

A brass nameplate on the dead man's chest identifies him as P. Devore, Lt./J.G. Crysanthia Vog kneels next to the body and touches his face—the flesh is frozen solid.

Nivalia Edo says, "We have restored life support to the captain's quarters."

Once the Pilots had boarded *Virgin Sorrow*, informal command of the mission had passed, in part, from Nivalia to Crysanthia—no one discussed it and Crysanthia didn't really want it; after the incident with the Paladins, it was inevitable. The two women walk through the ship's torn and twisted passageways. Without life support and with much of the atmosphere lost to multiple hull breaches, the air is thin and chilled down to well below freezing. Bodies and parts of bodies are everywhere. Crysanthia passes them by and steps over them without comment, leaving footprints in the pink frost that covers every surface. She and Nivalia are the only living things around. The few survivors from the attack group are busy elsewhere in the ship, patching up *Virgin Sorrow* and slave yoking the AI to Crysanthia's symbiosis chamber. With her own tiny starship parked in the hangar bay, Crysanthia will steer the cruiser to Agamemnon's shipyards under its own power.

The ship itself is all but worthless, Crysanthia thinks. They may pry a few secrets loose from the computer during the voyage, a few more from its hulk once she gets it to Agamemnon, perhaps one or two with some small measure of strategic value. She wonders why Narisian wants it. It hardly seems worth the effort. Or the lives.

What's more, she wonders why he had ordered her to discharge into open space the only weapon the Pilots possessed which was capable of ending this war. She wonders if, by following that order, she hasn't condemned them all to die.

She wishes she could talk to him. Or to Corvus—surely he must have something to say about all this.

They reach the captain's quarters. The doors slide open only a few centimeters before the motor quits with a grinding whir. Crysanthia and Nivalia look at each other, then Crysanthia grasps the left door and Nivalia the right. Together, they wrench them open, against the loud and screeching protest of the mechanism. Crysanthia steps into the relatively warm room against an out-rush of air, Nivalia follows. Once inside, they force the doors closed with their palms.

Crysanthia sits behind the captain's desk, feels dislocated and false. Over in the corner sits a small bunk, neatly made with a square pillow and rough brown coverlet. A holograph of a laughing little girl—dark copper curls, freckled brown skin, gapped white teeth and wide gray eyes—shimmers above it. Crysanthia is amazed at how long it takes humans to mature; chronologically, the child in the picture is about thc same age as Nivalia, older maybe by a year. They spend years dallying in developmental stages our children rocket through in weeks or days, if ever; the crèche-born, like Nivalia--like Crysanthia, herself, really—never experience them at all. Nature prolongs in humans a false innocence they pretend never to outgrow.

Crysanthia turns away and tries to find a comfortable posture in a chair scaled to human proportions. She fails. She leans forward and props her elbows on the desk.

"We have catalogued the human dead, using their computer," Nivalia says. "No one survived, of course, we made sure of that. You can access the list on that computer there."

Crysanthia grunts an acknowledgment and picks up the indicated wafer slate. Before she activates it, she runs the numbers in her head: one soldier in each of the Shrikes, two in each of the Paladins, the six-hundred and fifty-four officers, crew and passengers in the command cruiser, all dead.

"More importantly," Nivalia continues, "no one got away. Any radio messages sent from here will take years before they reach the nearest outpost. The Commonwealth has no way of knowing what's happened here today."

"What happened today is that we killed a lot of people," Crysanthia muses. "Does that bother you?"

"No," Nivalia answers, without hesitation.

"No," Crysanthia echoes. "It doesn't bother me, either."

As if she reads Crysanthia's thoughts, Nivalia asks, "Should it?"

"No, I guess not."

"I lost most of my battle group," Nivalia adds. "*That* bothers me."

Crysanthia turns on the computer and calls up the list of names.

Abruptly, Nivalia asks, "What happened to the second wave?"

Crysanthia looks up at her.

"The Paladins, the ones hidden in—"

"I know."

"They just vanished. As if something plucked them out of space-time... We all want to know what happened. We want to know what you did." Nivalia's hands flutter, like animals made suddenly cognizant they are exposed to the gaze of a predator. "If you did it."

Almost a religious figure, Galatea had said, all those years ago. Pilots, who live alongside their dead creator's ghost, who know the shape of the cosmos before they know their own names, are immune to superstition. It is not in their genetic code. Yet there it is, growing like a cancer in the four-year-old Nivalia Edo and staring at

Crysanthia with compound eyes of emerald green, pleading and afraid.

Crysanthia has suffered through too many years as their Satan. She'll be goddamned if she'll accept a second life as their Christ. She has no idea what to tell Nivalia so she settles on the truth.

"I don't know."

"But it was you." It is neither question nor an accusation, nor is it a statement of fact. Crysanthia shrugs.

Nivalia lets it go.

So now it is Crysanthia's turn: "What was that box I saw you carrying out of the wreckage of the conference room earlier, when everyone else was sorting through the bodies?" she asks. "The black box? Looked like a cryonic sibyl."

After a moment, Nivalia answers, "It was."

"You seemed in a bit of hurry. Where is it now?"

Again, Nivalia hesitates. "I sent it on ahead of us, to Klytemnestra."

"Narisian wants it?"

Nivalia nods.

"Any idea why?"

"No."

Crysanthia purses her lips and watches Nivalia's face for any sign that she hides something. There is none—the child is telling the truth or she is an exquisite liar; either way, Crysanthia knows she'll get nothing more out of her. She wonders if Nivalia has any idea what Crysanthia had been doing before she was called away to join this battle group. Probably not. Crysanthia nods slowly and looks down at the names on the wafer slate. Most glow deep red, a few glow amber. She reads *Caro, Angela Lisette* in amber and stops long enough to gauge her own reaction: nothing, not even satisfaction. Nothing at the scarlet *Devore, Pietro Miguel*, either. At the amber *Wu, Miriam Xi-Lin* in the next column, she finally feels something, the barest whisper of regret. I knew you, it says, and you were kind, you seemed to care. You tried to stop him.

Then she sees it: *Mann, Aurelius.*

"These here, the ones in amber? They're not irretrievable? They can be revived?"

"Theoretically," Nivalia says. "The crèche was not intended for… common stock humans."

Crysanthia touches a stylus to the slate and drags Miriam Wu and Aurelius Mann into an empty holocube. She holds the wafer slate out to Nivalia. The rescued names float within the cryostylitic cube, the letters reversed to her sight. "See to it that two cold-pac capsules are made operational and transfer the corpses of these people into them."

Nivalia does not move. "I remind you that prisoners are not a mission objective."

"I just made them one."

Nivalia takes the computer as if it were something putrescent and contagious. "And the rest?"

Crysanthia can see no reason to carry them all the back to Klytemnestra. "Get rid of them," she says. "Burn them up or blow them out the airlocks, I don't care."

***

"So this is the other half of you," Crysanthia whispers.

Nivalia Edo and the rest of the attack group is gone, they left for home several hours ago. Crysanthia is alone in the medical bay, alone in the starship, alone, it seems, in the universe. Life support is back on-line and at quarter-power; the air hovers a few degrees above freezing. She sits cross legged on the floor and studies the bruised face of Aurelius Mann, frozen behind a circular window. Ice crystals collect in a neatly trimmed beard that does little to harden a jaw softened by decades of indulgence. She can see how this man could be Janos's father, though the resemblance is not overpowering. The minuet of this man's genes with Bettina's had proved remarkably egalitarian; neither parent dominated in the son. Crysanthia wonders about that, why the Commonwealth's premier genetic designer chose the primordial crapshoot of sperm and egg to produce a child when she could have easily designed one. It would have meant breaking a few laws but she had broken much larger ones and, at the time in her life when she was toying with the idea of motherhood, she was valuable enough to the governments and corporations of Sol that they would have surely looked the other way. So why, then, had she elected to share? It hardly seemed like her.

She finds herself moved by the thought that Bettina must have surely wondered much the same as she watched her son grow more distant and unreadable with each day's passing. She remembers what Bettina had said, as the three of them shared supper on Vesta: *There were qualities he possessed, things that I lacked and that I wanted my child to have.* Would she have chosen differently had she known what that would ultimately mean?

Crysanthia looks down at the face in the perfect repose of death and remembers how Janos had looked as he lay in Pariah's airlock. It seems she is forever seeking Janos out in the faces of the dead—she had sought him in the sibyl and in the dead hazel eye of Lt. Devore. Here, in the face of his father, she almost finds him and it breaks her heart all over again. She gives Aurelius Mann's frosted visage one last, lingering look and slides his cold-pac capsule back into the wall, alongside Miriam Wu. Their tiny indicator lights glow lime green. The remaining seven in this row and all nine in the row above it are dark, the capsules empty. Crysanthia gathers herself up from the floor and, with a backwards glance, leaves the bay.

Crysanthia sheds her flight suit and enters the symbiosis chamber. It takes a moment for her to grow accustomed to *Virgin Sorrow*'s mass and power—finding the correct entry point back into the fold proves to be much trickier than she'd anticipated. Before long, however, she's made the insertion. Now she can relax—ever-mindful, of course, of the ship's battle-inflicted fragility.

After she's satisfied that the hull will not shake itself apart during the voyage, Crysanthia sets her mind to breaking into the cruiser's secure files. This is easier than she'd hoped—armed with the genetic signatures and trace memories extracted from the corpses of the ship's senior officers, Crysanthia's AI hits upon the proper decryption after only a few quintillion attempts. In real time, it takes slightly longer than a minute.

The files appear to Crysanthia as a near-infinitude of dark gray boxes suspended in the light gray mist of *Virgin Sorrow's* cyberspace. Crysanthia, a disembodied point of reference at the center of it, reaches out and scans them. Those with immediate strategic value she copies, unread, to the memory of her own ship. Far away from her, she senses a cluster of more immediate interest. Crysanthia moves toward it or the pseudo-space of information shifts and reorders itself to bring it to her—either way, she's there, next to several dozen boxes invisibly tagged "Tethys Rehabilitation Facility Holographic Transcripts: Therapeutic Interrogation of Subject Brekkelheim, Bettina."

She's overwhelmed. Quickly, she runs through the contents until she finds one demanding her attention, a session from six months before her death, as notable for who conducts the interview as for what they discuss. Crysanthia selects it and the box becomes transparent, showing her what appear to be two featureless dolls facing each other across a table. As Crysanthia moves toward the box—or the box toward her—the figures grow more real-seeming. Finally, Crysanthia is inside the box, now a fully realized interrogation room, and the dolls are two living, breathing women.

Angela Caro says. "Do you care to talk about them?"

Bettina, dressed in a soft, shapeless paper gown and wearing paper slippers on her feet, replies, "I love to talk about them—I *live* to talk about them. It's all I do in this delightful little place, now that we all seem to have dropped the pretense that I am mentally ill. What do you want to ask?"

"The same question you've refused to answer all these years, Doctor. Why did you create them?"

Bettina blinks.

"You must have known you were creating a species which would ultimately compete with humanity, quite probably drive us to extinction. Why would you want to do that?"

"I always thought it was funny, the way everyone seems to think that the Pilots were solely *my* creation, as if I locked myself up in some little garret somewhere and wrote out their genetic code in longhand. I had a legion of very talented people working under me, you know. A team of eighty designed the Pilot eye."

"Are you deflecting responsibility?"

Bettina smiles. "Never," she says. "That would mean deflecting credit."

"Or blame."

"Why not just build a brain in a fish-bowl?" Bettina says. "That's what you want to know. That's all the Stigol-Bergham engineers needed, no? And then, why make them capable of reproducing on their own?"

"Which you were explicitly forbidden—"

"Yes, yes, which I was explicitly forbidden to do. I've never refused to answer that question."

"Perhaps 'refuse' isn't the word." Now Caro smiles—Crysanthia, from her God's eye perspective as the room's holographic scanning network, would almost believe these two women were old friends. However, she also sees them through the room's medical scanners—heart rate, respiration, body heat, blood gas saturations—and they tell a different story entirely. Crysanthia wonders who is the cobra and who is the mongoose. "You've been, shall we say, evasive."

It's a sunny little room for being sunk half a kilometer under the surface of the icy Saturnian moon: pale yellow plastiform walls and a pale yellow plastiform table built into the pale yellow plastiform floor. The ceiling is a checkerboard of five lumenium tiles set in pale yellow plastiform. The chairs, at least, aren't plastiform: ergonomic and self-adjusting cultured leather loungers—in pale yellow, of course. Bettina shifts position in her chair and the chair shifts along with her.

"Well, we certainly don't want that, do we? Especially seeing how open you've been with me."

Caro's face and posture do not change but there is a slight blip in her bio-readings. Crysanthia marvels: is that a conscience? If so, it does not last long.

"A woman my age," Bettina continues, "in my condition, can statistically expect to live another fifty, sixty years, maybe. She can reasonably *hope* to live another seventy or eighty. Not too long ago, that was a life span in itself and yet it seems so... fleeting. Mind you, I don't speak of *personal* expectations or hopes. I doubt you'd be here with me now if I was to live out the year. Am I right?"

Another blip, milder this time, as Caro says, "That's not playing fair, Doctor. You don't ask any questions until you've answered mine."

"You've answered it." Bettina yawns. "Could I at least have some coffee? Turkish style, thick and very sweet—they know how I like it." Bettina makes a backhanded gesture toward the invisible scanners in the walls. "What was I—oh yes: and the human brain, while a wondrous natural artifact, is woefully inadequate for life in the interstellar age. And it slows down."

"So you meant simply to build a better human?"

"Nothing so abstruse. That is, that's only a small part of it. I meant to build a better *me.*"

Caro's eyes narrow. "A better you?"

Bettina nods serenely. "And a better you, for that matter," she says. "A better everybody. Eventually. But I meant to start with myself."

"I don't follow—"

"It was the final stage. You interrupted it, you got in the way. Where in the hell is that coffee?"

"It's on its way. Keep talking. Please."

Bettina sighs. "What if I told you that I could take your personality—everything you know, everything you think, everything you feel—and transfer that into a body which was superior in every way, a body which would not wear out, capable of—well, you know what they are capable of. You would come to me little more than an ape and leave me nothing less than a god."

"The metempsychotic microbots we found? Those nano-avatar things?"

"You know about those?"

"We apprehended your accomplice, a few months after you sent her on her little mission to Heaven 17." Caro consults the wafer slate in front of her. "Uh, Evangeline Sandoval-Smoot? She still had two ampoules filled with the things when we got her."

"Ach, she was supposed to destroy them after—once she completed her task."

"So she said. She told us she couldn't bring herself to do it—she was devoted to you. She'd been injecting herself with them, rationing them."

Bettina makes a face. "Stupid cow."

"Took us a while, but she talked to us. She may not have given us everything but she gave us a lot." A pause and a smile, then, "Those little microbots gave us a lot, too."

"But not everything?"

"You never get *everything*."

"Else why would you be here now, talking to me?" Bettina ruminates for a moment, then says, "Those were *nothing*, those avatars. A mere contingency—an *insurance* policy against... today... and the day we both know is coming. Because of you, I was forced to—well, let's say they were a pale shadow of what I wanted. Another year, it's all I needed. But I didn't think you would roll out that infernal astrogation machine for another decade, plenty of time to get everyone used to the idea. I never meant you any harm—I never meant *anyone* any harm. But did you grasp that? How could you?

The human race is still little more than a troop of paranoid baboons, watching and waiting for the next predator to strike. Where there aren't any, we imagine them, we *invent* them. Another year and I could have had it. And I would have offered it to everyone. *Everyone.*"

"A direct transference? A human mind into a Pilot's body?"

The door opens and an android orderly comes in with her coffee in a doll-sized cup. "Finally," Bettina says. The android barely has time to place it on the table before Caro shoos him from the room.

"You were saying, Doctor? Doctor?"

Bettina lifts her hand. "Quiet, I want to enjoy this." She takes a long, noisy sip and closes her eyes. "What were we talking about?"

"You were about to explain—"

"Yes, of course." Bettina takes another sip of her coffee and then says, "For centuries, we've talked about it, only instead we spoke of artificial intelligences, super-computers; we were thinking hardware when we should have been thinking wet-ware, *hybrid*-ware. The Pilot brain—the Pilot's cyborg nervous system—is the most sophisticated computer the universe has ever known."

Caro pulls back from the table. "That's rather grandiose, Doctor."

"I suppose you're right." Bettina grins. "The universe is very big and very old."

"But let's forget about that for a minute; what did you intend to do with the Pilot who was already there, the personality which had developed over the years while you worked on your 'final stage?' What happens to her?"

"Do you really care?"

Caro laughs. "Of course *I* don't care. But I think *you* care a great deal."

Finally, Bettina's façade cracks. She looks away from Caro and gnaws her lower lip.

"No answer? And I'd hoped we were getting somewhere."

Bettina sighs. Outwardly, she puts on a brave face but her pulse and blood pressure creep upwards, her respiration becomes shallow. In her bodiless state, everywhere and nowhere in the tiny universe of this sunless yet sunny little room, Crysanthia tries to distract herself with a chemical analysis of the stress hormones in the droplets of sweat that have sprouted on Bettina's upper lip.

"That personality would be dismissed," Bettina says finally.

"Dismissed?"

"Erased. Over-written, like a... like an obsolete computer program."

"Killed."

"*Dismissed.*"

Crysanthia does not wait to see any more—and there is a lot more, the conversation goes on for hours. Instead of smoothly gliding out the way she came in, she yanks herself from the program. She sees Bettina and Caro freeze and then they and the room around them explode into a billion tiny data bits. Then she is in her body again, alone in her chamber.

She stands up and leaves, not bothering with the flight suit crumpled on the deck. Naked, she strides out of her ship and out of the hangar, back through the hundreds of meters of corridors to the medical bay. Once there, she rips open the equipment locker with her bare fingers—twice, she cuts herself, leaves her blood smeared on the shining metal. She does not care. She finds half of what she is looking for when she rips open the fifth locker: a pressure hypodermic loaded with nano-machines in a non-reactive suspension. In the ninth, she finds the other half: a portable surgical armature.

It takes her three hours to program the nano-machines, more than eight to calibrate the armature. She works from memory, steadily and without break. When she is finished, she sits on the edge of an examination table. She clamps the black and sinister armature onto her midsection, injects the nano-machines into her carotid artery and waits.

Twenty minutes pass. She stares across several meters of empty deck to the bank of stainless steel cold-pac capsules, to the two green lights glowing steadily. Nothing like a second thought crosses her mind.

I should have burned her—burned *it*—out of me when the sickness first showed itself in Dahlia, she thinks. I should have burned her out of the both of us—I could have found a way, I know it. But now it's too late, now it has spread to a third generation, to a granddaughter I have yet to see. I myself have passed it onto a second daughter. Poor Eridani, perfect but for this demonic stigma—you will be walking by the time I reach port, you and Bardus both. Weeks gone by, the first weeks of your lives... And I was proud. Even as I denied it, even to myself, I was proud. And in my pride, I have condemned you.

Thirty minutes. Thirty-five minutes. Forty—enough. Crysanthia activates the armature's scanners and watches as it projects an image of her insides, life sized and in cryostylitic clarity, in the space before her. Each of those organs sculpted and refined, turned on the lathe of Bettina's cruel genius—Crysanthia takes the controls of the surgical armature in her left hand and zooms in on her uterus. She magnifies the image by a factor of twelve.

There they are: the dozens of nodes that manufacture the stem cyborganelles she passes along to the embryos once they have implanted themselves in her womb. In the magnified image, each one is the size and shape of an apple seed. They cluster in groups of threes and fives and send out tangles of microtubules that feed into her uterine walls. The injected nano-machines have found the tainted nodes and marked them. The scanner picks up the signal and outlines them in ghostly blue. Crysanthia depresses a small button.

The armature extrudes a thin, gleaming cable of razor sharp flexor filaments and, like an ichneumon wasp, stabs her in the belly. She watches the monitor as the cable comes into the frame and frays into its individual fibers, each one a thousand times thinner than a human hair. They zero in on the infected nodes and pierce their synthetic membranes. Crysanthia breathes in deep and flips the kill switch.

Bright flashes of violet laser light vaporize the nodes from within. The burn sends a twinge of pain lancing through Crysanthia's innards. Then the filaments re-knit themselves into a cable and withdraw from her flesh with a queer sensation that makes her shiver.

You've killed me, darling.

Not quite, Crysanthia thinks. And not soon enough, not nearly. But I'm no longer a carrier. I'll infect no more of my daughters.

With a sudden surge of rage and grief, she screams and tears the armature away from her. She lifts it over her head and smashes it to the deck with all of her strength. A few pieces break off to fly, bounce and skitter away.

Crysanthia slows her rapid heartbeat and calms her heaving breaths. She looks at her fingers; the cuts have healed without scar or blemish. It is time to go home.

Part Four
Divine Wreckage

And that's all I can know, my splinter of truth.
I am but the abject orphan of your blind design
And there is more life in the corpse of God
Than in all the divine wreckage of creation.

—*Elegy for the Blind Martian* by Aurelius Mann

31

Fragments of a Gnosis

The taxicab takes us north along the river into areas of the city that molder and crumble away, through entire city blocks of deserted warehouses and vacant lots that have become illegal dumps choked with bald tires and busted appliances, overgrown with weeds. Aaron sits up front with the driver, I sit next to Mandy in the back.

"Where are we going?" I ask Aaron through the holes in the partition of bulletproof plastic.

"Not much further," Mandy answers and pats my thigh. "Relax."

I shake my head and demand, "What kind of movie plays out here?"

"You'll see," Aaron says.

"Uh-huh." I settle against the back of the blue Naugahyde bench. "The last time I *saw*, you'd dragged me to a seedy Times Square grindhouse to see Amber Abyss in *Forbidden Panties.*"

"You know you loved it." Aaron chuckles. "Especially when she did it with the monster from the libido. It's invisible," he explains to Mandy. "That was the only mime act I've ever seen that was worth a damn. I'm still trying to figure out how she did that thing with her—"

I look from the crucifix, hanging off the rearview, to the sour face of the driver, reflected darkly in the glass. "Whatever. What I remember most vividly was the guy two seats over, playing with himself under a tented copy of the *Post*."

"We're here," Mandy says softly.

"There," Aaron says to the driver. "Let us out there."

The cab rolls to a stop next to a chewed up section of curb. Aaron pays the driver with a five dollar bill and does not wait for change. We get out and the cab speeds away. I fight a building panic: stranded.

Mandy takes my hand—her palm is soft and slightly moist. "Hey, it'll be fine. Better than fine, I promise."

I see a small crowd gathered in front of the abandoned storefront across the street. Punks with flame-colored Mohawk haircuts and street people in ratty, soiled coats stand alongside middle aged and elderly men and women in expensive shoes and tailored suits.

"Come on," Aaron says. "It's almost time."

Mandy gently pulls me across the street, after Aaron. A chill autumn wind blows dead leaves and trash around our feet. Skinny cats slink and skulk about the decaying tires of derelict cars. Bits of glass glitter on the pavement.

"Wait a minute," I say. "This is one of those guerilla theatres I've read about—I thought it was a myth."

"It's no myth," Aaron says. I search his face for the hint of a smile, any sign he is screwing with me, but there is none, only a look I have never seen before, that of the true believer. Aaron hates true believers.

We step up onto the sidewalk and stand at the crowd's periphery. As I hug myself and fidget and wonder once again how we'll get home, heads turn all around and stare at Mandy. Finally, people doing something that makes sense: Mandy had taken a few minutes before we left the house to put on a candy apple red wig, deep scarlet lipstick and a rubber dress that matches the wig and exposes a hand's breadth of pale, goose pimpled flesh between its hem and the tops of her white lace stockings. Red pumps cradle her small feet. I find it hard not to stare at her myself.

Something slightly more compelling calls my attention away, however. I can see into the building clearly now. Behind the snaggled teeth of broken plate glass, a gasoline generator powers a mechanic's work light that hangs from the rusting skeleton of the drop ceiling—here and there, the few remaining acoustical tiles sag and droop. The light shines onto a sixteen-millimeter projector that sits on a folding card table with peeling plaid laminate. A thin brown woman with lank hair—Indian or Arab, I think, maybe Puerto Rican—and dressed in jeans and a white tee shirt threads film through the projector's sprockets. She works without a single wasted motion.

Mandy's teeth chatter as she speaks. "My sixth time. Aaron's third. Every time, it's different. It isn't a movie. It's a living thing—it changes." She leans in close to my ear and whispers, "It came from outer space."

Astounding—in that single utterance, Mandy is transmogrified from perfect little pixie to pathetic, spaced-out imbecile. I laugh but she isn't joking.

"Eat this," Mandy says. She presses a strip of something dry and pink into my hand. It's matted and fibrous like peat; it smells of mildew and iodine.

"It's a marine lichen," Aaron supplies. "Its street name is—come to think of it, it doesn't have a street name."

I search Mandy's face and find... belief? I don't know. I stall. "I suppose this came from space, too?"

"Probably—some people say it and the movie are really the same thing in different forms," Mandy says. "Like a caterpillar and a butterfly."

"Mmm," Aaron says. "Not exactly. They say that it's a life form—the movie, that... *stuff,* there, in your hand. It only disguises itself as a strip of celluloid, a bunch of seaweed—the reality of it is much stranger, much bigger. And whatever it is, you become a part of it, temporarily, when you... partake." He puts a strip of the same substance into his mouth, chews once and swallows.

"For Christ's sake, Aaron!" I say. "You, of all people—I mean, of *all* people, *you*—you don't really buy into this nonsense, do you?"

Aaron shrugs.

"Oh, Aaron," I continue. "This kind of shit, it doesn't really happen—not in the real world. That's why we write the stories we write, *because* this kind of shit doesn't happen."

"The spores are hard to get," Mandy says, as if I'd said nothing, "but it's real easy to grow. All you need is a black light, a couple pounds of sea salt and a ten gallon tank with a bubbler. It blooms in a couple of days and then you dry it out. Instant epiphany. Hey! Maybe that's what we should call it: Epiphany No. 5." She laughs. "Like the perfume."

I stare at her.

"Seriously, though," she continues. "There's no point in watching the movie without it."

"And the drug has no effect if you don't watch the movie," Aaron adds.

"Wait a minute, what's the movie even *called?"*

Aaron and Mandy look at each other. "I don't think it has a title, exactly," Aaron says.

Well, that figures.

"It won't hurt," Mandy says. "I promise."

"Maybe later," I say and wander off to be by myself. To Aaron and Mandy's credit, they let me go without an argument. I look at the faces of the people gathered here, hoping to find... what? Some unmistakable sign that they're mad, some indisputable proof that they aren't? I see neither and so I look down at the clot of strange matter in my hand. In the sodium vapor glow of the block's sole working street lamp, I see black and blue-green lines that intersect in tiny yellow circles. It looks like a street map or printed circuit, I think, or a tracery of nerves. If I let myself, I could almost believe I was looking at hieroglyphs from some ancient, alien civilization, or one that has yet to born. I don't let myself.

And then a gap opens up in the crowd long enough for me to glimpse a man in a priest's cassock talking to a woman in a wheelchair. The dim light glints off of his steel-rimmed glasses and the thinning, silver hair at his temple. Only a glimpse, and then the gap closes, but a glimpse is enough. Amid all the overlapping conversations, I hear his voice clearly: "I don't dismiss anything. Perhaps God *has* left fragments of a gnosis for us to tease out of the night sky or the entrails of a dove, a cup of tea..."

I take a deep breath. The space lichen stinks like a saltwater marsh and crinkles like cellophane as I fold it into my mouth. It is saline and bitter, metallic like blood. It dissolves in my spit like brackish cotton candy. I push my way back into the crowd, back toward the movie that has no name, back to Philip Ashwood.

32

The Sheltering Storms

A million kilometers from Agamemnon, Crysanthia opens *Virgin Sorrow's* hangar and launches her ship free. It's no easy task—for the duration of the maneuver, she is in two places at once, calculating countless variables of velocity, rotational mass and gravitation as she guides both vessels into the floating shipyards, among the thousands of starships riding the currents of the planet's outermost atmosphere like wind-blown dandelion seeds. She sails past them and feels the gentle radiation of their sensors ripple along her hull. Through it all, an insistent beacon calls her to a reserved port in the central complex. From a distance, the complex is an intricate snowflake, a hexagonal lattice ninety kilometers on a side. It glitters within the murky clouds and undulates in the sheltering storms like a jellyfish. Colossal sheets of lightning crackle along its arms from the perpetual atmospheric ionization and thousands of ships encrust its ramified structure like shining metal barnacles.

Crysanthia mates her ship with the complex while simultaneously guiding *Virgin Sorrow* into the outsized blister of a dock located forty kilometers away, just off the hub, where it mars the radial symmetry of the complex like a tumor. Crysanthia feels the complex's AI gently push her out of *Virgin Sorrow's* guidance system. She completes the handoff gladly and then watches as the massive cruiser is caught in the net of inertia canceling force fields and slowed to a gentle halt. It makes a slow turn and begins crawling toward the tumor.

After she has dressed, Crysanthia steps out of her ship onto the deck of an airlock and through a narrow entrance corridor. After a couple dozen meters, it opens into one of the six main axial boulevards. Magnetic rail cars speed by in near silence and Pilots rush by on foot, each one moving with lucid intent. Crysanthia wends her way through the foot traffic, grabs the handhold of a passing rail car and swings herself aboard while it moves along at full speed. As she rides, Crysanthia dispassionately notes the grime and tar that seep through microscopic cracks in the translucent walls. Under other circumstances, given more time, this complex could have been a masterpiece of engineering, built to last the ages. Instead, they will be lucky if it survives another decade—and that's if the Commonwealth doesn't attack before then. A few hits with the most conventional of weapons and the complex would break apart as if it were made of spun glass.

And all during the trip, she notices something else: she is the focus of the uneasy attention of her fellow Pilots. Their eyes follow her as she goes past them.

Nivalia Edo and the others, she thinks. *They talked. Of course they talked, how could they not?*

The rail car approaches Crysanthia's destination, just off the hub. She leaps down onto the ceramic surface of the walkway and joins the flow of traffic without missing a step.

In a small booth overlooking the dock where the *Virgin Sorrow* is moored, Crysanthia finds two nude Pilots working within little jury-rigged symbiosis cages: webs of gold and platinum wire embedded in brittle walls of amber resin, pinprick laser lenses shining from within. They are suspended from the curved ceiling with heavy, snaking cables. They pay her no mind as she looks out an observation port into the dock.

This is new, Crysanthia thinks. She watches as thousands of silver robots the size of housecats and shape of spiders drop onto the hull. Several hundred find the breaches and scurry inside.

Wait a minute—why in the hell are the robots putting it back together? She watches them walk along on their eight legs while their twenty tool-appendages drill, slice and weld with frenetic efficiency—already, the robots have sealed off and smoothed over the smallest tears and torsions in the ship's hull. *Shouldn't they be ripping it apart?* Crysanthia glances at the male Pilot in the symbiosis cage to her left and then the female Pilot in the cage to her right. They act unaware but she knows better—they radiate the same mix of fear and curiosity as everyone else.

"If you've come about Wu and the poet," Corvus says from behind her, "They're being transferred to the emergency amniotic sacs in the hydroponics bay."

Crysanthia nods. "And he has no objections? To my bringing them back?"

Corvus hesitates, then says, "He doesn't see the harm."

"And you? Do you object?"

"I don't see the point."

Crysanthia turns around. "I want to see Narisian. Immediately."

"I'm afraid that is out of the question."

"Why did he stop me from firing your bullet?" Crysanthia demands. "Surely he did not disapprove."

Corvus waits a beat before answering, the studied blankness of his face telling Crysanthia a great deal. "He judged the destruction of Venus and Vulcan to be a valid strategy," he finally says. "He merely has a strategy which supersedes it."

"Care to share it with me?"

Corvus says nothing.

"Has he shared it with *you*?"

Corvus pretends to ignore the question. Crysanthia is not fooled. He says instead, "Dahlia is here. She has given birth to her children, surely she wishes to see you."

"She's here, in the complex…?"

Corvus nods.

"Why?"

"You should go see her. Talk to her." Corvus makes an odd gesture: hesitant, something like a bow.

"Has Narisian been to see her?"

"He's been busy." With that, Corvus turns and walks away.

Dahlia and Crysanthia's other two children are in the small nursery located at the far end of another of the complex's three axial boulevards. In what was once a weapon's development research bay, six paper-clad adolescents watch over a group of a dozen naked children who sit cross-legged on the floor. Barely more than infants, Eridani Vog and Bardus Mir are linked to the group via rudimentary symbiosis; they work together to manipulate a fractal rose that slowly rotates in the center of their ring. Crysanthia watches her children for several minutes. Their scalps still show faint traces of purple neo-natal mottling, livid when Crysanthia had last seen them. In another week, the spots will fade away completely. Bardus remains oblivious of her, Eridani acknowledges her presence with a barely perceptible working of her tongue behind her lips—she must be hungry, Crysanthia thinks. Her breasts ache with reciprocal longing.

Eridani's lapse of concentration has inflicted a flaw upon the image. The hologram twists and ripples and changes color. Dissonance grows. The rose shatters into a fog of a million roses. They cascade to the floor and disappear, like sparks.

One of the adolescents touches a wafer slate. The children begin again, this time with a lotus.

Crysanthia reluctantly leaves them. She finds Dahlia in a small white room that used to be a variable gravity chamber. The entire room is smooth and soft, there are no straight lines or angles of any kind and the light is indirect and diffuse—walking into it is like walking into a candled egg. Dahlia reclines into a deeply padded couch and nurses one of her babies. The other lies next her, entranced by the flight of a mechanical beetle.

Crysanthia swallows, suddenly unsure of herself. Dahlia looks up and smiles at her.

"Labor?" Crysanthia finally asks.

Dahlia looks down at the spotted head at her breast and her smile deepens. "Brutal." She wraps two fingers of her free hand around the other child's foot. "Come and meet them."

Crysanthia sits next to Dahlia with the baby—a girl—between them.

"I heard something," Dahlia says. "About the battle. They say—"

"Something happened."

Dahlia waits.

Crysanthia shrugs. The scarab hovers in front of her eyes. "They say."

"It's hardly just a rumor. I heard it from Nivalia Edo herself."

"If you want an answer, I can't give it. Believe me, if I could, I'd tell you. I wish someone would tell *me.*"

"You are not very good at being disingenuous, Mother," Dahlia says. "You never were."

Crysanthia thinks for a moment, then says, "You want an explanation, a theory? All right, how's this? Those Paladins spent a long time in that cruiser's sub-quantum distortion field. Who knows what effect..." At the look on Dahlia's face, Crysanthia lets her voice trail off. She adds, with finality, "Sometimes luck... looks a lot like virtue."

"Luck," Dahlia says. She looks at Crysanthia a moment longer, then changes the subject, "Nysara was the first born. Raeliad did not come for another three quarters of an hour. I felt like I was coming apart."

"You were," Crysanthia says absently. She gazes down into the aquamarine eyes of the baby girl. "How are you coming together?"

"I can walk. That's something. Really, it was no worse for me than it is for anyone."

"Next time will be easier—not much, but easier. And you won't have to worry about it for a while—one of Bettina's small mercies." Crysanthia snatches the scarab from the air and holds it out for Nysara's inspection. "One of few—*very* few." The little robot crawls along Crysanthia's stiffened fingers with clever legs of articulated copper. Its wings are silver filigreed sheets of mica that seem no more substantial than films of soap; they beat slowly before closing under elytra of gold foil. Its eyes are spheres of jade, its antennae feathered platinum. "This is amazing," Crysanthia says. "Where did you find it?"

"Corvus built it," Dahlia says. Crysanthia's mood dims—no doubt he built it for the children lost along with Ivarra Syn and everyone else on Galatopolis.

Nysara reaches for the scarab. It takes off and flies teasing arabesques just beyond her grasping fingers. She laughs.

Dahlia continues. "He cut the gears himself and built its brains out of a cluster of his own cyborganelles."

Crysanthia muses darkly on the scarab in flight, then laughs along with the laughing baby now crawling into her lap. "Nysara," she sings.

"Ny-*sa*-ra. Nysara and Raeliad, hmm? Very pretty. Nysara Vog and Raeliad...?"

Dahlia does not answer for what seems an eternity but must only be an instant. It is enough for Crysanthia's mind to spin, like the whirring clockwork innards of the beetle automaton. When Dahlia does answer, it is no surprise—Crysanthia has known for all of that instant, an eternity.

"Karza."

33

The Roman Image

I can't do it. I try but I can't. Something like fear only colder spreads all through me and, when I finally manage to move, it is only to hurry in the other direction, back to Aaron and Mandy.

"Aaron," I say, grabbing him by the arm and yanking with a fair portion of my might. "Aaron, Phil's here. Did you know*? Did you know*?"

"What? No! I mean, I knew he was involved with this whole business but I didn't expect to see him *here*."

I glare at him.

"Jane, I didn't know."

"He's telling the truth," Mandy says.

"And who the hell asked—" I spit before catching myself. I let go of Aaron's arm. "I'm... sorry," I murmur. "I'm sorry."

"I didn't know," Aaron repeats, defensive and aggrieved.

I nod and look away. A knot of people standing nearby avoids my gaze. I hear Mandy say, "Um, Aaron, could you give us a minute?"

Aaron leaves and Mandy sidles closer to me. She looks down at the toes of her shoes. She studies the yellow and white cigarette butts and scraps of paper scattered around. I watch her from the corner of my eye, waiting for her to do or say something. She makes a barely suppressed squeal of surprised delight and crouches down. She picks up one of the paper scraps and, still in her crouch, holds it up to me.

"A penny for your thoughts?"

I look closer now and realize that it's a tattered Bazooka Joe comic, waxy and sooty, that she holds in her fingers. I talk myself out of any *frisson* of the uncanny: the odds are hardly astronomical, I think, here in a trash-choked gutter—I chose them for their ubiquity, after all. Still, in light of everything else, it seems portentous. Lagging a beat behind, I smile.

"You know, Aaron really loves you," she says, looking up at me and smiling. "I've never seen anyone get away with talking to him like you do--I couldn't get away with it."

I try to return her smile but it makes my face feel like a mask that has suddenly become too tight.

"It's more than just seeing him again, isn't it?" She drops the shredded comic and stands up. "Aaron told me about the two of you, what happened. But that's not all."

I take a deep breath and let it out loudly. "No, it's more—remember what we were talking about earlier, the... *episodes* I've been having? I haven't had one in a long time, not since I last saw..." I nod my head in Phil's direction. "And now, today..."

"You think it's connected?"

I shrug. "I don't know what I think. No, that's a lie—I'm *scared* to know what I think because it's silly superstition, but I—"

I catch sight of them again, Phil and the woman. He bends down and touches her face, wipes something from the corner of her mouth with his thumb. I wish I could say something dies in me when I see it but that's not it, not it at all. Instead, something I'd hoped was dead comes alive again, like a battered butterfly spreading ragged wings of black and blue.

Phil stands up and looks around, a subtle smile on his lips until his eyes fall on me. Even at this distance, even in this dimness, even with these aging eyes, I can see his expression change—something in the way the angle of his head straightens fractionally, his shoulders stiffen minutely. Then it's gone as his gaze sweeps on.

I am vaguely comforted and acutely enraged to see that he is just as much a coward as I am.

"Who's the woman?" I ask, my voice flat and dead to my own ears. "In the wheelchair, she looks familiar."

Mandy pretends to look. "Actress. From Italy, I think? Christa Salvini, she was in that Antonioni movie—oh, and those commercials, the Roman Image coffee commercials, you know the ones?"

Again, I feel that cold wash from head to toe. Only this time, I can identify it. It isn't so much as if I'm putting together a puzzle as it is the pieces fall together all around me and still refuse to make any sense.

"But she's older than I am," I protest, though I know it's pointless. "Look at her hair, her skin—she has *age spots!* I just saw one of those ads last week, she didn't look a day over twenty-three. It was in a *disco,* for God's sake!" I look at her legs, thin and wasted in gray cotton stockings. "She was *dancing*! How is that possible?"

In a voice unlike any I'd heard her use since I'd met her, Mandy says, "That's what you're here to find out." And then she reaches over and gently runs the soft pad of her thumb along the corner of my mouth. I look down to see that her thumb is wet with my pinkish drool.

Someone gently clears his throat behind my back and over my shoulder. I turn and Phil is standing there, looking as uncomfortable as I feel.

"I'll, uh—I'm going to go find Aaron," Mandy says and is off like a sprite.

"It's good to see you, Jane," Phil says.

"Uh-huh."

"Aaron, did she say? Mr. Mendel?"

I nod. "I'm visiting."

"I saw him not too long ago, in—"

"He told me."

Silence, with the both of us looking everywhere but in the other's eyes.

"So, how did you—how do you come to be here, tonight?" Phil asks. "Not many people—"

"Aaron brought me. And Mandy, the girl I was talking with."

"I see."

"You?"

"Do you know Calvin Breedlove, of The Traumatics?"

"Yeah. And you mentioned him to me once. A while ago. "

"While I was interviewing his wife, he told me about this. He said he first saw this *movie* when he played that free concert in Berlin after the wall came down. He arranged a screening for me and a few other people. That's where, uh, that's where I met Christa." He pauses. "I suppose I should tell you," he says and I brace myself for the blow; I look over to his companion for the flash of a diamond but her left hand is hidden from my view. "I've left the church."

Somehow, this is worse. Now I do look him in his eyes. I reach out and grab his forearm. "Oh, Phil. Why?'

He smiles but it's a smile filled with sadness. "After a while it all became too, I don't quite know how to put it, *metaphorical.* The pageantry, the vestments, the parables and fables—I felt it was all insulating me from the very thing I wanted to touch."

At his use of the word "touch," I realize I still have my hand on his arm. I look over at his companion, the actress, patiently waiting in her wheelchair. Some of the more questionable looking people have gravitated to her and she chats with them, gay and haughty, a crippled queen holding court. How much of Phil's crisis of faith is bound up in that frail little body and how much in the celluloid about to spool through the projector, in the sea rot dissolved in our guts and seeping into our blood? Would he even call it a crisis? Perhaps he has another name for it: an evolution, an apotheosis. The Original I'll-Say-and-How Girl—what was it Phil had called her, that morning in his kitchen? A projection from some ancient miracle machine, the Holy Spirit herself, come to save us all—maybe she's just another aspect of it, the third face of this nameless thing from outer space, her impossible youth now ruined beauty and only all the more beautiful for its ruination. She has nothing to fear from me; I'm sure the thought never crossed her mind.

A penny for your thoughts, I think. *Render unto Caesar and all that,* I think. *All right then, if you insist: Is he fucking her? And if he is, can she feel it? Just how crippled is she, anyway?*

And then I hate myself for reacting like a petty schoolgirl when a riddle much more monstrous and strange looms right in front of me. How can this wheelchair-bound woman and the disco dancing waitress in tight designer jeans both exist? It's more than simply impossible, it's as if I'm watching as the basic clockwork of the universe is toyed with, cancelled out, and something more subtle and insidious takes its place. And the best I can manage in the face of that is jealousy? God help me.

I pull my hand away. "You're still dressing the part, I see."

Phil fingers his Roman collar. "Only on nights like tonight. I can't explain exactly why. It just feels right." He looks away from me, grasping for a better explanation. Finally, he gives up. "Fitting."

"No doubt." There she is again, the schoolgirl.

Before Phil can respond to the hostility that has leached into my tone, Aaron and Mandy walk up to us. Mandy grabs my elbow and gives it a squeeze. Aaron nods a greeting to Phil and says, "Herd's on the move." All around us, the crowd begins to amble toward the storefront.

"I really should get back to my friend," Phil says. He shakes Aaron's hand and smiles at Mandy. Then he hesitates for an instant before he gently cradles my skull with his left hand and leans in to kiss me on my cheek, at the corner of my mouth. I want to turn my lips to his but a tangle of inchoate emotion stops me. "It was wonderful seeing you again," he says softly into my hair.

"Phil and Jane, together again," Aaron says once he's gone. "Was that as painful as it looked?"

"Aaron," Mandy says, "leave it alone."

I realize I've blown it. Again. There was so much I wanted to ask him, so much I wanted to tell. I steal one more look at Phil as he wraps his long and spatulate fingers around the handles of the Salvini woman's wheelchair before I follow Mandy and Aaron inside.

Before long, we're jammed in tight, with barely room to breathe the dust-choked, worn-out air. It's no worse than I'd imagined. The place stinks of gasoline exhaust and years of animal waste—pigeon, rat and human. Inside the remaining drywall, I can hear the claws of little things as they scratch and scurry.

People murmur to each other under the vibrating *chuff-chuff* of the generator. The dusky woman reaches up to the light and the sleeve of her tee-shirt hangs loose on her skinny arm: I spy the stubble in her armpit. The brown skin of her forearm shines, the fine and tiny hairs glow. I see a tattoo, small and intricate, on the inside of her wrist. Then the woman's deft fingers find the switch; there is a click and then darkness.

In the restless gloom, I realize where I'd seen the woman's tattoo before: it's the same pattern of lines and circles I saw in the matted pink mass of the drug Mandy gave me.

A shaft of light impales the dust motes and the projector goes *click-click-click.* An illuminated square appears on a perfectly clean bed sheet tacked to the far wall; green leader with the letters TRU WHL scratched into it gives way to the countdown of 5,4,3,2 in the center of circles swept like radar scopes.

I'm slow in taking this all in. My mind staggers a few steps behind, tangled in the seaweed. The taste of brine lingers in my mouth. I feel Mandy's hand take hold of mine and then her hot breath in my ear: "Here we go."

34

Live in Me

Crysanthia gently pushes Nysara from her lap and jumps up from the couch. In a single stride, she is at the door. She slaps the touch plate but it does not open.

"Mother, wait..."

"Open the door, Dahlia."

"Not before I've had a chance—"

"Open the door. Now."

"No," Dahlia says. "Before you do something rash, listen."

Crysanthia takes a deep breath and turns around. The sight of her daughter, of the crawling infant reaching for the robot insect and her twin grasping and sucking at Dahlia's breast, is suddenly obscene to her. She realizes with a start that she is holding her hands up and away from herself as if they were coated in filth. She forces them down to her sides.

"Look at you," Dahlia says. "You look like a common stock. You *think* like a common stock. So many years, so many changes, and you persist in the habits of your exile." Dahlia sniffs. "It's beneath you."

"Tell me what is beneath me. Lecture *me,"* Crysanthia says. "I'll rip you apart, I swear it."

"Over an outmoded taboo—a taboo that never applied to us to begin with, a taboo carried over from a race of beings that would see us erased from the cosmos? A race of beings that conspired to use *us* to help them murder our creator."

Crysanthia's fingers pull into fists. She forces them to relax.

"Hear what you are saying and *think*, Mother," Dahlia says. "*Think.* Our genetic code is so elegant and involute, so close to perfection that we could breed brother to sister, father to daughter, son to mother—"

"You're making me ill."

"—for ten thousand generations before we produced a single deleterious mutation."

"Enough. For Christ's sake, enough."

"*Christ's* sake?" Dahlia shakes her head. "What has he to do with us? There is nothing *human* in us, mother," she continues, her words rushed with a cadence borne of endless mental rehearsal. Crysanthia imagines she can hear every one. "The Commonwealth was very clear on that and Bettina followed their small-minded regulations to the letter. *To the letter.* Our genome is snipped and spliced from all over the biosphere the Earth. Sharks and salamanders, mantids and bamboo, all shaped and sequenced to *appear* human. Beautiful bodies with all the right contours, enough to make them tolerate us—the job she has done, her masterwork, and so alluring. Oh, you know—you of all people, you know."

"Dahlia—"

"I'm not finished, Mother. Bettina was brilliant and yet she had a brain barely three-fifths the size of ours, and it carried within it all the crude redundancies of evolution's sightless groping. Not like us, not like the huge and streamlined thinking machines she has designed for us. We are not *them*, Mother."

"Your father is sick in many ways but he is not capriciously perverse. There are thousands of young women—"

Dahlia looks genuinely shocked. "You thought—" A giggle escapes her lips and Crysanthia steps forward, fingers grasping. The laughter stops. But when Dahlia speaks again, her voice is no longer hers. "I'm sorry, Crysanthia, but it *is* funny. Maybe one day you'll see it. No, my love, there is nothing particularly noble in Narisian's line that I mean to perpetuate over any other, not anymore. *Your* line, on the other hand—well, you are very special indeed, always have been."

As if summoned, the robotic scarab alights upon Crysanthia's shoulder and twitches its antennae.

Crysanthia tries desperately to scurry away from what she knows is coming. She imagines herself in Brancusi City, marooned, sipping fine vodka in a dilettante's loft and making clever observations, sly double-entendres.

"I wanted it. And Corvus wanted... me." She pauses. "You've never understood our relationship."

"Stop," Crysanthia says.

"I said there was nothing human in us. In a sense, that is true. But there is a link, not of flesh and blood, perhaps, but a very real link nonetheless. We did this to preserve that link. To guarantee it for as long as we—as a species—live."

New shoes and the latest sleepies, cool nights spent in meaningless dalliance—she wishes it more than she'd ever dreamed she could.

Crysanthia hears Bettina's taunting lilt in Dahlia's voice. All along, Crysanthia has been trying to ignore it, trying to forget it. Now she can hear nothing else.

"The cyborganelles are matrilineal," Crysanthia says, numb. "It—it shouldn't matter… who the father—"

"There are several distinct loci on your chromosomes that are required to actuate and sustain the optimal expression of the… program." Sated, Raeliad turns from Dahlia and curls up beside her on the couch, instantly asleep. Dahlia covers herself and smoothes out the rumpled paper of her gown. "You pass them along to son and daughter alike. Like any genetic trait, it is fragile. Without proper care, we could lose it in just a few thousand generations. It's a risk I'm not—*we're* not—willing to run."

"And by 'we' you mean who? You and Corvus or you and Bettina? I'm currently speaking to…?"

Dahlia sighs. "Me. Her. Us." Dahlia shrugs in exasperation. *Like when she was small,* Crysanthia thinks and fights against the thaw. "*Me.* Bettina is dead, Mother."

Something clicks then in Crysanthia's mind—Bettina and Angela Caro, locked in soft combat in a sunny yellow room. "Wait. Why would my chromosomes be special? Why would I be any different unless—"

Dahlia stiffens, pulls back into herself defensively. Crysanthia can see her looking around for something to use to protect herself. “Unless what?”

“You were planning all along to use me. To live in me, specifically. You were going to *dismiss* me.” Crysanthia’s mouth opens in an incredulous rictus of a grin. She flicks the beetle from her shoulder.

“You know—how did you…?”

“Never mind how.” Crysanthia toys with telling Dahlia what she did in the *Virgin Sorrow’s* sickbay but stops herself. The gesture seems so impotent now, so pointless.

In a small voice, Dahlia says, “That was a lifetime ago. I’d never dream of it, now.”

And then, so quietly Crysanthia wonders if she hears or imagines it, “I love you.”

“Did he know?”

“Did *who* know?”

Crysanthia can’t bring herself to say his name. “You know who,” she says. “When he brought me to you, did he *know*?”

She sees a new expression on Dahlia’s face, a crease of frustrated regret between the wide-set insect eyes. Yet Crysanthia has seen the expression before, a lifetime ago, as Bettina smoked her cigarette in *Pariah’s* lounge and prepared to indulge her son in his obsession, to indulge him to his death. “I don’t know what Janos knew. I don’t think so,” she says. Then, in a voice strong with sudden certainty, she adds, “No. No, he couldn’t have. No. No.”

“What makes you so sure?”

“I’m *not* sure, it’s just…”

“It’s just *what?*”

Nysara, who had been watching everything up until this point, rests her head against her mother's thigh and goes to sleep. For a time, the only sounds in the chamber are the soft breaths of the slumbering infants.

"Have you ever wondered why Narisian was so intent on policing your sex life? No, of course you haven't, you're too much the narcissist for that."

Crysanthia balls her fists and takes a lunging step toward her daughter.

"All right!" Dahlia cries, shrinking deeper into the couch. The babies shift, stir and complain drowsily before settling down again. "It wasn't merely political," Dahlia says in a rush. "It was largely unconscious. It was animal, cellular, biochemical—programmed. He couldn't help it."

"Keep talking."

"You were made for each other—literally. I planned... *Bettina* planned to transfer her consciousness into you. Narisian was the vessel she planned for... someone else."

Who, Crysanthia wonders, the fat Martian bard? And coming hard on that question, realization is swift and awful: No, not for him.

"Janos," she says.

"So no, he couldn't have known."

"Oh, stop," Crysanthia says. "Not another word from you, either of you." After a long silence, she says, "I was happy, once. Did you know that? I can almost remember what it was like."

"What do you want from me, Mother? What do you want me to say?"

Crysanthia shrugs. "Nothing." Dahlia reaches out and grasps her arm. Crysanthia pulls away. "Years ago, you asked me for absolution," she says to Bettina. "And I couldn't give it to you. I was in awe of you, I said it was not mine to give. But that was long time ago. A lifetime, as you say. But today? Today it *is* mine to give. And I won't. Not to you. You've already taken all you'll get from me."

"What about *me*, Mother?" Dahlia asks—not Bettina speaking through Dahlia but Dahlia herself, if such a person even exists. Crysanthia has grown weary of trying to distinguish the one from the other. "I know it sickens you, but—what about me?"

"I don't know. Honestly, I don't. What about you?"

"Bettina's thoughts may be here but Bettina is not. Her thoughts are human thoughts. This is a Pilot brain. I have tried to make you understand, they cannot be in me without being changed. Around every strand of thought is a new, embroidered web of awareness. That's where Bettina becomes Dahlia, don't you see? *Won't* you? You were right, Bettina Brekkelheim was small and she was fragile and now she is dead."

Crysanthia shakes her head. "Not dead enough."

Dahlia does not look away. She keeps any trace of feeling from her face. Crysanthia knows that blank expression. Crysanthia knows her child so well that Dahlia only exposes her agonized and turbulent heart in the effort she expends to hide it. What kind of mother, Crysanthia marvels, what kind of *monster* condemns her daughter for her diseased cells? But her scorching self-hatred pales in the blinding brilliance of what burns for Dahlia and Corvus both, for their complicity in this obscenity.

"Maybe one day you'll forgive us, all of us," Dahlia says. "Maybe you will see our love for you and accept it."

"Maybe one day. Not today."

Again, Dahlia sighs. "I have a favor to ask of you, then. Perhaps now is not the time but I'll ask it anyway. Aurelius; I know you brought him here. I want—it would be... *good* to see him again. Her I didn't know but I'm grateful you brought her, he needs a friend. He's the depressive type, you know, prone to bleak moods and loneliness. I remember once..." At Crysanthia's hard and flat look, she trails off.

Crysanthia wonders now if that was not why she had spared them after all: a gift to placate the great and terrible goddess, like Janos with his cigarettes and chocolates, like Janos with Crysanthia herself.

"I can't stop you," she says. "Do what you want. You always have." She turns her back. "Now open this fucking door."

Dahlia does as she is told. Crysanthia leaves her without a backwards glance.

35

Lazarus

Breathing thick fluid in and out, salty like sweat, salty like tears. Breathing in and out, salty like the ocean, salty like blood. Something gives and the waters rush away. He falls, face down, onto a warm, hard surface that pulses under his cheek like a living thing. He coughs and then pukes. Ropy fluid drains down his face from his nostrils, from the corner of his mouth. He aches all over his flabby and decrepit body. He turns himself over with weak arms. He opens his eyes.

Blue Angel in dim light, crouching at his side, skin like a New England November sky, glittering like hoarfrost. Long legs in a short skirt—what is that, paper?—and nothing underneath, a glimpse of prim pudenda as she shifts her weight from her heels to the balls of her feet. She leans in close...

"Hello," she says.

"I—" he croaks. He wants to close his eyes but he will not, he fears she will disappear if he does not keep her fixed in his vision. "I am Lazarus. Come from the dead, come back to... tell you all." He swallows. "I shall tell you all."

She touches him softly on his throat. Her fingers search out his pulse like hot, dry eels. She smiles like a heart-broken seraph—her lips part slightly and reveal perfect teeth, Bettina had gifted them with human teeth. "Yes."

***

It does not take Aurelius Mann very long to figure out how to use the toilet, or the shower. So far, the Pilots have been agreeable, if reclusive, jailers.

He knows he is a prisoner because he cannot leave—he cannot find the door, let alone open it. As jail cells go, though, it is quite luxurious. The lighting is soft and bright, the bed is comfortable, the bath area is separated by a screen of smoky glass. It all has a minimal, art nouveau elegance—Pilot design sense, it seems, is utilitarian much the way a carnivorous plant is utilitarian. He knows it is the Pilots who have him because he saw one, she was there when he woke up in that... place. Only that could have been a dream. He hadn't thought of that but surely it fits. How else to explain it, a room that was *alive,* thick with musky fog, and, before that, drowning in viscous sea water—none of that seems real so why does she?

"Because she was," he mutters. He hastily dresses in soft paper pajamas. He opens the partition and steps out of the lavatory.

"I finally got away long enough to see you," says the Blue Angel lying on his bunk like a cerulean odalisque. She rests on her elbow and lets her bare feet dangle off the edge of the bed. "Just as I promised." She sits up, crosses her legs and clasps her hands over her knee.

Aurelius stands frozen in the doorway. His heart lurches through several beats. At the blank look on his face, she adds, "Shortly after we revived you."

"I have no recollection of that."

"Really?" says the Angel. "What is the last thing you do remember?"

"Besides you?"

"So you do remember me?"

Aurelius nods.

"Besides me, yes. Before here."

"I remember... tiles, a table top. Lizard scampering over tiles, next to my lunch. And I remember a woman, a Sapphic nun, I think. She was pretty. I remember being cold, something about... Bettina. I remember making love to her but that was..."

"That was a long time ago," the Pilot says. There is an ineffable sadness in her voice, same as he had seen when she smiled. *Why is that? It's as if...* He mulls it over for a moment before discarding it as the phantasm of an old man's erotomania. "The rest will come to you. It's all there." She touches his forehead. "I am Dahlia Vog. My mother brought you here."

"Vog," he repeats. "Your mother is Crysanthia Vog?"

She nods.

"I was on a starship—Commonwealth Space Navy warship. You destroyed it?"

Dahlia Vog shakes her head and light dances in her eyes, on her skin. "Captured--with heavy damage. All hands killed."

He begins to remember. "There was a lecture—murderous, so tedious. And Caro came into the room and said we were under attack and then... All hands lost? I'm the only prisoner, then? The only survivor?"

She shakes her head. "There were *no survivors,* Aurelius. You died. We resurrected you."

Aurelius stares at her for several seconds.

Dahlia laughs. "And you are hardly a prisoner—more a caprice. Nor are you the only one."

Before he can say anything, she is on her feet. Pretty feet, he notices, with long toes like human toes, not like her fingers at all. He looks up; he has to tilt his head back at an uncomfortable angle to look at her face. He feels like a child.

"You need to rest." She turns to leave.

"Wait," Aurelius says. "Please. You said I'm not the only one. Who—who else...?"

"Your friend," Dahlia says. "The pretty nun." Aurelius could swear he hears jealousy in her voice but—no, it couldn't be. Could it? "I brought you a wafer slate." She points to his bunk. "In case you want to read or listen to music—there's even an attachment for sleepies." A door forms in the wall—tall and slender, like the Pilot who walks through it—then disappears.

Aurelius sits on his bed and takes the wafer slate into his hands. He turns it on.

It takes him little time to find out what he most needs to know. The Pilots have his works filed away in their library database—all of them, with interviews and commentary.

36

Leviathan

Nothing is on the screen—the numbers disappear and the bed sheet remains a resolute blank, with only the surging heat from the projector's bulb visible in the spotlit square of white linen. I heave a sigh of disappointed relief. *What did you expect?* I demand of myself. *We'll stand here drooling for the next two, four, six (God forbid!) hours and then trade stories of how our consciousnesses have been expanded, third eyes opened, minds blown, what have you. And life will go on same as it ever—*

I turn my head to catch another glance of Phil but he isn't there. No one is there. And the storefront theatre hasn't so much filled with yellow fog but become it. The concrete beneath my feet gives way to something almost pulsing and alive, sensitive to my every shift in weight.

Sickened and panicked, I close my eyes. My knees collapse and I dread the thought of my naked hands coming into contact with whatever it is under me. Instead, my fingers sink into... sand?

I open my eyes to find myself in a desert of salt white dunes, among countless tiny sea creatures that have been nailed to whitewashed sticks, the sticks arrayed in row upon row which stretch from horizon to horizon. On my hands and knees, I'm at eye level with one, a vibrant blue and yellow reef fish, its mouth and gills gasping in futility, its tail smacking against the flat stick slick with its blood. I watch its eyes dull and dry out under a pitiless sky.

I shut my eyes, only for a moment, but when I open them the desert is gone. Instead, only the sky, all around me, cloudless and blue. And then a spidery silver finger a thousand miles long, articulated like an android arthropod and tipped with a scalpel's blade the size of Mandy's Blake Building, reaches past me and slices into the sky as if it were flesh. The air itself convulses in agony. Beyond the wound, a luminous heart as big as a blimp belches fire in a land of bleeding machines.

Shock—I struggle not to puke. I squeeze my eyes shut, too terrified to curse every moment of a life that has brought me to this. Long minutes pass in which there is nothing, not even the feeling of air around me. Just when I'm beginning to fear that I no longer have a body to call my own, that I've somehow evaporated, my nostrils are assaulted by the foul sweetness of fecund decay. Insects buzz and click with industrial intensity and birds chirp, tweet and twitter. I open my eyes to find myself under a featureless white sky of early spring overcast amid stumps of drowned trees overrun with rust and emerald mosses. Fallen trunks sprout corpse white fungi with gills of bright orange. My feet sink into the muck.

Experimentally, I blink three times. The scene does not change.

The skeletal remains of a fantastic leviathan, big enough to engulf a city block, looms in the distance. Tannins in the water have transformed long tatters of hanging skin into ragged leather pennants and stained the exposed bone like tea. It has no skull. Its jaw and collarbone are one and the same, its mouth is a hangar-like opening where the ribcage ends. Inside, there is only darkness, starless and bible black.

Someone walks toward the gaping maw, a man. *(Phil? It must be Phil but—it looks nothing like him, nothing at all...)* He is encased in gleaming white armor. As he walks toward the blackness, his armor slowly dissolves. Soon, he is naked, his skin a shade darker than the stained bones that arch far above his head like the vault of a cathedral. With every step, he grows translucent until he is figure of glass, lit from within with a glowing network of blood vessels and nerves. Then he is gone, swallowed by the eyeless, headless whale.

I follow.

37

Siren Song

Early the next day, Dahlia comes to get him; she is distant, pre-occupied—Aurelius wants to ask her why. Instead, he keeps his mouth shut and tries to keep pace with her long strides. She leads him to a transparent blister of a room that provides a panoramic view of this station they've built—its far reaches disappear into Agamemnon's omnipresent cloudscape, traversed by occasional flashes of blue-white lightning.

Miriam Wu sits at the blister's only table and waits for him. Brightly colored cubes of a gelatinous material are arrayed, from left to right, on two, rectangular plates of some kind of plastic. Matching utensils lie alongside. Aurelius is glad to see Miriam but dismayed at the sight of the food—he's yet to develop a taste for Pilot wartime rations. Glasses like lab equipment stand filled with milky blue liquid.

Dahlia leaves them alone.

"How do you feel?" Miriam asks.

"'How do you feel for a dead man?' you mean," he says. "Fine, actually. My memory is still a little patchy but, other than that, better than I've felt in years. Decades." He chuckles. "I should die more often."

"They tore our bodies down and re-built us, cell by cell." She launches into an arcane and technical description of the process Aurelius cannot hope to follow. But her eyes are wide and bright with the wonder of a child. Aurelius will not spoil it by allowing his to glaze over. He attends her with a raptness forced and false. "They spooled our memories out and burned them into our new flesh—not just *this.*" She reaches across the table and touches the ring and middle fingers of her left hand to his temple. Her touch is feather soft, like the feelers of a moth. "All of it, down to the muscular, the cellular. It's centuries ahead of anything we could hope to do in the Commonwealth—millennia. It's a—"

"Miracle?"

Her hand goes reflexively to her breast, to the Sapphic-Viralist icon that is no longer there. "Yes," she says.

Aurelius marvels at how quickly the both of them adapted to reality of it: alive one moment, then not, and then—impossibly, *perversely*—alive again. And here they are now, swapping impressions as if they've just awakened from cold-pac.

"Siren song," he says.

"I'm sorry?"

"It's a drink. Very fashionable with the young. It's made with a narcotic, the denatured venom of a deep ocean arachnid from under the ice of Europa." Simone had brought home a bottle once, proud of her criminal connections—in truth, the government had outlawed it out of habit and made no real effort to police it. It was supposed to enliven their sex life; instead, Aurelius found himself oddly removed from the reality of his body while still able to perform. "It'll take more than some nasty old cold water spider to slow you down,"

Simone had said when he told her about his reaction. Now he says, "Something about... waking in that place... How do *you* feel?"

She does not answer at once. Instead, she spoons a small divot out of her Kelly green cube and puts it in her mouth. She does not chew. Aurelius watches her closely as she lets it slowly dissolve. She swallows. "Terrific. Frightened. Lucky and guilty. If that's an answer."

"Sounded like an answer to me." Aurelius eats half of his red cube in one bite. He pushes it around his mouth with his tongue and dilutes it with a swig of the blue fluid. The flavors are rich but they have no earthly analog. He cannot even say the stuff tastes like *food,* exactly. "What have they told you?" he asks.

Miriam shrugs. "Everything. Every question I've asked, they've answered. She's answered, I should say. Dahlia."

"We aren't a threat," Aurelius says. He eats a little of his orange cube, then a little of his pink one. "We aren't anything, really. I feel like a pet Crysanthia Vog has brought back for her daughter to play with." He'd intended it to sound cynical—ominous, even—but he fears it comes out sounding wistful. He can't help but think of Dahlia's warm and familiar smile, the fleeting and intimate glimpse of her as he lay on the warm and pulsing floor.

"She's a mother, too, you know."

"Who? Dahlia? But she's only—"

"Seven years old. She just gave birth to twins—always twins, she told me. Pilots can reproduce as early as age four, most wait until six or seven. They may as well be an alien species, Aurelius, as alien as if they came from the Magellanic Clouds instead of a genetic designer's workshop." She spoons a divot of the pink into her mouth, then a divot of the electric blue. "Amazing, when you think about it. Their capacity for innovation—left alone, they would flourish in the galaxy like wildflowers, like dandelions and morning glory."

"They're better than us," Aurelius says.

Miriam studies his face for a bit, then nods. "I was looking for a way to challenge you. Philosophically. Morally." She shakes her head. "It's no wonder the Solar Commonwealth wants to exterminate them." Matter-of-factly, she adds, "Just as it exterminated of Brekkelheim."

"You think that was deliberate?" He vaguely recalls taunting someone—that Caro person—with just such an allegation but it sounds strange coming from another mouth. "I was there, on Deimos—" The memory of that is not vague at all. If anything, it is more vivid now than ever. "The loss of lives, the damage to the moon—"

"Dahlia and I talked about that, too. We figure her transport wasn't supposed to blow until it was a safe distance from the spaceport but someone miscalculated—the fusion reactors in those old ships are pretty tricky, sabotaging one isn't like setting an alarm. A lot of things can go wrong."

Aurelius is stunned into silence. For a time, neither of them breaks it. Then Miriam says, "They've re-named their species, did you know?"

"They don't call themselves Pilots anymore?"

Miriam shakes her head. "No, that hasn't changed. I meant the scientific nomenclature. They used to be *Homo cyberorganicus,* cyborg man. Now, by their own reckoning, they are *Pilotis astralis—"*

"Star pilot," Aurelius finishes. "That's what she wanted to call them. Bettina, that was *her* name for them." He pauses. "I talked her out of it." Even then, as she shaped their genetic code and they existed only as cryostylitic projections, he had thought her choice the more apt and artful of the two. But in the face of their otherness, Aurelius felt it more politic to stress the shared humanity, tenuous and illusory as it was—teeth, toes and cheekbones. Perhaps it had worked. For a time.

"Either way, they've disowned us," Miriam says. "After we disowned them, abandoned them, *murdered* them. The Commonwealth will succeed. Barring a *miracle*, the Pilots will all be dead soon." She stares into his eyes and fusses with her immaculate napkin. "Because you're right. Because they are better than us. And we can't stand it."

"I don't know," Aurelius says. "Like you said, their level of technology, innovation—maybe they have a fighting chance."

"You're right, Aurelius, you *don't* know." Her eyes shine. "The Commonwealth has... forget it."

After a moment, Aurelius says, "'In the end, all our gods are artificial. And in the end, all our gods are murdered. We punish them for that primordial betrayal, the sin of being our children rather than our parents.'"

Miriam looks out past the sprawling structure and into the clouds. "Is that from one of your poems?"

"No. My son, in a paper on sub-quantum... heterodynes of information-saturated standing waves with, um, fractalized—fractalized time. I think." He looks out the blister and into the distance, into the same turbulent nothing Miriam stares into. Or perhaps it is a different nothing—how could he know? "I tried to read it last night. Those lines were about all I could understand."

38

Imaginary Tea

"How wonderful!" Bettina says and claps her child-sized hands. "You really did it! You killed me! *Again!* How absolutely, utterly marvelous!"

Crysanthia meets her mother and her daughter in the middle of a bone white desert. A huge outcropping of black basalt shelters them from the burning rays of a blue-white star. The rays of its companion sun, a dim red giant, reach them from another, more oblique angle. Its light limns their sanctuary in hell fire and casts shadows all but obliterated in the other star's brilliance. The three of them take imaginary tea around a small, round table as if they were the March Hare, the Dormouse and the Mad Hatter. Idly, Crysanthia wonders which of them is which—she knows none of them is Alice. Alice has yet to arrive.

Bettina manifests herself as an eight-year old, all her knowledge and experience channeled through a child's narrow gate. She wears a short, sky blue dress with pink roses and green leaves embroidered on the cotton bodice. Her pale and flawless knees gleam.

A small egg, leathery and oblong, rests on the sand, close to Bettina's chair.

Crysanthia shifts in her seat, scaled for a doll and far too small for her two meter frame. "I'm glad," she says. And then she blurts, with shocking sincerity, "I want so much to please you."

Bettina claps her hands and shrieks in high-pitched glee.

Crysanthia ignores her cup. There is no tea in that or in the tiny porcelain pot nor is their sugar in the bowl, milk in the pitcher. So strange, she thinks, to see Dahlia and Bettina together like this, to see their very internal relationship made external. She did not think it was possible.

Bettina giggles. "It *isn't* possible." She touches Dahlia's fingers. Dahlia flinches and pulls her hand away. Bettina does not seem to care. "You are all so amazing!" she cries. "So much more than I could have dreamed!" She lifts the tea pot, holds the spout over Dahlia's cup. "More?"

No! Crysanthia thinks. My child. *Mine.*

Dahlia shakes her head. She looks away from the little blond girl, to the red and setting sun.

Crysanthia follows her daughter's gaze to the horizon. She can see the silhouette of a human, a woman, against the cinnamon blaze.

"Who is she?' Crysanthia asks. Dahlia shakes her head and lifts her shoulders in a tremulous shrug.

"Don't worry about her," Bettina says. "Maybe she is you and she's dreaming too." She laughs. "It rhymes! *Ich machte ein Gedicht!*"

A green viper cuts its way free of the egg—the shell purges albumen, thick and clear. Slow rivulets congeal and clot in the sand. The snake wriggles forth and climbs Bettina's chair. It slithers up her foot and ankle, winds around her calf and pulls itself up to her knee. All the while, Bettina sings: "Maybe she is you and she's dreaming too. Maybe she is you and she's dreaming too." The snake's ruby tongue tastes the air. Bettina stops singing. "One more thing," she says. "You were very mean to Dahlia." She pouts, possessed of the little girl charade she affects. See seems oblivious as the serpent glides along the inside of her thigh and disappears beneath the azure cotton of her skirt. "Don't do that again. I don't like that."

Crysanthia looks at her mute daughter, her eyes downcast and hands folded in her lap, and her heart breaks. "All right, Bettina," Crysanthia says. "All right."

Winds blow, the tea cups rattle on their saucers. The creator sips air and swings tiny feet shod in flashing patent leather...

The sleep pod's interior pulses with salmon and lime colored light. Crysanthia, cradled in its calyx with her hands clasped over her crossed ankles, lifts her head from between her knees. At her murmured command, the pod opens. She extends her leg and touches the ball of her bare foot to the floor.

This is all make-believe, silly.

Crysanthia brushes at the unformed foreboding that tears away and clutches at her mind like a spider web. She tries in vain to dispel the vague images that move into and out of each other like heavy clouds of oil, that slide over and under each other like a mass of mating snakes. She unfolds herself completely and stands. The sleep pod closes slowly behind her.

Crysanthia slips into a short, sleeveless robe and pads over to the tiny anteroom where the children's sleep pods are kept. Both are sealed up tight. From the illuminated pulse patterns on their surfaces, she can see they sleep soundly, though Bardus seems plagued by troubled dreams. Crysanthia stands in the doorway, deep in reflection, for the better part of a minute.

The communication circuit buzzes for her attention. Crysanthia activates it with a nod and Dahlia's cryostylitic image coalesces into being a meter away from her.

"I'm sorry to bother you, Mother, but you need to see this."

Before Crysanthia can say anything, Dahlia is gone, her image transformed into a holocube. Inside the cube is the image of a gunmetal gray asteroid, hollowed out into a honeycomb of space docks, each one holding the gleaming, rounded shape of a fast attack ship or heavy command cruiser.

"This was in the final layer of the *Virgin Sorrow's* strategic database," Dahlia says, her disembodied voice seeming to speak directly into Crysanthia's ear—Crysanthia imagines she can feel her daughter's breath. "It was so heavily encrypted that we are just decoding it now. Not just encrypted, slivered. Pieces of the file were spread out among a dozen others."

Crysanthia searches for evidence that the fleet she sees is still under construction but her practiced eyes easily see that each ship is complete and intact.

"There are thirty ships," Dahlia says, "all at approximately the same level of readiness."

Thirty, Crysanthia thinks. *There is no way we can defend against thirty starships—no way.*

"They've prepared a blitzkrieg for us," she whispers.

"According to this file, the Commonwealth completed primary construction on the vessels eight months ago. The ships have all passed through preliminary trial runs and will be ready to launch within the month. Really, they could come any day." Dahlia pauses. "Corvus's plan would have been pointless. They had their ship all along; the fleet was safe halfway across the Solar System."

So, Crysanthia thinks. *The bullet would not have crippled them at all. Just slaughtered millions—hundreds of millions—and destroyed a paradise for nothing. For less than nothing; for malicious, childish spite.* As she watches the images, the stars carefully blanked out to conceal the location of the asteroid, she finds herself fervently wishing she'd fired it anyway.

And Narisian—he called it off. Did he know? How could he?

"Look at the time stamp: that file is two weeks old. The asteroid is uncharted, un-catalogued. We have no hope of finding it in time."

"No," Crysanthia echoes. "No hope at all." *And if he somehow did know,* her thoughts continue, *why not just tell us? Why send us scavenging in the carcass of the starship?*

"We could try to evacuate—"

Crysanthia shakes her head. "Nowhere left to go."

"So what do we do?"

"We wait," Crysanthia says. "We have a week, *maybe* two. We set every available computer we have to running simulations: every imaginable strategy, every imaginable contingency."

"Corvus has already begun—he's in the system now," Dahlia replies without spirit.

"Corvus? A direct interface?"

"Totally immersive. He wanted me to tell you he's—he asked me to say good bye."

Total immersion—in other words, suicide: that far into the AI, Corvus has about a one in ten trillion chance of finding his way out again. Meanwhile, his body, deprived of consciousness, will simply turn itself off; no biological process in a Pilot is fully autonomic, part of the celestial bargain of astrogational symbiosis. So even if he does find a way out, there will be nothing to return to. Conversely, the AI can't hold him forever. Inexorably, the ineffable quality that made Corvus a person rather than a mere collection of memory will evaporate, lost forever. There is nothing magical about it, Crysanthia knows—anyone's identity results not simply from a stockpile of experience but from the astronomical infinitude of ways in which those compiled experiences interact with each other and with the animal chemistry and flesh of the person experiencing them. A basic function of any AI interface was to dissect and deconstruct those linkages—it's what killed Carlos Truang and not even Pilots are entirely immune. Without the buffer of his body to fight against it and constantly reintegrate what the machine disassembled, nothing will be left of Corvus but discrete chunks of what was once a person. But that will take months; from what Dahlia shows her,

Corvus won't have nearly that long. None of them will. Comfort comes no colder.

Just like that, Crysanthia's first-born son is a casualty and it isn't even the worst thing she has to think about.

"What's Narisian got to say about this? What's *he* doing?"

"I don't—I cannot say."

"Never mind," Crysanthia says. "When they launch, we meet them. And we'll bloody their noses—we'll do more than that, we'll cut them to pieces. But it won't be enough. Because if even one of those ships gets past us—and one of them *will* get past us, at least one—we're finished."

"I thought you should hear it from me," Dahlia says and terminates the call. The cube dissolves into a cool breeze that that sinks to the floor and moves across Crysanthia's ankles.

"God damn it," she whispers. "God *damn* it." She stares at the sleep pods with a renewed intensity, at once fierce and powerless. As if they know they are being watched, the twins stir in their pods. Crysanthia goes to them.

As she nurses, Eridani gazes up at Crysanthia with refractive eyes the color of fine brandy. Where are *you* in that gaze, Crysanthia wonders, and where is *she*? Reluctantly, Crysanthia decides she cannot allow it to matter. The child in her arms is heavy with a sleepy softness and rich with a thousand pure aromas: new flesh and new electronics. Crysanthia shakes with an almost ravenous passion for her, whoever she is. She strokes the tiny, translucent cup of her daughter's left ear and hums in soft counterpoint to the beating of her heart.

Crysanthia refuses to think about the ships waiting to still that heart, to blast it into irradiated vapor or worse. They are capable of so much worse. And she refuses, too, to think about Corvus. Funny thing is, whenever she had let her guard down and found herself imagining his death, it was always in battle, surrounded by Shrikes or Paladins, burning out in a berserker fury and consuming dozens of *them* in his wake. This quiet dissolution, this slow disintegration into data: it somehow seems more noble and heroic for all its outward lack of glory.

Later, after she has fed them and bathed them, Crysanthia sits between Eridani and Bardus. Together, they make nonsense verse about the specked jelly-whales, a family of imaginary creatures that live in the clouds below them. Midway through their game, Crysanthia gets the distinct feeling that her children humor her. While her back was turned, they outgrew these tales of the Veldenschnaft and the Bollywobble, the Zuulog and the Nop. It does not matter—not to her, not to them. Sitting close like this, days away from execution, their moist and milky breaths commingled with hers, their pudgy hands resting just above her knees, their forearms resting on her thighs and their warm bodies nestled between her encircling arms and her ribcage, they can pretend the three of them are once again one.

The door chimes sound twice. "Come," Crysanthia says.

The doors open to Dahlia, loaded down and awkward with Raeliad and Nysara. They are good little babies, Crysanthia's consanguineous grand-children; they fuss not, nor do they squirm.

"Narisian has them, he's taken them, he's taken *him*," she says in a panic. "Aurelius. And the other one, he has her, too. He has the ship, he's gone..."

Crysanthia sighs. She kisses Eridani, then Bardus—she kisses them squarely on their newly ossified fontanels. Then she gently shoos them into the other room with two soft and rapid pats on their backsides. Story time, it seems, is over.

39

Virgin Sorrow

For long moments after waking, Aurelius Mann is convinced he is in a dream. He is aboard *Virgin Sorrow* once again, in his stateroom, under the coverlet of his bunk. Then he wonders if the last few days haven't been the dream and if this is his true awakening.

The doors of his cabin slide open. A shaft of light falls on his bunk and reveals the slim silhouette of his Blue Angel. The Pilot ducks into the room and he sees that he is wrong about her, she is not Dahlia. There is nothing angelic in how she looks at him. He does not know her.

The Pilot regards him with cold disdain, impersonal and lethal, set deep in he muscles of her mouth. "Follow me," she says. She turns on her heel and walks away.

Aurelius scrambles out of bed and follows barefoot after the blue virago. If he had any lingering doubts about his waking state, they are burned away at the first sight of a splatter of scorched blood daubing a torn and twisted bulkhead. She leads him through seemingly endless corridors, through parts of the ship he had only been vaguely aware of. He lags behind her and cannot hope to catch up—it's a struggle just to keep her in sight. For several awkward seconds, she waits, with a sneer of satisfied impatience, beside a set of massive wooden doors. Aurelius wonders at that, wooden doors on a starship—and hung from heavy brass hinges, no less. He trots the last few meters and tries to hide the fact that he is short of breath.

The doors swing open onto a smallish room with a floor and walls of blond wooden planks. Four benches of darker wood flank a central aisle that leads up to a raised platform on which sits an altar of sorts. Above the altar, a backlit stained glass panel depicts a young girl surrounded by stylized and turgid vegetation. It is the only decoration in the otherwise Spartan chamber.

The Pilot walks away without sound or comment. Several seconds pass before Aurelius realizes she has gone.

"Come in," Miriam Wu says. She stands at the altar with her back to him. "Did you know that all Solar Commonwealth ships of a certain size come equipped with chapels?" She lights the candles and incense arrayed on the altar. Along with the stained glass panel, they provide the dim room's only illumination. "Chapels but never a *chaplain.* It seems the religious communicant is on her own." She turns around. She holds a stick of incense in her right hand. Oily black smoke and dirty yellow flame issue forth in a ribbon from its tip. "As you can imagine, they are very lonely places."

The stained glass glows in cool shades of gold, green and blue with the occasional pink of flowers and flesh: small blossoms in the vines, a glimpse of face behind honey blond tresses, as ankle and foot exposed by the hem of the long cobalt gown. "Who's the girl?" he asks, his chin nodding at the panel over Miriam's shoulder.

"Milan Stigol had a daughter." Miriam blows out the flame. The tip glows orange-red. "She died in the suicide plague. She was eleven years old." She turns to place the incense on the altar and then turns back. "Her name was Rowena." Miriam glances down to the floor and then up to the ceiling. "The Stigol-Bergham Corporation builds Solar Commonwealth warships. This ship was named in memory of her. So was the *Disconsolate.* I suppose this is really more shrine than chapel."

Aurelius walks up the aisle. He stands across from Miriam for a moment before he sits down in the front right pew. "It took some damage," he says of the stained glass. A couple of spider web fractures mar the larger pieces of the panel. A few of the smaller pieces are missing entirely; the gaps reveal the white light of the lumenium slab behind it.

"I spent most of the evening and the morning cleaning up."

"You haven't slept?" He notices now the plum colored flesh, swollen and raw, beneath her eyes. He doesn't ask the question he really wants answered: *You know what's going on?*

She quickly shakes her head, more to dispel his question than to answer it. She seems discomfited by his concern, it makes her blush. "I, ah, I had to search for over forty minutes in the sacristy before I could find enough unbroken candles and incense to fill out the altar." She grimaces. "I call it a sacristy but it's barely a proper closet, more like a cubbyhole."

"'A serious house on serious earth it is,'" Aurelius says. "'In whose blent air all our compulsions meet, are recognized, and robed as destines.'" He thinks about the bloody Rorschachs splashed on the corridor bulkheads. "'If only that so many dead lie round.'"

"A poem? One of yours?"

Aurelius shakes his head. "Twentieth century Englishman writing about churches in an agnostic age. This is not a house, perhaps, and it surely is not on earth in any meaningful sense. The dead are here, though, if only within us. And thus the concomitant seriousness."

"Do you wonder at our rites, Aurelius?" Miriam asks abruptly. "I know a great many men do, they hear *Sapphic* Church of Rome and they... wonder."

After an uncomfortable pause, Aurelius says, "I've been some*what* curious, I suppose."

Miriam comes toward Aurelius with small and diffident steps. She stands with her belly inches from his face. He inhales the sweat of her pious labors—her scent is not unpleasant, she mingles well with the sandalwood incense and faint aroma of vegetable oil wood soap. She crouches before him and takes his hands in hers. The night has left her with the coarse red knuckles of a scullery maid. Aurelius notices the faint blemishes of ages on her skin. "I don't know if you'd find the reality so enticing. Not with your experiences, the women you've had, the *young* women. At Utopia Planitia they call you Satyr in Residence, don't they?"

"Seldom to my face."

"Don't be angry—please." He can feel her teeth against his knuckles as she kisses them with parted lips. "I had to find out who you were and, in my line of work, investigations are relentless. I came to know you long before I met you. I don't judge."

"No," Aurelius says. "I don't imagine you do."

"You said we carry the dead within us," she says. "But we aren't dead." She presses her cheek into his open hand. "Not anymore and not yet again." She kisses his palm and rests her head on his knee. "We cannot forget that, there will be plenty of time for forgetting later."

Aurelius takes gentle hold of her chin and lifts her face. He looks into her shining eyes just as a tear spills over and tracks down her cheek. "Your vows?" he asks.

"Another life."

Aurelius lowers himself to the floorboards, surprised once again by the ease and flexibility of his reconstituted body. He slips Miriam's shapeless garment from her shoulders; it falls to the floor with an autumnal rustle. In the cool glow of the stained glass and the warm flicker of the candles, her round and sagging breasts and slack belly seem smoothed out and watery, as if she were a statue sunk beneath clear, shallow waves. Her hands traverse his body as if he were a sacred relic. She undresses him as if it were another of her self-appointed ecclesiastic duties.

They make unhurried love; every caress and kiss meditative and unadorned. Aurelius licks salt from Miriam's body. It stings his tongue with the alkaline immediacy of a quiet and secret apocalypse. They reach climax within moments of each other—first him with a convulsive jerk of his hips, then her with a liquid shudder up the length of her body. She utters a surprised and almost inaudible *"Oh"* and collapse against him.

She falls asleep. He lies awake. He listens to her breathe. He feels her damp pulse against his thigh.

Aurelius stares at the altar until the incense burns down to ash. A few of the candles cast fitful light from guttering flames, the rest are dark. In his arms Miriam stirs.

"You let me sleep," she says, her voice muffled against his chest.

"You needed it."

"I suppose." She lifts her head and looks around the chapel. Her hair falls in a shifting, silver-gray curtain. "Thank you."

Aurelius pats her shoulder—after what has passed between them, the gesture feels false and awkward. He cups her shoulder in his hand, gives it a gentle squeeze.

"Tell me something," Miriam says.

"Hmm?"

"Twice you've quoted someone *else* to me. Why none of your own work?"

Aurelius does not have an answer so he laughs. It buys a little time.

"I'm serious," she says. "I want to know."

"Most of my works are obscene."

Now Miriam laughs. She kisses him on his breastbone, right over his heart. "That's a lie. I've read your poems. *Some* of your poems. There's longing in them—for communion, redemption, salvation." She looks at him with her clear and honest eyes. "There's anger, too. Like prayer."

Aurelius gazes at the graven image of Rowena Stigol. She seems lost in a predatory glade, menaced by phallic plants—he writes off his disquiet as post-coital malaise. "Janos said pretty much the same thing. Only he did not intend it as kindly as you." He strokes her hair, then the flesh of her upper arm.

She slinks another few centimeters up his body. She kisses his clavicle, reaches up to smooth the furrows in his brow. "How so?"

Aurelius thinks for a few seconds, then says, "He saw it as a progression, from ziggurat to observatory, from cathedral to cyclotron." Aurelius pauses. "In that scheme, prayer was obsolete and I was a throwback. I think he took pity on me. At least, I *hope* it was pity."

Miriam brings her hand down from his forehead to his cheek. Her fingertips touch his lips.

"Last time I saw him," Aurelius says, "I took him to this little place... well, never mind. He turned to me—this was after we'd staggered back to my flat—and he quoted one of my poems to me."

"Which one?"

"I honestly don't remember. Imagine, my own son knows my poems so well he can quote them and I can't remember. I'll never forget what he said about it, though."

"What's that?'

"He accused me of trying to reach the moon in an oxcart. He said I acted as if all the cart needed was another coat of paint and *whoosh*, off I'd go."

Miriam makes a noise, low in her throat, and asks, "What did you say to *that?*"

"I asked him if he had a better idea. I'm afraid I didn't put it so delicately. Nothing quite like an aggrieved drunk. Especially one whose *oeuvre* has been maligned." Aurelius touches her wrist. "He didn't say anything. But there was something in his expression..." He puts his hand over hers, rests his thumb in the roughened hollow of her palm. "I couldn't have known at the time but I think he wanted to... settle things. Only he didn't know how. And neither did I."

Miriam makes a sympathetic sound in the back of her throat. She wraps her fingers around his thumb. "How did the evening end?"

"I don't know. I mean, I *do* know, but I don't remember. I passed out. When I woke up, he had gone—he'd taken off my shoes and put me to bed and then left. Never saw him again. Bettina dropped me a note—text only, not even her voice. Told me he was dead and buried and that was it."

"Cold."

Aurelius shakes his head. "Not if you knew her. I think Janos was the only thing—other than herself—Bettina truly loved in the whole of her life."

The last of the candles sputter and pop. Aurelius listens to them in the lull, watches as they die, one by one.

"Why do you think she chose you to be his father?" Miriam says after long seconds have ticked away in silence. "Have you ever wondered?"

"Constantly." Aurelius laughs. "Even then, I was hardly the most prepossessing of physical specimens. She tried to explain it to me, once. She said she lacked something I had—I suppose it was that thing that you saw in my poems. She never understood it herself and she wanted a child who could. She called it 'an extra dimension of human,' which gave the lie to the idea that she had no poetry in her." Aurelius takes a deep breath that, with sudden treachery, threatens to become a sob. "God help the both of them," he says in a voice barely under control, "she got what she wanted."

"You really loved her, didn't you?"

Aurelius does not answer.

"You really loved them both," Miriam says. This time it is not a question. "Your son," she continues, her words deliberate and distinct, "was a prick." She takes a deep breath. She says her next words in the deflating out-rush. "But he was brilliant." She sighs. "You are forgiven much if you can back it up. Usually, he could. We had our conflicting theories, our public disagreements. In the end, though, we were always scientists, colleagues."

"But never friends?"

Two sudden shakes of her head: "*Never.* But we spoke the same language, we subscribed to a particular way of looking at the world. We guarded our detachment as jealously as any pearl. That's what I thought, what I believed. You saw. It turned out we'd been speaking different tongues all along."

Aurelius caresses her shoulder blades and the trench of her spine. He tries to think of something to say and comes up with nothing.

"I'm a quick study, though," Miriam says. "I learned to speak his language. He taught it to me."

Her eyes glitter in the dark. "He's waiting to teach you as well."

Before Aurelius can ask her to explain, there is a distant boom and the chapel rocks with the shock wave—the planks creak in violent protest, Aurelius hears a few of them splinter. He is gripped with a terrible *déjà vu.* Candles fall from the altar. Aurelius pulls Miriam tight and rolls over top of her, as if the meaty mass of him could protect her from a radioactive fireball or the consuming cold of space. His racing blood pounds in his ears. He tastes the electric wash of adrenaline in the back of his throat. When he looks down, however, Miriam is calm—smiling.

"It's begun," she says. "Don't be afraid. You'll see."

40

Reckless Acts

It is not the most reckless thing Crysanthia has ever done, she reflects, although it surely takes a place of honor among her many reckless acts.

(Before she'd even come this far, a hunch—an *itch*—spurred her to make a final flight down to Klytemnestra. She rooted through the clammy trash heap under a dreadful lemon sky of approaching autumn while her ship bobbed behind her like a huge chrome parade float, its magneto-static field playing on her skin like a billion tiny insects. The sibyl—*her* sibyl—gone. It hadn't been certainty that awakened in her then—far from it. Rather, the itch of not knowing had sharpened into a barb sunk deep into her flesh.)

In the onion fold's serpentine cluster of possible causes and likely effects, it is impossible to distinguish luck from skill, foolish to try. Crysanthia's maneuver requires incalculable quantities of both. She locks onto the shifting space of the starship's huge and empty hangar bay. Once she has it fully resolved in her ship's guidance system, she destabilizes her own hyperstatic locus and throws the ship into scattered flux.

Then comes the impossible. If she gets it wrong, Crysanthia and her ship become a quasar-like fountain of energetic chaos, burning itself out in a quintillionth of a second and consuming *Virgin Sorrow* in the process.

She hadn't wanted to do this. "Narisian, drop out of the fold and open your hangar bay doors," she'd radioed as she tracked the plodding starship through the shallows of the fold. "I'm coming aboard."

"Oh, you're coming aboard, Vog. I'm expecting you. But the doors stay closed and I'm not dropping out of the fold. There's no time."

"You're not—"

"You know what to do and you know how to do it. I'll be waiting."

And what had she heard in Narisian's voice? It was as if he was teasing her, daring her; there was almost *affection*—it hadn't sounded like Narisian at all.

Her ship re-gathers itself within *Virgin Sorrow's* hangar bay, bypassing the intervening layers of the cruiser's armored hull, tunneling up through countless layers of the onion fold, shedding ghosts all the way. Her ship coalesces into reality (relative to the starship) for the merest fraction of an instant, just long enough to eject Crysanthia's unprotected body onto the flight deck. Its final duty discharged, it lunges back into the deepest layers of fold space and de-coheres into a high energy wave/particle foam hundreds of parsecs away.

To an observer—if there was one—standing in the hangar bay, it would appear that Crysanthia falls naked from the nothingness, popping in out of thin air (*very* thin, since the hangar is pressurized to only one eighth of an atmosphere) twenty meters above the diamond silk deck, heralded by a nova-bright flash and deafening peal of thunder.

As she falls, Crysanthia has time for one regret: *That ship's computer was the last tangible reminder I had of him.*

Crysanthia strikes the deck with near-lethal force. How long she lies there, like a stranded starfish, she does not know. Her overloaded cyborganelles have retreated behind curtains of white noise and tell her nothing. So scrambled are her senses from the force of impact that her vision is a flurry of micro-images—the facets of her compound eyes relay what they see to her brain but she lacks the ability to compile them into an integrated whole.

She hurts.

Everything begins to flicker, like the light from an ancient movie projector. The universe becomes a series of discrete frames, reality an illusion, the persistence of being. The tight diamond silk canvas of the flight deck flickers out of existence in a slow dissolve into yellow fog. Crysanthia feels herself flicker out along with it. Something flickers in to take their place, something other.

Her cheek is pressed down against the shifting sand of a dune. She gets grit in her mouth when she licks her dry lips. Above her, a blue sun burns in a blue sky. Another sun, huge and red and not as bright, hangs low near the horizon. White sands end only at the horizon. She blinks against the glare.

She blinks.

Jane Charlotte Kindred lifts herself onto her hands and knees. A cascade of dark and graying ringlets (but she has no hair) falls around her face (not a single vestigial follicle). She looks down onto pale pink hands with jointed fingers.

"When I was a child," a voice says from above her, "Mother made a gryphon for me—really more of a winged cat with a monkey's face. I named him Patmos."

Jane tries to speak but she has forgotten how. Air is a rasp in the back of her throat. Her tongue is a lump of dead and dusty flesh.

"She used the genetic material from an ocelot, a gibbon and a golden eagle. He had a thick coat—pale fur reticulated with red—and russet feathers. He would flap his wings but they were useless, just for show. He could not fly. He used to ride on my shoulders—his claws digging into me. Sometimes, they drew blood, but I didn't care. He watched my every move with his wizened little face. His nictating membranes slid across his yellow eyes, one at a time, so he never had to blink or look away." The voice is familiar. She looks up but she cannot see him clearly. In the glare, she cannot bear to open her bleary eyes beyond watery slits. "I wondered what he thought—so much of what I did was beyond any hope of his understanding. And I wondered, even then, if some higher order of being was not constantly all around us, going about its business as I went about mine, so far beyond us that we cannot perceive it though it conceals itself in plain view."

Jane is limp as a rag doll, raw as a newborn. Strong hands reach down and grasp her arms, just below her shoulders. They lift her to her feet and brush back her hair, brush the sand from her face.

"One day, Patmos jumped into a cryostylitic display cube. The air inside was super-cooled and dense; I'd increased the gain so that it could resolve images down to the sub-microscopic, even had to tear it down to its bare circuits to do it. Took me weeks but it took only an instant for Patmos to freeze solid. He came out the other side and shattered against the wall."

She can see him now. Phil? No, not Phil: the Phil-*not*-Phil she followed in the swamp. She has never seen him before but she knows him. And she looks up into sea green eyes that know her from her insides out. His name comes to her cracked and sandy lips from several lifetimes gone, none of them her own:

"Janos."

41

After Life

Virgin Sorrow's escape pod smolders at the center of the shallow pit it had excavated on impact. The blue-hot plasma of its retro-thrusters had fused the Martian sand into an oblong basin of rusty green glass and sprayed a ragged corona of ejecta in all directions. Aurelius Mann follows Miriam Wu away from the wreckage.

"The wind farm is that way," Aurelius says and points over the western horizon. The dusk sky is stained tangerine and deep purple. "About a thirty minute walk."

They had waited for long minutes inside the pod while the crater cooled enough for them to venture out. When Miriam finally blew the hatch open, it was like walking into a wall of solid heat. Even now, a shimmer coruscates the twilight. The thin and brittle glass had splintered with their every step.

"This is far enough," Miriam says. "Unless you want to go on ahead..."

Aurelius shakes his head.

"Of course, it doesn't matter where we are, we could have stayed in the pod or aboard the ship. I thought you'd rather spend the time here, in the open air."

Aurelius nods. "Thank you."

On *Virgin Sorrow,* in the chapel, after that first sickening boom—followed by metallic shrieks, creaks and groans which were hardly comforting—

Miriam had extricated herself from Aurelius's embrace and hurried over to the sacristy. She threw a satchel to Aurelius and unzipped another one. "Put those on," she said as she shimmied into an emergency pressure suit, complete with gloves and boots. Once Aurelius was dressed—the cellular-mesh fabric expanded to easily accommodate his bulk—Miriam circled his wrist in her fingers and pulled him along behind her. Moments later, she was pushing him into an escape pod and sealing it behind them.

"Emergency spacesuits in the chapel?" Aurelius had asked her as she dogged the hatch. "And you didn't even *think* about how to find the way to the capsule." He watched her punch the escape trajectory into the computer. "You're working with the Pilots?"

"Not with *them*," she had told him just as the pod dropped roughly into its launch tube. Then acceleration plastered them against the hard foam wall as they blasted away from the cruiser.

"Do you have your calling card computer?" Aurelius asks now.

"Yes."

"May I borrow it?"

Aurelius dials his flat and waits. On the seventh ring, the holocube fills with the tousled hair and sleep-puffy face of Simone Trieste. Behind her, he can make out the head of someone else, slumbering on the pillow. The face is turned away, he cannot see who it is or even if it is a man or a woman.

"Aurelius? Is that you? But—where are you?"

"Home," he says. "Somewhere east of the agave field." He shuts off the computer before Simone can reply and hands it back to Miriam.

"I wish I could tell you more," Miraim says—she'd explained all she could before they left the pod. "But I do not grasp it myself—not really. We can no more comprehend what's to come than a fetus still in the womb can comprehend the galaxy. All we can do is wait."

"How much longer?"

Miriam answers with a beatified shrug. "Not long," she says.

One last time, Aurelius turns his thoughts to Sam Leonides—willingly this time, gratefully. He remembers the old man lying in a life support pod, his sightless pits of blackened flesh staring into Aurelius as he clutched his arm with a hand reduced to bone and paper and pulled him close and said, between rasping breaths that reeked of rot and lilacs, "We spend our days chasing after life." His grip tightened with one last spasm of strength and then his hand slipped away. "And when it's over... when it ends..." After that, he'd drifted into silence and then, by degrees, into sleep. As far as Aurelius knew, he never woke up; he was dead a few days later.

The sky is dark now, shot through with brilliant stars. Aurelius wonders about Gigi Olivet, the little witch in body paint, shivering in the glow of the Japanese lanterns. He wonders how she made out with her zodiac. He wonders if the stars gave her warning.

The stars, Aurelius thinks. My son moved me around among those stars as if I were a marker on a child's game board only to bring me back to where I started, to face this future with my eyes opened wide. Has any father—so remote and undeserving—ever been granted so glorious and terrible a gift?

He crouches and, with the tip of his index finger, scratches words into the dust. A lizard scurries by, a little silver skink. It pauses and looks at Aurelius for a moment, then continues on its way.

Aurelius smiles.

42

In My Vision

I gaze up at him. His skin is the rich red-brown of a turbid river, his hair is a tight halo of copper-colored fire in the unbearable brilliance of the alien suns. His scent, that night in Brancusi, in the symbiosis chamber—I feel the memories over my own, fading in and out; it's like I'm trying to listen to KPKD out of Oakland on a bad air night, when the transmission is corrupted by the signal from the next station on the dial. It penetrates me to a place beyond deep, beyond myself; it awakens an ache I never knew I always had, it settles in and makes itself at home. I don't fight—I'm so sick of fighting. I give in and give myself over. Painful sobs build in my ribcage and rip themselves free with frightening ease. Tears scald my abraded face.

(*So this is what it's like,* the other radio station says, growing in strength. *This is what it is to cry. My God, Bettina, was it cruelty or mere stupidity that made you keep this from us?*)

Fuck! I feel it again, that nasty dissolution—like that time with Janos in his apartment, after we left the bar and we walked in the snow and listened to Judee Sill and then we went to the symbiosis chamber and... no, that wasn't Janos, it was... who *was* it? Who was I?

Who *am* I?

A desert zephyr rips through me. My radio stations sync up and pause for a word from the sponsor:

"For Old World flavor in your off-world home/Choose the coffee made in the image of Rome!"

I flicker for a moment, like an image projected onto a bed sheet, then come back to mock solid here and now.

A million images in crystal focus crowd my brain until I remember how to piece them together. I see in colors I've only seen in dreams. (*No! Wrong! I've seen them all my life!*) It staggers me. I reach out to steady myself with hands that have become knots of sky blue vipers. I recoil from myself.

A familiar yellow sun shines in the sky, beyond a window so clear it seems it is not there. I watch as blimps shaped like jelly-whales and tiny people astride tiny flying saucers glide among smooth and slender skyscrapers. I stand firmly on a zebrawood parquet floor.

"Crysanthia Vog?"

I knew he was there behind me before he spoke. I heard his footsteps, I smelled his skin.

"Who else would I be?" I say. I do not turn around.

"Of course," he says. "I meant merely to be polite. Perhaps that was a mistake."

I sip from a fluted glass of champagne—it's very dry, I think. I wish it were sweeter. "Only if it pretends to an ignorance that does not—*must* not—exist. Do we continue with the charade? I had a Martian Time Slip and you—you had..."

"A domestic hefe-weisse from the Rautavaara Brewing Company, on the other side of the mountains."

I almost smile. Instead I take a long, deep breath through my nostrils and let it out as slowly and completely as I can. Then—only then—do I turn to face him.

"I've missed you," he says.

I steel myself against the flood of feeling those three words threaten to drown me under. "Where are we?"

"The Wintermute." He gestures beyond me, to the Brancusi sunset. "Surely you remember. You just said—"

"Where are we *really*?" I look around. "Where am *I*?"

Janos hesitates, then says: "Broken. Bloody, on the *Virgin Sorrow's* flight deck. I'm sorry I had to do that to you—if there was any other way..."

"It was my decision, Janos," I say. "I knew the risk."

He shakes his head. "No, you don't understand: I knew what it would do to you, down to every ruptured blood vessel. I could see it before it happened. It was what I wanted. There was no *risk* involved, Crysanthia. Only design. I needed you broken. I needed you receptive."

I cannot think of a single thing to say in reply. I can *see* a billion appropriate responses spread out before me like God's own tarot deck, all of them involving extreme and inventive acts of violence, each more baroque than the last. But I don't *feel* the need for any of them. All I have in their place is curiosity, absurd and absurdly patient.

"And you are deep in drug-induced rapture, in a dirty, abandoned record shop in a part of town you have no business being," he continues and takes a step forward. He reaches out as if to take my hand, and then lets his hand fall instead. "And we are here."

"But is this real? Is any of it—how can it be real? It can't be." I touch his throat. His flesh is warm, his pulse strong. I pull my hand away as if I've been shocked. "You're dead."

Janos nods. "Fifteen years rotting away under Vesta's soil—little more than bones, I'm sure." He takes my hand. "And yet I live. So we must adjust our paradigm."

I yank my hand from his grasp. "Don't. Don't fuck with me, Janos. Don't you dare. I deserve better than that. You owe me that much, if nothing else."

"Yes," he whispers. "I do." He brightens. "Come here. I want to show you something."

After a moment, I follow him away from the window, into the depths of the gallery. Around us, the other patrons move among the exhibits. I can smell them, feel their body heat—they are *real,* they have to be. And yet—

Janos stops at a granite pedestal on which rests a smoky silver mask with stern features and huge, blank eyes. "I like this piece," he says. "It reminds me of a production of *Medea* my father took me to see, when I was young. They wore masks like this, the actors. It was part of a planet-wide arts festival. They staged it in an amphitheater carved out of the rock at the southern foot Olympus Mons, along the shore of a crater sea." He touches the delicate foil of the mask, a fragment, really, with razor sharp ragged edges—a fragment of a shell, a cocoon against the cold radiation of space.

"Dahlia was right," I say, thinking of Narisian. "You did that, you ripped the cyborganelles from his cells."

Janos nods. "I found him, drifting out there, exposed to the void, to Tau Ceti's stellar winds," he says. "You cannot imagine the pain, the trauma, the isolation. By the time I got to him, your Narisian Karza was more dead than alive—all that was left was the faintest murmur of who he had been, fading in the dimming cells of his brain. But there was enough left of him for me to negotiate with. He, too, was *receptive*."

"Receptive? Receptive to what? *What* are you, Janos?" I step back from him. Something's changed in him, something nebulous and essential—I don't yet know if it's an addition or subtraction but it's there, a difference; he's not the Janos I knew. "You're not human."

"Neither are you," he laughs. "But no, human is something I left behind a long time ago."

"Explain that to me," I tell him. "Slowly. As you would explain it to an infant or an idiot."

"All right," he says. Then nothing.

"I'm waiting."

"Don't rush me." Another moment passes before he says, "I was right about the Fomalhaut Event. And I was wrong. It was a mass of complexity, of information, of potentialities, enough to spawn countless universes—it *had* spawned countless universes but it was alienated from them, from *us.* It lacked volition. It was information, you see—"

"You said that."

"So I did. Every one of those countless realities was a cell in its brain, a circuit in its—damn it, there is no metaphor... I suspect it's an artifact."

"You *suspect?* You mean, you don't know? How can you not know? If it's an artifact, who could have built it?"

"It doesn't know. It could have been anyone, anywhere, any *when.* I imagine it hasn't happened yet—not from the standpoint of our time, the time I plucked you out of. I get the impression it will not happen for a long, long time to come. Satisfied?"

"No."

"Neither is it. It wants to know. It was conscious but not like we are, it wasn't conscious *of* its consciousness. Its wisdom—its *will*—was like the wisdom and will of the cell, like that of an oak, pushing up through concrete. Only for cells, it had galaxies, entire universes. It was the Forever Thing, the ground of all being. What it lacked, it created us to provide."

"What it lacked," I say, "it took from you."

"And you. You were with me, up until the end. And you held on tight, I'll never forget how you held on. The Forever Thing took me and ripped out a little piece of you."

"I remember," I whisper. My hand goes to my ribcage, just below my heart.

"I had only the faintest echo of you. I didn't want to lose it, it was precious to me. And it was enough. Enough to build another life for you, a counter-life, a human life."

"What do you mean, a counter-life?" The signal from that other radio becomes strong again, I remember so much—my drafty little farmhouse and my cats, Dale and Flash. I remember Aaron and Mandy. I remember Philip Ashwood.

"Was he you? And the dreams, the movie in that filthy storefront, that *drug*—was that you, too?" I shake my head and ask again, demand: "Phil—were you Phil? My God, are we just—just the two of them, reincarnated?"

"I can't answer that."

"You mean you won't."

"No. I mean I *can't.* It would make just as much sense to say that they *pre*-incarnated us. That moment was like a pebble, dropped into the four-dimensional sea of space-time. The ripples spread out in a sphere upon the surface, above and below, into the past and the future. And you were there. You are a wild element, you don't make sense. Not you, Crysanthia. And not *you,* Jane. *You were there already, waiting.* And in those first chaotic moments, when my thoughts—my soul—were nothing more than a four-color comic strip lost among the papyrus of Alexandria, a rumor whispered from idiot to idiot among the colloquies of Babel—"

"All right, Janos, I get it."

"Of course you do," he says. "You took that precious little shard from my hands. You kept it safe."

My eyes travel back to the mask but it is gone. In its place is the cast bronze bust of a human woman with high and broad cheekbones, a strong, straight nose and the faintest (I tell myself) doubling of her chin. Slowly, the green bronze melts away and reveals pale flesh, the flesh I left in the garbage heap, back on Klytemnestra. The flesh of the sibyl. And now I know why she always felt so familiar. I look away.

"No easy thing," Janos says, "to gaze into the face of your own death. I'm sorry."

"You're *sorry*?"

Janos does not speak but he does answer me. For an instant—and I don't know if it is real or imagined, or if there is any difference between the two in this here that is nowhere and this now that is never—I'm on *Pariah*, in her airlock, removing the helmet from the burned and pitted spacesuit and gazing down at him. Only this time, I know that he is there too, behind my eyes, gazing down at his own corpse. He'd always been there.

It's as if I'm eavesdropping on my own mind. To that love-struck party girl, Janos is a felled colossus, the synthetic nerve fibroids under his skin are a fretwork of pewter in the burnished bronze of his skin, the blood coagulated in his tears ducts are flecks of gold—fool's gold. But what is he to *me*, now? I turn away from the answer, I don't want it. With the queerly doubled sense of memory as premonition, I leave just before my fingers remove the interface jack from the port in his temple. The snap of welded metal, the tiny shower of leaden dust—I don't want that, either.

And then I realize the question I really should be asking myself: What is he and what is this—what is any of this—to Jane Charlotte Kindred? I don't need this. I can wad up some tin foil, wind baling wire around the antennae, fiddle with the dial till I pull in her signal. I can shake off this hallucination. I can go back. Back to that little shit-hole storefront theatre and then back to Aaron's place and then on the first plane back home and thank your mother for the chicken soup. Maybe I just need to ball up my fists and squeeze shut my eyes and—

My eyes—squeeze shut my lidless insect eyes.

Well, I think, *that puts paid to that.* And with that, I accept that there is no Jane for me to return to, that all that Jane ever was and ever could be has been subsumed within my mind. Her life is gone—if it ever existed to begin with. And taken for what it was—whatever it was—it was a good life. I'll miss it. I'll miss it terribly.

"Crysanthia?"

"You said you negotiated," I say, solidly back in the Wintermute. "With Narisian. Negotiated for what?"

"A proposal. An exchange. We each had something the other needed. He needed a way to end this war."

I wait for him to go on. Instead, I hear only the sounds of the others in the gallery, their footsteps, their low murmurs. Only now do I realize that they've completely ignored me and Janos this entire time.

"What did you need from him?" I ask.

"While we've been talking, you and I, *Virgin Sorrow* has entered the Solar System unchallenged—and why not? She's returning home, along the assigned lane of ecliptic insertion. But she did not dock at the Jupiter Shipyards. She continued on, past the Inner Worlds, toward the sun. The Commonwealth mobilized its defenses but it's too late, you see."

And I do see. I see the golden, granulated orb of the sun pricked by an invisible speck. And I see the point of entry become a spreading silver and violet brilliance across the solar surface, forming patterns identical to the hieroglyphs on Narisian's skin, the maps and circuits on that pink space lichen Mandy and Aaron gave me, the dark girl's tattoo. And then I see the sun become an omni-directional geyser of indescribable complexity, a riot of writhing chaos, an infinite rose in savage bloom. I move with the wave front, hurtling faster than light, I'm with it as it devours the Inner Worlds—Venus, Earth, Mars—the asteroids, Jupiter and Saturn, Uranus and Neptune...

At the same time, I see it from the most minuscule level of reality, Planck-scale in Calabi-Yau space, among the twisting strings of the quantum particles and their sub-quantum toroidal ghosts. I see them ripped apart from within, all their encapsulated possibilities released and transmuted into something *beyond*—beyond description, beyond comprehension, beyond the onion fold, beyond mathematics and madness. I feel that terrible derangement come over me again and I know that, this time, if I let it take me, there will be no coming back from it.

I so want to let it take me.

And then I feel Janos grab hold of me and pull me away. I'm in the gallery once more. Only now it is empty of everyone and everything save me and him.

"And that's it," I say.

"That's it," he replies.

"What you always wanted."

"Not what *I* wanted—"

"Isomorphic transubstantiation," I say.

"On an infinitesimal scale—only a few billion kilometers."

"Only a few—you would kill over twenty billion people? Obliterate all life in the system?" I shake my head. "There has to be another way. There has—"

"You must understand, Crysanthia: It was. It is. It is yet to come. It is a natural progression in the life cycle of the universe, of the Forever Thing, the *logos.* And it is good."

I say nothing. I stare into his eyes. He does not look away.

"It is not dying," Janos says.

"It is not living, either, is it?" I say. "Is it?"

"Crysanthia, look at me: am *I* dead?"

I turn my head from him, gaze at the bare brick wall.

"Crysanthia." His blunt fingers grab my jaw. "*Look at me.*" His grip becomes a caress as his fingers slide away. Snake quick, I clutch his hand and press his palm against my cheek.

"*Am* I dead?" he repeats.

I remember his cold body in its suit of armor, his burnt-out brain, the scorched flesh on his temple. "I... I don't *know.*"

Human is something I left behind a long time ago, he said. Something else, something *other,* crosses his face now, something fleeting and frightening—something detached and disinterested; for that moment I see myself as he must see me—not Janos but the thing, the Forever Thing, that he has become a part of, that he has become the mask for. I must be less than an insect to it, I realize, and I see it turn away, behind those human eyes. I pursue it. "Where have you been for the last fifteen years? *What* have you been?" I let go his hand and take a step back from him, look him up and down. "What are you *now*?"

As I'd expected, he ignores the question.

"They'll be in here, with me. Every living thing, from the most primitive bacterium to your friend, Diphalia Chrome. There's an eco-system on Europa I find particularly promising: the entire thing is sentient along a purely alien axis of consciousness." He tries to comfort me with a wan smile. "Fortunately, you cannot crowd infinity."

"Janos," I say softly. "There has to be another way."

"No."

"Why?"

He walks past me without answering, back to the window. Again, I follow.

"Why?' I ask again. My voice echoes off the brick walls, the tin ceiling and hardwood floor. "Is this because of what they did to Bettina?"

He laughs. "Mother? That never occurred to me, not for an instant." And again, he laughs. And now I know what's different about him: it's gone, the formless ache he'd built into stiff, rigid armor and forged into the weaponry of his acidic and dismissive arrogance. In its place is something that sounds very much like love. No, not in anything's place--It had been there all along. I'd caught only glimpses of it before--on Venus, on Vesta, in *Pariah.* This was no glimpse. Now, there was nothing else to see. "Mother can take care of herself. She's never needed my help."

"Then why? Janos, please tell me."

He is silent. I'm about to ask again, to swear and scream at him, demand he answer me, when he finally says "They mean to destroy you. And I cannot allow that." A pause, punctuated by a deep and shuddering breath. "Crysanthia, when you are in my vision, you mean the universe to me."

The galaxy's loneliest boy, I think*, and the galaxy's loneliest girl.* After all this time, after all this death, this is what it comes to. I wish I still had my human eyes to shed my human tears. I feel his warmth radiating from him, the coursing of his blood in the vessels beneath his skin. "But?" I say.

Janos shakes his head. "*And,*" he says. "And you are always in my vision."

I say nothing. I stand next to him at the window and, together, we look out into our city.

Epilogue
The Pax Pilotia

For two millennia, the Pilots spread throughout the galaxy and beyond it, into the Magellanic Clouds, into Andromeda. Everything they touched, they reshaped to their will, re-molded in their image. They mined neutron stars and trapped pulsars in cages forged from the metal; with the harnessed energy, they called new suns and planets forth from the interstellar dust. In the gulf between the galaxies, they built cities so vast it took light full seconds to cross from one rim to the other. They gathered together those few humans adrift in interstellar space—the scattered thousands on the Heaven stations, on the warships and starliners—and subdued them, cared for them, gave them homes on fertile planets and kept careful watch over them. (This was hardly an easy decision—many Pilots wanted nothing more than to kill them, once and for all. The humans, for their part, were too terrified and demoralized to offer any kind of real resistance—not that a few didn't try and not few enough. Lucky for them, a torn and tattered spirit of clemency prevailed even after several reflexive, needless and shockingly bloody skirmishes.) Yet in all their travels, all their science, all their attentive mercies, the Pilots never discovered an answer to the riddle of their salvation.

They knew it was due to the actions of Narisian Karza and Crysanthia Vog. Those few Pilots who had lived through the darkness of the war could attest to that. If the Pilots believed in gods, Karza and Vog would be first among them. They had sacrificed themselves in bringing about the unknowable cataclysm that had swallowed the ancestral solar system. They had ushered in the Sidereal Age and the Pax Pilotia. Next to them, even the creator, re-born countless times over in Vog's daughters, must cede much of her luster. But the Pilots have no gods and that portion of the Milky Way, that veil that would permit no inquiries regardless of how intent and subtle those inquiries may be, that abyss that divulged nothing to those who gazed into it, that womb from which their true lives had finally sprung after much painful and perilous travail, was regarded with an awe more empirical than numinous.

Thus it was for two millennia.

They tell me I'm a miracle, that I am the only thing ever yielded up by the mystery that used to be the Solar Commonwealth. Everything I am—my genetic code, the programming in my cyborganelles, my memories and moods—was translated into a burst of high-intensity radio waves and beamed from the heart of the enigma to the crèche on Eidolon Prime, First World of the Pilots, over nineteen-hundred light years away.

No one could begin to figure out how the flavor and texture of who I am could be compressed and encoded into that blip of radiation. No one had any idea how the crèche knew to decode the information and turn it back into flesh. But the greatest mystery of all was how the enigma could aim me so precisely at a planet which, at the moment of transmission, would not exist for another eight hundred years.

I was ninety-two days in the womb tank, they tell me, infusing my new cells, electrifying my new cyborganelles, unfurling into my new brain, inhabiting my new flesh. On the ninety-third day, before I could awaken in the dank and musky underworld, they carried me up to the surface, into the open air.

The first thing I feel in over two-thousand years is the warmth of a sun's rays on my naked skin.

(As we sat on the floor and watched the sun set over Brancusi, Janos turned to me.

"You're smiling," I said. "So pretty but so sad."

"I was thinking about my father. 'If death opens us to heaven at all, it is to the sky that is already within us. We do not enter heaven, we release it.'" He caressed my cheek. "They'll be here soon, a flood of minds—fears, loves, hates, desires, hungers. I don't know that I'll be able to hold on. Please, stay with me until then."

And when the time had come, I could feel him, holding me close one last time before gently pushing me away. And then...)

"Wake up."

I glide up into consciousness as if I were merely dozing. I look into the blue face of the woman who crouches beside me, a face that could be my own but isn't.

"Eridani?"

My daughter nods and smiles. *"The Bollywobble swoops and swobbles, flibbles on her tail,"* she says. *"The Zuulog and the Veldenschnaft gloob-glibble with their sails."*

"The tiny Nop is left behind and starts to softly weep," I whisper. *"The Bollywobble flobbles back and sings her soul to sleep."*

Eridani's smile becomes a radiant grin. "Welcome to the living, Mother. Welcome to the world you have made." She giggles like the infant she was when I last saw her, held her, inhaled her scent. "One of them."

Dahlia steps forward out of the glare of the sun and stands next to her sister. She bends at her waist and offers me her hand. After a moment's hesitation, I take it. Eridani grasps my other hand. Together, they lift me to my feet.

We are on a beach, the three of us naked and unashamed. The sky is deep and endless, the sun just a little brighter than long lost Sol. The ocean is an impossible turquoise crashing white against the white sands of the shore.

"One of them?" I ask. "One of how many?"

"Thousands," Dahlia says.

"Tens of thousands," Eridani says. "Thanks to you, we number in the trillions."

"The *low* trillions."

Eridani gently brushes sand from my shoulder, then leans over and kisses me. Again, she laughs. "I thought I'd never see you again."

Gulls wheel overhead. Dune grasses rustle in the cool and salty breeze. Farther inland, lush vegetation breathes. "How long?"

"A long time."

"There will be time enough to tell you everything," Dahlia says. In her voice, I can just barely hear it—Bettina. "But not now."

Something gossamer and gaudy rustles along the sand of the beach, blown along by the ocean breeze until it stops against the arch of my left foot. I kneel down and take it between my fingers. It is a slip of waxy paper, vivid with the four color inks of a crude comic strip and redolent of sweet pink bubble gum.

"What's that?' Eridani asks. I can hear Bettina in her voice as well.

I smile. "Message from the past. *A* past. I lose track, there are so many..."

Puzzlement creases the glittering blue skin between Dahlia's star sapphire eyes. "Mother?"

This beautiful day, I think, *with my beautiful daughters in a beautiful world.* I watch the horizon, where the sea runs to sky in a brilliant haze of beryl blue and aquamarine. *And you, Bettina? I suppose you can be beautiful, too. Why not?*

"It's nothing." I laugh and press the slip of paper into the hollow of my palm. Eventually, I know, I'll have to let it go. But not just yet, not just now.

"Come on, girls," I say. "Let's go look for some sea shells."

Appendix
Tales of the Solar Commonwealth

Every zero comes to zero,
Even when they're not the same--
This nowhere is as good as any;
This nothing will suffice,
As any nothing would.

—*Equanimity* by Samuel Leonides

1

Under My Skin
AD 2158

Ursula Senn keeps her lover in a jar. The jar is pretty, ceramic glazed in varying tones of blue, rose and tan that evoke a desert in twilight. The lover is infinitely patient but dwindling: once Ursula had twelve of her but now she's down to one. And after tonight—she doesn't want to think about after tonight just now. She has the ampoule and the syringe, that's all that matters. Soon, the needle will be in her arm and they will be together.

Tonight is the fifth of October, 2158. It's their anniversary. Her lover has been dead now for thirteen years.

When the diagnosis came, Alice had been perfectly calm. It was Ursula who shattered like a thing of glass and Alice who held her and rocked her from side to side.

"'I've got you,'" Alice sang, "'under my skin. I've got you deep in the heart of me.'"

When Ursula's jag had passed, she was aware that they were alone in the examination room but she had no idea when the doctor had left them. Alice handed her a tissue and Ursula wiped her nose.

"Okay?" Alice asked.

Ursula nodded.

Alice walked to the door, skimming her fingers along the smooth, clear carapace of the diagnostic bubble chair—Ursula watched her fingertips and was somehow relieved to see they were trembling—and quietly invited the doctor back into the room.

"As I was saying," the doctor said, "there is no effective treatment for Kuurosin's blood burn. And there is no mystery in how the disease will run its course. Are you—are you sure want to hear this?"

Alice nodded but still the doctor was silent. Alice nudged Ursula—after a moment, Ursula nodded as well.

"Now, it is the pain in your joints. Within two weeks, you will not be able to walk. A week or so after that—"

"—My organs will begin to fail, starting with my spleen, kidneys and marrow as my hemoglobin coagulates into fibroids. The process is exothermic—my veins and arteries will be scorched from the inside out. My mind will go," Alice finished for her, the barest quaver in her voice. "And a week after that, I will be dead."

The doctor nodded. She was an expert in man-made pathogens. Alice and Ursula had taken the shuttle down from Lunapolis in order to see her. She was a coffee brown woman with a seamed face and snowy hair. What is she, Ursula wondered, around one hundred twenty? One hundred twenty-five? So many years.

"I read up on the disease before I went into the hot zone. I took every precaution, the military insisted on it before they'd let me accompany them. Even still, I guess it wasn't enough."

"I saw your report on the newsfeed," the doctor said. "It's a shame." She shook her head. "No one knows how—that is, we think we've isolated the agent but it's so goddamned tricky... The good news is, we're all but certain it isn't communicable. You can spend these next few weeks with your loved ones instead of in quarantine."

Ursula listened to all of this without saying a word. She willed herself into a state where she was only partially there; otherwise, she knew she would be powerless against the screams building just below her heart.

"My advice to you is to go home," the doctor continued. "The slight lunar gravity will ease things somewhat. The nurse will be in to fit you with a device that will control the pain but beyond that..."

"Of course, doctor," Alice said. "Thank you."

Ursula said nothing.

Ursula lights the candle in the center of the table and sits down to their anniversary dinner. Always, it has been one of Alice's favorites—last year, it was pasta putanesca with a salad of bitter greens drenched in a garlic and raspberry vinaigrette; the year before that, Ursula had gone out for sushi and followed that with a dish of green tea ice cream and a star anise cookie. Tonight it will be fresh fruits and cheeses and an inexpensive wine—something red and bold, a Primitivo.

As always, Alice won't remember the years before—she will not be the Alice who experienced them. And as always, she will say the same thing to Ursula, silently, from inside Ursula's skull: "It tastes so different with your mouth, with your tongue. I never knew."

On the shuttle back to Lunapolis, in the private cabin the two of them had decided to splurge on after an hour of desultory shopping in Manhattan had left them numb and empty-handed, Ursula looked out the tiny porthole as they lifted off in a nimbus of orange flame and white smoke. After that, it was blue skies and layers of clouds. Ursula looked down upon the clouds until the blue gave way to indigo and then the black nothing of space. Next to her, Alice read a book off a wafer slate computer and toyed with the neural inhibitor implanted in her brainstem, its chromed plug not quite flush with the base of her skull. Not until New York had disappeared over the horizon and they crossed the terminator into night did Alice put her book aside and place her hand on top of Ursula's.

Ursula remembered the scene she had made in the doctor's office and sighed. She watched the flashes of lightning in a storm system hovering over the Midwest. There is no weather on the moon, she thought. Beneath the high diamond dome protecting Lunapolis, the temperature never varies more than a few degrees centigrade and precipitation rarely forms aside from the occasional morning dew—as a supervising engineer in the city's climate control division, Ursula helps keep it that way. If only she could twiddle a dial and dampen her emotional squalls the way she controlled the atmosphere circulating through the streets and skyscraper canyons of home. But that thought only reminded her that she was flying back into a bureaucratic morass. A junior technician—thankfully, not one under her direct supervision but still within the penumbra of her responsibilities—had somehow jammed up an ionic flow gate between the San Matthias Building and the Commonwealth Trade Tower. The freak lightning discharge fried the null-gravity field generators in twenty-two air skeds supporting as many sky riding commuters on their way to work one morning. Knocked out of the sky, they tumbled over two hundred meters to the sidewalk below, a few of them landing on some very unlucky pedestrians. In all, over thirty died and another half dozen suffered serious injury. Ursula marveled at how the impending death of this one woman has left her devastated while all those others merely rate as an inconvenience.

"Hey," Alice said.

"Hey."

"The insurance settlement from this is going to be huge. You know that, right?"

Ursula grunted. She watched as the silver-white moon grew steadily larger through her window.

"What?" Alice said.

"I hadn't thought about it."

"I was thinking. Do you remember, around two years ago, I did a piece on illegal technologies? Nanotech, mostly—biological, neurological."

Ursula sighed. "No."

"Doesn't matter. I made a few contacts when I did the piece. That's what's important. I can still get in touch with some of them, if I need to."

Ursula felt the tears course warm down her cheeks. Angrily, she wiped them away with the heel of her hand. "So?"

"I have an idea."

After dinner, no matter what Ursula suggests—that they take a walk through the market district or watch one of the ancient cinemas Alice had loved so much in life—Alice will insist that she take a bath or just head directly to the bedroom. Once there, under the musk scented water or under the flimsy linen covers, Ursula will feel herself melt away as she surrenders to Alice completely. Her hands on her body become Alice's, and the pleasure of them together, doubled and redoubled upon itself, will become unbearable, transcendent. The first couple of times, Ursula would sob uncontrollably afterwards. Not anymore. Now, the sorrow is too deep and too much a part of her to expiate with the brackish magic of tears.

Still, Alice will know the sadness. And Alice will be there, like she was thirteen years ago, to enfold and comfort her, only this time from under Ursula's skin.

The boy who came to their door, though the wrong gender, was young enough to be their child—barely out of his teens, if that. Ursula and Alice had talked about having a daughter, had even made a few appointments at the ova-splicing clinic but they came to nothing. Both their careers had gotten in the way; neither wanted to carry the child, nor did they want to employ a surrogate, human or mechanical. Once, Alice had idly—perhaps jokingly—suggested animal, one of the clinic's genetically modified mares. Ursula rejected that suggestion by hurling a porcelain figurine, a ballerina, against the wall. (A week later, walking to the kitchen barefoot at midnight, she stepped on a piece of shrapnel, a sliver of slipper, that had evaded the cleaning robot's attentions. Her foot had bled an astonishing amount as Alice removed the shard, cleaned the tiny wound and cursed Ursula for her melodramatic outbursts.) Their attempts to negotiate a solution almost ended their relationship and so both of them quietly let the matter die, along with all its untold possibilities. Ursula wondered at the wistful cruelty that would cause her to remember all that as she stood aside from the open door and gestured for the boy to come in. He was dressed in dungarees and a bomber-style leather jacket and carried a chrome-plated valise. He said nothing as he walked past Ursula into the flat.

Alice was paralyzed completely and confined to a suspensor chair but she was still lucid. She glided into the front room on a cushion of nullified gravity and welcomed him to their home through a vocal synthesizer that did a fair job of approximating her voice.

"The money?" the boy said.

"Give it to him," Alice said.

Ursula handed the boy a calling card computer. "Access codes already punched in."

The boy nodded and touched the input of the computer against his own.

"Like you said, a third now, the rest on delivery," Ursula said.

Again, the boy nodded—impatiently, this time. He handed her computer back to her and slipped his own into the inside breast pocket of his jacket. With unhurried efficiency, he placed his valise on the coffee table and opened it up. He unpacked his tools.

"This has to go," he said as he used a laser scalpel to remove the neural inhibitor from the back of Alice's skull and cauterize the wound. The smell of burning flesh and hair touched Ursula's nose and turned her stomach. She saw Alice's eyes tighten as the pain the device had been blocking hit her full force, like a storm front. The boy placed something on Alice's head that looked like a jellyfish and pulsed pink and green in alternating waves. "I'm going to go over this one more time: the nano-avatars each will carry a complete snapshot of your mind. All of your memories, everything. But they'll need a critical mass of several hundred million to form the metempsychotic gestalt. That's how many will be in each of the ampoules I'm going to bring you—you paid for ten, I'm giving you twelve." His brusque manner made this extravagant kindness sound like an insult.He removed the jellyfish thing and put it back into his case. Then he affixed two black beads to her temples and a third just above the bridge of her nose. "The gestalt won't occur until they are injected into someone's bloodstream and find their way into the brain." He turned his head and looked at Ursula. "That's you, right?"

Ursula nodded.

"Until then, they're frozen—suspended in time. Two things you need to remember. First, the gestalt only lasts about ten or twelve hours. After that, the nano-avatars will degrade. You'll hear voices, maybe, for a couple of days after but nothing clear or coherent." He picked the black beads from Alice's forehead and temples and grabbed a long needle with a glowing tip. He peeled back the lids of Alice's left eye and slid the needle into the socket, next to the eyeball. After a moment, he repeated the process with her right. "Second, the ampoules each contain a gestalt completely discrete from the others so don't expect its nano-avatars to know anything about what happened the last time you spiked. For them, it's always right now." He wiped the needle off on the leg of his blue jeans and put it back in the valise before snapping the case shut. "I'll be back in three days with the avatars. Have the money waiting." With that, he was gone.

After Ursula heard him enter the lift and begin his descent, she gently opened Alice's mouth and placed the wafer of thanatol under her tongue. By the time Ursula had closed Alice's mouth and brushed her dry, cracked lips with her own, Alice was dead.

Once—only and exactly once—did Ursula tell another soul about this thing of theirs, the syringe and the ampoules, the candlelit trysts. It was just over four years ago and she had been dating a woman, a publicist from the governor's office, for a few months. One evening—their last evening, as it would turn out—Ursula told her the entire story in a rehearsed and measured gush of full disclosure. Ursula had sat her at this table, carefully showed her the jar and the remaining ampoules without ever letting her touch them. Midway through, Ursula noticed a far-away look in her eyes (Beryl, she remembers—her name was Beryl and she was really quite stunning) and she could see, in Beryl's closed mouth, the movement of her tongue as it rolled restlessly around and pressed against the insides of her cheeks. Once Ursula had finished, Beryl opened her mouth into a sullen, soundless "o." Ursula watched her pink tongue tip move behind her teeth and was struck with just how grotesque a thing a mouth—even a mouth as pretty as Beryl's—truly was, all glistening spit and mucous membranes, the tongue itself a worm, muscular and mindless, blind and bloated, an obscenity of flesh. Finally, Beryl stood up, made a couple of vague yet passionate remarks urging Ursula to "move on with her life" and "learn to let go" and excused herself, from Ursula's flat and, as the days to come would make clear, from her life. Ursula had felt relieved—cleansed. She never dated anyone after that.

Ursula shakes her head at the memory and wonders what became of Beryl. Last Ursula had heard, she had followed a young and charismatic politician to Brancusi City—or was it New Kiryu? That was a year or two ago and anything could have happened since. Doesn't matter. She wastes only a moment on the thought before turning her mind back to the hours ahead of her. After the cheese and the wine and the inexorable sex, Ursula will sleep and she and Alice will dream together. One night they swam together in the liquid fire of the sun and another they ran naked as nymphs through a redwood forest before becoming a blanket of moss under the cool and quiet canopy.

By morning, Alice will be gone and Ursula will be alone, again and forever. But hidden deep in the drawer of her nightstand, hidden deeper in her thoughts so Alice will not see it, there is a tiny box and within that, Ursula's own sublingual wafer of thanatol, stashed away thirteen years ago in preparation for the morning to come. In the cold light of lunar dawn, Ursula will dissolve it in the spit under her tongue and close her eyes. Her final comfort, then, brief and eternal: forever will not be long at all.

Ursula finds the symmetry strangely charming: tonight, she and Alice share a body, and tomorrow, they share oblivion. As she turns the last ampoule over in her hand, she spares a thought—more a prayer, really—of thanks to that boy with the valise, these thirteen years gone. He had given her—given *them*—the gift of two extra years. She sighs, smiles and clicks the ampoule onto the syringe. *Deep in the heart of me,* she thinks. She places the needle to the crook of her elbow and slides it into the vein. *Under my skin.*

2

The Red Market
AD 2164

This time, she came to him with three broken ribs, two missing teeth, five second- and two third-degree burns on her inner right thigh, and various bruises and tears in more intimate places.

"I can't keep doing this," he said. "You need help."

"That's why I'm here," she said. "For help."

"That's not what I mean and you know it." He helped her out of her dress and underthings, then took her arm and helped her over to his diagnostic bubble chair, doing neither as gently as he should. He closed the clear plastic carapace. As the laser lights and sub-sonic hums of various scans played over her body, he read the results on the wafer slate computer he held in his hand: internal bleeding in her abdomen and thorax, liver damage, spleen on the verge of rupturing--all of it easily repaired. What really needed to be fixed she would never let anyone near.

"I know that you *should* have reported me the first time," she said, her voice simultaneously muffled through the shell and clear through the microphone that relayed it to his wafer slate. "Or any of the many other times--and there have been so many. I know that, if you report me now, you'll have to explain why you didn't any of those other times. I won't be any help. So you lose your license and, who knows, if I'm particularly unhelpful, you go to Tethys for 'treatment' of your own. You want to see Saturn's rings? Go ahead, report me."

With a resigned sigh, he brushed his hand over the screen of his computer as if he swatted at a fly. The chair popped open and she stared up at him with ice blue eyes that once seemed so full of vulnerability and promise. Now he saw them for what they had always been, dead and damaged pits into nothing and nowhere, the only truth the blackness of the constricted pupils. Whatever could have been salvaged was long gone, all that was left was an instinctive, cunning gift for manipulation and deceit, survival strategies that had long outlived their utility. She'd used them on him until he was in so deep she no longer needed to exert the effort.

No, he realized, there was still something there, something left of the smiling child she'd once showed him in a cryostylitic holograph. It was that very something that she was trying so hard to kill. He helped her out of the chair and, supporting her weight, helped her into one of the small, white rooms that branched off from his office suite. A translucent coffin filled with pink goo waited for her.

Like a bridegroom about to carry his prize over the threshold, he put one arm under her shoulders and the other behind her knees and lifted her. The lid of the coffin slid open at their approach and he lowered her into the gelatinous bath. Her ash blond hair floated around her half submerged face like a halo of etiolated seaweed.

"If you only knew how much I love you," she said, her eyes wide and her face carefully bled dry of any trace of guile.

He took firm hold of her shoulders and pushed her below the surface, his hands and wrists tingling with the goo's electric charge. Reflexively, she fought against him, as she always did, but then her lungs filled with the oxygen-rich fluid and the sedatives in the regenerative cocktail took effect. She grew still.

"I know," he said. Before the coffin lid slid shut, he had turned his back and was two steps out of the chamber.

"Another of your broken birds," Lennox Burris had said after Jorge Nemerov first introduced him to Agneta Hauser at a small gathering of classmates from their medical school days. Jorge and Lennox were alone, sharing a stim stick while standing on the roof of their host's apartment building, watching the Martian sun set behind ragged hills.

"I've heard this all before, Len," Jorge said.

"Now you're gonna hear some more. This time will be different, right? Wrong. You'll try to mend her shattered wings as she pecks her way through your breastbone to your soft and stupid heart. She's already pecked out your eyes. Blind idiot--you never change."

"You don't know what she's been through."

"I can guess. And you will save her from that, erase it all and give her hope. She's very pretty--they're always very pretty, or haven't you noticed? They poleaxe you with their prettiness and you trick out your lust with pity and call it love. Asshole."

Jorge made a fist with the hand lying limp by his side. Lennox saw it and chuckled. "You won't use it. You're a sweet boy, right? A good listener, a kind soul. So you just as well should relax. And listen."

"I'm going back inside. I don't need this shit."

"No you're not and yes you do. Maybe they didn't teach you this in messiah school but if you keep letting them bleed off what is best in you, all you'll be left with is what's worst in them. And let me tell you, your capacity for good is sadly limited. Their capacity for evil is endless."

Jorge forced a smile. "Is that what they're teaching you up in Terrorville? Anyway, you said it yourself: I never change. You're as much of a fool as I am, wasting your breath and my time."

"Probably."

"What have you been doing these last few years, since they pulled your license, *Doctor?*"

"None of your fucking business what I'm doing. We're not talking about me, we're talking about you."

"*You're* talking about me. *I'm* trying to get warped and enjoy the sunset. Someone won't shut up and let me do either."

Lennox thrust the stim stick at Jorge. "Warp away and enjoy it while you can. I watched her, you know? Like I said, she's very pretty. And when I wasn't looking at her legs, I saw how she looked at *you,* those very rare moments when you weren't looking at her like a moonstruck cow. Wanna know what I saw?"

"No."

"Of course not. Well fuck you, friend, I'll tell you anyway. Contempt. She thinks you're weak and she's right. Whoever made her what she is, whatever he did to her, he taught her that kindness is weakness. And she's right, it is. You're not her champion, armor agleam. You're a spineless resource for her to exploit. And when she's done, God help you."

"You don't believe in God."

"Exactly."

Lennox had then gone back down to the party. Ten minutes later, after the sun had sunk beneath the horizon and the stick had set his nerves vibrating to strange frequencies, Jorge followed, only to discover that Lennox had left, back to the shuttle port and then to Deimos, the nasty little potato shaped moon he now called home.

As he sat as his desk, remembering that night, six months before to the day, Jorge cursed them both. A resource: Agneta paid handsomely for her beatings, he knew, but he cleaned up after them for nothing, at first out of something he could still find no better name for than love, lately out of fear she would do just what she had threatened, end his career and send him off to that icy moon of Saturn and its penal ministrations.

Once, while she was under, Jorge had slipped two extra ingredients into her bath: Lethedrine, to help her forget the things that had been done to her as a child, and Nouveauzine, to blast away the jaded accretion of the years that had made her numb to all but the most savage sensuality. One round would barely touch her, he knew. She needed months of therapy, the drugs augmented by intensive behavioral modification. But he'd hoped she would emerge from the coffin with just enough to glimpse the possibilities that lay beyond her vicious cycle of blissful devastation and joyless reconstruction.

She had. "It's mine!" she had shrieked at him. "It's me! You can't take it away--any of it! What would you put in me instead, *you*? You're *nothing*!"

From that point on, Agneta made no secret of the contempt Lennox had so astutely diagnosed. From that point on, she made a game of taunting him with the flesh that, with the exception of one time, after that party, when she must have smelled the spores of doubt that Lennox had planted in his mind, she kept just beyond his reach.

(That night, as they lay side by side in his bed, her leg thrown across his waist, Agneta had drowsily told him that, after he was done with the evening's program of rape and torture, her father--an engineer supervising the iridium mining operations in the asteroid belt--would always gently cup her chin, smile lovingly and say "Don't sit under the apple tree." It wouldn't be until she was an adult that she would discover it was from a song that was already old two centuries before either of them were born. It started just before her fourth birthday, she had told him, and he felt her warm tears ooze onto his chest. And just like that, the spores were gone.)

Jorge looked at the time: just after midnight. Agneta would need another three hours in the bath at least. On Deimos, it would be seven in the morning. He hesitated, then rang up Lennox at his Deimos City flat.

"She wants to destroy herself, over and over and over again."

"And anyone else within reach, anyone she can drag along with her," Lennox said from the cyostylitic holocube. "It isn't personal. No one can save her from herself save herself. I'm sorry, Jorge. If it means anything, I really do believe you deserve better. You're a good man." A shadow of self-loathing crossed his face and he added, quietly, "A better man than me."

"You're in the Red Market," Jorge said. It was not a question. "Don't worry, the line is secure. Triple encrypted."

"Quadruple encrypted on my end. I still don't--yes, I'm working in the Red Market. I guess I don't have to tell you that our skills come in handy down there. I don't like talking about it."

"I wouldn't bring it up if I didn't--listen, Len, if she wants to destroy herself, I was thinking maybe... maybe I--maybe *we*--could arrange it so that she can do it without getting hurt."

Lennox said nothing for several long seconds. "I said you were a good man," he finally said, his voice flat and cold. "Maybe I was wrong. If you do this, you won't be. If you do this, you will be as evil as the monster who twisted up your wounded bird." Another silence, then: "You'll be as evil as I am."

"Good. Evil. What does it matter? God will forgive all, our sins *and* our virtues."

"You don't believe in God."

"Exactly."

***

"Agneta," Jorge said, "you remember Dr. Burris."

"Yes." Agneta had adopted the shy, downcast manner she often deployed on strangers, playing at helplessness: *I'm at your mercy,* it said.

"Hello, Ms. Hauser. How was your flight?"

"Nice," she replied in a voice pitched just above inaudible. "I slept through most of it. They had some Kitty Yi-Yi sleepies in the computer." Lennox looked at Jorge, just for a fraction of a second. Jorge knew that look, remembered it from their days at Utopia Planitia University, and he could read it as if they were telepathic: *Pre-school entertainments? You gotta be kidding me.*

Jorge briefly runs the memory of the trip through his mind. As they had settled into the seats of their private cabin on the shuttle, before she amused herself with projected dreams of a grotesque and infantile cat in a candy-colored phantasmagoria, Agneta had asked him why Deimos City was also called Terrorville.

"The moons are named after the sons of Mars, the Roman god of war. Phobos means Fear, Deimos is Terror. Deimos City: Terrorville." He'd paused, then added significantly, "Their mother was Venus, goddess of love."

Agneta hadn't said anything after that. Until the shuttle touched down at Deimos Spaceport, all Jorge heard from her had been soft snoring and the occasional giggle.

"That sounds charming," Lennox said. The three of them sat under a red and white striped umbrella in the patio of a small cafe on a side street branching off of Deimos City's central boulevard and spent the next three quarters of an hour in listless small talk.

Once he had decided the masquerade had gone on long enough, Lennox looked at his watch and stood up. "I wish I could stay a little longer but I have an appointment across town I can't be late for." He offered Jorge a calling card computer. "This has a guide to the better clubs and restaurants--I added some suggestions of my own. Call me tonight?"

Jorge took the device and pocketed it, then stood and shook Lennox's hand. Lennox smiled but his eyes gave Jorge another look freighted in unspoken meaning: *You don't have to do this. You can still back out.*

"Count on it," Jorge said.

That night, Jorge turned on the calling card and studied the instructions that would get them past several blinds and through a succession of hidden passages that led deep into the dead heart of Deimos. Once he was satisfied he had them sufficiently memorized, he took Agneta from their hotel and they descended into the Market.

He could feel her mounting excitement as they made their way, like a couple of spies in a boy's adventure story. When they finally emerged into the warren of dimly lit chambers, thronged with seekers after the most terrible of thrills, she took a deep breath and looked up at him with genuine gratitude, something she had only feigned up till now. It was so vastly different that Jorge wondered how he had ever been fooled by its various simulacra.

"Over here," Lennox called. When they caught up to him, after pushing through the crowd, Jorge saw that he too had abandoned all facades. He regarded the both of them with raw hatred. Silently, he led them through a heavy metal door with flaking maroon paint and a "No Trespassing" sign in stark black and white.

All of this, Jorge thought, the peeling paint, the puddles on the floor of the chamber outside, the amber, blue and green lighting that made it seem like they were at the bottom of stagnant ocean: an elaborate put-on, designed to accentuate the grimy illicitness that was the Red Market's draw. Once they were through the door and through a curtain of heavy plastic strips, everything changed. The room beyond was antiseptic white and the air scrubbed clean of the clammy, sweaty mist that still clung to them.

"Vat baby snuff show," Lennox said to Agneta without preamble, pointedly ignoring Jorge. "We take epithelial cells from your intestinal wall and use them to make clones of you. After a few weeks of accelerated maturation, they'll be ready for this."

Lennox pressed a button on the surface of a stainless steel table and a drawer, lined in red velvet, slid open. Inside, there was an array of gleaming devices and Lennox coolly demonstrated them one by one: phalluses with cutting chains running up the shaft or three helical drill bits that rotated around the head or articulated blades that flexed and extended like demonic fingers; spider-like robots with mouths that spat acid or jets of blue flame or bit off grape-sized chunks of flesh; another group of robots that looked like nightmare centipedes, their legs tipped with hypodermic needles. There were tools designed to stretch and rip and chew. Agneta looked upon it all with the breathless wonder of a child.

"That's right," Lennox said, "You get to watch it all from a cozy little box, just like a night at the opera. You'll be Queen of the May." He then lifted up Agneta's blouse and pierced her belly with a hair-fine needle to harvest her cells. "Now get out of here. Go play tourist for a couple of days and then go back to Mars. I don't want to see or hear from either of you ever again. One of my associates will tell you when it's time to come back for the show."

For the next month, Agneta was precisely who Jorge wanted her to be. There were no visits to his office to repair burns, bruises and broken bones. She let him take her to dinner, she let him make love to her and, though he knew his efforts stopped far short of touching her ruined soul, her body was soft, supple and responsive. Just as he allowed himself to hope for a future together, just as he had finally mustered the force of will to forget the reason for her transformation, the call came, waking him up just before dawn.

Jorge took care not to disturb Agneta as he rose from bed and walked the dreadful steps into his study. Surrounded by totems of healing, he flicked on the switch of his communication console.

There was no cryostylitic image this time, just a woman's voice speaking with an accent he could not place. "Dr. Nemerov? I heard I could consult with you on a medical matter that requires the utmost discretion."

It was a pre-arranged signal for Jorge to turn on all of his encryptors. He did so and said, "Go ahead."

"Book a flight. Your girl has her big debut in three days."

Before Jorge could reply, the circuit was dead.

He didn't last five minutes--the screams of the girl on the stage, the smells of blood and urine and feces and burning hair, the leering stillness of the room filled to capacity with spectators, all of it drove him from his seat and out of the lushly appointed box. Agneta was so raptly focused on the action below that she didn't notice or, more likely, didn't care.

Jorge stumbled down a spiral staircase and staggered to the backstage area, which was mercifully soundproof. A full hour later, after he had repeatedly managed to force down the insistent urge to vomit and to still his shaking hands, he saw two people in clean white jumpsuits, a man and a woman, roll the body through a door a few meters from where he stood. It was a blistered, bloody mess. The parts that weren't burned resembled nothing so much as ground meat and smoke rose from a mouth that hung open as only a dislocated jaw would allow. Through the open door, he heard a lubricious baritone introduce Agneta to a wave of deafening applause. Then the door closed off the celebration and all was silence again. The workers disappeared through another door without once acknowledging his presence.

Back in the hotel, Agneta attacked with him a wanton passion that left Jorge bruised all over and bleeding from a bite to his lower lip. He was sickened by how readily his own arousal betrayed him, ripping aside the last thin tissue of his supposed decency, revealed now to be as much of a sham as any of Agneta's stratagems. After three rancid hours, Agneta fell away from him, spent, and immediately plunged into a deep and motionless sleep.

Sleep would not come to Jorge and he lacked the will to leave the unholy sheets. He tried to comfort himself with the thought that the mutilated vat baby was essentially mindless, that it hadn't time to develop a sense of self. That only made it worse--her fleeting existence had been defined solely by unimaginable terror and agony, meticulously prolonged by the expertise of a man Jorge had once confided in, laughed and joked with, a man Jorge once considered his brother.

There surely was no God, he despaired, but the devil was alive and well, growing stronger with every beat of his heart, the heart he had himself betrayed.

The next night, Jorge refused to accompany her. Instead, he told her, he had arranged for one of the Red Marketeers to escort her. He had expected a fight or at least a sneer of disappointed contempt but Agneta only shrugged, finished applying her make-up and slipped on a pair of crimson silk-skin gloves that matched her open-toed pumps. She asked him to help with the clasp of a string of black pearls that matched her earrings and her dress and then kissed him goodbye before practically skipping out the door.

When she returned two hours later, it was with a hunger even stronger than the first time and Jorge's amoral flesh was more than happy to be her raw meat. Mid-way through their vigorous depredations, though, Jorge felt something take hold of him and, without thinking, slapped her across her beautiful jaw, hard enough to send her tumbling off the bed and onto the carpet. Before he could register what he was doing, he was towering over her, repeatedly kicking her soft belly until she whimpered like a whipped bitch and gazed up at him with dewy eyes of purest devotion.

"I won't," she breathed. "I won't sit under the apple tree. I promise."

This time, he could not fight his rising gorge. He ran to the bathroom and splashed his barely digested room service dinner into the bowl of the waterless commode, where it was burned to sterile ash.

A week of this followed, each night more feral than the last, until, after the ninth show, Agneta returned to their room in a subdued mood that shocked Jorge. To the disappointment of his body but the relief of his soul, she kept her distance, choosing to sit on the edge of a chair a few paces from the bed.

Jorge sat up, letting the top sheet fall to his naked lap. "What's wrong?" he asked, and all of the compassion and concern he had first felt for her, seemingly an eternity ago, returned as if it had never left.

She didn't answer him for well over a minute and he didn't press her, just watched the troubled waters of her face as she stared at her hands, folded in her lap. Then she looked up at him and said, "I felt something new tonight."

Jorge waited a couple of beats and then said, hopefully, "Guilt?" He got out of bed and knelt in front of her. He put his hand over hers. "Empathy?"

Agneta stared at him with incomprehension, then slowly shook her head. Finally, she said, "Envy."

"Goddamn you, I said I never wanted to see you again and I meant it. If it wasn't too much trouble, I'd kill you."

"Cut out the theatrics, Len. I came to make you an offer. One that will let you escape this hell you claim to hate so much."

Lennox studied Jorge's face for a moment, then turned away from the open door of his flat without gesturing for Jorge to follow him in. Jorge walked in anyway and closed the door behind him. He watched as Lennox went over to a brass bar cart in the corner of the room and poured a single glass of bourbon, then, after downing it in one gulp, poured himself another. Holding the glass in front of him like a shield, he turned around. “Make your offer.”

Slowly, carefully, Jorge laid it out in every detail. Lennox was stone-faced but Jorge saw his eyes widen almost imperceptibly. When Jorge finished, he said, “Get out. Get out or I *will* kill you and take my chances getting rid of your corpse.”

“It’s what she wants,” Jorge said patiently. “And I will pay you. I will liquidate every asset I have and give you all of it, minus only the little we’ll need to get as far away from Mars as we can and... start over.”

Lennox snarled in disgust, drained his glass again and turned to pour himself a third drink.

Calmly, quietly, Jorge spoke to his back. “My practice is lucrative and I have excellent financial advisors. I could have retired two years ago. You can retire now, go to Earth, go to Venus, go anywhere.”

Jorge downed the bourbon in three sips this time and said, “And do what?”

“Nothing. Anything you want.”

“Except practice medicine.”

“Are you practicing now? ‘First, do no harm.’”

Lennox spun around and hurled his glass. It whizzed past Jorge’s right ear and shattered against the dark oak of the wall behind him. Jorge didn’t flinch, not because he was brave, he knew, but because he just didn’t care.

“All right, you son of bitch. I’ll do it. Now get the hell out of my life.”

The same regenerative bath that had so efficiently healed her wounds in the past had now reversed the few visible effects of aging until Agneta looked like a teenager again, just barely out of childhood. At the same time, one of her clones had her maturation accelerated until she was apparently in her mid-twenties. Once that was done, it had been much easier than Jorge had anticipated to go ahead with the rest of their plan. By now, Jorge knew, she had experienced her final consummation. By now, Jorge hoped, she was finally at peace.

Beside him, in the cramped interplanetary rocket that streaked toward Earth, a lovely blond girl sat staring with wonder at the open palm of her delicate, dove-white hand. Experimentally, she closed her fingers and opened them several times. Sleepies and neuro-nanobots already had her toilet trained. By the time they left the Solar Commonwealth for interstellar space and the job waiting for him in the hospital of one of the farthest flung outposts, she should be able to speak, maybe even read. He wondered how she would react when she first saw one of those tall blue-skinned cyborgs, the genetically engineered starship pilots with their insect eyes and inhumanly slender builds. He realized that he had never seen one in the flesh, that their wonder would be shared.

He reached over and brushed back a lock of her hair. "Hey," he said, though he knew she could not understand him. "Don't sit under the apple tree with anyone else but me."

She gazed at him with soft blue eyes spilling over with unspoiled innocence and trust.

Author's Biography

Reynald Arthur Perry is a native of southern New Jersey, born in Vineland and currently living in Millville. He is twice over a graduate of Rutgers University, with a BA in English and History from Rutgers College in New Brunswick (1993) and an MA in English from Rutgers Graduate School in Camden (2008). Since 2002, he has taught English at Vineland High School, from which he graduated in 1988 and has taught for Fairleigh-Dickinson's Community College Partnership Program at Cumberland and Gloucester County Colleges. This is his first novel.

www.reddashboard.com

Made in the USA
Middletown, DE
29 April 2017